EDUCATION 101

EDUCATION
101
One Man's Journey to the Final Four

Ron Mayberry

iUniverse, Inc.
Bloomington

Education 101
One Man's Journey to the Final Four

iUniverse books may be ordered through booksellers or by contacting:

iUniverse
1663 Liberty Drive
Bloomington, IN 47403
www.iuniverse.com
1-800-Authors (1-800-288-4677)

ISBN: 978-1-4620-2963-1 (sc)
ISBN: 978-1-4620-2964-8 (e)

Printed in the United States of America

iUniverse rev. date: 07/22/2011

This book is dedicated to my wife Jeany. She put up with me and my pursuit to be the best basketball coach I could be in the State of Texas. We should have been in the real estate business as we bought fifteen different houses over the forty five years we have been married. She is the bottom line reason for any success I have had. I was blessed to have a younger brother Mike who was always there for me when I needed support.

ACKNOWLEDGMENTS

Thanks have to be extended to all the schools that I have coached for in my life time. That includes Perryton Junior High School and Mr. Mize for giving me my first job out of college. Paul Robertson, the Superintendent at Adrian High School who saved my life one night along with Sheriff Wheeler. Jay Spears who was my mentor at Midland High School. Dee Windsor for giving me the opportunity to coach at Albany High School. A big time thanks goes to Buster Brannon and Phil Reynolds for the lessons learned coaching at Van High School. Thank you Larry Wartes and Larry Dipple for the lessons learned while coaching at Hereford High School. Gil Bartosh and the Mojo football coaches and Mojo supporters for the opportunity to coach at Permian High School. Chester Story and Dr. Al Langford for hiring me at my first college job at Midland College. Dr. Phil Speegle for hiring me at Odessa College giving me my first opportunity to be a college Head Basketball Coach. Bill Hardage and Gary Goodin for their support and ability to help me get the Wayland Baptist University Athletic Directors position and Head Men's Basketball Coach. Jim Campbell for hiring me at Kilgore College and giving me the opportunity of a life-time coaching in East Texas. Joe Tubb and Dr. Baker for hiring me at South Plains College where I would retire for the first time. Rob Winkler for hiring me as the Athletic Director and Head Basketball Coach at Trintiy Christian High School. Mark Cotton for giving me the opportunity to coach as a Girl's Basketball coach at Stanton High School. Thanks you Bill Hood and the board of education for hiring me at Robert Lee High School. Steve Taylor for hiring me at Ozona High School. Bruce Yeagar and John Cornelius for giving me the opportunity to coach at Wellman Union High School. Dr. Sherry Sparks for hiring me as the Head Women's Basketball Coach at Howard College. Tom Manning for the wonderful experience I had coaching at St. Michaels High School. Todd Duncan for the opportunity to be the assistant basketball coach at Trinity Christian High School. Ray Morris for the chance to help him at Shallowater High School. The entire administration at Kirtland Central for the opportunity of a life time to be the Head Girl's Basketball coach. A great deal of appreciation goes to Todd Duncan for allowing me to be the Head Girl's basketball coach at Trinity Christian High School and just being a part of his life and family. Special thanks to Mike Bennett for hiring me as the Athletic Director at All Saints Episcopal Middle school in Lubbock, Texas.

Special thanks go to all the players that I have coached. There are too many to mention but all have made an impact on my life and this book is about them. If they read the book they will identify what is real and what is not real.

Last but not least, I want to thank my wife, Jeany and my youngest daughter Marcy for the support they gave me during the four years that it took to get all this done. Without them, this would have never happened.

INTRODUCTION

Tiger Woods was the ultimate hero until he was caught cheating. Who can argue with that statement? What if the world of "March Madness", the entire millions upon millions of basketball fans and supporters found out that their favorite University was cheating. Tiger was cheating out of lust and used his power and money to satisfy his lust. Coaches, Boosters and Fans cheat for the same reasons but it happens to be called something else. Their cheating is all about getting to the "Big Dance", during March Madness. It doesn't take a rocket scientist to understand the market for my book, called "Education 101." One man's Journey to the Final Four.

"Education 101" One Man's Journey To The Final Four is about Ron Young, a coach that starts his career in coaching on the junior high level and advances as a coach all the way to the Final Four at North West State University located in Amarillo, Texas. This story is about two issues, one the Big Time players Ron Young recruited, the recruiting stories, and the different methods used in the recruiting wars. The other issue is about Ron Young and his struggle to learn what it takes to win big, how he learned his lessons and the results from his lessons. After many years Ron Young finally gets his opportunity, makes the most of his opportunity coaching his Cinderella team into the NCAA National Division One Championship. Ron Young has his days of glory and then the tables turn on him as he has to deal with the NCAA Investigators for cheating violations. After that, it gets worse as he is forced to deal with the FBI for mafia connections and gambling investigations. Ron Young's basketball career, which covers over thirty years of dedicated service, honest hard work is destroyed after one year of trying to make it to the "Big Dance."

For three weeks, The Final Four March Madness is the most watched sporting event in the world. No one is exempt from its excitement and intensity from the young to the old. It is a unique sporting event. The interest is clear from coast to coast and country to country. The potential is unlimited, particularly if you can present a good story. I have a good story and you are going to be hard pressed not to find readers that would not be interested in my story about success at the Final Four. I have witnessed several basketball coaches reading my book, and I can honestly say I am excited about the response I received from them concerning my book. This book could be used as a tool for learning how to coach for beginning coaches. It's time to give readers a little "Education 101" about what it takes to get a team to the Final Four.

Ron Mayberry, author of "Education 101", one man's journey never coached a game on the division one level. However he is proud of fact that as a head coach in basketball his teams won-lost record are 908 wins and 325 losses. He doesn't feel that fact alone makes him special but since he did it at 24 different schools, he feels that puts him in a different category. Not only that, he has over 1000 wins when you include his head coaching wins on all levels of basketball. He feels he has experienced the ultimate journey in coaching as he has coached on the pro-level, university level, junior college level, high school level and the junior high level in both boys and girls. He feels strongly that for some reason or another, the good Lord above has taken care of him because he feels he has always had good players. What he is most proud of is the fact that he never had a losing record at any school where he was the head basketball coach on one of the above levels of play. Coach Mayberry feels this gives him some distinction among his peers that puts him in a different category of coaching basketball. Coach Mayberry had most of his success on the college level mainly because he had several players (17) go to the pro-level. Because of that Coach Mayberry was recruited as well as his players. He feels he learned from the best how to bend the rules of the NCAA without getting caught.

Although Coach Mayberry never made it to the Big Time, [Division One Basketball] he really feels he has a story to tell and it is a good story. Coaching players that can play in the NBA is a story within a story but he does not feel that makes him special except that he did it on a Junior College Level of basketball. Coach Mayberry has rubbed elbows with the best in Division-One basketball coaches and has mentored several coaches that have made it to the top, some who were his assistant [7] coaches at one time or another.

Another fact that coach Mayberry is proud of is the way he worked himself up the ladder into college coaching saying he did it the hard way. He started his coaching career at a Junior High school which is not the normal path a coach should follow if he wants the kind of success that coach Mayberry has accomplished in his coaching career of 50 years.

The book is really three separate stories. One story is a fiction story with half- truths spread in and around a story about taking a team to the final four, recruiting those players and results of the players that are recruited. The other story is true stories about how a coach learns how to coach, how to win, and what a program is all about. The true stories are hidden in the book by changing names, teams, and schools. The third part is about breaking NCAA rules, how they are broken, why they are broken and results that come from breaking the rules. All violations of rules are true and are lessons coach Mayberry learned from the best NCAA coaches in America. Again the stories are real but the people are made up and the schools involved are a figure of his imagination. The coaches that really do the job of coaching basketball are the 96% that never obtain a division one position. They never will be considered for a division one position but they are the ones that coach hard day after day trying to develop young girls and boys into basketball players. All the above is what gave him the motivation to write this fiction story about the journey of winning a National Championship in the NCAA, and all that goes with the recruiting of big time basketball players. He feels he is qualified to teach a course call "Education 101" by giving a story of one man's journey to the final four. .

Ron and his wife, Jeany live in Lubbock, Texas, have been married for 45 years and she is his one true love in his life. She is an ex-English-Drama teacher and has a passion for books and literary events. His daughters, Kim, Mendi, and Marcy were raised in an athletic family meaning the seasons were not fall, winter, spring, and summer but instead, football, basketball, track, and baseball/golf. The tradition continues with 6 grandchildren, four boys that participate in football, basketball, track and baseball, and two girls just waiting to be cheerleaders.

The bottom line in this book is about "Big-Time Basketball", and the pursued of trying to make it to the "Big Dance", but it is a lesson in basketball that can be used by all coaches of all ages on any level of basketball. The book clearly demonstrates how Coach Young learns his skills and then uses those skills to further his basketball career. It is the expressed desire of this author that young coaches everywhere learn from Coach Young and his experiences. In order to covey that message, Coach Mayberry underlines specific points about coaching throughout the book.

Table of Contents

ONE

The sound that I heard was one that I was waiting for and could identify. It was a little past midnight and the click sound was a door coming open in the Hilton Hotel. First, I called Darryl on my cell and told him to be on the alert. As I thought, I pretty young co-ed was leaving a room going in the opposite direction of my location. I did not want to shout or make too much noise, certain that I would disturb innocent people, but I wanted to catch her before she got out of my sight. She made a direct right turn into an open area where the vending machines were located. She disappeared and then I ran. Just as I was getting close, she came out of the vending area toward me. She had a diet coke in her hand, and I stopped dead in my tracts. I stared without any guilt, and realized I had made a mistake. I was looking at a woman, not a young co-ed. I called Darryl back on my cell and said to him, "False alarm."

"March Madness" has become an American tradition, a tradition that brings with it emotional highs and excitement beyond belief. But at the same time it can bring about the lowest, most dejected feeling that a human can endure. One side gets it and the other doesn't get it, and they usually hit the opposite walls at the same time. You can experience this "March Madness" several ways. Most folks tap into the madness through television, but some lucky people get to be a real part of it, living the moment with another thirty thousand at an official NCAA basketball venue. The excitement is unbelievable.

I happen to be the luckiest man in the world as I get a first-hand vision of the game on the bench as the head basketball coach. At least that is what the Boston Globe stated in its two page spread about the "Big Dance", but right now I am not sure that I feel that fortunate. I am in the Hilton Hotel in New Braunfels, Texas, and it is 2:00 a.m. I am situated on the north end of the third floor and Darryl Johnson, one of my assistant coaches, is at the other end. All of our players' rooms are located in between the two of us. Another assistant coach, Soapy Hudson, is in the lobby hiding, and Eddie Bryson, the final member of our coaching team, is perched in a car scanning the outside entrance. We are on guard because we have heard a rumor that several young ladies would be trying to visit our guys tonight after the coaching staff goes to sleep. Typically, we heard this rumor from the coaching staff at Memphis University, our opponent for the upcoming championship game. It's either a plot to wear all of us down or just something to worry us. A little cash here and there and some coeds would do anything to help their team win. This type of action is not uncommon in our competitive world. Wake-up calls have been changed or cancelled before and prank midnight calls to the coaches are par for the course. The win-at-all-costs philosophy is common at this level of competition. To me, it's just another night at the office.

The game is set for 7:15 p.m., central time, at the Alamo Dome in San Antonio, Texas. Dome officials have added fifteen thousand extra seats for this game. When it comes to Texas and putting on a show, no one does it any better than the San Antonio Chamber of Commerce. Because of all the media hype and constant circus-like distractions, I decided to move our team headquarters away from the center of this activity in San Antonio and into New Braunfels, about a thirty-minute drive from the dome.

Director of Basketball Operations Bryson demanded that he get the car watch. He said, "I want to be the first to stop this little deal," so I let him do it. Eddie is one of the finest assistants I have ever been around. His loyalty to our program and to the coaching staff is unmatched. The funny thing is he never played a quarter of basketball in his high school or college days. As a matter of fact, he was an outstanding college football player at Texas Christian University in Ft. Worth. He still looks like a football player, standing six feet tall and weighing about 240 pounds with not an ounce of fat that the eyes can see. Eddie is a big-time division-one personality with energy to boot. He can work 24 hours a day, never complains, and can sell anything to anybody, but his most important asset is that he loves the players and they love him. I have a bad habit of nagging our guys about doing the right things off the court as well as during the game. My assertiveness about off-the-court behavior can go a little over the top. It's just that problems on the court seldom happen unless we as coaches try something stupid, but off-court difficulties crop up on a regular basis.

My other two assistant coaches were both all-Americans in college basketball. Darryl played at St. Johns University and Soapy at Washington State University. Neither feels comfortable when I start confronting players about attitude problems, so they usually just stay quiet. After all, their primary job is recruiting, so sometimes my words hurt their efforts more than help. At any rate, they both provide what I want from a recruiting standpoint, so I do not get upset with them about their reluctance to confront players about off-court behavior. I hired both of them because of their connections with big-time prospects. Their job is clear: Find the best players on the planet and do whatever it takes to get them to attend and play for our school.

Eddie's job is simple too; after I tear a player down; he has to build him back up. That might sound easy to do, but I have found very few coaches who can do the task justice without making the head coach look stupid. It's called undermining in our business. Eddie has that kind of talent to lift the player while not lowering the coach, and we all appreciate him a great deal.

Finally Eddie calls me on his cell phone and I notice its 3:15 a.m. He and Soapy have surrounded a group of college coeds in the lobby and confronted them. With the on-site security officer by their side, it is easy to disperse the invading troupe. They had brought three six packs of beer and a bottle of cheap vodka hidden in a backpack. Of course, we got no names of anyone involved, who had organized this party or any other details. They were just looking for some fun at the Final Four.

After they left, we all hit the rooms to get as much sleep as possible. While I was lying in bed, my mind roamed and I started thinking about my job as the head men's basketball coach at North West State University, one of the largest Division One NCAA schools in area, but one that had never been to the Final Four of the NCAA National Division One Championship, much less played for the title. A small smirk came over my face as I thought how it all happened but the smile was more about how this yellow bird had finally made it to the top.

It all started for me in a second-grade classroom in Odessa, Texas. My father was a semi-pro baseball junkie and we moved around a lot. I was so excited to finally have a real school that I could call my own, where I could make friends. I will remember my first day for the rest of my life. I particularly remember Susan Elliot, who was the prettiest girl in the second grade, or at least that is what I thought. She had a pretty pink dress with a pink bow tied around her ponytail. Finally the bell rang and we all went to our respective rooms. After the announcement and the pledge, our teacher, Mrs. Reynolds, assigned each of us seats. I had a brand-new desk that had a smell of just cleaned fresh wood; it was shiny like the surface had just been varnished. I guess it was all the excitement of it, but I kept thinking about how lucky I was to be here. After we were settled in and Mrs. Reynolds had taken roll and so forth, our class and the other two classes of second-graders assembled in a large room where the chairs were already placed in different rows. I noticed that all the seats were set in circles separated from each other into three distinct sections of the room. The teachers started calling out names and placing students in each circle. My name was finally called out and I had to take a seat in one of the outside circles. Once we were settled, I remember to this day what happened next. One of the teachers began "Now students, this will be your reading group this year." She went on, "This group (pointing to the circle that Susan was in) will be called the blue birds; they are the fastest readers. The group in the middle will be referred to as the red birds, and they are the next-fastest readers. The group on the outside (pointing to where I was seated) will be called the yellow birds. They are our slowest readers." Suddenly, it hit me with a start: I was dumb. It had never entered my mind until that very moment. I looked over at the other two groups and all my friends were in the blue birds or the red birds. It seemed like my group had a cloud over our heads and they had clear skies and bright lights over theirs. My two best friends were in the red birds and, of course, Susan was a blue bird. I felt I wasn't as good as them, that I was inferior. The desk that I had loved so much turned stale, the teacher was mean and I was a yellow bird. My first day in a real school "taught" me that I wasn't good enough.

TWO

To me, there is nothing unusual about being born in Los Angeles, California, and raised in Texas. That is until you find out that my mother, one of thirteen children, rode horses from the I-20 McDonald's Observatory to the Carlsbad Caverns just for fun, learned to shoot a tin can in the air from 30 yards away, could rip off a chicken's neck in a New York minute, and often drove an 18-wheeler from Pecos, Texas, to El Paso at 18 years of age. I would say that gives her some level of distinction. During the early years of my life in this small town called Kent, Texas, you would never have guessed I would become a coach; my future would involve work in the rodeo, maybe farming, or perhaps ranching? – All these seemed more likely outcomes. This was where my mother was raised and this was where my upbringing took place as well. My parents were poor following the Depression and really could not afford to have a baby, as times were tough. Matter of fact, my uncle Todd has told me that I slept in the drawer of a dresser. He said that my Mom and Dad could not afford a baby bed. I was the first grandchild in this family but no one would have known it, because with so much love and compassion around, I was just treated like another one of the brothers and sisters. When you are raising thirteen, what is one more mouth to feed?

If you blink your eye, you will miss Kent. It sits around 150 miles east of El Paso and about 50 miles west of Pecos. The town contained one large food store, one small post office, one train station, one service station and a small one-room schoolhouse, just like viewers read about or saw on "Little House on the Prairie." I was both lucky and unlucky to attend school in Kent. I was lucky because I was loved and cared for with tender care; unlucky because I didn't receive a very good education. The one-room schoolhouse had six rows of desks, each row representing a grade. I was in the first row, where first-graders sat. Including my family, twenty-five families or so lived in and around Kent at the time. Most adults were employed as extra hands on local ranches, while others worked old highway 80, which ran from Texas to California. My grandmother ran a boarding house for laborers working around the area or anyone who was unlucky enough to get stranded in Kent. She also served as the Justice of the Peace for the county. Between getting meals ready, washing and putting dishes up, cleaning up after people, washing clothes, and also listening to complaints from ticketed speeders brought to the house to be sentenced by grandmother, life in this small town was not boring. She was one tough old lady. Grandma saw no gray in driving too fast on the highway and she would fine most violators the maximum. The highway patrolmen really liked her as she would not put up with anything.

Finally, I moved with my parents to Odessa, Texas, where mother got a job working at Smith and Quicksilver, a really nice clothing store, and my Dad started his own business as a dental technician. The line of work was a hand-me-down trait that he picked up from his father.

After the move to Odessa and the school transfer, I was quickly established in the yellow bird group. Right off the bat, I was held back because of my educational background. Needless to say, I was not overflowing with confidence in the classroom. Instead, I developed a real underlying panic attack mode of thinking about my intelligence. I was simply convinced I was dumb, backward in comparison to my classmates. Before being classified as a yellow bird, I had no fear. That is why I loved going back to Kent in the summer because they all accepted me just as I was. I always felt confident among my family members in that little town. The only other place I felt comfortable was on the athletic field. I seemed to have some natural ability when it came to running, catching, jumping, hitting, and all the things that go along with third- to sixth-grade athletics. I excelled in any sport that I participated in. I was respected and it seemed that everyone liked me. Sports provided a relief, because in the classroom, I took a backseat to everyone.

My father was born in Merkel, Texas, to a family that had arrived there in covered wagons, but they moved to Los Angeles when they got tired of the dust storms and felt moving to California offered more opportunity. Dad came from a family of seven, with four brothers and three sisters. He stood six foot two, was very handsome and a very likable person, witness by how he always got along with the Boyd family. He never had a run-in with any one of the thirteen brothers and sisters. Everyone liked him and always wanted to be around him. I guess he learned his street-smarts in fast-paced Los Angeles. He could con a mailman to go for a walk on his day off as he was a smooth talker, and had a sharp, curious mind that led him to many adventures during his lifetime. He was the kind of person who never doubted his ability to get something done. He would do it. I remember when I was in the fifth grade; the Harlem Globetrotters were coming to town. Every day, the paper would advertize the event, advising readers to get their tickets early because they would sell out. Day after day, I would say something about wanting to go. Sure enough, two days before the Trotters were scheduled to arrive, the paper posted the news that the tickets were just about all gone; I was so disappointed. But the night of the event around 7:00 pm, Dad asked me if I wanted to go. Of course I said yes, assuming he had tickets. When we got to the game, the line was about two blocks long and I just knew we were not going to get in. All those people waiting to get a ticket and we were at the back end of the line. But it was like my father didn't even see the line because he walked right up to the front and worked his way in like we belonged. Then he bought the best tickets in the house right behind the Trotters' bench. I still do not know what he said to them but that was my Dad.

He loved horse racing and it was fun to go with him to the racetrack. He knew how to study the racing forms better than anyone I have ever known. He would get a form the night before and spend two or three hours poring over it. He was a piece of work. It was from him that I learned my first lesson in coaching: <u>Be prepared in the heat of the battle, and know your opponent better than they know you.</u> He always played the horses to win. He would tell me that that is what it is all about: <u>"Play to win."</u> The last thing he taught me was to play your cards close to the vest but <u>always have something in reserve-an ace in the hole or a backup</u> plan. He would bet on one horse that he had studied and felt confident in, and then he would make a secret bet that none of us knew about. That was his sleeper bet (his ace in the hole). Of course, he would win on the sleeper more often than on the regular bet, and it always paid more money. Like I said, he was a piece of work. He taught me a lot about life and winning. It really paid off for me as I started getting older and began to realize there is a fine line between winning and losing. Dad may have been a red bird, but he carried himself like a blue bird.

He was an outstanding athlete as he won the Los Angeles city tennis championship and was drafted out of high school by the Brooklyn Dodgers in baseball. The Dodgers had an AAA farm team in Los Angeles so he never had to move. World War II came along and he enlisted in the Navy. While he served they put him to work as a dental technician. He had a love for boxing, and competed in several amateur events, and later became a referee. That's how we ended up in Odessa, as he was playing baseball for the Odessa Oilers, and served as a boxing referee for the Golden Gloves. On the side, he would do dental work. I can remember going to the baseball park and chasing down fly balls and home runs that went out of the park. For every ball I brought back they would give me a nickel. I enjoyed every minute of it. Since my father was either playing baseball or working as a dental tech, and my mother was working at a clothing store, I had lots of free time to myself. I ran the streets with my buddies when I was in the fifth, sixth, and seventh grades. We did just about what we wanted to with little or no supervision. It was not unusual for one of us to spend the night with any of the other guys and stay out past midnight or later. We never thought anything about it. It was so different in those days.

I experienced first-hand one of the biggest lessons I could ever learn about coaching when I was in the fifth grade taking swimming lessons from Coach Blaine. Coach Blaine, my elementary coach was so <u>patient and understanding, teaching each of us differently because we were all at different levels.</u> Some were scared of water, some not; some were advanced, some not; some could float, some not; but he taught all of us how to swim. Coach Blaine was so good with everyone and never lost patience with anyone for what they couldn't do. Rather, he just had each swimmer work at the level where he or she could have some success. I learned three very important lessons from Coach Blaine: First, have organized methods of teaching; second, teach the basic fundamentals first and move to the more complex later; third, remember that learning is a process where people improve at different rates and different times. Do not give up on someone who cannot perform the way you want them to the first time. Funny thing, later as I advanced from the fifth through the seventh grades, I came across many of those same people who had taken those swimming lessons. You know what? They could all swim.

It wasn't until I was in the seventh grade that I realized I was as good an athlete as anyone in my class, but I was skinny and weak. Most of my friends were so much stronger than I was and that really bothered me a lot. At that age, two boys will play-fight by pushing and shoving one another. There were heavy-set guys who could push me around if they wanted to. I had to learn to think quickly and figure out ways to use my mind to negate their brute strength. That alone helped me become a better coach in my later years. I learned how to handle situations where an adversary had more ability than I did. I learned that when you are overmatched in talent, you had better be smarter than your opponent, or otherwise, you are going to get a whipping.

Being a yellow bird, I soon figured out that I was much better off in the streets than in the classroom. It was so much easier for me. Don't get me wrong; the streets are very different places now than when I was growing up. The greatest danger lurking back then was that you'd get beaten up by older guys who were more interested in scaring than actually hurting you. It was a different world. There were no guns, knives, and explosives, at least in my neighborhood. Violence had a different type of meaning. You were as good as you could run, and I could run faster than most young people my age. I very seldom got caught. My experience in Odessa was something that helped me the rest of my life as I developed the ability to have a second sense about people. You learn to survive that way. In the seventh grade, I realized for the first time that physical strength is a huge asset in sports. I loved to play football and was pretty good in my early years until my friends started passing me by in weight and strength. All of sudden, football became hard. My first painful encounter on the gridiron came on a kickoff return that year. I always played the back person to receive the kickoff because I had speed and good hands. I received a kickoff and started down the middle of the field. Out of nowhere, someone hit me and the next thing I remember I was on my back trying to breathe. That was scary. I thought I would never catch my breath. Of course, now I know that I had just gotten the wind knocked out of me. I quickly developed a respect for the game of football.

In the second-grade, I found out I was a yellow bird and then in the eighth-grade, I was defeated. My family moved to Amarillo, Texas at the start of my eighth-grade year in school. As soon as football season came to an end, basketball tryouts started for eighth-grade students. I was scared to death as I was shy and did not know too many of the guys trying out. I will never forget what happened on that fateful day that the coach finally decided who had made the team and who hadn't. He lined us up facing him on the baseline and went down the line pointing to the guys who were cut. When he pointed to me, my heart sunk to the floor. I just knew he had made a mistake. I was heartbroken and stunned. I had never been cut before, I thought I was better than most of the guys playing, and the failure completely floored me. I was a little scared of football, but I had not expected to be cut in basketball. I went home with tears in my eyes. Of course, the first person I saw was my mother. She could tell that I was hurt so she just put her arms around me and comforted me. Mom had the heart of a pure blue bird. When my father got home from work, he asked why I was not at basketball practice and Mom told him what had happened. I was in my room when I heard the door slam. I rushed out to ask my mother what was going on and she replied that Dad was going to see the coach. I had never yelled at my mother, but I did this time. Seeing the panic on my face, she quickly chased after him, and thankfully, convinced him to turn around and come back. I was very embarrassed but at the same time so proud of Dad. We all three sat down and talked things over. I decided that with the help of my parents I would show the coach I was good enough to make the team by working hard over the next year. That was the deal we made or otherwise, my father was going to talk to the coach. I was hurt and not too eager to get back on the court. This would help me later as a coach. When you have to cut someone from a team, always do so with compassion and encouragement. No one likes to cut young people but sometimes you are forced to do it. When the unpleasant task falls to you, always remember what it would be like if that were your child being cut.

Two weeks later, David Clark, one of the guys trying out for the team who had also been cut, approached me and asked if I would be interested in playing on a team organized by the local Boys Club. I said yes and we became friends; we are still close to this day. I started playing, and often got my name in the paper as the high scorer. And the Boys Club became a second home for me. I would have my parents' drop me off every Saturday and Sunday morning, and they would pick me up when it got dark. I started spending every hour I could at the Boys Club. To this day, I am a good shooter because of that formative experience. I learned a great deal about being a good shooter playing by myself. To become a good shooter, you need to spend lots of time shooting the ball, over and over. Accuracy does not become second nature by accident. I even expanded my shooting lessons at home. I did not know what I was doing but since I had so much free time on my hands, I would go outside and shoot at the corner of our apartment building. The apartment managers would not let us put up a basket so I pretended that the top of the apartment about twelve feet high was the goal. If I hit it just right, the ball would bound off the corner and back to me. If I missed, the ball would go straight down or over the house and I had to chase it down. Soon I made a game of it; if I missed it either way, short or over the top, I would sprint forward or around the house and try to catch the ball before it hit the ground. Unintentionally I was not only improving my shot, but also developing great eye/hand skills and good footwork at the same time.

Needless to say, the next year in the ninth grade, my last year in junior high I made the team and was the leading scorer. I also played football that year, but it had really hurt me being so weak because I was behind most guys my age. Not only that, I have allergies and the grass brought on outbreaks. I always had problems with my allergies and still do. My body just did not react to playing outdoors very well in the fall: It seemed I was sick with the allergies all the time. I was doubly excited then for basketball season because I knew the cold weather was coming. Of course, if I had not played baseball as well, my father would have been crushed. So I played the game through my tenth grade. My best position was the outfield, especially left field. I was fast and I felt I could catch almost anything. After that, I gave baseball up. In hindsight, I wish now that I hadn't have quit it, but my father was cool that I had tried, and he did not demand that I play. Instead, he supported me in all the other sports. He never had a negative word to say about any coach I had. Although Dad missed lots of games that I played, I always knew he supported me.

Going from junior high to high school was scary for me. Polk High School was the only choice in town at the time and it was one of the largest high schools in the state of Texas. The other thing that really intimidated me was that we had to make an early choice as to which sport we were going to play. I disliked deciding on a sport I wanted to play ahead of time, and I felt trapped by the coaches. Both football and basketball had early training and as a freshman, I had to work out that spring in the sport I had chosen to play. It was then that I received a little help from the second coach who made a real difference in my life. He was the freshman coach and I loved him like a father.

Coach Keel was kind and he had a caring attitude about all kids in the school. He advised me what to do. He knew that I wanted to play football but suggested that basketball presented me the better opportunity to play a sport at Polk High. As it turned out, he was right. All the better athletes from the other junior highs played football, and I would have been hard pressed to make the team. I'm sure that neither he nor I realized that I would turn out to be one of the better athletes in the school. I had the skills and smarts but not the strength or size. Soon it was clear that all the work that I did at the boys club, and shooting practice at my house, paid great dividends for me because I quickly established myself as the best sophomore basketball player in the school. It helped that a new high school called Southside opened my sophomore year. Some of the better players transferred to that school. The coach at Polk became my third mentor; one I have fondly remembered my entire life. Teddy G. Hill was a mechanical drawing teacher and ex-football player who had played at Hardin Simmons University in Abilene, Texas. He ran the city swimming pool in the summer and he put me to work as a lifeguard during the warm-weather months between my ninth and tenth grades. Hogan Park Pool was in the tough part of Amarillo, and was a hangout for the young "Flyboys" who attended Amarillo Air Force Base, which was located in the Southside school district. The pool was a meeting place with girls too, and oftentimes the Southside boys and the Air Force guys did not see eye to eye. It was obvious to me within a week of working at the pool what Coach Hill's initials had to stand for: He was "Tough Gut Hill." Coach was in his sixties and getting ready for retirement but that did not stop him from picking up a large wrench when he had to discipline a few fly boys or some of the "Hoods" that made the pool their hangout. It did not matter how tough it got; Coach Hill could handle it. I was amazed. I gained a great deal of respect for him. He was as kind of a person as you could ask for, but if you crossed him and he was in the right, you had better start backing down, because he certainly wasn't going to.

He was a very good man, but not a great coach. I did not realize this until years later when I went to college on a basketball scholarship and found out that most of the other players on our team knew a little more about game than I did. But Coach Hill did do some good things and I will be forever happy that he coached me in high school. I was lucky that I learned from a good Christian man who stood up for what was right. He has influenced me a lot going forward with my life.

When I was a senior, Albert Fudd, an all-American from Oklahoma State and an ex- Polk athlete, came to the high school to do his student teaching. Part of his teaching program was to help Coach Hill. Mr. Fudd was an ex-Olympic team member who had played for the late Hank Iba, and later in life he would become the president of two major tennis shoe companies. I was lucky because he took a liking to me and he spent a great deal of time teaching me the game. He taught me the bottom line for success in offensive basketball. He did that in less than three weeks but it would carry me for my entire playing time and coaching career. From him I learned how to catch the ball, face up to the basket, and do one of three things: shoot, drive or pass. Then he taught me how to fake, and to read a defense. Next, he gave me lessons on how to apply that concept inside or outside. In short, he taught me the simple but complex method of playing the game of basketball. Albert Fudd was a blue bird without a doubt.

When I turned sixteen my life changed. My mother had just announced that she was pregnant. Boy was I excited. I was the only child and spoiled rotten, no doubt about it. There had been another baby born before me but he died two days after birth. Mother's RH negative blood and Dad's O positive did not mix well, and my older brother died back when the medical world hadn't yet figured out how to overcome the complications that occur when the two blood types appeared together. Later, my mom told me that I almost died as well. It was just a fact of life back then. In early June, my baby brother arrived before anyone had figured out what he should be named, nor did we know mother was going to deliver a boy. I was in favor of naming him Mickey after Mickey Mantle, the famous Yankee baseball star. But in the long run it didn't matter what any of us wanted to call him because an Irish nurse started calling him Michael before he was born. The same dreaded blood-borne complications threatened him, although the doctors had assured us that medical knowledge had progressed since 1937 and the birth should present no problem. But there was some difficulty with the delivery regardless, and this nurse just took over and saved my brother's life. So, on June 9, 1955, Michael Boyd Young was born in Amarillo, Texas, at St. Anthony's Hospital. The life I had known would never exist again, but really it was not all that bad. Even though there were sixteen years' difference between Michael and me, little did I know that that age gap would cease being a factor in no time.

Proud as we were, we just had to show Michael off, so we went on a family vacation to California. It was then that I found out for the first time about my father's side of the family. I learned that I had more aunts and uncles in the Los Angeles area that I had never known about. It was neat to stop at places along the way and visit with Dad's bothers and sisters and hear old war stories. I met my other grandmother and saw things that I had never anticipated I would ever see, but what impressed the most was that I watched TV for the first time in my life. And what was equally impressive was that I got to watch Sandy Koufax pitch for the Los Angeles Dodgers. I met some of the players and it was a thrill of a lifetime. Although I was a basketball player, I loved baseball. My idea of a good game was a 1-0 game thriller with all the pressure that builds into that kind of game. "Nobody handled that kind of pressure better than Koufax."

As with many young men, I was starting to feel my oats in basketball so to speak. I was getting to be a smart-ass and too good for my own business. It was clear to me that I was good enough to play on the varsity as a sophomore, but Junior Varsity Coach Brown kept me humble and under control. I learned two huge lessons this year. <u>One, this new coach used a performance chart of pluses and minuses on each player's game performance to decide who would get playing time.</u> It was a "Come to Jesus" moment for me. If I was really the best player, then I should come out with a high grade. And I did actually, but some of my best friends did not. The truth was that I had developed the habit of shooting the basketball only when a shot opportunity presented itself. In addition, I was a good shooter, so my shooting percentage was high. I was very good at the free throw line, and I did not turn the ball over very often. I was not a reckless passer; rather I passed the ball quite well. I had learned to fake a pass early in my life so I did not telegraph my passes as many times as some of the other guys did. When you take into account that I also was one of the better rebounders on the team, it was no surprise that I always graded out the highest on the JV team. Needless to say, I liked this system, which I would later adopt when I started coaching. But one night at the dinner table, I learned the second big lesson. I was griping about Coach Hill and Coach Brown and how hard they were on us, telling my mother and father how mistreated I was, and so forth. I guess I was hoping to get sympathy from one of them, but although I did not yet realize it, my parents were getting fed up with my immature attitude. This particular night Mom stood up from the dinner table, went over to the phone booth, got the telephone directory and started looking up a number. I asked her what she was doing. She said, "I am looking up Mr. Hill's phone number. I am fixing to call him and tell him that you cannot handle playing basketball for him because he is too hard on you." I yelled at my mother for the second time in my life: "No!" I quickly reversed myself and pleaded with her that I could handle it. She put the phone book down and softly said, "I do not want to hear anymore about this again. Do you hear me?" I went to my room and told myself that I would never again bring that subject up. I grew up a little right then and later thanked Mom for setting me straight. I never complained to them again, even when I went to college to play basketball.

I had to take geometry that year and I was intimidated by other schoolwork, much less this new subject. I was lucky that I was seated next to a guy who would later become one of my best friends. Delbert McKenzie was very smart, a blue bird without a doubt. He was not an athlete but was really smart about sports too. We hit it off right away. I found out he lived only two blocks from me so I started going over to his house at night in order to get help with geometry. With Delbert's help, for the first time I started to believe that I had some smarts in the classroom. I met his sister June and her best friend, a girl named Jennifer Bennett; both girls were in junior high. But the minute I saw Jennifer at Delbert's house, I knew she was special. As it turned out, she would end up becoming my wife. But at this point, I was a true jock, someone who thought about sports twenty-four hours a day. My life revolved around the playing field. I had no time for girls, except when it was convenient for me. That's not to say that I did not like girls because I did, but I had other things to do. I just looked on girls like a typical immature boy does. When I saw Jennifer for the first time, I thought she was so beautiful and sweet. She was a blue bird for sure. I thought, "Can a blue bird like a yellow bird?" But oh well, I had other things to do.

Although playing basketball at Polk High School was a high point of my life, I did not really learn that much about the game. Coach Hill ran lots of drills that were fundamental in nature. Fake one way, go the other, things like that. They were all good, but he never explained what we were doing and why we were doing it. I'm not sure that he understood the drills enough to explain. Also, the drills were not vigorous or intense at all. The only way practice became dynamic and exciting was if the players started getting competitive with each other. But I did start one tradition that would help me become a better coach, and that was to attend the Texas State Basketball Tournament in Austin. I started attending these my sophomore year and did not miss a state tournament until 35 years later. I always wanted to know what winning teams grasped that I did not know. I had a real desire to learn from the best performers. I needed to find out what the secret to winning was. This burning desire pushed me into and along my career for a long period of time. I finished my senior year as the leading scorer and assist guy on the team, first-team All District, All- State, Most Valuable Player and with a full scholarship to Texas Christian. Not bad for a young man who was cut from his team in the eighth grade.

THREE

BACK AT THE BIG DAY, my phone rang at 7:30 a.m. for my wake-up call. I was sweating from the top of my head to the bottom of my toes. If I had gotten any sleep at all, I couldn't remember it. Regardless, I was energized as today was the day. We had already set our plan into action the night before with an 11:30 late-night lights-out, punctuated by an "in your room or I will kill you when we get back" ultimatum from me. The coaches would be exhausted, but the players should be rested and ready for the battle ahead. I would guess we do not have a player who routinely goes to bed before midnight seven nights a week. The morning featured a scheduled shoot around at nine o'clock at the dome. We were assigned this time slot by Final Four officials following Memphis's shoot around an hour earlier. The hotel offered a hot breakfast from six till nine that morning and we told our players to get a quick bite before gathering on the bus for the drive to San Antonio. We were scheduled to leave the hotel at eight-thirty that morning for what I figured would be about a thirty-five-minute trip, perhaps even longer with police escorts and over fifty other guests following us. The tardy arrival was part of the plan; we really did not need a full hour for this shoot around.

Coaches differ about the value of a game-day shoot around. Some insist it loosens up the team and gives them more confidence. Others call it a waste of time and energy. I have always been a strong proponent because it gets the team out of the hotel and into the environment where they will have to do battle. It helps release a little steam and momentum built up inside both the coaches and the players.

I was in the breakfast room writing down what I wanted to accomplish during our hour when Bubba Peek and Sammy Burleson walked in. It did not surprise me that they would be the first to arrive for breakfast, but seeing these two wide awake and joking with each other so early did seem strange. Bubba and Sammy were always the last doing everything. They were the last ones on the bus, the last ones to get dressed and the last ones to leave the gym. They were constantly on the dean's list for tardiness.

I thought it was also ironic that these two would be in the line to eat first, not only because they were habitually late but also because they were the main reason I had been hired at North West State University. This was my first year as the head coach at North West State, or any NCAA school. I had been a high school and a junior college coach, and had also run the show at a small National Association of Intercollegiate Athletics (NAIA) college. Everything was a first for me at this level. There seemed to be no way I could get hired at a large university of any basketball quality coming from a junior college. I had applied many times before and never gotten to first base. Athletic Directors (AD) in Division One colleges and big-time schools don't feel comfortable hiring a junior college coach, regardless of the candidate or his strengths. It was not in the best interest of the university. A junior college coach had little knowledge about playing big championship games with big-time talent. Another stigma was that junior college coaches could not recruit big-time players because the restrictive and microscopic rules established by the administration and the NCAA were different for Division One coaches. I had arrived on this hot seat by an unexpected accident.

I was the head coach at Great Plains Junior College, located in Pampa, Texas and just about 40 miles from the North West State University campus located in Amarillo, Texas. I was in my ninth year and we were playing the fifth-ranked team, at our level, in the United States. With my team being ranked second, it was a big game for both teams. Our group could have more than held our own with most Division One conferences, with six guys being eagerly recruited to transfer to big-time schools; our opponent was suiting up four players in a similar situation. The contest attracted a very big crowd for a junior college game. I would guess about 4,500 people. Our sports information guy informed me that it was the largest crowd he had ever seen in the Great Plains Dome. There were over 100 college scouts from all over the country in attendance. The teams played a great game, one that wasn't settled until the last few seconds. We won 66-62 and the Great Plains crowd went home happy. After the game, it was almost impossible to get out of the gym. Scouts, sportswriters, administrators, family, and other issues had to be handled one at a time.

It was at least an hour before I started leaving, saying my usual good-byes to the custodial staff cleaning up after the game. I always expressed interest in the custodial staff and I encouraged the assistant coaches to do the same. We typically would give them Christmas presents and, occasionally, we would treat them to some coupons to take their families out to eat in the big city of Pampa, Texas. When I left the dome and started walking to my car, I noticed two gentlemen wearing nice suits and ties walking toward me. They spooked me a bit as neither had the look of a spectator; rather they looked like two businessmen, and serious ones at that. One offered his hand to shake mine, saying. "Good job, Coach."

"Thank you," I replied, scanning their faces for a minute to see if I recognized either one.

The second man piped in, "Coach Young, we have been waiting outside for the last hour for you. We are here to give you this card. Our boss's name and phone number are on the card, and you are invited to call him at your earliest convenience. We're certain you'll recognize the name and thank you for your time." Once I got into the car, started the engine, and fumbled with the interior light, I was stunned when I read the name on the card.

It belonged to JJ McFather, president of the North West State University Booster Club and CEO of Shell Oil Production Company in Amarillo, Texas, whose father was considered the fifteenth wealthiest man in the world. The older Mr. McFather started out as a cotton farmer and got rich in oil, and now owed the world's largest collection of windmills, for wind energy collection. His son JJ served on just about every financial committee at North West State; he was also involved with the present state governor, assisting with his finances for his campaign the next year. JJ was by far the most influential man in the area. The next morning at eight, I called his office and talked to his secretary. She put me on hold and thirty seconds later JJ was on the phone; I was suddenly very nervous when he said, "Hello." I could barely speak, but relaxed when he said I am excited to hear from you. With my curiosity running rampant, I was wondering what he would want with me? As you would expect from a good businessman, JJ got to the point quickly.

"Coach Young, my father, Steven McFather, and I are very impressed with the job you do and we would like to talk basketball with you, particularly about recruiting and about the North West State University basketball coaching position. We would like to arrange for you to be picked up by my father's private plane, travel to Dallas, let us pick your brains and then we will bring you back to Amarillo It would take a full day. Can you give me a date that you can make this trip?"

I almost yelled back, "How about in the morning?"

JJ replied, "Can you be at my building at 8:30 a.m. sharp tomorrow?" I eagerly agreed and JJ had his secretary set it all up. "See you at 8:30."

As soon as I put the phone down, I started getting excited and I walked around in a cloud the rest of the day. I had applied for the North West State University head coaching position several years earlier but had not even come close to getting in the front door. It was an old-school institution with a current old-school head coach. He was a really great man and an excellent coach but just could not get the program over the top. Time had caught up with him. His teams were not stocked with talent like the other schools in the conference, which was one of the best and deepest in the United States. He was honest, and as far as I knew, he had never cheated, but if he did bend the rules, he didn't do so well enough. He had always coached his players well, but had not done a good job of recruiting. He had never learned that recruiting is what college athletics is all about: The one with the best horses usually wins.

I knew where the Shell Oil Building was so I had no problem finding my way. I was sure my meeting with Mr. McFather was the start of something big for me. JJ met me in the Lobby and told me that something had come up and he was not going to be able to go to Dallas, but not to worry as his father would take good care of me. He winked at me and said, "My father is the key anyway so do not worry about me not being there." He took me to the top of the building where a helicopter was ready for takeoff. The next thing I knew I was in Dallas. The flight took fifty-five minutes.

My meeting with Steven McFather was not what I thought it would be. We talked about basketball nonstop for four hours. I have never spoken with a businessman who knew so much about college basketball, particularly big-time college basketball. Afterwards, he took me to the country club for lunch, where we continued to talk about the game. It was a delightful meeting, one that surprised me a great deal. The bottom line was North West State University basketball and how to get the team on the same level as other great programs in the United States. I told him point-blank how to do it and that it would cost a lot of money, but it could be done. Money was not something that scared him, nor did pulling whatever strings were necessary. What concerned him was who to hire to pull all this off, and I could tell he had spent countless hours trying to figure that part out. The present coach's contract would lapse next year and it would not be renewed. He told me that I would be considered for the position but it would not be an easy sale to the administration. Then in the same vein, he hinted to me that if I could build the program to where he wanted it, he would do whatever it took. When he said that, I let him have it with both barrels. First I said that there are more criminals in the NCAA than in the prison system. I then began to tell him how, who, and what was done to get players nowadays. He was a rapt listener, and sat back and took notes. I told him about how college coaches did everything within their power to steal players from other teams and to buy players from other schools.

He had just one question: "How do you know all this?" I went down the list of each player I had coached who was recruited by a Division One coach. I told him the different angles that were used to get them to sign. I told him about James Plunk. James was credited with 18 hours of college work without ever attending a class. To top that off, he received a large amount of money to go to summer school. He never left his house that summer and received the hours and the money. I continued that I was in the middle of it all, watching my players get used and bought while I was trying to figure the proper way to handle everything. I had too much first-hand info for him not to pay attention. I had been bribed, bought, and even sold by big-time college coaches and recruiters trying to get players so they could win.

Then when I started naming names, he became very quiet. I had gotten his attention, and I came across as someone who knew what I was talking about. After all, I had recruited, and coached, twenty-two school athletes who had gone on to play in the NBA. I knew something about talent and something about recruiting, things I have been learning from my first job right up through the just completed big win. My Dad taught me to have an ace in the hole and I felt I did. I became bold and told Steven McFather that I would help him turn the program around right now if that would help my cause when the time came. He looked at me very funny as though I had taken words out of his mouth: "OK, tell me what to do."

I told him that I knew where to find two of the better players in the country, both of them looking for the right place to go. I revealed what I knew about Bubba Peek and Sammy Burleson, both great players from the Bronx, New York. Bubba was six foot eleven inches tall and weighed a little over 300 pounds. Sammy stood six foot three and weighed 190. I was convinced Sammy was the best point guard in the East. I had recruited both out of high school while I was the head coach at Great Plains Junior College. Neither had the grades, nor could they pass the American College Testing (ACT) Assessment or the Scholastic Aptitude Test (SAT). I told him that I had made home visits with both players and both had visited our campus during their spring break last year. They liked me quite a lot and trusted me, mainly because I did not try to buy my way into their lives. When I visited Bubba, he had three brand-new cars sitting in the street or driveway. It was not uncommon for a big-time basketball recruiter to use every bit of incentive to get a player to attend a prep school, or a junior college, of their choice. That way, the player could gain their eligibility and, at the same time, he would be under the control of the big-time university that had put him there. Bubba just smiled when I asked him about the cars;

he did not know how to drive. I told him I taught driver's education and would teach him how if he wanted. He liked that, but declined the offer. That kind of broke the ice and from that point on, I was welcomed in his home. His mother was as sweet as could be and she acted like she really liked me. Later on, when Bubba visited our school, I found out that his mother had Alzheimers. Bubba and I really connected when he visited our school in Great Plains. The afternoon of his first day on campus, several of the guys got together for some pickup basketball. I was right there because I was curious to see how he compared to my current players. Halfway through one of the games, Bubba stopped and ask for a sub. I thought he was just tired but instead he came over to me and asked if we could talk in private. I told him to follow me and we went to my office. I was thinking *this is good: Am I going to hear that he really likes our school and is ready to commit? Why else would he want to talk in private?* We entered the office and I shut the door.

We sat and I said, "OK, Bubba, what is on your mind?"

He said, "Coach, I think I have the crabs," as he was scratching his groin area.

This was hardly what I expected but I did not want him to know I was disappointed, so I asked, "Have you been sexually active with a girl?"

"No," he replied, but he and some of his buddies had gotten together with a crazy woman in the park. He finished with, "She screwed all three of us."

"Bubba have you seen any crabs on you?" I asked.

He looked puzzled and asked me, "Can you see them?"

"Sure," I replied, "but you have to scratch them off your skin and then they will run to another part of your body."

"What do they look like?"

"Well, they're black and about the size of a pinhead." Without thinking I added, "Pull down your pants and let me see what I can find." When Bubba lowered his pants and stood there naked with his private parts hanging out for me to inspect, I realized I had made a huge miscalculation. Finding those black crabs on Bubba's dark skin was a more difficult task than I had envisioned. Bending to get a better look, I lowered myself closer to the affected area. Of course, just as I did this, the door opened up and office secretary Betty Reid stood looking at me inspecting Bubba in all his glory.

I panicked. *"Bubba has the crabs and I'm trying to locate them, Mrs. Reid!"* I called out, as she just froze in her tracks. The yell was unfortunately loud enough for the athletic director and almost anyone within a mile to hear. We all agreed I needed to go to the pharmacy and get some medicine that would kill the crabs. I have never been so embarrassed in my life. To make matters worse, when I went to the drugstore to pick up the medicine for Bubba, the clerk behind the counter was all smiles and grins as he handed me the medication. The pharmacist was one of our regents and it pained me a great deal to watch his facial expression. The next morning the sign on my office that used to say "Head Coach" was covered by a hand-scrawled one that read, "Head Crab Finder." Still, two positives emerged from this experience: Bubba, who was clearly one of the best 3-point shooters for a big man I had seen in my life, and I had bonded, and I learned you can't find crabs on a black person.

Now it was a totally different case with Sammy. He was a street kid, and quite good at it. Sammy had so much cool in him. Nothing seemed to bother him at all, regardless of how tough it got. I gave Sammy the nickname of "smooth" and he warmed to it right away. It certainly fit him. Sammy and Bubba played on the same high school team, which won the state championship going away in the large-school division. The biggest problem with Sammy was that his Dad was one of the prime-time pimps in the neighborhood, and he was being indicted by the grand jury for murder one. My home visit lasted about ten hours because Sammy did not show up for our 8:30 p.m. appointment that night. I was determined to see him so I asked if I could wait and his mother agreed. She fixed me some tea and we had a good long talk, mostly about Sammy. She said that Sammy was extremely worried about his father and that he left just before I came to go visit with his girlfriend and talk it all over. I fell asleep on the couch and soon after midnight, Sammy woke me up. I awoke to find him apologizing for everything. He was upset and did not want to talk to any basketball recruiters; he said he was sorry but he just could not concentrate on recruiting. I said "OK, let's talk about your Dad and what you want to do after college."

Sammy talked a long time about his father and it was clear to me that he loved the older gentleman very much. My patience won out and we stayed up past three in the morning just talking about everything, except Great Plains College. He did want to play on a Division One school, one that would give him the exposure to be drafted and to play in the NBA. I had watched Sammy play against the Russians during a special event where the best high school players from New York took on some of the best players from Russia. It was no contest, as the local kids won hands-down. Bubba scored 22 points and pulled down 15 rebounds while Sammy lit up the court for 12 points, 15 assists, and 11 steals; he drew three charges as well. Of course, I had first seen them both play in the state finals where their team took the championship. Sammy was an athlete, and one hell of a competitor. There wasn't a coach alive who did not want Sammy, but at the same time, not many coaches were willing to take a chance on him because of his background. It did not take me long to explain to Bubba's and Sammy's families why I felt they would be better off with me as their coach, even if it was in Texas. It was simple math. The fact was that if they attended a junior college, they needed to graduate from that institution to receive a Division One scholarship to play. I had the NCAA records to back it up: We were first in graduation rates among junior colleges, and first in retention, which was about players staying in a four-year college once they transferred from a junior college. That was my selling point and both families liked what I had to say. I had gotten through: Both realized graduation was a must if they decided to go the junior college route.

When it came time for these two kids to make a decision, they decided on Northern New York State Junior College. Bubba told me he got $2,000 when he signed and another $3,000 when he arrived. He said that he could not afford to go very far away because his mother had Alzheimer's. Sammy would not tell me the exact details but he said he got two of his friend's scholarships to go with him. I told Mr. McFather, "Both these kids know that they will never graduate from junior college and they are looking to transfer now, so they can sit out one year and be ready to play the next year." What I was telling Mr. McFather was that these two kids could become North West State players if he could find someone that could handle the off-the-record stuff. I said, "It is simple but expensive and I know for a fact that two big-time universities have already contacted them about coming to their school next year."

I continued, "You contact them and let them know you are willing to pay for their schooling next year as a student, you will get them a job, and you will take care of their expenses while attending North West State University in the fall. After they attend school for a year, they become eligible and you have two great players on your team who will be ready to play when you hire a new coach." I continued, "You will have to use good judgment and you will have to buy your way into their hearts but if done right, you can get them. I will be around to make the kids feel comfortable and encourage them your way if you will allow me to help. Of course, all of this is against NCAA rules, and you need to know that. I imagine in your business deals, you know how to handle such an undertaking." With that, I gave some more advice and gave him some more thoughts on the process and then we went finished our lunch.

As I watched Sammy and Bubba eat, I wondered how Mr. McFather got the deal done. I never heard from him after that and only could guess at the deal. I had told him exactly what I would do and that was to make the first contact, and encourage them to attend North West State University. But after that, I never heard much about what was had transpired. The rumor I heard from some of our players was that Sammy's father was cleared of any wrongdoing with the help of a big-time lawyer from Dallas who was North West State University alum and that Bubba's mother was moved into a nice high rise apartment in the better part of the Bronx. I did not know all the details, but when the North West State University basketball position came open, Steven McFather kept his word and I got the interview I was looking for. Not only that, his son JJ was on the search committee; as a matter of fact, JJ was the chairman. With JJ McFather on my side and my having won the National Junior College Championship with some of the best recruits in the nation, I was feeling good about my chances of getting the head basketball coaching position at North West State.

Of course, here I am in black and gold, North West State University colors, enjoying the moment while the rest of the players start coming in the breakfast hall. By this time, my assistants should be in full swing making sure that all rooms were clear and that all players and managers had made their way down. Darryl was the first to come down the hall into the breakfast room, sitting next to me. Darryl and I were very close as he had been with me since my first year in college. He was a Junior College All-American basketball player at Tall City Junior College, located in Midland, Texas. His freshman year was my first year as a college coach and his presence always reminded me of that. I was the assistant basketball coach and the head golf coach that year. Man, was I a rookie.

FOUR

orth-eight hours after I accepted my first college job I was trying to fit my long legs and arms in a tiny seat right behind the cockpit of a private jet. I wanted to watch the pilot operate the jet. I have always been fascinated by planes. Deep in my heart I wanted to be a pilot and loved the thought of flying. Soon, I was turning my head and holding on for my life as we went over the mountains near Albuquerque, New Mexico. As the jet was going up and down with huge jumps in between the air pockets, my thoughts went back to high school coaching. Two days ago I was coaching a spring football game and now, I was on a private plane headed to Albuquerque. Chester Stamp, the Athletic Director at Tall City Junior College put me to work as soon as I said "I will". He said, "You are scheduled to catch a plane to Albuquerque to recruit Nancy Garcia, a young woman golfer graduating from high school in Albuquerque, New Mexico." Chester had already made contact with Nancy and her coach, setting up a meeting at the high school. For information purposes, Nancy Garcia was not an ordinary golfer. She was the best golfer in New Mexico, regardless of gender. She was considered by many golf experts and scouting reports as a sure bet for the WPGA Tour. The private plane I was on belonged to one of the primary boosters at Tall City College. He was very involved in women's golf and he had made contact with Nancy Garcia himself. He made a huge donation to the college as long as the college started women's golf. Very few universities gave full scholarships for women's golf, much less men's golf

30

and even few junior colleges offered scholarships for women's golf. Tall City College was in a class by themselves.

As soon as we landed, I caught a cab to her high school. I was excited and nervous at the same time. I had a briefcase with me with information about Tall City College, but had never recruited nor even coached women before. When I arrived at the high school, I went straight to the office and asked for the head girl's golf coach. He came to the office and we met. He was a very nice guy and we had an easy conversation as we went to his office. We sat down and he says to me "Coach, I am sorry but Nancy signed a Letter of Intent last night to attend the University of New Mexico." She sends her regrets and wishes you the best. When I called Chester to tell him the bad news, he said, "Welcome to recruiting!"

My job description at Tall City Junior College was Head Men's and Women's Golf Coach, Assistant Men's Basketball Coach and Physical Education Instructor. I taught tennis, weight training, and bowling. I loved every minute of teaching on a college level. To me, it was not a job. It was so different than teaching on a high school level. College students cared about the course and the grade they were going to get, therefore creating a different attitude and performance level. I never considered it work to teach at the college level.

Chester told me that in the fall, I would be busy with golf and not to worry about basketball. That was an understatement. The first objective was to recruit a women's golf team. Tall City College competed in men's golf last year and they had every player back so at the present time, my main focus was recruiting women. Chester had already recruited one girl from Midland, Texas so I had to go to work. The girl's team was easy to get because no one in our area played women's golf. I picked up two really good players from Temple High School, and one decent player from Amarillo High School.

Four weeks into recruiting and I was finished. <u>My first lesson to learn about recruiting is that you are never finished.</u> Two weeks before school was scheduled to start, I got a phone call from one of the girl's parents in Temple, Texas. Seems that the two girls from Temple changed their mind and decided to drop us and go to Tri State Junior College, in Temple. Tri

State was the only other junior college in Texas participating in women's golf. Not only that, the girl from Amarillo decided to join the other two girls. Everyone involved with Tall City College was upset, but the really unhappy person was President George Lang. The next day, Dr. Lang told Chester that we were going to have a women's golf team or Tall City College was going to need a new AD and golf coach. He said, "Tell Ron to get a team together regardless". It was now a week before school was to start and I was in a deep panic. I started calling everyone I knew that I thought could help. Everyone tried to help and some gave me leads to follow but each time, I came up empty handed. It was so late in the recruitment for girls because they usually have their college plans completed by this time of the year. Then it hit me; age is not a problem with the National Junior College Association. You can be fifty and still qualify for participation if eligible. With this in mind, I started advertizing for women's golfers [any age] that wanted to play college golf. I sent flyers out to all the golf courses within a 100 miles radius. I finally got four women, Nana Jones forty-seven, Judy Reese thirty-eight, Becky Duran thirty-one and Lacy Mann thirty-two. They received scholarships and carried a full academic load, because the NJCAA required all athletes to carry twelve hours to be eligible. They were from the West Texas area and all were married. We were the most consistent women's golf team in college golf that year as we always finished last. Golf season was a riot!

My wife and I bought our fifth house at Midland. Since the girls were so young, ages 6, 4, and 2, Jennifer tried to stay home with the girls, but finances were tight so she went to work part time for Tall City College in the Registrar's Office. We found a home with three small bedrooms, and one large master bedroom. It was simply made for us, as the bedrooms were like a dormitory. You had a long hall way, with each bedroom connecting with the hall. All the bedrooms were alike with the same floor-plan. At the end of the hall way, there was a large bathroom and a large playroom. We could not pass it up.

I owe much to Chester Stamp for any success I have had. He gave me a chance to be a college coach and he believed in me. Anyone who knows anything about college coaching knows that the key to winning in college is all about recruiting. Chester recruited Darryl and the first time I saw him in the gym, Chester pulled me over and said, "This type of athlete is what we want to recruit at Tall City." Chester sent me to Kentucky and Illinois on a week recruiting trip. He gave me some solid advice and told me where to go but other than that, I was on my own. I made my plans and attended several high school tournaments in Kentucky and Illinois, going from one high school to another talking to coaches about players. I found out two things: one, people in Kentucky knew very little about junior colleges, and two, they would lay out the red carpet if you were a basketball coach. Kentucky people love their basketball and they don't mind telling you how the game should be played. In Illinois it was not much different than Kentucky except they were a little more distant. One thing Chester emphasized over and over was that I should be careful not to recruit players who can't make a difference in the Western Junior College conference. The year before, West Texas Junior College, a team that was in our conference won the National Junior College Championship and the standard was set high. I was proud of Steve May who was the head coach of West Texas Junior College. Steve's first coaching job was as my assistant basketball coach at Ford High School, in Hereford, Texas. I came back excited from my trip with a long list of names of players that I thought could play basketball in our conference. I gave my information to Chester but I could tell that Chester was not as excited as I was. Ten of my top recruits signed with Big Time division one schools and the other five signed with a lower level division one schools. Three of the top fifteen went on and had a tremendous career in the NBA. I was so embarrassed and felt so bad once Chester explained everything. I wasted all that money and time for nothing, except for me to learn a very valuable lesson. <u>Don't try to recruit someone you have no chance to get.</u> Yes, all those players could play and were the kind of player we needed in our program but no, they were not the kind of player that we could get. They had grades, they had passed the ACT and they all could qualify for division one scholarships. I simply didn't do my homework enough to know the most important concept of all is the question "Can Tall City College sign-this player?"

Chester was one of a kind. He never said a lot to me about my failure as a recruiter on that mission. Instead he just stayed the same kind good natured guy. Now don't get me wrong, I have seen the bad side of Chester Stamp. When he gets mad, he turns red and when he turns red, no one including me wants to be around him. We were playing a game at Midland in the P.E. facility, and were beaten by a poor call at the end of the game. I saw Chester turning red so I tried to calm him down and it worked up to the point until we were entering our dressing room. Then all of a sudden he grabs a basketball and bounces the ball on the floor in anger that the basketball goes straight up to the ceiling, hits the hanging lights, dusts flies everywhere into the crowd leaving the gym. He was that strong and powerful when he got mad. We were playing Abilene Junior College at Abilene for our first game of the season. It was the first game of the year for both teams and it was very clear that the Abilene officials needed more time to clean the gym. Everything was dusty and dirty. Chester received a technical foul for questioning the official's judgment on a charging call. The more he had time to think about the call, the angrier he became. The half ended and we started walking to our dressing room when "Bang" Chester hit his fist on the wooden scorer's table. He hit it so hard that dust flew everywhere and everyone in the gym stopped whatever they were doing and looked. Next, Chester shouts to the crowd where the officials could hear him as they were walking to the dressing room. He looks at the crowd and says, "You want to see a charge, I will show you a charge". Then turns to me and says "Coach Young, run over me". I just looked at him with a huge question mark on my face, as I was not about to run over him. Thank God, we finally got into the dressing room. Chester gave me my first victory as a college coach. We were playing Valley Junior College in Big Spring, Texas. My wife and his wife were setting right behind our bench. Chester got a quick technical foul in the first half on a call that anyone would question. For some reason, Mandy, his wife who is just a sweetheart of a person, turned to Chester and they started yelling at the official together. It was obvious that Chester and Mandy had a run-in with this particular official before. I had never seen Mandy act that way and it just seemed to turn Chester on that much more. Chester was kicked out of the game before the first half was over with us leading by four points. I had to take over and coach the game. I wish we would have been behind but we were ahead and that put more pressure on me. It took forever to start the game again because Chester refused to leave the gym and stood in the entrance doorway with both arms stretched out from side to side of the doorway as to block anyone leaving or entering because he was a huge person. At half time I received notes from Chester telling me what to do. I know things were going to get tough as Valley does not lose at home. It was a really small gym with no room on the end line or side line. It was a great full court pressing gym which is exactly what Valley did best. Grey Wilder was the coach and his team would pick up at the baseline and cover you like a blanket for 94'. I decided that we were going to spread the court and try to penetrate on each possession since they were applying so much pressure. I tried at halftime to explain the four corner offense. I looked at Darryl and told him to penetrate every time he got the ball and everybody else, to create passing lanes for him to pass the ball and get ready to score. He could penetrate on most anyone, but what separated him from others was he could pass the ball to an open man when he penetrated. We won in overtime by 111-110. It was an unbelievable game. Darryl scored 42 pts and had 12 assists. Chester forgave me that night for the blunder in Kentucky.

That spring, Permian Basin Junior College in Odessa, Texas reassigned the Men's Head Basketball Coach, Marcus McDougal. They did not fire him but moved him into the Physical Education Department. Coach Mac was on the way down. He was a good coach in his day but the conference had long passed him by. He was a sound smart coach but just did not have the players to win in the conference. The bar was raised by Steve May. I called and put in my application for the position. Fred Gibson, who was on the school board and the father of Jamie Gibson whom I coached at Odessa Permian, went to work trying to help me get the Permian Basin Junior College Position. Matt Wilson, who was on my Permian High School team that went 28-4, was now a sophomore to be at Permian Basin College went to the president office and talked for me. Of course, the Odessa American got information that I had applied and they put their stamp of approval of" my being selected head coach." This went on for a month. By now, Burns Roberts, the golf coach at Permian Basin College and athletic director was a good friend of mine so I called him several times concerning the position. I felt I had a good chance to get the Permian Basin College job because of my connections and because of the negative background concerning the basketball program at Permian Basin. There was no history of winning and Permian Basin was the doormat of the conference, always finishing last or next to last. I found out that Steve May had applied and that just floored me, as I could not figure out why. I called him and we had a long talk. He told me not to worry because he was just trying to get a raise from West Texas Junior College. Finally one day, I received a call from Dr. Dave Smith, the president of Odessa College. He asked me to come over for an interview. I did and the interview went well, I thought. The interview was on a Friday and I did not hear from anyone until Wednesday. Dr. Dave Smith called me and explained I had come in third in the race for the job. He asked me if I would still be interested in being the head coach at Permian Basin if the other two declined the invitation. I said yes and forgot the issue. Four days later, I get a phone call from Dr. Smith asking me if I would accept the head coaching job at Permian Basin College. I said that I would have to talk it over with Jennifer and would get back to him within twelve hours. I called Steve May and asked him what happened. Steve said that they offered him the job; he turned it down and then got a raise from West Texas Junior College. I called the president back the next day and told him that I would love to be head men's basketball coach at Permian Basin Junior College. After the conversation ended, I asked Dr. Smith what happen to the second choice, as I already knew what happened to the first choice. He said that they did a background check and found out their second choice was gay.

FIVE

BACK AT THE BIG DAY the trek to San Antonio from the hotel in New Braunfels was the most exciting bus ride that I have ever been involved with. Flashing red and blue lights from our police escorts set the tone with more than 500 fans scrambling not to be left behind by our entourage. The scene would have been laughable except it was dangerous as well. The college kids were beside themselves with excitement and enthusiasm, screaming at a decibel only the young can achieve and maintain; at least half were probably still hung over from partying into the wee hours. Darting into and out of the lanes both in front of and behind the bus, trying to get the attention of some of the players, they fed a scene comic yet frantic. I felt bad for the bus driver, but he kept driving as if most of his rides went something like this. It was the print press, the broadcast media, and the families upon families that provided most of the laughs. We had imposed a gag rule on the players and I had the coaches take their cell phones away from them at ten the night before. This treatment was new to the players but we decided we had no choice, what with the unrelenting press coverage, not to mention friends and family members trying to remain connected to the their heroes. In reality, the players were just as glad for the semblance of peace and quiet, and we set it up so they could blame the coaches for not being able to talk or visit with family, friends, and other interested parties. All twelve players had family attending the big game and this group posse was growing by leaps and bounds before the tip-off to start the game. The last time I counted we had over 250 people claiming they were family who just had to have tickets. The gag rule gave us coaches at least some control over the chaotic situation. There was nothing new in big-time college basketball about confiscating everyone's cell phone. I had learned the hard way years before those players, regardless of how sincere or well-intentioned they were, will stay up all night talking to girls, buddies, and family if allowed. At any rate, the total news blackout was effective. No one knew what was happening except us, and as soon as we headed toward the bus, the panicky swarm sprinted to any method of available transportation to join the caravan. No one wanted to lose contact with the bus. It was a mad rush not to be left behind. Think Black Friday in the mall or the Oklahoma Land Rush. The race was on.

We were not far away from San Antonio when Willie "White Shoes" Warnell came from the back of the bus and sat down beside me. Willie was a solid six foot one inch guard who wanted to be six foot three. The first time I met him, he was decked out in high-heeled men's shoes and an Afro haircut, and I thought he was six foot six. Further inspection indicated a frame about six feet tall and weighing 170 pounds. He was from Los Angeles where he attended East Side High School. He was a very cool guy and if Willie wanted something, he had a way about him that got results, exasperating you but making you smile, all at the same time. He was an excellent salesman and always had a smile on his face. He would simply hint at what he wanted, expecting you to figure it out. We called him White Shoes because he loved to wear all-white tennis shoes. He liked all sorts of clothing, but the shoes were his trademark. Everyone knew him at school; everyone called him Willie White Shoes. I wouldn't be surprised to learn that almost none of his schoolmates knew his last name. He loved being called Willie White Shoes, and we all obliged him.

Like many involved in college coaching, I started recruiting Willie long before his sophomore year in high school. He was the second-leading scorer in the city of Los Angeles as a freshman, and by the time he was a sophomore, he was no longer second. He had the best pull-up jump shot in basketball and he could shoot the ball from any angle on the court, but his specialty was a step-back shot move going to his left. That move alone raised Willie to another level as far as recruiting goes. Of course, he was an outstanding athlete also. What made him more interesting and hard to guard was that Willie played differently than most right-handed players. While most with that dominant side invariably made their move to the right, Willie worked his moves to his left. He told me one day that he threw a baseball with his right hand but he would write with his left. He said he batted lefty but played golf righty. He could play to either direction; no one could cheat on him defensively. He was a big-time recruit for us at Great Plains College. Recruiting is so much luck and in this case, I was very lucky. His high school guidance counselor happened to be my uncle on my mom's side of the family. That is how I heard about him and the truth is that is how I got him on the dotted line. When our family had its annual reunion, numbering around 100 people, Uncle Howard told me all about this kid named Willie Warnell. Howard got to know him very well. Willie was beset by recruiters and would come to Howard for some relief and advice about what to do. The two became close and Willie learned to trust my uncle. Howard would call me and tell me who was recruiting Willie and what they were offering. I would tell Howard how to reply, whom Willie could trust, and so forth. Willie thought Howard knew it all when it came to college offers and that opened the door for a deep friendship between the two. This coincidence got me in the door, a place few recruiters would reach. I was just waiting to see if he would pass the ACT or the SAT.

Willie lived in the projects on the east side of Los Angeles. He always dressed to the hilt, always had nice clothes and I learned that that was something that was important to him. He liked nice things. In my opinion, Willie was the best guard in the United States from the standpoint of being able to both pull up and shoot and to drive to the basket. His decisions were solid, his court sense developed; the only weakness in Willie's game was his defense. He simply wasn't interested in defending. That did not bother or surprise me because most great scorers were the same: They do not want to play defense, but they all want to play. I made it simple for them; play defense or you do not play. I even worked out a means of determining their defensive performance on the court, so it was not something that I worried about. I used a system of pluses and minuses that I learned in high school and refined along the way. I carried it over and used it to rank how a player performed defensively in a game. All aspects of defensive play were totaled up and the players with the best defensive grade got into games first. They were my starters. A low grade did not mean that you would not play. But you would have to wait your turn to get in the game. It wasn't a gut feeling, or a result of any personal likes or dislikes--the highest grade got you the first opportunity. Defensive rebounds, steals, deflections, charges, blocked shots, and defensive stops—they all helped your score. If a player contributed on the defensive end in a measurable way, they played. I made it even fairer by dividing the number of minutes played into the total defensive score, which would give each player an objective grade. With my system a player could play only five minutes but still score higher than a player who played thirty minutes. The players hated it but I loved it. They had to play hard on defense in order to keep playing. .

Despite Willie's reluctance to play defense, recruiting him fit my philosophy perfectly. To my way of thinking winning in basketball was simple. Just ask yourself two questions. First, can you win a championship without a talented scorer? My answer to that question is no, a lesson I learned the hard way time and time again, just like other coaches have. It just doesn't happen. The team with the most talent that can do the most positive things on the court wins, yes, but it a paramount that they have somebody who can shoot and score in difficult situations. I have been teaching myself this one for years: Make sure you have at least one, and hopefully more than one, player who can shoot and score. The other question is can you win the game without getting good looks at the basket? The answer here is no as well, although I do look at that question from a defensive viewpoint first. If you can deny your opponent good looks at the basket, you will win most of your games, given roughly equal talent. Of course, some coaches, and many players, come at it the other way: Work your tail off to get good looks at the basket, and the wins will follow.

As I had guessed he would, Willie made good grades but did not pass the ACT. That put a lot of pressure on the decision of what to do next. There was a limited amount of time he had to make a choice. He had already signed a letter of intent with UCLA and they wanted to place him in a local junior college close to their school. They tried to talk Willie into a prep school but he didn't want to do go that route. Because of my uncle, I knew more about Willie than he knew about me. I recruited Willie's best friend, Victor Brown, who played on his high school team; we signed Victor to a part scholarship, part financial aid agreement. It was a gamble, but I did have inside information that if Willie had to go to a junior college he wanted to go wherever his buddy went. Recruiting his best friend gave me the opportunity to recruit Willie in a casual way. It was a way that Willie very much appreciated. He was a steal for me and it happened just like I planned. He visited our school, liked what he saw, and decided to sign a scholarship agreement with Great Plains College. We were lucky because things usually do not turn out the way you plan them when it comes to recruiting, but every once in a while it does work out.

I remember the battles Willie and I had over his defense to this day. I demanded he play it, and he stubbornly refused to do so. At one point, I even told myself that I had made a mistake recruiting him. He simply was too immature to understand that we could not win without him doing his part. He would say to me, "Coach, you recruited me because I was a scorer and now you want me to play defense."

"That's right, Willie," I would reply, "and now I'm trying to raise your level of knowledge in the game of basketball, so we can win as a team and you can become a complete player." Our arguments were hopeless, with both of us insisting we were right. It wasn't until Willie saw that, right or wrong, he would have to sit on the bench if he did not play defense that he finally came around to my way of thinking. Once he did, he was a monster defensive player. His scoring went up and our winning went up. He was the main factor in our National Championship. His sophomore year, he came in first in the scoring title and won the Defensive Player of the Year award in the National Junior College Athletic Association (NJCAA). I was so proud of him, and he was very proud of himself.

Willie averaged twenty-six points a game his sophomore year at Great Plains. His play was one of the reasons I got the position at North West State University. He was by far a better player than anyone on the current Black and Gold team and he was very popular in this part of the state. You might think that it would be an easy transition for Willie to go with me to North West State University, but it was just the opposite because he started feeling his oats and getting a big head about his game as big-time schools came knocking on his door. All were willing to go the distance to get Willie, which meant they were willing to buy him if necessary. It really impressed him, and now convincing Willie to sign was a difficult deal to close. I remember the day; I called JJ McFather and told him I needed help in getting Willie's signature. Of course I knew what Willie liked so I told JJ what some other schools were doing. I felt sure that if we were going to have a chance of signing him, we needed to compete. During spring break, when Willie was at home, the doorbell rang. He opened the door to find a shoe box with instructions that it was to be opened by him, but he had to sign for it. It was neatly gift-wrapped with a note that said, "Open as soon as you get this." Willie of course couldn't resist, opening it to reveal a pair of white Nike tennis shoes with black laces with "Black and Gold Lions" written on them. Along with the shoes, there was a nice card telling Willie how much the North West State University Lions wanted him to be a part of the State family. And it closed with the statement that "we always take care of our family." No signature or identification of the sender was included, but when Willie grabbed the shoes to lace them up, he was shocked to find a hefty sum of money hidden inside the shoes. It was more money than he had seen in his lifetime, and it came with an unlimited account credited to Willie at the best clothing store in Pampa. It stated that the card was good as long as he played for the Black and Gold Lions. Willie told me about it when he signed. He said, "Coach did you know about the tennis shoe deal?"

I said, "No, but I knew that 'Something was going to happen,' because I had passed it on that we were going to lose you if we did not compete."

"Funny thing," Willie added. "There was more money in the left shoe than in the right. Do you have any idea why?"

I didn't know I confessed, but his game was becoming known. Just to be funny I threw in, "Perhaps you're more valuable going to the left than to the right."

Now Willie was sitting next to me on the bus ride and it did not take a rocket scientist to figure out what he wanted. He said, "Hey coach, I got family and friends in town and I want to take them out tonight to a real nice restaurant and go first class. I want to celebrate our National Championship in style. How about a small loan? I will pay you back."

I said, "Willie, you know I do not loan money out to individual players. You know that that is against my policy."

He replied, "Yes, sir." The players knew that no loans would be coming from me. It just wasn't going to happen. It was not because I did not want to or because I could not get the money, but rather because I did not want to discriminate one player from the other. Whatever I did for Willie, I had to do for any of the twelve on the team. It was a concrete die-hard absolute team rule for me.

But to cushion the blow, I said, "But I will call JJ McFather and have him handle this situation for you." I then said, "Check your mail later and I suspect you will have received something that will ease your problem before the day is over." Willie smiled and went back to his seat.

As Willie moved back to his seat, I thought to myself how terrible I had become. I could not sleep at night. I was always restless, breaking out in sweats, just knowing any day now; someone was going to blow the horn. I was disgusted with myself and how I had allowed my self-esteem and my sense of ethics to become so compromised. *I have joined the other criminals who cheat every day in order to get the job done. I have joined the group which I hate and cannot stand,* I thought to myself. I rationalized that the only ones who do not cheat were the ones who could not afford to. As one of college basketball's Hall of Fame ex-coaches has said, "The integrity of NCAA coaches is a joke. It's all about buying players to win." To me, it's almost like you're playing the role of a big mafia boss in the movies. There he is attending mass while at the same time his henchmen are murdering people in the street. Big-time coaches hide behind different types of smoke screens while their players are stealing, robbing, mugging, buying, and selling dope. Then the same coaches are put on a pedestal and regarded as exalted beings qualified to teach Sunday school classes. It is a disgrace to our society and the NCAA.

I was not always this way. I can still remember my first year as a head college coach and how I worked so hard trying to do the right thing. I stood for everything that was right: for honesty, hard work, and integrity. Those were the first tricks I used to influence the young men in my care. Getting the position of head basketball coach at Permian Basin Junior College was like a dream come true. I didn't care that I got the job by default; I just knew I had the job. I was excited about it and I had to figure out what to do. I called several of my close friends who were coaching on a Division One level and picked their brains with pen in hand, perched to jot it all down in a notebook. I knew nothing except from my experience at Tall City College in Midland, where I had been an assistant. According to my notes it would come down to my ability, 1, to outwork my opponents, which I felt confident about; 2, to find players that had division one talent but could not sign with a division one school because of grades or other situations; 3, to promote my program within the town community and within the school community; 4, to get the school administration, particularly the president, to make a commitment to my program; 5, to find players who can fit into my style of basketball; and 6, to get these players graduated and moving onto big-time schools. Now that I knew what it took, I needed to go to work.

My first college coaching job was anything but easy. I dreamed big and knew if my dreams were ever going to be real, I would have to prove myself over and over again. I was not in a network such as North Carolina, Duke, Kentucky, and all the big major schools where their graduate assistants get jobs with other colleges if they hang in there long enough. The program at Permian Basin College was bad as it gets. They hadn't had a winning record in five years and it had been twenty years since they had been in the playoffs. The last time they won twenty games or more was twenty five years ago. Permian Basin was considered to be the floor-matt of the conference, and the city of Odessa was a football town. Junior college basketball did not interest the city much at all. It would be easy for a basketball coach to stay on 'cruise' at Permian Basin College. Not much was expected from the coach, other than to be competitive. Permian Basin College was a good place to get a college education.

None of this bothered me at all, because I just wanted a chance to show what I could do as a college coach. One thing that I learned is that everything is relative. It didn't matter if you were coaching at North Carolina, Texas Tech or a small high school. Everything matters the same to the people involved, coaches, players, parents, administrators, and fans. They are involved and could care less what is going on somewhere else. Losses are lows, wins are highs and the emotions are basically the same. They all have the same feelings and everyone wants to win.

The first thing I had to do was to figure out what was wrong and then find ways to change it. The first thing I noticed was that Permian Basin College did not have a good recruiting budget at least compared to other teams in the conference. I knew two of our opponents so I had a fix on that issue. There was no assistant coach at Permian Basin College, whereas most of the conferences schools had assistant coaches. This of course leads to limited effort in recruiting and virtually all aspects of coaching. When Permian Basin did get a player that could play, it was usually chance or situational. The coach before me simply did not have the funds or the time to do the job correctly and it really was not his fault for not having talented players. Next, there was a lack of discipline in the program. Very few players continued their basketball careers after Permian Basin College. They either did not have the grades or were not good enough to play at another level. The last thing that hurt the program was the reputation of the Permian College basketball players. The community of Permian Basin College and the city of Odessa considered the athletes to be social misfits who could not fit into a community environment. The overall life of the basketball players centered on the fact they did not regularly go to class and their public behavior was not acceptable to most of the community. Some of the guys would be playing a pick- up game in the gym and all you could hear were four letter words coming out of their mouths as loud as they could scream. It was embarrassing when visitors came to the gym. This alone was the main reason that the previous coach was reassigned. Most people felt he had lost control of his players. To make things harder, the head men's basketball coach did not even have an office where he could work. With all this knowledge, I began a series of necessary changes. It is not easy to change the way people think or act, but I needed to go at it full blast with no regrets. There is an old saying that goes something like this:

"It is almost impossible for people within a structure to correct a problem when they are the reason for the problem."

First, I talked to the president, trying to get his attention directed to some of the problems if he really wanted to have a winning basketball program. He was nice and professional but I could tell he wasn't going to do anything immediately. I did talk him into making an office for the men's basketball coach, with a phone line out of a boiler room next to the gym floor. Once that was done, I left the door open and every time, I heard a four-letter word come out of a players mouth, I sprinted into the court to attack the group involved. I instructed them to leave the court and not to come back for a week. It did not take too long to stop the foul language. Next, I made the entire basketball team meet in the morning for breakfast, then go to class. If they went to breakfast and not to class, they had to go through two stages of discipline. One, I would break their plate, meaning I would not feed them in the cafeteria and they were on their own for one week, and two, I would release them from their scholarship if it happened again. It did not take long for that to stop. All this happened in the last three weeks of school so I really did not get my full momentum into them but it was enough that six guys decided not to come back. It did get the attention of the administration and some of the professors which was the best thing that could happen to our program. We had zero money for phone calls so I talked our athletic director into a deal where we could use a phone watts line in one of the large business downtown Odessa. We could use it at night only, but it did allow us the phone at no charge to Permian Basin College. They allowed us two nights a week so I signed up for Wednesday nights from 5:00pm-11:00pm and Sundays from 4:00pm-11:00pm. I loved it as you could call anywhere in the United States with no charge. I stayed organized and used my time wisely. Players, coaches, and others soon learned to expect a phone call from me on those nights.

I laugh now but at that time in my life, I decided to concentrate my recruiting in San Antonio, Houston, West Texas and New Mexico. From my limited knowledge, that was where big time players could be found. I had no budget so I had to be very conservative in my spending. My reason for including San Antonio was that my parents lived there and I could stay with them saving money. Also, it was hard to believe but San Antonio was the tenth largest city in the United States and very few colleges recruited players in San Antonio, especially junior colleges. Houston was a no-brainer, simply because of the talent and the size of the city. At that time and period, Houston had the best talent in the state and was so large that lots of good kids were left out in the cold. Being very conservative, a good friend of mine, Julian Spears my mentor at Midland High School, lived in Houston. He was not coaching any more but working as a stock broker. I could stay with him and save money. Recruiting in the West Texas area was simple for me as I knew the players, coaches and communities. New Mexico was new to me but we had two players returning from Albuquerque, NM and I really liked both of them. That led to one of the best connections in recruiting I have ever had in John Houseman, who was the high school coach at Albuquerque High. John was a legend and soon we became good friends which led to finding other players. John's teams played in the state championships year after year and he was the reason behind it. He was a military man, clean cut, a nice dresser, and ran a disciplined ship. He was an honest humble man and a guy I trusted a lot. I concentrated on just three cities in New Mexico, Albuquerque, Hobbs, and Clovis, but John was the key to any evaluation I had.

The last part of my plan was the hardest. I knew deep down to have success I had to have one-on-one contact with the players I was recruiting. I needed to use my personality to create a relationship with a player and the parents. For that to happen, I had to get a recruit on campus or get into their home. I felt if I could get a home visit, I had a chance. At Permian Basin Junior College, we did not have funds to fly athletes in to visit the campus and that was a huge problem. My motto was 'where there is a will, there is a way'. I decided I would recruit four or five players at a time. I would travel in a twelve-passenger travel van on Sunday to San Antonio. I would spend the night with my parents in San Antonio, pick up a load of recruits on Monday morning and head back to Odessa. Of course, I had already made my contacts, visited with the parents and players on the phone. This always helped everything to go smoothly. On Wednesday night, I would take the players back to San Antonio, drop them off and head to Houston. I would spend the night in Houston, and then on Thursday morning, pick up players and bring them back to Odessa. On Saturday night, I would drive back to Houston and drop off the players, then go to San Antonio to pick up another group of prospects on Monday. I did this for six weeks in a row. It was a ten-hour drive to Houston and a seven-hour drive to San Antonio. I concentrated on inner-city schools in Houston and San Antonio and by the end of the six weeks; we had over fifty players visit Permian Basin Junior College.

Early in my career, my greatest asset was my wife, Jennifer. One night, we had the three recruits from Houston at the Barn Door, a nice steak house across from Permian Basin College. Jennifer came with me because I needed to attend a conference meeting that was being held at the same place. We arrived at 6:30pm, ordered our food and I went to a private room for the meeting. Somehow, the meeting took a long time as several issues were debated over and over. I would leave the meeting and check on my wife and the players every once in a while but I had to leave Jennifer without my support. I finally got away from the meeting around 8:30pm and when I returned to my seat, the recruits had a pen in one hand and said "Coach, we're ready to sign." My wife was a better recruiter than I was.

My first year at Permian Basin College, I signed four players from Houston and three from San Antonio. I thought I was lucky at the time when I signed my first big time athlete, James Knight a transfer from Houston University. He was my first big time athlete to sign and I learned a lot from that experience. One, when you sign a big time blue bird basketball player, there is a price to pay. Since he was one of the better athletes in the state, he had been pampered a lot and he demanded some things before he signed. We could not pay him what he wanted but we could provide him his Pell grant and work study money which were legal. I found a summer job for him at Permian Basin College in the bookstore. I had to drive back and forth from San Angelo to Odessa every Monday and Friday that summer. He had an uncle that lived in San Angelo so on the weekends, he would stay in San Angelo and during the week, he would stay in Odessa. Two, if they are unhappy with you or your school, they are going to let you know it every day.

I picked up another six-foot-five transfer from New Mexico University and a six-foot-one guard from Clovis who was a very good athlete. I finished my recruiting with three kids I coached in high school that I felt could play on a college level. What is funny is that in my first recruiting class, not a one could start for my team at North West State University. What I learned later as a college coach that I did have a good recruiting class for a team like Permian Basin and I had outdone what was done in the past by Permian Basin standards. The only problem with my comparison was that I was comparing our team to a team that finished last. We were not very good. It was a very hard lesson to learn and it took me a long time to learn it. You are only as good as who you compare yourself to.

The next thing I did was a huge gamble as I was breaking out of my comfort zone when I took over the scheduling of classes for my basketball players. I wanted to make sure that they were taking at least eighteen hours of academic work, and wanted to make sure that they had the right instructors. I did this so when they dropped a class, they would still have enough hours to be eligible. Also, I wanted to make sure I knew when they dropped or added classes, and what time their classes were held. I became their counselor. I took over their Financial Aid Grants and Pell Grants, Work Study Program making sure that all of the paper work was correct. If right, the person that qualified for a Pell Grant would have plenty of spending money for the fall semester. All of this was a lot of work for a "yellow bird," but to be honest, I never put any thought into the process. It was something that had to be done. I soon learned how to handle each situation and I thought, "Just maybe, this yellow bird is developing red bird wings." After all, I finished my M.Ed. at West Texas State University and was starting my doctoral degree at the University of Texas at Permian Basin.

My first year as head coach, was a great year in basketball by Permian Basin standards. It was not a great year by my standards. We won more than twenty games and set twenty-two new records at Permian Basin College. We won our own tournament but finished fifth in the conference. That was not good enough to make the playoffs. It bothered me a great deal that we did not make the play-offs because I felt we were good enough.

Little did I know at that time, but my teams would qualify for the play-offs for the next twenty three years in a row.

I look back at my Permian Basin College coaching experience and am grateful and lucky to have started at a college at the bottom instead of at the top. I had to suck it up and be creative in order for us to survive. Now don't get me wrong, I learned over the years that it is harder to stay on top than to start from the bottom, but for me, Permian Basin was a great starting point.

A sad thing happened that year at Tall City College when the entire coaching staff was fired in the middle of the year. It could have been me as I was on that staff the previous year. It seems that some grade changes were made to help some division one players gain eligibility that summer. Little did I know at the time but I soon learned this was another way the big time coaches manipulate and pay for players to get benefits they do not earn. It hit me hard and I felt for the coaches, particularly Chester. Tall City hired an interim coach to finish out the season named Paul Persons who later became the athletic director. Tall City College finished strong and made the play-offs, but we all were very sad for the coaching staff.

Although we finished fifth in the conference, we did have two players make the first team All Conference team. James Knight, a Houston University transfer and Charles Johnson, a Houston Wheatley by-product both received full scholarships to play at a division one school. James attended San Diego State and Charles went to New Mexico State. Both got drafted and both played in the NBA for one year, and eventually got cut. Charles is in prison right now and James was killed in a drug deal that turned bad. They were my first two guys that I coached that you could call big time players. It was clear that I did not get the most out of them and I did not feel comfortable coaching them. I was worried about both issues because I knew deep down that I failed with those two guys.

Both Charles and James had a drug problem and that was something that I did not know how to handle in my early years. I had never had to deal with drugs in the schools that I coached, so it was a new challenge for me. I was clueless how to stop it. We had a team that could have won the conference championship but because of drugs, and drug attitudes, we finished fifth. One thing for sure, I was going to find a way to stop it.

The next lesson I learned at Permian Basin College was something that would stay with me forever. That spring, Tall City College started looking for a basketball coach. I received a call from Mr. Paul Persons, the athletic director and he asked me if I would be interested in being the head basketball coach. Tall City was building a huge basketball arena, new dorms, new classrooms, a new student center, and other new facilities and they had the money to back everything needed to be successful. On the phone Dr. George Lang, the President of Tall City College and Paul Persons came across very strong. They made it clear they wanted to win and they felt I could get the job done. Of course I was interested, so we set up a date to meet. Now, I really liked Dr. Lang and Mr. Persons. Both men were my kind of people and I felt comfortable with them. Dr. Lang was an ex-football coach and Mr. Persons was an ex-basketball coach. They offered me the job and would give me a huge raise if I accepted. Dr. Lang was from the old school of thinking. He did not mean any harm but he said something I did not like in terms of how many whites and how many blacks should be on the court at one time. No doubt about it, Midland was a better job, better facilities, better future, but I was not sure that I wanted the job. Dr. Lang's statement really bothered me. As soon as I got back to Permian Basin College, the administration from the president, vice president to the athletic director came into my office. They had already heard about the meeting at Tall City College. Mr. Persons had called and told Permian Basin Officials that they offered the Tall City College position to me. Dr. Smith, the President looked at me and said "Tell us what we need to do to keep you at Permian Basin College." I thought it was strange that all of a sudden Permian Basin Officials were interested. I know I had been a pain all year long to all of them about changes that needed to be made. It was clear to me that this was my chance and I let them have an earful. I hit on them about the drug problems, money problems, assistant coach problems, teaching problems, travel problems and academic problems. They told me to wait at least twenty-four hours before I made a decision. I agreed and the next morning I met with Dr.

Smith. After meeting with Dr. Smith, I was stunned that I received help on every issue I had. Bottom line, when you got clout, you can get someone to pay attention but if you don't have clout, your chances of something happening, are slim.

On the drug issue, Dr. Smith came up with some answers. One, he wanted to hire an assistant basketball coach and let him be the dorm director. Two, he wanted to hire drug dogs to go through the dorm with a special agent to run random drug checks. Three, he wanted to provide educational programs concerning the use and the abuse of drugs in their life. To top things off, he gave me a raise, upped my recruiting budget, and took my classes away from me. He gave me the title of Head of Community Relations at Permian Basin College. I turned the Tall City position down.

That spring, I went looking for a guy that could be a dorm supervisor and assistant basketball coach. I knew whoever I hired was going to have to be a special person and one I trusted. Also, I knew exactly where I was going to find this particular person and it was in San Marcos, Texas. He happened to be my brother. Mike and Betty were living in a trailer house on edge of San Marcos where you could actually see the sun set in the west. He was my youngest brother by sixteen years, and in my opinion, the most talented one in my family He was very smooth in all respects of life situations and attitudes. Most importantly, Mike had already decided that he wanted to coach so that did make my job easier. That afternoon, Mike cooked steaks on his outside grill, we had a few beers and I talked Permian Basin College Basketball. Betty had already graduated from Southwest Texas State University with a teaching certificate in Elementary Education. Mike lacked a year to graduate so my plans included the opportunity for Mike to finish his education at the University of Texas at the Permian Basin in Odessa while being a dorm supervisor at Permian Basin College. With administration help, we could get Betty a job teaching elementary school in Odessa and that gave me confidence I had a good plan for Mike and Betty. It would be an early start on his coaching career and should help him obtain a job the next year when he finished at UTPB. Two weeks later, Mike called and said "It's a done deal," so we went to work together at Permian Basin College. Little did we know or understand, but a brother and brother team can really be a strong team.

The next year at Permian Basin College, we started the same routine in recruiting but this time, we had an early jump as Mike and I were recruiting the entire year on the phone and going to games where we scouted players. This time we moved out on my original territory and included Ft.Worth, Dallas, and East Texas. We got a nice tip from an ex-player about two players from Marshall, Texas. We followed up and signed those two from East Texas, two more from Houston, two from San Antonio, and one from Dallas and one from Ft.Worth. We continued and picked up two really good athletic basketball players from New Mexico. It was by far a better recruiting class than the year before.

Again, I learned a huge lesson in recruiting; one that would carry me for life. I got involved with a kid from Midland Lee High School. His name was Jimmy Ray Dennis. Jimmy was six-foot-one and weighed about one-hundred-seventy-five pounds. He was a scoring machine and tough as a boot. In high school, he had a terrible attitude in games, always getting technical fouls and a negative attitude so most college coaches stayed away from him. Jimmy had been kicked out of several games and the people in Odessa hated him on sight. This was not good for me since I was thinking about recruiting him. His competitive nature really got my attention with the fact that he could score. He could score inside or outside and it did not matter who they were playing. It was an all-or-nothing type of deal. I was not sure about him from an attitude standpoint and I wondered why Tall City College was not recruiting him or at least not signing him. After all, he lived in Midland. I found out later they were concerned about his attitude. To make things worse for me, Jennifer worked at Midland Lee as an English teacher. Finally, I asked her to find out what was going on with Jimmy Ray and the next day she told me that he had no one showing any interest and he really wanted to attend Permian Basin College. That was not hard for me to figure as Jimmy and one of our current players, Albert Herring were good friends because they played on the same Outsiders team in the summer. Albert had told him that I was a good coach and he should come to Permian Basin. I really liked Jimmy's game but not his attitude, so I had to find out for myself. I went to Midland Lee expecting to find a troubled young man, but instead I found a young man that was a leader in the school. I was confused, so I sat down with the principal, assistant principal and head basketball coach. I thought it was odd that they were so willing to help this young man when all I had heard was negative. Jennifer talked to several teachers about Jimmy Ray Dennis, and to my surprise, we found nothing but positive comments about him from all the people we visited. He was a leader at the school and everyone at Midland Lee just loved him. In my research, I found out that he would stand up for people and fight if necessary. He stood up for Midland Lee and often went overboard. He did have an emotional problem on the court, one that had to be corrected but I enjoyed everything I heard and from that day on, Jimmy Ray and I became very close. <u>I learned right there that you can't judge a book by its cover.</u>

My second year at Permian Basin was totally different. We finished second in the conference and made the playoffs for the first time in over 20 years. Jimmy Ray was a first team all conference pick and I was coach of the year. Not only that, we broke all existing records and filled the gym each night we played. We lost in the first round of the playoffs against McLaren Community College. They had a player named Delbert Johnson who went on and made a career in the NBA. He was a big time player and we could not stop him. I did not realize it but we had established a winning record at Permian Basin two years in a row and were slowly bringing back pride into the community. We received many headlines in the newspaper and our players were graduating from college. That spring I was selected along with my dear friend Coach Stamp to coach the Texas-Oklahoma all star game in Shawnee, Oklahoma.

My third recruiting class at Odessa College was my best ever. I did the same things I always did, but got better quality players. I had Mike helping me so together we picked up the pace. We found out that parents liked a brother-brother coaching team so we used that a lot in our recruiting process. We finally hit pay-dirt as we picked up two kids from Melba High School in Houston. Melba was one of the better teams in Houston and this was a first for us. I really liked the head coach at Melba and felt we had a lot in common as far as basketball. He coached fundamentals, defense, and attitude. We picked up six-foot-eight, David Johnson and six-foot-five Josh Savoie. We also signed another six-foot-eight, Marcus Ivy and then signed the MVP guard of San Antonio, Ivy Anderson, a six-foot-six scoring machine. I was starting to understand the concept of staying in a certain area to recruit. Back at home, I picked up five-foot-nine point guard Cubby Kitchens from Hereford, Texas, and Tim McLemore, a six-foot-six post from Permian. We also picked up a big time athlete from Hobbs, New Mexico. I really felt good about this class of recruits and was excited to start the year. It was by far the best class of recruits since I had been at Permian Basin College. I expanded my recruitment to Chicago, Los Angeles, and New York. Every year I was expanding my recruiting but I had not been back to Chicago since my first year at Tall City College. I still wanted to go back to Chicago so I did some research and used Boyd Ball's scouting report and headed out to Chicago. I felt I knew exactly where I wanted to go and who I wanted to recruit. I was ready this time. I did do my homework.

I was excited about the trip and made plans to stay five days. I was not going all that way to not do any good. I made sure that I had the best of clothes, packed them in a brand new suitcase and went on a plane to Chicago. When I arrived, I went to the baggage claim only to find out that my luggage was lost. I checked into a motel close to the airport and ran into an old friend named Carter Pennyton. He and I hit it off when he was a high school coach at Cross Plains High School and I was coaching high school at Albany High School. He was presently the coach at Hicks County Junior College. HJC always had guys on their team from Chicago and they were always good. He let me borrow a couple of shirts so I could have something different to wear. Every day I called to see if they had found my clothes and I had no such luck. After five days on the run, in freezing weather with clothes that smelled like rot gut, they found my clothes. I came back with fresh new clothes. I tried to explain but I know Jennifer wondered about that trip. I did sign two players from Chicago. They were different and I had to learn all over again. Little did I know but you do not have to go to Chicago to learn a big lesson about college recruiting which can be learned just around the corner.

I was in my office with David Johnson, my favorite recruit from Houston. David was now my fourth big time player. He was a guard-forward type player as he could pass, and shoot with the best of them. His only problem was speed. He already had division one schools lining up to recruit him and had not played a quarter of college basketball. It was in the early part of the fall and I told him that his grades had to improve. The good part was that he had no absences but the bad part was that he had four "F's". I asked him "What is the problem?" He would just shake his head like "I don't know." Of course, I tried to motivate him by telling him about the division one coaches interested in him and all he had to do was to make his grades. I talked to him about how proud or how disappointed his mom would be about his grades. After talking over half an hour about his grades, I told him that I was going to talk to each professor to find out and get back to him later.

My mom and Dad moved to Odessa that summer to be closer. They were getting older and I felt better with them being closer. After the death of Jennifer's parents, my parents were all we had left so Jennifer and I decided to try our best to take care of them. I helped my mom get a job in the cafeteria at Permian Basin College and she loved the job and everyone loved her. I asked her if David was rude or not coming to breakfast. She said that he was one of the nicest ones and always came to breakfast. I thought," he comes to breakfast, is polite, goes to class and has four "F's." "Now, that was a first for me". After talking to each professor one on one, I knew the problem. I called David back into my office and this time I was not so nice. I raised my voice and said, "David, every instructor said the same thing. They say you turn tests back in without any answers. Is that true?" He had his head down and said, "Yes." I couldn't help myself as I went off at him and told him point blank that was the worst excuse for failing a course that I could think of. I told him that either he started answering the questions or I will get a bus ticket with his name on it to Houston. I was totally confused because nothing made sense. He was the smartest player on the court and picked up things quickly. His learning curve was the best on the team from a basketball standpoint. He was unselfish with the ball, an excellent rebounder and one of the better defensive players. I hated it when all four teachers called my office and told me that he had repeated the process again with no answers on test papers. My golden rule is "Never say you are going to do something and not back it up." What I learned with all players and particular the best players, that if you say something, you better back it up. I had tears in my eyes when I went downtown and bought a one way ticket for David Johnson to travel back home to Houston. I called David into my office and to be honest with you, I was not prepared for what happened next. I said "David, I talked to your professors. Each one said that you still do not answer the questions on tests. Is that true?" He said "Yes". I pulled out the bus ticket to Houston and handed it to him. I told him that I was sorry but I could not justify his actions in the classroom. I handed him a drop card where he can drop the classes from Permian Basin College and told him to fill it out and sign. I explained that by dropping his classes now, his transcript will be clean in case he decided to attend college somewhere else. He had tears in his eyes by now and I just went along with my business and waited for him to fill the card out and sign.

This is the hardest part. Your heart tells you one thing and your mind tells you another. He just stared at the card for a long time and I kept waiting for him to fill it out. It seemed like a life time waiting but after ten minutes, I gave up and said, "David what is wrong?" He broke down crying and with an emotional bust of energy, he yelled, "I can't read this so I can't fill it out." There was a long silence with both of us just staring at each other. I was trying to figure all this out. Then, I said "David, you can't read". He said "No, I can't read". I then said, "David, can you write?" He said he could not write. I looked hard at him and really did not know what to say. Finally I asked, "How did you pass in high school?" Now, all this time, he has never raised his head or looked me in the eye. He looked up and replied, "They passed me because I was nice and not a problem in class." The first thing that came out of my mouth "Does your coach know about this?" and he said "Yes". Then I asked, "How did you pass any tests if you could not write or read?" He said they gave him oral exams and he could pass them. I thought to myself,"What have I got myself into with this recruit?" Something hit me hard and I told David he was not going back to Houston, just go back to your room and I would get in touch with you later. I said, "I have no idea what I am going to do, but I'm going to do something." As soon as David left, I called Doc Walton, health instructor who was also the athletic trainer. I told him the entire story and asked him if he would give his last test to David orally. I explained his situation and to my surprise, Doc agreed to do so. I called David and told him to see Doc and explained to him that we were going to try to do something to keep him in school. I said, "We were fixing to start all over." I then told him that Doc was going to test him orally in health. Doc called me as soon as David finished the test and told me that David made a ninety-one orally on the test. I went crazy. My first thought was that this kid is a genius and we do not know it. Of course, I was a yellow bird so this fight was easy for me to understand. He thought he was stupid and had been told that all his life. It is all about how you perceive yourself.

After getting approval from the administration, I personally went and talked to each teacher David had in class and asked them to help us this semester by giving him oral tests. To my surprise, each one agreed. Two of the professors really got on me about recruiting a kid that can't read or write but I had fallen in love with Permian Basin College. Each teacher really wanted to help him. They all liked David a lot and were equally excited as I was when he could answer most all of the questions asked. It was unbelievable that he could digest lecture and visual learning to the point that he could answer verbally. He finished the fall semester with a 2.8 grade average. The next semester he was placed in low level reading classes and math classes. He had extra classes he took to improve his writing and reading. David did all this without anyone on the team knowing it. He really wanted to do something about his life and he went to work doing just that. He would get up early and go to classes that were designed to help him learn to read and write. From that day, forward, I was a huge David Johnson fan. I loved the guy.

No one loved him anymore than his teammates as he was always making outstanding passes to them so they could score. He was blessed in some ways that many of our players would never understand. He was the ultimate team player. Now you put him with Jimmy Ray and Josh Savoie, you can have an outstanding team. All you lack is a good point guard and we had one in Cubby Kitchens. He was better than I thought and he fit with those guys like a glove. It was without a doubt, the best team I ever had in my coaching career. We won over twenty-five games easily and broke most of the records ever set. Jimmy Ray Dennis became the all time leading scorer in Permian Basin College history. Cubby Kitchens set records for assists and we made it to the finals of the regional tournament. Our conference was as tough as it gets.

West Texas Junior College, coached by Juan Rodriquez had a great year led by Ryan Paul who played in the NBA ten years. We could not get past them. Coach Rodriquez had a team that went to the finals for the national championship. I learned more about coaching when my teams played against Coach Rodriquez than any coach I ever coached against. Of course, he went on and had tremendous success in several different NCAA schools and eventually he won the Division One championship while at Arkansas. He had his guys sold on pressure defense and coaching against his teams made you a better coach. Not only that, but Coach Julius Stone was now in his second year at Tall City College and had an outstanding team. Somehow, Julius would get the best players out of Dallas year in and year out. You could not beat Julius in Dallas. It was just a matter of time before Tall City College would dominate in basketball. They had the best of everything and Julius was just the right guy to lead them. I knew deep down I was getting close to what it is all about or at least that is what I thought.

The last story I want to relate at Permian Basin College was when I learned that luck plays a huge part in the recruiting process. We had four starters back from a very good team. Also, we had Anderson Cooper who had to be held out due to injury. Needless to say, we were in very good shape. Mike took a coaching job in Moloch, Texas as the head boys basketball coach and assistant football coach. I relaxed in my recruiting because I felt good about the coming year. I learned the hard way that would be a mistake. Simply put, I felt comfortable with the players returning. I really did not see anyone that I could recruit being better. I learned later in coaching, that kind of thinking will beat you every time but I did not know it then. I went through my usually process of recruiting but did not have the same intensity or heart. I signed some players from the large cities as I always did, but the highlight of my coaching stay at Permian Basin College was just around the corner and didn't know it.

That year, the North Regional Texas High School Championship was being held in Abilene. Grey Wilder, coach at Valley Junior College, Julius Stone, coach at Tall City Junior College and I decided to attend the tournament and share expenses. Monterey High School was one of the favorites to make the Texas High School State Championship as they were led by a player named James Hoch, a six-foot-six guard. We all teased each other about who we were trying to recruit but we all were interested in James. He had all the basketball numbers you wanted and the size to go with it. The only problem was that he was white and we questioned the talent level of any white player coming from the West Texas Area. All of us had been burned many times by some great white player that was supposed to be everything, only to find out he was just an average player when he had to go against quick black players. Not only that, what followed was angry parents calling you at all hours telling you how you were cheating their son. As we watched the game that afternoon, all three of us kept looking at each other to get a feel of how we felt about James. To me, it was not like he was having a bad game, but he was just too slow and not athletic enough to play the college game. I thought, just another white kid that over- achieves. After the game, we all challenged each other about our honest evaluations. We all agreed that James was not a college prospect from the standpoint of making a difference in a program. Yes, we all felt he could play but not a making a difference.

Two weeks later, I had my team at Permian Basin college going through a spring workout when one of our players cornered me and said "Coach, did you see James Hoch play this year?" His name was Cubby Kitchens and Cubby had played against Hoch in high school. I said "I watched him play at the regional tournament last weekend." "I was not very impressed with him." Cubby then followed "Coach, was he hurt?" "If you were not impressed with him, something was wrong." Then I said, "Cubby, he was slow on foot and I do not think he can play at our level of competition."

Cubby looked at me and said as he walked away, "Coach Young, if he can't play on this level, I can't play on this level." Besides that, Cubby said "I do not remember him being slow." This conversation bothered me. No one thought Cubby could play either and he was without a doubt one of the better point guards in the conference. I thought a long time about it and out of reaction to Cubby's attitude; I called James Hoch on the phone and asked him to come for a visit to Permian Basin College. It was just a "gut feeling" I had when I called him.

He said that no one was recruiting him except a couple small four year schools. Then he said, "I am really open to anything right now." We set a date and I told him to bring his basketball shoes because we would play some pick up games. I told him to come around noon and my mother would take good care of him in the school cafeteria. On the day that he was supposed to visit, he did exactly as I said. He went to the school cafeteria where my mom worked, and she made sure he received all he wanted. She called me and told me that James was in the cafeteria. I went to the cafeteria and met him for the first time. I was very impressed with him and I told him that we would start playing around two-thirty that afternoon. The guys on the team loved it when we had recruits visiting our campus. We would always play pick up games and they would rather do that than go though a tough off season workout. To be honest with you, I loved it too, for all I had to do was keep score. Cubby picked teams that day and picked James to play with him. What I witnessed next is a true Cinderella story. Three times down the court and I could not believe my eyes. James Hoch was a true blue bird big time basketball player. The greatest thing was that James did not know how good he was. How could he, because no one was really recruiting him. That night, I went home with James to visit with his parents about coming to Permian Basin College. It was not easy as his parents had their heart set on a large four year school and the idea of him going to a Junior College was not something that set well with them. I did the best sales job I have ever done in my life. It was easy because I believed in Permian Basin College and certainly believed in his talents. I worked as hard as I ever worked in those two hours. Two weeks later, James signed a letter of intent to attend Permian Basin College. After James signed, I asked him why he looked so slow at the regional tournament. He said, "I knew I must have looked bad because I felt bad. Coach, my legs were gone by the time we reached the high school regional's. Those three and four hour workouts every day at the end of the year just took a toll on my legs and strength. I had nothing left during the play-offs. " Enough said because I knew he was telling the truth. I had been there myself.

James was the best player that I have ever coached up to that point in my career. He was so fundamental, so sound, and so competitive. He was by far the best player on the team, and what separated him from so many other players was his mind. He was positive in his thoughts on the court and his body just followed. We were playing San Jacinto in the semi-finals of a tournament. San Jacinto was on a winning streak after winning the National Tournament the year before. Ronnie Irons was coaching them and to this day, Ronnie and I are good friends. It was a game that I will remember the rest of my life. We beat them by two points and stopped their winning streak. James scored 18 points, got 10 rebounds, had six assists but more importantly drew five charges in the game. After that game, James Hoch would never be the same from a recruiting standpoint. He became one of the top recruits in the country.

We were playing NMMI at the military institute and the military cadets started making fun of his hair. James had golden blond hair and the cadets started calling him 'Goldie-locks'. He scored 26 points, got 12 rebounds, eight assists as we routed New Mexico Military Institute. We only lost one game in the fall semester and won two tournaments. We were good and had our share of Division One players but West Texas College was above our level. West Texas College beat us twice by one point each time, then went on with a 36-0 record and won the National Junior College Championship.

The next year, Tulsa University had four players recruited from West Texas College and won the National Invitational Tournament. That opened my eyes and I knew we were getting better. James Hoch was a really big time player. He went on and played in the NBA 13 years and had success. I was lucky in finding him and recruiting him but it was not luck in identifying him. In four years at Permian Basin College, I had five players that played in the NBA. My start as a college coach was not a normal start.

As soon as we finished the regional tournament, I came home to find a message from Gary Smart, Vice President at Panhandle Baptist University. I called him and he said that some officials at Panhandle Baptist had asked him to contact me to see if I was interested in being the athletic director and head men's basketball coach at Panhandle Baptist University. He contacted me at just the right time as I was down about the season ending at Permian Basin College and the loss to West Texas Junior College. I said yes, I would be interested. Of course, Jennifer was not happy but I felt I needed to look into it regardless just to honor their interest. Panhandle Baptist offered several things that made the job appealing to me. One, being athletic director was something I always wanted to do. There was a chance of my becoming athletic director at Permian Basin College but Panhandle Baptist was a university and Permian Basin College was a junior college. The challenge was different and somewhat stronger at Panhandle Baptist as Panhandle Baptist had several issues facing them. Two, my chances of going to a Division One school would be greater at Panhandle Baptist than Permian Junior College and that was still my main goal. Three, my recruiting style was a better fit at Panhandle Baptist than Permian Basin College. Although I did a good job of recruiting at Permian Basin, other coaches in the league did a better job as they seem to have better contacts than me. Four, recruiting was different in a four-year school as you did not have to bring in a new team each year. You might have a year where you are just recruiting two or three players. Five, the program was in a slump just like Permian Basin was when I first went there. With all this in mind, I accepted their job that spring. I was going to Panhandle Baptist University as their athletic director and head men's basketball coach. This was a huge step.

SIX

BACK AT THE BIG DAY, arriving at the Alamo Dome was as exciting as playing for the championship. The place was packed with fans everywhere screaming for joy. The Black and Gold was much in evidence among all the banners and pennants strewn around the venue. Having just completed their shoot-around, the Memphis team was exiting as our entourage entered. Memphis fielded a huge, fast, quick, and talented squad, ranked ahead of us the entire year, at times as high as No. 1 in the nation. They had knocked off perennial power North Carolina 82-72 in the semifinals, which was no fluke. From my perspective, it appeared as if Memphis outplayed North Carolina from the opening jump ball right until the finish. The closest game, and only real scare, for Memphis in this tournament occurred in their first round vs. Marymount, where they were stretched into an overtime period before winning. Since then, it had been pretty much a cakewalk into the finals for them. Not only was Memphis anchored in the center by a six foot eleven and a six foot ten player, both big bodies were quick and strong, and could score with their backs to the basket. Add into the mix the plays of probable, according to most experts, first-round draft pick Winston Smart, a six foot two slender and lightning-fast point guard. The trio proved their mettle in the win over the Tar heels, as Smart scored a game-high 23 points, and the two big guys inside brought down 31 rebounds between them. Memphis was as talented from top to bottom as any team in the United States, a judgment that was amply backed up by their 29-2 record.

As was understandably fast becoming an obsession of mine, I couldn't help wondering how they managed to get all that talent on one team. How had they managed to get all those players to commit to their school? It wasn't like any of those guys was not extensively recruited. When the top teams in the country all want the same player, I always wonder which school will win out, and how. Multiple factors come into play: school tradition; programs that had players who went on to win the most NBA titles; location; weather; quality of the conference in which they play; how many players are returning for another year; coaching style. But the bottom line is money, and lots of it. Money is requirement number one to get the job done, some of it spent legally, some not. I already knew some of what we had been doing, but what about Memphis, I wondered?

The dome was huge, with a seating capacity of 45,000. Ticket scalping was going on in earnest as far as the eye could see. Fears or no fears, it was moments like these that had you smiling and just thrilled to be a part of it all. Arriving at our dressing room--"North West State University Lions - Championship Dressing Room"--we plowed in, soaking in all the buzz and excitement. Each player had a designated locker and dressing area with his name on it, with all kinds of gifts and freebies filling their space. Banners were hung everywhere, North West State University signs too, and the middle of the room, awash with ribbons and decorations, was dominated by a huge basket of fruit, candies, and cold drinks--just about anything you could want. A giant TV screen showed last year's final four championship game. This state of the art video system was yet another toy, provided in this area just for our use. The room bubbled with excitement.

Before you knew it, the door burst open and the Dome manager called out, "You're up, North West State Lions." We rushed as a group to the gym floor in a burst of energy that had me concerned. I wanted to yell to the players to slow down, to bring it all under control, but this moment of exuberance got the better of us all. The players ran on the court to a burst of emotion and cheering from the fans, who seemed to be perched everywhere and who liked our team quite a bit. For a moment, I let myself forget the task at hand. We were the Cinderella team. It seemed most everyone in America supported us in our role as the underdog. Easily

15,000 people had showed up for our morning shoot around. The clock said just after nine in the morning, but the noise and excitement seemed to scream nighttime, prime-time, the big time.

I was proud of our guys. They had withstood a lot of negative hype to get here. It would have been easy to forget that the players on the court had each had a choice and they picked State. There is a huge difference playing for North West State University on the one hand, and UCLA or Duke, for instance, on the other. From an early age, kids dream of hitting the championship-winning shot for one of those big-name programs, but not for North West State. Our panhandle Texas school was not high on the list of where players wanted to attend. North West State University had no tradition of winning basketball. If anything, school history prepped a player for more of a win-some, lose-some tradition. The school was not a pipeline to the NBA with just one ex-player on a current big-league team. Compare it to me and my situation: Just a junior college coach, I had more guys playing in the NBA than this Division One School did since it was organized in the early 1900's.

The weather in Amarillo was as unpredictable as the fortunes of their past teams. One day it would be sunny, the next day cold with winds blowing 40 to 50 miles per hour. Making matters worse was what we all referred to as Dr. Death, the dust storms in the spring. One good storm could dampen an athlete's enthusiasm to play here quicker than a bullet through the head. Not only that, the population in Amarillo was mostly white and Hispanic, making some of my strong African American players feel overwhelmed and out of place. They were a special group of talented players, and now they had just won five straight games in the National NCAA Division One championships. Neither overconfident nor cocky, they all realized that each game had been a war and could have gone either way. The winning was fun, yes, but what made it special for me was the fact that I was 100 percent convinced that this group of young men had done it by outworking each opponent we had faced up to this point, the final game in the Final Four. I had put these guys through hell and back in the fall in practices and in weight training, and all the hard work was paying off.

I felt one advantage I held over many coaches was my experience coaching football in Texas high schools. I'm not actually sure if I'm a better football coach or a basketball coach. Most college round ball coaches could care less about football. If asked to help with their school's football program, they would decline, perhaps politely, perhaps not. To my way of thinking, to learn the ropes in a basketball-only coaching environment is to be pampered. Luckily, that had not been my fate. In Texas if you wanted to coach basketball, you had no choice but to help out with football first. Basketball just does not hold that special a place in the state. In Texas, high school football is king. None of which bothered me in the least: A true child of the state, I really enjoyed coaching football too. It was no punishment working the kids on the gridiron, it was a privilege. I find it ironic that I wouldn't be as good a coach if it wasn't for football, because in Texas, that is where all the great coaches are found. A typical Texas football coaching staff employs between four and eight men. High school basketball programs are lucky if there are two coaches; often there is just one. With all that expertise in the football programs, I was learning from some of the best in a way I never could have just in round ball. In high school and college, it's all about player development. Football coaches work night and day trying to groom and improve their players. Player development is coaching job number one. I was lucky because I learned from the best, the Texas football coaches. Learning what makes a good program and how to set one up separates all the men and women doing this job. It's not possible to really know what program will work and why until you've been in the middle of a good one. Teams do not win year after year by accident. It is a learned trait and one that comes from having developed a good program.

I was hired at North West State University because of my winning record in basketball and my connections but what school officials did not realize was that my strength was in building and evaluating a program. It takes lots of work and I was experienced enough to help evolve the way things were done at North West State University without making a big fuss. I had had my first exposure to a really solid situation years before when I was hired to be the head boys basketball coach and assistant football coach at Permian High School.

I remember I was at the Texas High School State Tournament being held at Gregory Gym in Austin, Texas, home of the University of Texas Longhorns. Built in 1935, Gregory Gym was old and worn out, but it had been the best place to play basketball in Texas back in that day and time. But by this point in time, let's just say that it was less so. Gregory Gym had been the home of the state basketball tournament since the University Interscholastic League (UIL) organized in 1935. The UIL governs all high school athletic school competition in Texas. Held in three sessions as it was, getting tickets and finding seats to the state tournament games was a mad house. You had to exit and return for each session. All Texas high school coaches received free tickets so that took care of half the problem, but finding a seat was still murder. With close to 5,000 seats and a host of schools competing at these games, it sometimes became a case of standing room only, and long lines for tickets. We in coaching had formed a little group who would always sit together on the north end of the old gym. They weren't particularly good seats but we didn't care. At least we didn't have to fight for a place to catch the action, and generally one from our group got there early enough to save some seats.

To make the time spent there a little more interesting we came up with a game, where we would each bet one dollar (big-time spenders, I know) on each game and try to predict the total points scored. Closest to the correct figure would win, so even if one team dominated in one of the tournament games there was something to pique our interest right to the end. We might have anywhere from ten to twenty coaches participating, and it was fun riding each other on terrible picks and talking trash. More often than not, I would be the guy holding the pot, and keeping a record of everyone's picks. One day there was a gentleman sitting behind me whom I did not know, but we started talking round ball and coaching, and by the third quarter, we got to know each other pretty well. He had grasped our little game right away and joined in; like it was something he had done at games before. I just assumed he was a friend of one of the other coaches playing. But we finally shared introductions and I found out he was none other than the Athletic Director and current head football coach at Permian High School. I didn't know why a football coach was in our midst at the state basketball tournament, but he was obviously enjoying himself so I never asked. Little did I know that within two weeks of this delightful afternoon, Permian High School would be welcoming new Head Boys Basketball Coach and Assistant Football Coach Ron Young.

Permian did not yet have much of a school basketball tradition when I arrived, but I set myself the task of changing that. Although I thought that I was there to set things up and teach everyone how it was done, I ended up learning more and more about running my own program every day. I thought I knew maybe 95 percent of what I needed to know when I arrived, but what I really discovered was how much I didn't know. After an early stumble or two, it became a learning experience that would better prepare me for what I would face in the rest of my coaching career. When I left Permian I took a very good idea of what I wanted to work with going forward with me. I used concepts I learned from football coaches at Permian and Brownwood to develop a solid college basketball program. It must have been at least somewhat effective because at the next few stops in my coaching career I would use the same techniques and setup to bring six different schools from the lower rungs in their respective leagues and conferences to the top. By the time I accepted a Division One head coaching position, I was very confident I could turn a school around if given the time and some talent.

The fans don't see all the hard work players put into a team, and that is why it is so rewarding to see them enjoy success and get their due from all the hard work and commitment. I introduced an off-season program that was second to none in the area of development of athletic talent. Along with this off- season routine, I developed an in-season one as well, one that focused all our attention on developing player skills and talents to the maximum. The work was hard, and I was pretty demanding, but it was rewarding to see players who stuck with it. And to think it all came from my early experience at Permian High, home of the "Mojo" and "Friday Night Lights," along with my vicarious adventures at Brownwood High School, home of the legendary Gordon Woods.

When I got the chance to find out first hand why the "Mojo" always wins, I jumped on the opportunity. I wanted to know how they win year after year after year. My first clue happened the first day I reported to Odessa Permian for spring football drills. I thought I misunderstood him but it was clear that I would get my regular salary they quoted, no classes to teach, and all I had to do was coach spring football. As the Head Boys Basketball Coach at Permian, I was going to get full time pay and coach football in the spring. I far as I knew, that was totally unheard of the Texas.

The day that I arrived in Odessa, Gilbert Branch, the Head Football Coach-Athletic Director decided to leave Permian to coach football at Texas University. Now, I knew what he was doing at Gregory gym. I really did not understand the impact his resignation had on everyone at first. Two days later, I realized that at Permian High School, when the head coach leaves, no one has job security, and that meant me. That was my second clue to what a real program is. That night, Coach Branch visited with me and promised that I still had a job and not to worry. It finally hit me that all the other coaches, eight in fact, might be gone once Permian decided who they were going to hire to take Coach Branch's place. I was beginning to get the thought that this place was different than any place I had been in high school. Since spring training was going to start on Monday, the administration made John Sparks the interim head coach. Now, everyone had three weeks to clear the air and get something done for next year. As a head basketball coach, I couldn't have entered the picture at a worst time. John was nice but distant, and very demanding. His assistant coaches were all into keeping their job so friendliness was out of the picture. It was clear after one day that is was going to be every man for himself. We did nothing but work on football and coach kids to play football. I was completely taken in by the intensity of the entire staff. It was just spring, we started early and finished late and it was nothing but football. John Sparks was the most intense coach that I had ever known. When he would get excited, his voice would go up a notch and you would pay attention. He spared no one, coach or player his intensity or his sharp mouth. .

For sure, football at Permian High School was an eye opener for me. I did not have enough money to stay in a motel during this period of time, so I just slept in the Permian Field House. I had plenty of room and would not bother anyone on the basketball side so that is where I made my home. I rented a roll-away bed and put it in my office. I had a shower and plenty of room for my clothes. Besides that, at Permian no one uses the basketball side in the spring. It was just not a popular thing to do. I was learning quickly that a solid program is made up of little bits and pieces that create a special feeling within the program. Coaching spring football at Permian was something that I would never forget. Remember, I always had the philosophy of trying to learn from other coaches. Well, I had nine coaches I could learn from and I got a masters degree in coaching. A simple football practice alone would draw between four hundred and six hundred spectators. It was something that I was not used to. Shot- gun alley would draw about five hundred people in stands that were enclosed just for that drill. Shot- gun alley is something that all football coaches do in practice. It is aligning up a center, a blocking back and a running back on one side of the line of scrimmage, and then getting a down defensive lineman and a defensive linebacker on the other side of the scrimmage line. The offense has three downs to make a first down. If they do not make a first down, then coaches change the lineup for what ever purposes they desire. The difference at Permian was the intensity level. Permian had two portable stands that would sit about two hundred spectators each. Most everyday that we had shot gun alley, the stands would be filled. Peer pressure is the greatest of all pressure that young people face and this event was no exception. Fans, parents, teachers, administrators, and anyone watching would get on their feet and start screaming, clapping, even booing sometimes for their favorite player to "Hit somebody". Not only that, the coaches would get into the act. It was something to watch at Odessa Permian. Remember, it's not what you do but rather how you do it. One of the major differences at Permian was a football coach could do just about what he wanted to in practice and get by with it. I was floored by our workout schedule as we would work every morning from six-thirty to seven-thirty and every afternoon from three to six. After morning workouts, players would have to shower, get dressed and get to class on time. Twenty Blow dryers were installed to help. Students would attend classes and then start over that afternoon. The morning workouts during spring training were set up and organized in such a way that we worked on the fundamental techniques of blocking and tackling. I was getting an education of a lifetime in football management. John was very organized and each coach had an assignment. What really excited me was the fact that each coach was very good at what they did. They did not try to do everything but instead only what they were supposed to do. If they did not perform very well, then John would have a meeting with them after practice and go over their mistakes. He wanted it done right. It went like clockwork and before the end of the spring training every player was well schooled in the art of blocking and tackling. In the afternoon, we would then put those techniques to work in live blocking and tackling. Again, it was not what they did but how they did it. Other coaches do the same thing but not the same way. The intensity level was so high that many athletes just drop out of the program. It was a survival course which creates an atmosphere of competitive greatness. Over one-hundred-forty athletes would start off the spring training with the hope and dreams of being a "Mojo" football player. By the time those athletes would be seniors; only about fifteen to twenty would still be around. Trust me; those seniors maxed out on their talents. At the end of spring training, John was named the Head Football Coach at Odessa Permian High School. Everyone was happy for John and themselves. They would get to stay at least one more year.

That summer, I finally got an opportunity to look at the basketball players coming back next year. Not bad I thought as the numbers were good. About thirty young athletes came to the gym each night we had open gym. I had two athletes that caught my eye that seemed to be a little ahead of the others and both were seniors. One was a six foot seven post player and the other was a six foot one guard. The only thing that I did not like was I thought they played soft. Of course, that is something that is hard to explain but it is easy to spot. It does not always mean that the athlete is soft, but means they just don't understand how to play basketball with aggression. I found that to be typical for football players playing basketball. Ken Hawkeye was going to be my assistant coach. Ken was moved up from junior high to junior varsity assistant coach and when asked what second sport he wanted, he picked basketball. Come to find out, he had been the head ninth grade basketball coach at Nimitz, the year before. Nimitz was one of the major feeder schools for Permian. Ken was a great guy, loved to play golf, and he loved the kids that he coached in junior high. He really helped me in identification concerning which kids played basketball and which did not. He told me that our best player was not showing up for summer basketball. His name was Darryl Bunting, who was the starting middle linebacker, at six foot five and two hundred forty pounds. Of course, I got to know him during spring training and he was a physical specimen for sure. He had speed, quickness, and a nose for the football. He loved contact and was an excellent competitor. I thought, great! But where is he? Ken also told me that our sophomore class was loaded with good basketball talent. That news had a good ring to my ear. Ken became a person I could trust. He was married and had a little girl about the same age as my oldest daughter, Ann. My wife and his wife hit it off, and we soon all became good friends.

At Permian, football season did not start at the beginning of the school year but right after the fourth of July. The entire coaching staff would meet with football players at different parks in the city of Odessa. We would take roll, as they were expected to be present. We would run sprints, do agility drills, work on a few pass patterns, and then let them play touch football. We would start around seven in the evening and finish around nine. Of course, this was always in the gray area whether it was against the UIL rules which govern Texas High School Football. I never knew and never questioned. When regular workouts started, we would do three workouts a day until school started. We would workout early in the morning, that afternoon and then later that evening. It was twenty-four hours a day of football. What was the most interesting concept about this work ethic was the fact that "it was expected and demanded". No one thought anything about it or questioned it. It was the "Mojo" way. Once school started, we would go back to working out twice a day as we did in spring training. The only difference was the morning workouts were more intense than in the spring workouts. I was in complete shock. It was clear to me why Permian always wins in football. The ultimate sacrifice is made by the players and coaches, not to forget the parents. I had never worked that hard before nor had I ever witnessed players working that hard. By the time, a player reaches his senior year; he has reached his potential or something was wrong with him. In other words, when he finishes his senior year, he is as good as his talent would allow him to be. That is what the "Mojo football program" creates. A complete football player that has survived a program that allowed him to become the best he can be.

I coached the Junior Varsity linebackers and assisted with the secondary. On offense, I coached the offensive ends. We had four junior varsity coaches and each of us had our own assignments. We were the varsity scouts as we worked in groups of two. I was assigned with coach Spears a veteran football coach of twenty-five years. We would scout an opponent for two straight weeks and then another opponent for two weeks. Not only that, we would get films on each team we played and we would study the opponent. When we played a team, we usually knew what they were going to do. The first game we played was against El Paso Andrews. Coach Spears and I scouted them in their first two scrimmages. We were going to have our first booster club meeting and John ask me if I wanted to present the scouting report to the booster club. Now, I have always had a lot of confidence in my ability to speak and I wasn't a rookie. I had presented scouting reports before at several schools I had coached so I said "Yes, I would be happy to give the scouting report". John was pleased that I agreed and said "After all, it will give the booster club a chance to meet you". The night of the first booster club meeting, all of the coaches and the players met in the field house, and then walked through the high school into the high school cafeteria where the boosters were meeting. It was a grand entrance by the coaches and players. I can't begin to explain to anyone the goose bumps and cold sweat that went through my body as we entered the cafeteria. Over one thousand football boosters lined up on top of each other clapping and screaming for a ten minute standing ovation when we entered. I could not believe my eyes and my ears and I thought how great it would be to play for people that excited about football. What about basketball, I thought? When it came time for me to give my report, I was already exhausted from fear of giving the report. I thought, "Great start Young". That night in front of the one thousand or so boosters, I was a pure yellow bird. No doubt about it.

Odessa had a football stadium that seated around twelve thousand spectators for all of the Ector County Football teams. When Permian played, there was never an empty seat in the stadium. Jennifer and I had a hard time getting used to "Friday Night Lights" in Odessa. It was so big, that the wives of the coaches had to have assigned seating. The varsity coach's wives would sit with each other and the junior varsity coaches wives would sit with each other. Last year, Permian won their third state championship so expectations were high. We were a good football team that year as we finished with 9 wins and 1 loss. Midland Lee was the District Champs as they beat us 13-6 in Midland. The morning after the season was over; John had 24 for-sale signs in his front yard. Enough said about "Friday Night Lights."

Everyday during the last period of the day, I got to work with the basketball guys. I really liked the group of guys that I had. We had some talent, but something was missing. I could not really put my finger on it. They were really nice kids and they tried to do what I asked them to do. The young group was really a good group of basketball players. Ken was right about the fact that the sophomore class was strong. On October fifteen, I was released from football practice but not scouting. What was sad about that, I really did not mind. I enjoyed football a lot because it gave me a release from worrying about basketball. Darryl Bunting told me that he was planning on playing basketball. He told me that he went to Ector High School that summer to play basketball. Ector was an all black school and in my opinion, they had the better athletes in Odessa and they were the dominant basketball school in Odessa. So I thought that if Darryl really did play with the Ector guys that summer, he and Permian were better off.

I never was big on the magic thing most Permian fans felt about the "Mojo" until our first basketball game. We were playing Lubbock Monterey High School in Lubbock. We had all our players which was something new for Permian basketball. Last year, the football guys that played basketball didn't get to the gym until after the Christmas holidays. Now, I never really believed in the "Mojo" but that night I started wondering. We trailed most of the entire game, until the fourth quarter when we started to make a run. Monterey was a good team and they stepped up and stopped the run with about three minutes to go in the game. Our fans started yelling Mojo, Mojo, and more Mojo. All of a sudden, our player's attitude switched to no fear and we went on and won our first game on the road against a good team. The last three minutes were the best we had played the entire game. It was a great start for our team and me.

Everyone always asked me how I liked Permian knowing that Permian was such a football school. I always said the same thing. I would say, "Permian on a scale of one-to-ten is a ten on a football basis. Basketball on the same scale is an eight, and that is higher than most high schools in Texas, and we have enough athletes to go around." Not only that, "Permian wants to win at everything, not just football." The tradition of hard work was already in place. There were lots of athletes walking the hall because of the type of program Permian had in football. I know that I was not unhappy with the prospects that I had in the basketball program. We had a good year for my first year. We finished third and won more games than we lost, which was better than they had done in the last five years. We really did not do all that bad. Ken did an outstanding job with the junior varsity. They won twenty-three games and finished first in the district with five sophomores playing. Ken was a coach that demanded that they do it right and he was a blessing for me. Darryl Bunting and David Combs had a great year. David averaged fifteen points per game and signed a scholarship to play basketball at McMurry, and Darryl average fourteen points per game and was the leading rebounder in the district. We were still soft at playing basketball and that bothered me a great deal. Somehow, someway, I had to find a way to teach the guys to play hard.

Coaching basketball took a turn with me when I went to a clinic in Lubbock during the school year to listen to my good friend Larry Brown. Larry had led to high school teams to state championships and he was speaking about basketball. I was really impressed with his speech. He said some things that were good. He had four books that he used in his talk and asks if anyone had read any of the books. One of those books was John Wooden's <u>Practical Modern Basketball</u>." I was embarrassed to admit that I had not read any of the books. His challenge was simple. "Are you keeping up with the game?" From that point on, I started reading every basketball book that I could get my hand on, and John Wooden became my mentor. It was during this time in basketball history that the passing game/motion offense started becoming popular in Texas. I read books and studied film, talked to coaches and even got a Bobby Knight film. My education had slipped. I was living in days of my college coach and those days were long gone. It was time for me to make a change. I started playing pressure defense on a half court basis forcing the offensive player to the baseline, and started teaching a match up two-three zone. I went to a structured passing game with a numbered fast break with a secondary attack. I developed drills to teach my offense and defense where we did not waste time. I used the same method that the football coaches used to develop their program to develop my program. But the main thing I did was develop a delay game that I could sell to the players. I studied Dean Smith's Four Corner Offense and bought into its concepts. Instead of calling the offense Four Corner, I called it Four to Score. In short, I became a brand new coach.

The major influence I had were the football coaches I worked with and the football program. My thinking was "If they can do it in football," "Why can't we do it in basketball." I made an announcement to the players that things were going to be different from this point on. That spring, I bought 15 weighted vests, two blocking dummies, 25 blind folds, 25 weighted jump ropes, and three huge pyrometric boxes that the players could use to improve their jumping ability. Jack Brown, the Athletic Director of the Ector Country School District called me in to his office and questioned me about what I was doing. I explained what my plans were and he just smiled and told me to get after it and he supported my thinking one-hundred percent. I simply was doing what the football team was doing and I really believed that I got his respect by doing just that. I started working the basketball players out in the morning, and the afternoons just like football. In the mornings, we would work on techniques of shooting, dribbling, and passing. In the afternoons, I would put them through one hour of hell with weighted vests on each varsity prospect. It was not easy and my intentions were clear. I was developing a basketball program where the players could develop to the best of their ability. Soon, the players started taking pride in their work ethic and assumed that it was supposed to be this way. After all, the football team worked this way, why can't the basketball team work the same way. We had a real program where the players in the program were paying a price to be in the program. I finally figured out what was wrong and I felt that I was getting it right. It became clear to me that when you work that hard, you learn to play hard.

Football season the next year was easier for me. I felt comfortable with all the coaches and with my assignments in football. We really had a super football team as they won the district and advanced into the playoffs. They were back making the normal run for the "State Football Championship". Darryl became the top linebacker in the state of Texas and would eventually sign to play with Oklahoma University and then later with the NFL Houston Oilers.

That fall, I worked the kids harder than I did in the spring using the weighted vests for conditioning and the heavy ropes for conditioning. The results were unbelievable. I watched players get stronger, jump higher, become quicker and developed a strong mind-set. John Mark Woods developed into an excellent athlete. He became strong and then all of a sudden, he could dunk the ball. He was only five foot ten, but his hops became something special. His fundamentals were ten times better than the year before. Van Weaver, another senior grew two inches and got stronger. His shot was better than ever before and his toughness was totally different than the year before. Sam Catfish Jones was a much better basketball player. His work ethic and commitment was no longer a question. He was a player waiting to get the opportunity to show what he could do. Carl James and Art Diddle were excellent play makers and shooters. Carl had a sense of toughness that we lacked the year before and he had a desire to be as good as he could be. The real surprise was Steel Rodman and Garrett Forest. Garrett was an excellent penetrator and Steel really had a good head for the game. All of a sudden, it hit me like a bolt of lightning. "Oh I see" and the light bulb came on. We had developed mental toughness as a team and now, we were ready to play hard. For a surprise, we got a transfer from the Houston, Texas by the name of Al Weems. He was a strong six foot three player that really understood the game. His strength was defense and rebounding. Al fit right into the group with no let down from mental toughness to work ethic. After all, now the entire group expected to be mentally tough so anyone new had to be that way. That is what a good program does when expectations are set properly.

Needless to say, we were ready to see if all this hard work would pay off. I was scared because we still did not have a big post man as he was still in football. Well, we got him sooner than we thought as the football team got beat in the quarter - final game. We had already played four games and won all of them. After football, Darryl came to me and told me that he wanted to play basketball but had lots of conflicts. First off, he was tired and wanted to wait a week before he started, then he wanted to take all his football recruiting visits [five] during basketball season. He had them already planned out. We talked about it and I told him that I understood his situation but I had to think about whether I was going to allow him to play with him missing so much. Darryl was very mature about everything and he understood why I would question this situation. Darryl understood what program meant better than most guys his age. It was not so much him missing practice and games but it was more about him not being on the same page as the rest of the players. I certainly understood his needing more time to heal from football. This was a very difficult decision because I really liked Darryl. Not only that, Darryl was not being an asshole or anything like that, he was being honest and doing what he needed to do in order to take care of himself and his football career. The next day, we met and I told him that I could not allow myself to let him play with all his conflicts. I told him that I wanted him to play badly and so did the guys on the team, but I could not allow someone to miss that much and be fair to our basketball program. My decision was about the basketball program, not Darryl, not the team, not me, but the program. We had come a long way and I was not going to take a chance on losing what we had worked so hard to accomplish. My answer to Darryl was "You would not expect to miss that much in football and expect to play, then why do you expect anything different in basketball". I do not think you can bend when you are trying to establish a program. If you do, you will be bending so much that you lose your program. Now if we had an established program, then I think we could bend but not now, it was too early. This was big news to anyone and everyone within 200 miles. I was the bad guy and many people let me know it. The local paper, the administration, the football coaches and even some of the players on the team let me know I was not a very popular guy.

Much to my surprise, our first loss was in the Brownwood Tournament when we lost the first game to Copperas Cove. Then we went on to win the consolation tournament. We beat Monterey again and then played in the Odessa Tournament. We won the tournament by beating cross town rival Ector in the finals. It was the first time that Permian had beaten Ector and at the same time won the Ector County Basketball Tournament. Guess what happens next, the kids were now starting to believe. By the time district came along, we had lost only one game. By this time, most everyone had forgotten about Darryl and was on our band wagon. We finished with 28 wins and 4 losses and the best won-lost record percentage wise at Permian. What was even better is the fact that we had the top four players back with a great junior class coming. I coached the sophomores that year and we lost one game and won the district going away. We finished with a 14-1 record. I had a new assistant coach by the name of Eddie Wink. Ken was moved to a varsity assistant coach and he did not have to coach a second sport. Eddie knew nothing about basketball but he was still a great assistant coach. He was a gentle kind man with a personality that the players loved. He was a people person and he would play a big role in our success. Every time I would get on one of the players, he would come around and built them back up. He understood his role and he was good at it. I thought it was ironic and funny that I was in a football school, and had what I considered to be the best assistant coach I ever had. Eddie coached the junior varsity to 24 wins and only 5 losses and the district championship. Permian football boosters started supporting basketball and it was fun. We would fill the stands up for basketball which had not happen in many years at Permian. It was a complete turnaround for the basketball program and I was named the "Coach of the Year" by the Odessa American newspaper.

Chester Stamp was the new basketball coach at Tall City College. He was a huge man at six- foot- six, two hundred sixty pounds and not hard to recognize. He attended several of our workouts and games during the season. We got to know each other and I really liked him. We would talk basketball and recruiting and almost anything about anything. He had a lovely wife by the name of Mandy and they had three children. Tall City College was going to open up next year in competitive basketball under his direction. Dr. Lang was the President of Tall City College. Chester was recruiting one player from Permian, one player from Hereford and one player from Monterey. Of course, I knew all three players very well. I even knew their parents and coaches. As soon as basketball season was over, Chester offered me the Assistant Basketball and Head Golf Coach's position at Tall City College. After talking to Jennifer, I said I would take it. Chester told me that it had to be approved by the president and the board before I could tell anyone. I do not think that I have ever been so excited about coaching. I could not sleep at night and it killed me that I could not tell anyone. I am glad I did not tell anyone because a month later, when the board met, they rejected Chester's request. There reason was that it appeared that Chester was hiring a basketball coach and not a golf coach. I was upset and heart- broken. Chester was upset also. He found out later what really happened was that Dr. Lang had already committed the position to someone else and Chester really did not have much to say about it.

Fate has a way of directing our lives and during this time period, our football coach John, became upset with me concerning two players that decided not to play football and just play basketball. Neither one of the two players told me about this so it caught me off guard. John called me into his office and in front of several other coaches in the office, really threw a fit as he felt I had something to do with their decision. He threw a chair across the room to get my attention. He had my attention but in the wrong way. When I left that room, I knew I was not going out on the football field to assist in football anymore. It was uncalled for and unfair. I knew why he was upset but it was the wrong way to handle me. I knew the pressure that John had but he handled me wrong. I was a guy that totally supported the football program. Red flags were everywhere. Even though I knew it was over at Permian, I still talked to those two kids. I felt that they both would regret not playing football at Permian so I made sure that they knew what they were doing. The funny thing about these two kids quitting was that neither were very good at football. One had a deformed arm and the other was too weak and skinny to make a difference. They barely got to play in Junior High School. Most everyone said that he acted like that to run me off. That never entered my mind but basketball had made a major turn. John was an emotional guy and an intense guy and he just was mad as hell to see two kids go over to basketball. One thing was for sure and that is if he was trying to run me off, it sure worked.

I did not know what I was going to do but I did know that I was not going to coach football under John again. To my surprise, Jim Buttons our varsity linebacker coach got the Borger Athletic Director and Head Football Coaching position that spring. Jim and I developed a very good working relationship as we both were "Linebacker Coaches", Jim was on the varsity and I was on the junior varsity. To my surprise, Jim asked me to go with him that spring to Borger as his First Assistant Football Coach. Jim was in the room the day John threw the chair and both Jim and I had some laughs over that incident. We had developed a very good friendship. Jim was a nice guy and I really liked him. He was a true Christian guy and lived his life as an example to follow. Jim and I were on the same page and I felt comfortable with him. I talked it over with Jennifer and we decided it was not a good move for me. We both felt I needed to stay in coaching as a basketball coach. Jim and I talked again as spring training was getting close for both schools, Permian and Borger. He told me that it would not hurt his feelings if I looked for a basketball position when spring training was over. He would not lock me up in football. To this day, I do not know what came over me but I said yes. I resigned my position at Permian and when to Borger with Jim Buttons as his First Assistant football coach.

Everyone was floored including Jennifer as she really did not buy into this deal. I got a card from Chester and Dr. Lang congratulating me on the move. Regardless, of what anyone thought, I was in Borger that spring coaching football. Going to Borger that spring was not like going to

Permian last spring. I had to teach classes and coach everything. We were into the spring football game at Borger, when one of the football managers came up to me and handed me a note. He said I had a long distance phone call. I continued to coach the spring game and as soon as the game was over I looked at the note. It said "call me ASAP", Chester Stamp. As soon as I got in the field house, I picked up our athletic phone and called. We talked a little while with small talk about some players that he was trying to get signed and then he ask me "Do you still want to come to Tall City College as my assistant coach?" I was standing there with sweat from the spring game in football gear and I said "Sure I do Chester but how can you do that? He said "Well, since you are now a football coach and not coaching basketball, we can hire you for this position." He said "The guy we hired quit right after he signed on." "The job is yours if you want it." For the first time in my married life, I did not ask Jennifer what she thought. I said yes to Chester and I became a College Golf/Basketball Coach. Little did I know that my career as a college coach was just beginning?

SEVEN

BACK AT THE BIG DAY, our shoot-around and pregame warm-ups are very different sessions, and the players know this. After all, this was already the thirty-seventh time we had been in this situation. So when it started up as if we were doing a pregame warm-up instead of a shoot around, I knew the team's heads were not on straight. It was nine o'clock in the morning, and who does their pregame drills 10 hours before tip-off? I called the team over to the bench and put a stop to that. "What are you doing?" From the tone of voice they knew I was unhappy. Skunk knew exactly what was going on, and with a quick smile said, "Come on guys, we can't forget why we're here. Let's get it together." Right away, basketball sense was restored; they huddled up and broke into assigned spots for a shoot around. I could yell all day long, my assistants could talk to them all night long, but when Skunk said something, the guys all listened. That Skunk was the only one of the starting five who was not bought and paid for must have carried some weight with them, or at least that was how I explained it to myself.

Everyone called young Stuart Keith "Skunk" because he had a white birthmark in his hair right at the front part. It stood out, and since he was black, that birthmark gave him a look that you couldn't miss. He was six foot eight and weighed 250 pounds, with no fat showing anywhere on his body. Once you met Skunk, you did not forget him, because of his hair, yes, but also because of the way he carried himself. He was just a freshman, but everyone loved Skunk. He very seldom spoke but when he did, everyone on this team listened.

Mr. Keith was from a small town in Louisiana called Smyer. He picked up his nickname back there, and everyone knew him as Skunk both there and when he arrived on our campus. Smyer won the High School State Championship in Boys Basketball all four years Skunk attended. In addition, Skunk's cousin, a guy we were recruiting, was also one of the other players on that team. Arnold was just the opposite, just five-foot nine and about 170 pounds. A darting ball handler, I gave him the nickname of "Jet One." He was so fast and quick, particularly in his first ten yards, I couldn't resist the handle. He was by far the quickest player I have ever seen from sideline to sideline. Basketball has a lot of players who are quick and many who can run fast but very few are both quick and fast. We didn't recruit Jet because of Skunk; I thought he had real potential in his own right. I had been recruiting him, and then both of them, since their sophomore year when I saw both play in a tournament in Baton Rouge. I attended that same tournament all three years they played for the varsity at that high school and they won it all three times. By the time the third year came around, I knew quite a few folks in Smyer. One I met the first year and really became quite close with was Danny Williams, the owner of the City Drugstore in Smyer. We started up a conversation that first year, and he showed interest when I told him I was a college recruiter. One thing led to another and before long we became friends. Every year he would sit exactly at the same spot as the year before so finding Danny was not difficult. He knew everyone in Smyer and kept me informed about what was going on in the town, particularly anything that involved Jet One and Skunk. He really liked both guys a lot as human beings, not just basketball players. He shared with me that he didn't think that Skunk had ever had a girlfriend and that his Momma would kill him he ever did have one. It was his opinion that Skunk was overprotected by his mother, and that he was very naive about life in general. I first recruited the two of them for Great Plains College. I worried that Skunk wouldn't pass the tests to qualify for a Division One school, but I figured Jet One had the smarts all along. I had noticed Skunk right away, but I became familiar with Jet One as the three years went by. When I found out he was Skunk's cousin, I knew what I had to do.

Just as I had expected, the first time they took it, Skunk failed the SAT, and Jet One passed it. Arnold was a straight "A" student; Stuart was a "C" at best. Skunk was very depressed over his test results and got down on himself, developing an attitude that he couldn't pass if he took the test 100 times. I didn't tell him so, but I tended to agree, but I still encouraged him to take it again and again if needed. Of course, he did not want to do this, and each retake did cost money. I flat-out told him to take it as many times as he wanted and I would help pay for it. That impressed him, and from that point on, he started trusting me; we had a different kind of relationship. It is a funny thing about relating with recruits. You never know what button to push that works with them, but once you do, you know it.

It was a nervous time when the ACT test came up in early June. If Skunk failed this one, he would have to forget about Division One basketball for a while. Meanwhile I had gotten the job at North West State University that spring, and everything had changed for me. Well, not everything. I did continue to recruit both players but now it was for Northwestern State. Through the three years of observation I had either been smart, or at least doggedly persistent, and I was not backing out now. Sometimes in recruiting, you get too far into it to back out. Another thing that had changed was that I now had a different attitude about Skunk passing the ACT. I solicited help from everyone I could find to try and help him pass. He had not signed with anyone at this point in time because he was waiting to see how he would do. This was hard to swallow as a junior college coach, but now at a Division One school, I was happy about it. Arnold was also waiting; they had decided they wanted to go to school together. Junior colleges across America were recruiting Skunk. When lots of schools compete for a player, the recruiting process can yield strange results. Because Skunk and I had already gotten close, his mother liked me. Her name was Minna, the same name as my mother, and we talked often about that, and lots of other things too. Minna was concerned that the move from high school to college for her boy from a small community like Symer would be a dangerous transition. And she wasn't only talking about basketball. His impending social life outside basketball worried her. I couldn't blame her: It is where most young athletes fail in college.

Once a young basketball player's social life becomes more important than academics or the game, there's a domino effect. Every aspect of his young life affects the other and so forth, until all aspects of his college life are challenged.

Junior colleges, meanwhile, would be scrambling to attract Skunk with money: a certain amount when he signs, so much when he arrives at school, and again, more when he stays one semester. Throw in some payments in cash and goods and it added up to a lot of money. I had not mentioned any money at all. I felt it best not to get into that game. As conversations progressed, however, it did invariably come down to cash. They were poor folks, good folks, with a nice clean home and good Christian values. But finances were an issue.

Arnold had decided to take the ACT test both in solidarity with his cousin, and to see if he could make a better score on the ACT than he had on the SAT. He thought it would look better on his transcript. I gave Danny Williams some money to allow them to take the test and he in turn actually paid their filing fee for the test. I knew my involvement was a violation of rules so I am as guilty as anyone, but with Danny making the payment, it looked aboveboard. I justified my actions to myself by saying they needed to have hope and this was their last hope of both of them attending a Division One school and playing basketball together. I did not expect Skunk to pass but I was looking toward his future. My plan would be to place both of them at Great Plains College so I could keep an eye on them. It seemed the best idea if I could not recruit them this year. Of course, I was not the only Division One school representative thinking that way. It was going to be competitive, an all-out war.

There was surprise aplenty all around when the test results came in. Skunk passed and Arnold failed. Wow!! Although you had to have your doubts about what had transpired, we had the results and they stated that each of them had now passed a necessary test. The next few days were as hectic as it gets. Skunk could now become a Division One player, highly recruited, not signed and awaiting someone to seal the deal and get his signature. I sent both Darryl and Soapy to see what they could to do. There are so many restrictions placed on recruiting by the NCAA, we had to be careful because this time we would be watched. We had already mailed both of them a scholarship agreement form. Neither sent the papers back. Twenty-four hours passed and I did not hear from either young man. I was worried: That was not a good sign. I had my two assistants in a motel not more than five miles from their neighborhood trying to keep up with whatever was happening. I couldn't take it, and picked up the phone and dialed Minna. I asked her what was going on. She was evasive, and I could tell right away something was different. *Who has gotten to her?* I thought. It's just a sense you develop when recruiting, and I became paranoid. It is a learning process, one I had become very good at. I started asking questions and got very few good answers. As soon as I put the phone down, I flew to Baton Rouge, rented a car and drove to the motel where Darryl and Soapy were staying. My gut feeling was one that I have had before, I just knew someone had sold her, and I had to do something about it. You get these uncomfortable sensations in recruiting when decision time nears, certainly once you've had the experience of getting burned by someone with a little money, or better goodies, to offer. I called Arnold and talked to his mother, whose name was Mabel. We had a nice conversation. I told her why I had called, and asked her to meet me at the local grocery store in thirty minutes. The Smyer One Stop was the only grocery store in town, so it wasn't hard to find. Mabel was my one hope to keep the lines of communication to the greater family open. We could no longer visit the family as the other coaches were doing because we had already made the maximum legal amount of visits per NCAA rules. When we drove by Skunk's house, you could see all the rental cars and even some of the coaches waiting outside for their shot to top the best offer the family was mulling over. It looked like a parking lot just for rental cars and college coaches.

At the grocery store, I met Mabel. She would shop for food while I talked. I wasted no time and got right to the point. She and I have already discussed the two boys attending North West State University together, and Mabel really liked that idea. They could look out for one another. I found out that what it all boiled down to was that Minna was enjoying the attention and the prospect of a higher payday for her boy along the way. From what Mabel said, it appeared all the offers had gone to Minna's head. She was the center of attention and liked it. Mabel confessed that she was a little disgusted with her sister because, after all, the only reason that Skunk was even getting so much attention was because Arnold had tested and passed the test for Skunk. I tried to act like I did not hear that and even looked the other way, but I had already suspected it of course. I told her to go back to the house and I would call her about all this later that day.

I turned to Danny Williams. The owner of Smyer Drug was excited to hear from me, as I expected he would be. After I filled him in, Danny told me he would help in whatever way he could. Time was not on our side, I knew, because a big-time coach with his foot in the door and a receptive ear would come through with a signature if we didn't get something done ourselves, and soon. Division One or not, North West State University did not have the resources to match what several of the big-time schools could offer. They knew it and I knew it so I had to do something quick or I was going to lose Skunk. I told Danny that I had a gut feeling it was now or never. Together, he and I came up with a plan. I called Mabel and Arnold and talked to their entire family. I invited the whole gang to meet me at the drugstore and bring the scholarship papers with them so Arnold could sign with Northwestern State. I urged them to invite Minna and her side of the family to witness the signing. Danny was to witness the event and take pictures. Of course, I could not make an appearance by NCAA rules so we hung out in Danny's office in the back while it all came down. Arnold signed and everyone was so happy for him. The whole gang was there, and Skunk's family with his two sisters and several more aunts and a few uncles were gathered as well. A party of fifteen relatives and friends celebrated Arnold's big day. After the signing, I had Danny tell Skunk and Minna that we were in the back office if they would be kind enough to join us. Danny was a trusted and respected businessman in Smyer and that he was on my side carried some weight.

Minna, Skunk, Danny and I started talking it all over, like we had done many times before. But now it came down to money. Minna had changed some of her earlier tune and wanted quite a bit to sign, more to get Skunk there and then again at end of a year. Of course, I was ready for all this. It was not my first rodeo, so to speak. With every good player that gets recruited, it sooner or later comes down to money. Working in that kind of atmosphere was wearying, and frustrating, something interference from the NCAA was doing little to remedy. They made me so angry, but I had learned over the years to keep my cool. It is hard for an honest coach because you usually come up short, and lose out on the good players. It is sad but true. I can count on one of my hands how many times I have prevailed under similar circumstances, and to be honest, I felt deep down inside we would lose out on this one. These weren't inner feelings I was enjoying, but after so many times of getting beat playing it straight; it had turned my stomach sour.

Playing by the rules wasn't hard for me since it fit my personality. That was one of my main calling cards from the time I started coaching until now. Everyone who knew me knew you were going to get exactly what you saw. I had been coaching on the college level for years when I took the job at Northwestern State. I must admit that I was getting tired of getting beat by people with money, schools with money, coaches' with money. My attitude was changing over the years. I could feel it but I couldn't do much about it. I had been a sometimes successful recruiter with an honest philosophy long before I made Mr. McFather's acquaintance. I had made up my mind I was not going to change when I was hired at North West State University. If I couldn't do the job the way I knew was right, then I would just quit. I believed in doing the right thing with respect and fairness to all parties. I may have wanted to cheat but I really did not know how. It did not come naturally to me. Skunk was my first recruit at North West State University and I did not want to cheat. Of course, I had already more than bent the rules, though I wasn't totally aware of it. But here we had made contact and I was meeting the family in the back room of this office. Although I was aware that I was violating rules, deep down I felt justified because I had made a connection. I felt strongly about Skunk being with me instead of the other coaches who were just recruiting him based on his name and his high school numbers only. They did not know him. Signing and coaching him would be just a job; to me it was a commitment.

I had fostered Darryl, my right-hand man, over time. He is a black man same as Minna, Skunk and the family, and he was in the middle of a conversation with Minna. But little did Darryl know, he was doing just what I had planned he would. He had no clue what was going to happen next. Darryl is a very personable guy, and he had become good friends within the family, particularly with Skunk. I looked at Darryl and said, "Now Darryl, what are we going to offer to compete with all this money other colleges have? Now that you know what they want, I want you to make them a better offer. What have you got?"

Of course, I knew Darryl was a straight arrow, innocent of any shady dealings whatsoever. He knew we did not buy players. Darryl looked at me and he acted just as I had expected him to. Looking back in shock, he replied, "Coach, we don't buy players." It was impossible to look into that face and not know he was sincere.

"That's right," I said. "And you and I know that, but I want you to say it in front of Skunk and Minna."

Then I turned to Minna and looked her right in the eye, "You bet we are going to make you a better offer!" I could feel the surprise and tension rising in Darryl, and in Skunk and his mom too; they were all wondering what I meant. I had center stage and I used it: "We are going to offer your son an education. That's right, an education," I continued. "We will promise you that Stuart will graduate from North West State University in four or five years, whatever it takes. That education will be worth all the money and more that you will ever see right now by his signing with any university, but most important, that education will last the rest of his lifetime." I knew it was now or never so I rushed ahead, "We will know his teachers; he'll get the best, we will monitor his classes, and we will not allow him to become overloaded. If Stuart misses as much as one class, I will know about it. The same holds true if an assignment is not turned in time. We will do whatever we can to motivate him to go to class, and get him the help necessary to do class assignments. We will provide tutors and teacher's aides to help him with all his schoolwork. We will also keep you in the loop with regular academic progress reports so that you can relax and feel good about his being at Northwestern State, and not worry how he's spending his time. And last but not least, our staff will personally make sure your son stays out of trouble, inside the classroom, and outside the classroom and of course during practice and games. If he and his buddies sneak off to some shady bar or nightclub, we will know about it and we will do something about it." Then I attempted to close the deal with, "I daresay none of those big-time schools or universities vying to buy his signature now will be able to give you what I have just offered you."

It was time to let my speech sink in and wait for a response. Tears rolled down from Minna's eyes, and after what seemed like an eternity, she turned to Skunk and asked, "Stuart, what do you want to do?"

Skunk looked at her and said, "Momma, I have already told you what I want to do; I want to go to North West State University with Arnold."

"OK. Go home and get the papers and let's get this done right now." The ever-cooperative Danny yelled with joy and handed Stuart his car keys so he could run home and get the papers. The entire family was waiting in the main part of the drug store as the celebration began. I gave Danny an envelope in which to mail the papers from Skunk along with Arnold's paperwork so that everything would look on the up to our watchdogs back at State. We shared hugs all around, and Darryl and I left through the back door, heading back to Amarillo with huge smiles on our faces. From that point on, Skunk and Jet One became two of my favorite players.

Of course, it wasn't that easy, and right off the bat I developed a love/hate relationship with my new responsibilities. Anyone aware of how protected and isolated he was at home had to expect that Skunk's first week at North West State University would be a disaster, and the young man did not disappoint in that respect. One night he and some of the guys on the team got their hands on some beer, and Skunk lost it right away. He had never had a drink before in his life and he went crazy when he got drunk. Feeling his oats and no pain whatsoever, he started showing off and jumped on top of a car, dancing around like a monkey, and following one move, the top of the car simply caved in. It did not improve the situation that the car he damaged belonged to the dorm supervisor. Of course, I got a call from her around midnight telling me to come to the dorm, because we all had a big problem. By the time I got there, the campus police had everything under control. Of course, I couldn't miss the crumpled roof on the Toyota Camry sitting in the parking lot as I pulled up. The entire top of the car was resting on the seats and the rest of the interior.

The next day, the North West State University Dean of Students read the riot act both to Skunk and to me inside his office. He was furious with Skunk about his behavior, just a few days after arriving on campus. And it was hard not to see the dean's point. The gift certificate for a quart of his favorite bourbon I slipped him probably wouldn't have been enough to keep Skunk in school. I liked the dean and he was a fair man, but there was administrative pressure on him not to condone or leave unpunished bad behavior from student athletes. He had overreacted a few times in the past and I feared he would do so again. I kept repeating that this was a good kid on his own for the first time, and let's just give him a chance to correct his behavior. He finally relented, accepting my plea, and gave Skunk three months of probation with a sentence of cafeteria duty every day for the next 60 days. Of course, whatever money he made would be going to pay off the extensive repairs need on the dorm director's car. We actually caught a break there, one that was understandable, because Stuart really was a sweet kid. The dorm director just loved him and refused to press any charges. Her understanding was helpful in my argument with the dean. Skunk apologized all around, and then to his teammates, and everyone warmed to him.

Then one day Skunk really got everyone's attention. It was during a practice session. Being just a freshman, Skunk did not yet command the respect of his teammates the way I wanted him to. It was normal that this was a process that took time, so it did not bother me. He was clearly a superior player to others sharing the same position but he was a freshman and would have to prove himself. He would have to earn the respect of his teammates, including the ones with whom he would be competing for playing time. I was disturbed by the behavior of the other two players on the team who shared his position. They were both seniors, and had played with the varsity the last two years even though neither one was really good enough to play on even a good high school team. Making matters worse, they did not realize they weren't very good, and they were determined to cause Skunk problems in workouts. Not only was neither half the player

Skunk was, both were lazy, and always took shortcuts in workouts, trying to make their play look good. They would pick on Skunk and try to find ways for him to look bad.

One of the two, the main protagonist, was a tough kid from Louisiana named Jonathan. He had played basketball for one of the largest schools in New Orleans, a school in as tough a neighborhood as any out there. He loved to brag about how tough he was, how he had done well both on and off the court in an environment more difficult than most of us could even imagine. I certainly had no argument with him on that score. I knew where he came from, a notorious precinct in the big city on the bayou. Few white people spent time at his school or in his neighborhood, and visiting teams would leave as quickly as they could after a game. Jonathan was a nightmare to coach. He stood six foot six and carried around a 245-pound body with tattoos all over. I didn't agree he was as tough as he thought he was, but I was careful with him nonetheless.

Of course, neither Jonathan nor Cameron, the other senior who played that position, was happy that a freshman had been recruited to play with them. Although they acted poised, they had to realize that Skunk was the better player. He would surely eclipse them in playing time eventually, and both players let us know how unhappy they were about it every day. I consider a workout to be a practice in which the player has to learn by doing. I staged tough workouts, physical to the extent that players would lose their cool and get into it a little with one another. I believed that competition for each position was critical for team improvement. I simply insisted on competitive workouts each and every day. All my players knew how strongly I felt about this.

One particular day, the usual was happening: We were having a physical workout, and Jonathan and Cameron were really beating up on Skunk. I was aware of it, the assistant coaches noticed it, the players knew about it. I had discussed the situation with the coaches, and we all felt it was in Skunk's best interest and that of the team, that we back off and let the three of them do battle. If we had tried to protect Skunk from the tough stuff, he would have lost respect in the eyes of his teammates: not good for Skunk and certainly not good for the team.

I learned a long time ago that when a fight breaks out during a workout, the worst thing a coach can do is hurry over and break it up. When you do that, before long, you have a fight happening all the time. Deep down players do not want to fight but they will not back down due to peer pressure. So when you witness rough play turning into a shoving match, then maybe a fist or two flies, no one backs down. I've learned the hard way over the years that if the players know the coach is going to stop it as soon as it starts, the fights will be nonstop. But if they realize that if they start something, no one is going to help them put a stop to it, they think twice before responding to that hard shove with a fist. It had become a no-brainer: My philosophy was not to stop it, to just let them fight. Once a struggle was lost, we would restore the peace, but never before the two players have had a chance to duke it out. Knowing that, players are very reluctant to fight, no matter how tough the workouts get.

Of course, the day came when it got different. Jonathan started pushing Skunk early in practice and it got rougher by the minute. I would say something to the entire group about backing off, no cheap shots and do not foul on purpose, but my words were not reaching the ears they were aimed at. Before long, without any notice, Jonathan and Skunk squared off with fists ready to do battle. Jonathan, the older player from the toughest part of New Orleans, faced Skunk, a baby out of high school from a little town called Smyer where everyone loved each other and everyone knew your name and where you lived. I thought to myself, *God, I wish I could stop this!* But I knew I couldn't. I had to let it play out regardless of how bad it looked for Skunk. Everyone's attention was on those two guys; it was clear that at least one of them was going to get hurt. My assistant coaches looked helplessly at me and I gave them the thumbs-up signal, meaning let it play out. Jonathan made the first move, trying to hit Skunk in the head with a hard right with a closed fist. To everyone's surprise, it was over in an instant. Skunk just backed off as quickly as a cat, and when Jonathan's blow missed, Skunk suddenly landed a hard blow to the side of the senior's head with his right foot.

The kick was strong and powerful, and found its target, landing directly on Jonathan's nose. He went down, bleeding, and looked knocked out. But he sprung to his feet almost immediately. Still, Jonathan called out, "Fight's over, Skunk wins, I quit." I was stunned, as was everyone. Skunk looked to be in shock as well.

I stepped in; saying, "Practice is over," and everyone yelled and put their arms around the victorious freshman's shoulders. They were so proud of him, they respected him, and certainly none of them wanted any of the medicine Jonathan had received. Here I was, assuming I had taken in a defenseless waif from a small town. That was before I found out that Skunk had earlier earned a black belt in karate.

So it was little wonder now months later that it was Skunk who got everyone out on the court, in front of about 15,000 fans, working the kind of shoot around routine we all knew they needed. We always start these with individual spot shooting. Specialized shooting was worked on next. Each coach would work their group on the shots we felt they would need to make in the coming game. We were a well-organized coaching staff: Each of us knew what we were supposed to do.

Each shoot around had a different feel, and rightly so. We planned our shots according to the kind of defense our scouting told us we could expect to see. After working on specialty shots, we went into the meat-and-potatoes of the session. The assistant coaches had gone over the scouting report and each position coach worked with his players on what we needed to do in order to win. We would practice the scenarios they had drawn up over and over. These drills were by far the most important thing we covered. Coaches needed to be familiar with our opponent's team tendencies. We needed to learn their weaknesses and how best to attack them. Any team can play the way they've been coached to, but when the pressure is on in a tight battle in the later minutes of a game, they will fall back on the tendencies they've always relied on to try to get a win. <u>Our basic defensive objective was if they like to play a certain way, then that was not the way the game would be played unless it was the way we felt we could win.</u> We would deny them their favorite scoring plays. Of course, we had been doing this in practice all year. But now we eased it down into slow motion and took it step by step. After practicing that, we would shoot free throws. I had always been an advocate of free throw shooting games and contests.

Anything we could do to encourage them to shoot as many foul shots as possible, and then a few more, was the idea. Using the peer pressure from their wanting to outdo one another from the line worked in our favor. It is impossible to get the same kind of game pressure you get in a game, but peer pressure is the next best. .

We finished our shoot around right on time, went back into our dressing room and I let them dig into all the goodies stashed there. Each player was happy; you could see it in their eyes. They glowed with excitement. I couldn't help but think of how I would feel if I was a player in the game that was to come. I knew that I had never had the opportunity to do what they were about to, but I could identify with them in some ways. I had to be the most naïve player to attend a Division One school to play basketball. No player, not even Skunk, was as naive and ill prepared to play big games, and I was raised in a city of 150,000 people. I started thinking about my first year at TCU. I had in fact remained hopelessly naive through all four years at that Texas school. Going to college as I knew it was nothing like going to college today. It is two different worlds.

I still remember my college days like it was yesterday. Times changes, people change, but going to college for the first time never changes. The only thing to fear is fear itself. That is exactly how this yellow bird felt when he stepped on the campus of Texas Christian University in Ft. Worth, Texas as a freshman. I felt fear! I was scared that I would flunk out academically and then everyone would know I was a yellow bird. I thought about it all the time and had built up a phobia. I was scared to death about passing college school work. I should have been scared of not making the basketball team but that never entered my mind. I was not scared of anything except failing my classes, so, I developed a plan of action to challenge the fear I carried inside me. My plan was to approach college as though I was working and getting paid for my work. After all, in my mind that is what I would be doing if I had not received a scholarship. I decided that I would study extra in the mornings and extra right after dinner. I have always been a morning person and not a night person. I figured I would conduct my own study hall in the evenings in the library and hopefully, might be able to keep up with the other guys on the team. One thing for sure, I was not telling anyone how scared I felt.

For me, going to TCU was the biggest wake- up call a person could
have. Nothing was what I thought it seemed to be, or at least what I
thought it was going to be. I realize now it was because I was so innocent
and pure of heart, so immature about the real world, especially life outside
my environment. What else could you expect from a boy that was raised
in Kent, Texas by his mother's family of thirteen brothers and sisters? My
family life was simple; we were taught to work hard, respect everyone,
believe in God and do the right thing. The second night I was in Fort
Worth in my dorm at TCU, a knock on the door changed my life for many
years. My roommate, Doug Hood from Waxahaxie, Texas answered the
door. Doug and I were paired together by the coaching staff. He was a
first team All State guard that was a great shooter and excellent playmaker.
He had played in the state Tournament and if he had a problem I thought
was that he was sold himself a little too much. Little did I understand that
was an asset instead of a handicap! He was easy to like and deep down
a really good guy. When Doug opened the door, there were two of the
varsity players wanting our attention. They told us to come with them
because we were having our first team meeting. Of course, Doug and I
tagged along as though we knew what was happening. We went across
campus to dorms where upper classmen lived. We walked into a nice and
big dorm room, but not big enough for seven new scholarship freshmen,
and twelve varsity members. We really did not know each other very well
but we got to know each other very well in the next two hours and as we
went through freshman initiation. All us freshman, buck-naked crawling
on our knees, blind folded and being hit by clothes hangers on the butt
doing odd and funny things. Of course, the varsity players were yelling all
kinds of encouraging words to us that usually contained four letter words.
We became very close before the night was over. I did not have much time
to notice anyone or anything, but I did get a feel how some of the guys
on the freshmen team took in it stride and others got mad. I just laughed
at myself along with the others. I thought, they are just having fun at our
expense and I assumed it was something that had to be done so I just kept
my mouth shut and absorbed everything. They broke my ego fast. It really
was not that bad and afterwards we all went out to one of the clubs on the

Jacksboro Highway, in Ft. Worth. I had never been to a club much less drink a beer in public. We had a few beers and lots of laughs. I acted like I knew what I was doing when in fact, I didn't have a clue. I did not drink in high school at all until my senior year, and that was after basketball. Some of my buddies and I would sneak off into Palo Duro Canyon and drink beer. It would consist of drinking three or four beers, getting silly, talking about girls, going to eat a late night snack and going home. We thought we were bad. It only happened once and I was scared to death of getting caught.

The next evening the same thing occurred, and this time Doug and I were prepared. We did not answer the door. We had it figured out so just turned the lights off and shut up. That lasted for about twenty minutes when all of a sudden there was a click on the door, and in walked the hall monitor and behind him some of the varsity players. The hall monitor had master keys and could open any room. This time the guys told us that they were going to take us out on the town and to get dressed. No problem and we got dressed fast. We went out to another club on the Jacksboro Highway. It was dark inside and I was a little nervous after the night before. I was scared that we were getting into something that we shouldn't be doing. Doug was nervous too and that made me feel comfortable to some extent. As we were looking for a place to sit, I looked on the dance floor, and recognized Donny Reed who stood six feet seven inches and weighted about two-hundred-sixty with no fat. Donny was a starter on last year's championship team and was named to the first team All Southwest conference team as a junior. I was stunned. I punched Doug but he couldn't see anyway because he was half blind and he was not wearing his glasses. After all, last night, Donny was busting my behind with a coat hanger, and now he was on the dance floor dancing up a storm. I might add that he appeared to be a very good dancer. He and his sexy girlfriend who got my attention were doing something they call 'The Ft. Worth Push.' For the first time, I realized that I was in a different world; not knowing to relax or be scared. We sat at their table and soon, Donny sat down from the dance floor and introduced himself and his girlfriend. He ordered us beers whether we wanted one or not. Everyone seemed to know him, know us and it made me nervous. It was beyond my belief. He was not the only varsity player at the club and soon we got to know some of them a lot better. We drank a few beers, they danced and we laughed about the night before. Doug and I just watched as I think he was in shock as much as I was. There were tables close to us that were loaded with young ladies all wanted to get to know us. It was not long before we were all together getting to know each other better. Welcome to TCU.

Registration is the heart of frustration in college. Everyone should have to go through college registration. It is a maturing process. No one can explain it but you have to do it in order to understand how frustrating the process happens to be. You go out of one line and into another line. If you are lucky, you wait thirty minutes in a line to find out that the class you need is closed, or the professor you want for that particular class is not available, or the time slot you needed for a class is not available. You go from line to line, in a panic and hoping everything will work out to your benefit. By the time you get all your classes worked in, you are so happy to get a schedule done, you will accept almost anything. Being a yellow bird, it was very important that I get the right professors so registration was critical in my mind. One thing that I did like about registration was the fact that it did not matter if you were a blue bird, red bird, or yellow bird; everyone was in a panic mode. That always put us yellow birds on equal footing. I had no clue as to what my major would be. My Dad wanted me to be a dentist, and mom just wanted me to go to college and hopefully graduate. Since Doug was one of the big time recruits at TCU, the coaches gave him a game plan during registration. He shared that information with me so I just did what he did. Other than the regular classes freshman take, TCU required Orientation, Physical Education, and Military Science. Because we were a Christian orientated school, we had to take two semester of Religion.

Coach Bill Batch, my third mentor was one of the most respected coaches in the Southwest Conference. He had written some basketball articles and his teams won several championships. A championship was expected this year as he had five seniors back from a Southwest Conference championship the year before. That was the main reason I decided on TCU as I had tremendous desire to be with a winner. His specialty was post play and the development of post players. He was like a 360 degree turn around from Coach Hill, my high school. Coach Batch cussed, smoked, and drank alcohol. He did not hide his drinking from anyone and was open about it. I ran into him one time in the elevator on a trip and he was so drunk he did not know who I was. Most coaches give their players a break during workout in order that they can get their breath, but he gave us a break so he could have a cigarette. He would sit on the score table and smoke while we hurried to get a drink of water. He used four letter words like they were part of the English language. I was known by him as the "Little Shit". This was a shock for me coming from one environment to the other. The NCAA had a rule in those days that freshman could not play on the varsity. I thank God everyday for that as I was not ready for Coach Batch.

Delbert Swanson was the freshman coach. Coach Swanson was a two time All Southwest conference player at TCU and we all liked him. He was tough but kind and he knew his basketball. He was an easy guy to like because he would spend extra time with you if you asked him for help. He individually worked with me and talked to me about typical college issues. I am sure now that he knew I was over my head. I didn't know it at the time but he must have. I started on the freshman team that year but was disappointed because we were not as good as I thought we should be. We were beaten by several junior colleges but won most of our games when we played other freshman teams. I was mad because we did not beat Texas University. What made it bad for me was the fact that I played terrible with two good friends playing on the Texas freshman team. I averaged 7.4 pts per game and really did not have many games in double figures. I felt I was having a hard time adjusting to the college game. The truth was that the other players on our team seemed to know more about basketball than I did, and their skills were better. They seemed to understand little things that I should know. Doug, my roommate could shoot as well as I could, if not better, but he also had a better feel for the game than me. Daniel Jr. Wells from Houston was a six foot six inch player loaded with talent. He was skinny but a natural scorer. I was more impressed with his passing and knowledge of the game. He knew how to draw a charge. We never even thought about drawing a charge when I was in high school.

The biggest difference in my days and the present day was that I never had to compete with blacks. None of us did. The Houston guys knew a little about black players but most of us were totally clueless. Of course the reason is that the blacks played in their league and we played in our league. To the average young person now days, that seems impossible but I had never seen a black person play basketball until I was twenty. If I had to compete like all the other kids do now days, I would have never been able to play in the Southwest Conference.

On our trip to Baylor, I had a friend, Bert McKenzie from high school that played on the Baylor freshman team that invited me to go clubbing after the game. I got home rather late and definitely could feel the effects of our partying. The next morning, we had breakfast as a team and got on the bus back to Ft. Worth. Our team always flew everywhere we traveled but Waco was a short distance from Ft. Worth so we took the bus. Freshmen had to sit in the front on the bus and I was one of the last ones on the bus so I sat by Coach Batch and Coach Swanson. I was really feeling bad from the party last night and before long, I had to throw up. I pulled the window down and threw up all over the outside of the bus. We were on the road, and the wind and speed of the bus kept all the pieces I threw up on most all windows on my side of the bus. The damage was done and created a domino effect on some of the players. It seems that I was not the only one on the team that had too much to drink and soon several other players started throwing up. It was a comic effect that I started. You could hear players throwing up their breakfast and yelling and shouting at each other not to throw up. I looked over at Batch and he was grinning as was Swanson.

I was spoiled for life as we won the Southwest Conference my first year at TCU. The varsity was very good. H.E. Kemp, a six-foot-eleven, two-hundred-ninety-five pound post with a right or left hook shot with touch and direction was the key to another Southwest Conference Championship for Coach Batch. H.E. was smooth with the hook shot. It was like he could catch and shoot while getting his body ready for a hook. What made him different was that he could shoot the hook from ten feet away from the basket. He was something to watch. This was my first exposure to a hook shot as an offensive weapon, and he was one of the best in the world. Watching this team taught me so much about basketball. I loved the roles each of the starters played. One of my favorites was Dee Nile, a very athletic six foot four swing man from Childress. He could have played football as well as basketball because of his body strength and athleticism. He was more athletic than any guy on the team and he often would show off at practice by dunking the ball. The next guy was what gave me hope. He was built just like me except he was two inches taller but his game was very similar to mine. His name was Larry Bowen and was an outstanding shooter. He was our zone buster. That's not to mention the other two keys to the success of this team, Donnie Reed and Bear King. Reed, as mentioned before was outstanding at the high post. He was a great feeder and an excellent rebounder, scorer and shooter from the high post area. Of course, the guy that was the anchor and soul of the team was King from a class "B" school called 'Ava'. He was six-foot-two of pure basketball and tough as nails. He scared me to death and was without a doubt one of the better defensive players I have ever been around. He didn't know it but he taught me a lot just from watching him every day in practice. He was a team player first and foremost and an excellent ball handler and passer. With that mix, you have a championship team. Coach Batch was an inside-out coach. Everything centered at the post and everyone that played knew their roles. Little did I know but I was learning something that would carry over into my coaching for the rest of my life. Inside play, roles and assignments. In high school, all we did was go out and play. At TCU, each guy fit a role that Batch had and then he coached those roles. Coach knew exactly what he wanted at each position and when they did what he wanted, they won. I did not realize it but I was getting a first class education in basketball.

As a freshman, I went to the library every night after supper. I would stay about two hours and outline my assignments, which I learned in freshman orientation. I was amazed how much it helped me remember what was said in the class room and then it just made me feel much smarter the next day in class. When I had a test, I would study for about two hours, in the evening and then get up early and study in the morning. I always felt better about what I could learn in the mornings. I was like hermit, because I did not go out very much at all my first semester of college. I was so scared of failure that I would not risk it. Finally, the first semester was over. There were seven freshmen on the team and I had the highest grade point with a 3.2 for the first semester. To my surprise, everyone started thinking I was smart, even the coaches. I made a 'B' in English, History, Religion and Military Science. The first semester helped my confidence and I was proud of myself. I hoped, just maybe, this yellow bird was moving up.

The NCAA pairings came out in early March for the National Championship Tournament and we drew Cincinnati in the first round. Cincinnati had a black player named Oscar Robertson. He was a first team All-American and the first black player we had to play against. I had never played against a black player in my life. Bear King had to guard Robertson, and I thought to myself that Oscar Robertson would meet his match. I was dead wrong, as Oscar did just about what he wanted to and scored a team high 34pts and Cincinnati beat us 84 to 63. It was not even close. I saw another world as I watched the game film. I have never seen such a display of skill and athlete ability. I wondered if there might be more guys in the world like Oscar.

The spring semester of my freshman year, I did something that changed my life forever. I joined a fraternity named Delta Seta Theta. It was by God's grace alone that this happened to me. I did not know what a fraternity was when I went to TCU. I met a guy named Jim Perkins who was a Delta Seta who played basketball with me on the freshman team as a non-scholarship player. We started hanging out together and he asked me to go through spring Rush. He told me about the intramural program where they played football, basketball, baseball, track and golf. That was something that I wanted to do as I really wanted to play football in high school and I saw an opportunity to have some fun playing football again. Besides that we had several athletes at TCU that were in Delta Seta. After Rush, you attend fraternity parties and meet all the members, I decided I wanted to be a Delta Seta. What I did not know was that it would be their choice and not mine. That is just how naive I was about TCU and about fraternities. I had two more fraternities that wanted me but I wanted to be a Delta Seta. I wanted to follow in the footsteps some other great athletes that played at TCU. After Delta Seta decided that they wanted me to join, I joined and then they told me I had to go through a semester of being a pledge. I had to learn a brand new alphabet, carry a brick around with me at all times, learn a new way to talk, a new way to walk, go to study hall, go to meetings, go to dances and go to socials with other sororities, I wasn't so sure I really wanted to do all that. I had to learn how to engage in politics within the fraternity and wear a tuxedo. I had never worn a tux on in my life. I had to go through hazing once a week and eventually got so involved that I helped kidnap an active and took him to Old Mexico, dropped him off like I knew what I was doing. In short, my life turned completely around in a short period of time when I joined. It was fun for me and it completely took my mind off basketball. My social life turned up a notch and my mind opened up to another way of life. Looking back on all of it now, it was one of the best things I did in college. When it was over, I made a 2.8, and formally became an active Delta Seta at the end of the spring semester. It was a moving experience for me and one I will never forget. Little did I know it was going to be the main factor in my decision to become a coach?

To my way of thinking, intramural football in college was the best thing since sliced bread. I loved the competition. I could not play because Coach Batch made intramural football off limits. That did not mean I could not coach football, so I became head coach of the Delta Seta. My first year as the head coach, we won the football intramural title. That is how I became a valuable asset to the Phi Seta. Next came fall Rush which I was excited to be a part of because I was looking for athletes to join. I wanted another championship, so I recruited guys who were good athletes into Delta Seta. It just happened by accident that the start of basketball NCAA workouts and Rush were at the same time, but I was not worried about any conflicts. I had really prepared for the start of basketball and was in excellent shape, my basketball skills were as sharp as ever. Playing against players who were better than me really helped my game and I got better. We started our workouts on October 15th, and I was ready. The day before we started, I had an accident that would change the course of my basketball career. I sprained my right ankle very badly playing a pick- up game. If you have never sprained your ankle, you do not want to do it as it was the worst pain I ever had in my life. I thought I broke my ankle and when I found out I sprained it, I wondered what the pain would be if you broke it. What I found out later on in years to come, a bad sprain is worse than a break. I went to the trainers who lived in the dorms and they quickly went to work on my ankle. Our training staff knew it was a bad sprain, and their advice ran through me as they said, "Whatever you do, stay off your feet for the next 48 hours:" I wanted to say, "Guess what, we had Phi Seta Rush parties scheduled tomorrow that will start at 8:00a.m.and will go until late into the night." What I did next was the dumbest thing I did at TCU. I attended the Rush parties and stood on my feet the entire time. That was the turning point of my sophomore season as I never recovered from my ankle sprain. I would have been better off breaking my ankle.

The trainers at TCU did everything to get my ankle healed including shots but it just could not be done. Any basketball player that has ever suffered an ankle injury knows that this injury creates a problem in your shooting. I could never really cut like I needed to which meant I could not gain the confidence I needed. I lost lots of confidence and had a terrible year. I did get to play a little but it was because we were terrible. I think we won seven games all together and Coach Batch turned hostile. I was just one of the guys he turned on and it was easy for him to find fault in me. I was terrible from the beginning and I forced opportunity after opportunity and lost a lot of confidence. It all started from the ankle injury and got worse as time went on. Needless to say, at the end of the year, I was on Batch's 'Black list'. It was then that he started calling me the "Little shit". I was 6'2", and weighed 170 pounds.

The next basketball season I thought it was a dream and pinched myself to make sure I was awake when Coach Batch told the entire team that I was going to be one of top eight players. Batch always had his eight players that he coached and that was the elite group. 'Batch's boys' would consist of his starters and first line subs. He never went to the other guys unless we were winning big or losing big. For him to make that statement to the players was a thrill for me and something that I had been waiting to hear. Two days before practice started, I tore a hamstring muscle playing intramural football in practice. Of course, this did not set very well with Coach Batch. I went from the first eight to the bottom of the group and it took me forever to get my leg ready. The trainers and I were becoming good friends by now as they taped me every-day and whirl-pooled my ankle because it was not the same. Seems as though I developed a pinched nerve in my ankle, or at least that is what a real doctor said. I finally made up my mind that I was going to get back on the good side of Batch so I set out to do just that. I had one thing going for me that very few of the guys on the team possessed and that was a desire to be good defensively. I figured if I could guard our guards in practice, then I could guard any guard in the conference. We weren't winning because we did not have good guards but we just didn't have the kind of post play that coach Batch was used to coaching. Also, my sore leg and poor ankle would not be as much of a handicap on defense as offense because defense is more about desire and attitude. My plan worked and I soon became one of the top eight players. I played nearly the entire game when we played Texas Tech at Lubbock. Soon, I became one of the better defensive players on the team. I started studying defense and really picking up on man to man techniques and zone concepts. My junior year was a real turning point in my basketball career as I soon learned the importance of defense.

My grades picked up as I made a 3.0 in the fall semester and a 2.9 in the spring semester. I received several nicknames from the crowd during each basketball season but one that stuck with me was 'Dingle-Berry'. Two buddies I had on the football team gave me that nickname. I didn't like it but I didn't fight it. At TCU, all athletes became good friends as we all lived together, ate together and shared rooms together. That was something I really liked about TCU. When we played Rice, the game became dead and boring. At first it was the football team, and then some fraternities and some spectators started yelling that they wanted Dingle-Berry to play. Batch went to the end of the bench and pointed for me to get in and the crowd went crazy. I made three of four free throws in the last few seconds of a game, and the entire student body went crazy and carried me off the floor.

That spring, I started playing golf with some of my fraternity brothers. I was surprised that I really liked the game and started visiting with Richard Simmons from Stamford. He was on the Taxi Squad when I first met him. The Taxi Squad at TCU was made up of scholarship players that did not make the teams but were kept on scholarship. They would do work in and around TCU and travel in a truck. Richard was a natural athlete that went to TCU on a basketball scholarship. He did not like Batch and his ways, so he gave up basketball and turned to golf. They put him on the Taxi Squad. I used to go over when he was practicing golf on the putting course and we would talk about his life as a basketball player and my life as a basketball player. We had lots of similar situations and that created a strong friendship. I got to know him better during the Colonial Golf Tournament held in Ft. Worth every year. It was part of the PGA tour, and the athletes at TCU got to work all four days if they wanted. I started off working at parking cars. Next, I lost a flip and had to work cooking and selling young kids hamburgers and ice cream. It was more of a baby-sitting job than anything else. The benefits were the good looking mothers that would tip you when you took good care of their kids but the down side was the spoiled brats who made the job hard. Finally, my senior year, I worked in the bar and was a runner. I just helped deliver drinks outside to special people. I really enjoyed the tips and excitement of the Tournament. It was an experience I will never forget to this day. I became a huge PGA and golf fan, but Richard Simmons made it very special. My Dad loved golf just as I did and he started following Richard when he went on the tour. I always appreciated Richard because he was always nice to my Dad. When Richard Simmons won the Masters in Augusta, I thought my Dad was going to have a heart attack.

Starting my senior year, all I wanted to do was make a difference in the TCU basketball team. That summer in workouts, I worked as hard as I could to work out. I was ready for my senior year and looked forward to helping the team in anyway I could. Once the season started, I was out of Batch's rotation again. I worked hard to get my shooting touch back and finally did, but by this time, Batch had decided to go with the younger guys. He developed an attitude about me to justify his actions. He felt I was a great practice player but a poor game player. That really hurt. He was not completely wrong as I never had much success as a shooter when I did play. What he never realized that the only chances I did get were on his terms in the most negative situations possible and I was in poor physical condition. It was always a situation where I had everything to lose and very little to gain. My confidence was low and high confidence is the key to a good shooter. This really helped me in learning how to handle shooters in basketball and quarterbacks in football. I had excuses with injuries, but I was not the kind to look for excuses as I learned that from my mom. When Christmas break came, our team was making our annual trip to Oklahoma City to play in the All College Basketball Tournament, and I decided I was finished with TCU basketball. I knew I had no value with the team so I just went home. I did not tell Coach Batch and I knew it was wrong but I didn't care. I had never done anything like that before and it shocked the entire team. If anything, I had always been a solid team leader to this point. I told the guys he would not even know I was gone. Yet when he was handing out rooming assignments, he found out I was AWOL. To say he was pissed off would be an understatement. When we met in his office after the team returned from Oklahoma City, he told me that I could finish the year, but wouldn't get to play in another game. I had to suit up and work out to keep my scholarship. That was all he said. He was very upset with me and I didn't blame him one bit.

Just as I did in the 8th grade when I got cut, I started playing basketball again. This time, it was a semi-pro basketball team called Harley's Cleaners. They played on weekends, usually Friday, Saturday, and Sunday. They played their games in Ft. Worth, Dallas, Austin, Waco and Denton. I went from not playing for TCU to playing full time for a semi-pro team. It was nice to feel good about myself again, but my ankle looked like a watermelon thirty minutes after each game. I didn't care then. The team was a semi-pro team mostly made up of former TCU players with regular jobs in the area. They all knew who I was and that made me feel good. To my surprise, most of the guys knew the conflicts I had with Coach Batch. It was like old reunion days for me as each and every player playing on the team would tell me war stories about their years of playing at TCU. The problem I had with all this was that I was not bitter about Batch because I felt I caused most of my own problems. Of course they didn't care because now I was one of them. Soon after I started playing with them, our coach was transferred to Atlanta. After long discussions they all decided that I was the only one that had the time to coach because most of the others had jobs or some kind of commitment.

That is how I became a semi-pro coach. I could not play two games in a row because of my ankle so it seemed the right thing. Besides, I thought it would be a stepping stone in my career. I was sure now that I wanted to coach. Harley's Cleaners provided free cleaning and $5.00 per game. Not bad because $5.00 could get you a lot in those days. We wore their uniforms and we paid for our own travel. They provided the uniforms. We were a good team but we could not past an all-black team from Houston. They beat us in the championship game to go to the national finals. We played well, I learned a lot and it was a start for me. It was a nice deal for a guy like me just about to graduate and thinking about coaching.

The last home game at TCU was something that I would never forget. It was Parent Day and my parents and Mike were there along with my Uncle Richard and Pauline. During the third quarter, the crowd started chanting for me to get into the game. It got louder and louder. I looked up and saw the entire football team, the baseball team, track guys, fraternity guys, and even some professors that I knew getting in on the chant. They stood up, and then everyone stood up and started chanting,"We want Young, not Dingle Berry!" Coach Batch turned all shades of red, and pointed to his ankle as to say that I was hurt. Of course, all the athletes knew that I was not that hurt so they just kept pouring it on. It lasted like a life time to me but I am sure it was only about a minute or so. My parents were proud as was my brother Mike. It was a great moment in my life. Of course, I did not get to play, but it was a moment that eased all the emotional scars that I developed over not playing at TCU. The press made a big deal of it and that made me feel good. That spring, my Delta Seta established a plaque for the most outstanding intramural athlete on my behalf. They named it the 'Dingle-Berry Award'. I was honored and I still remember many of my fraternity brothers to this very day.

That spring, my advisor called me in and told me that I lacked a three hour physical education course in order to graduate. The only time they offered the course was in the fall semester so I put my new plans on hold and decided to go back to TCU. My plan was to take that course, and graduate in December and then try and get a teaching or coaching position close to Ft. Worth so I could finish another year of coaching Harley's Cleaners. First, I had to make some money because TCU was expensive. I went back to Amarillo that summer and found a job as the Head Life Guard of the Amarillo city pools. The pay was good and I could handle the job. I taught life guards how to teach swimming and how to become certified to be a life guard. I gave personal lessons and helped with organization of the city pools. I was twenty-two now and starting to think about my future and career. One of the pools that I was responsible for was Carver Swimming Pool. It was an all-black pool and located in what we used to call Palo Duro Park. Everyday that I went over to the Carver Pool, I would have to pull someone out of the deep water while I was teaching swimming lessons. We would be giving lessons on the shallow end of the pool and all of a sudden, I would hear sounds of "Help me, I can't swim!" Sure enough, in the deep end of the pool would be someone that couldn't swim. Someone for no reason at all would just jump in the deep water. It was scary for me, but at the same time very rewarding. I soon became very good friends with some of the black lifeguards. They even invited me to come play some street ball at Palo Duro Park. I was thrilled to death because I had always wanted to play with them but was scared to ask. Playing basketball on the playgrounds of Palo Duro Park was a learning experience. It was rough, and no fouls were called. If you did call a foul, then an argument started and then time expired. I especially would not call a foul. I was determined not to be a cry-baby but I sure took a whipping. Most of the players were very athletic and good. They were a lot better than I was when I was in high school. I thought something was wrong with our world that they could not play or swim where I could play or swim. Something was not right. Little did I know that my world was starting to change?

As the fall semester was ending, I did manage to send out about seventy-five letters around the area to see if I could get employment. To my surprise, I did not get any replies. Since that did not work, I sent out about twenty-five more letters to schools around the Amarillo area. That was too far but I was now desperate and hoping someone would remember me from high school. Sure enough, I got a reply from Perryton Junior High School. They needed a 9th grade PE teacher, and a 5th grade Science teacher. My major was PE and my minor was Biology. I didn't know it at the time but I found out later the only reason I got the reply for the position was that Mr. Mizer, the superintendent knew who I was as he followed basketball in the Panhandle and remembered when I played for Polk High School. He knew T.G. Hill and called Coach Hill about me. It seemed that they both attended the same college. When I went for the interview, Mr. Mizer asked me if I wanted to coach and I said yes. They had no openings then, but you never know about next year. I told him up front that I was coaching a semi-pro team called Harley's Cleaners and planned on finishing the season as their coach even though we were far away from Ft. Worth. I had already looked at the school calendar and explained that I would need to take three Friday's off. He told me that I would have to pay the substitution fee and we signed the agreement for my employment.

Even though it was hard, I did complete my coaching agreement with Harley's. We finished the season better than the year before. We only lost two games but we still could not beat the all-black team from Houston. I installed my grade- out system and it was successful. We had only eight players so it was easy.

Ron Penny was the head boys coach at Perryton High School and Roy Runnells was the head junior high coach. I was lucky to have the opportunity to observe both of them in action. Ron Penny won the State Championship at Perryton and Coach Runnells went on the win a state championship at Dumas and Kerrville. They were both 1-3-1 zone people as was Batch at TCU. Although we played a lot of man-to-man defense at TCU, we ran the 1-3-1 most of the time. At any rate, I was very fortunate to start at Perryton Junior High School. That spring, I started trying to get a head basketball coaching position. I did not know what to do, but with Jennifer helping me write letters, I got some replies. One day, I got a reply from Adrian High School, a class B school where basketball was very important. Little did I know how important. The superintendent wanted to meet with me at a track meet on Saturday at Hartley. We met and had a great visit. He had heard from Coach Batch who gave me a great recommendation. I had heard from the older players at TCU that if Batch liked you, he would go all out to help you get a job. I finally knew he liked me. He, Mr. Hill and Mr. Mizer gave me a great recommendation. Phil Roberts, the superintendent asked me to come down for an interview. I knew nothing about interviewing and little about Adrian except they had a reputation for playing good basketball.

Perryton had a track meet that weekend so I went out and helped with the meet; not because I wanted to but because I had to as part of the job. I talked to Ron and Roy about the job, and also visited with Mr. Mizer. I guess my enthusiasm showed because all of them tried to soften the blow if I did not get the job. I could not understand why they thought that I might not get it because I thought I would. The night I interviewed for the job, I understood their thinking. There were five of us in a room waiting to be called in to talk to the board. All were at least fifteen years older than I was and some were well known coaches in the area. I was excited and nervous at the same time. I just kept saying to myself, "don't choke". My time came and it was not half as bad as I thought it would be. Everyone was nice. Mr. Roberts, the superintendent was trying to make me feel more at ease as he introduced me to the board and explained my situation and what Coach Batch and T.G. Hill had said about me. Batch was the one that got their attention the most, because he had called Mr. Roberts and the president of the board. He told them I was destined to be a great coach as I had all the tools necessary, but needed a starting point. That really got their attention. It also got my attention as I realized for the first time how lucky I was to have played basketball for Coach Batch. He had his faults but from a basketball standpoint, he was a class act. He also was a good influence on my coaching philosophy. They had one problem with me being hired and they were honest about it. They wanted me to explain what I was going to do as a coach since I had no experience. I thought it was a fair question. T.G. Hill taught me when we were working at the swimming pool that

when someone asked you a question and you are not sure how to answer
that question, ask a question in return. I asked the board what they wanted
in a coach. It worked as they explained what they wanted and that gave
me a clear picture of what they wanted to know. I explained I could not
tell them that I knew what to do, but I could tell them that I knew what
not to do. I then proceeded to explain what a coach should not do. It sold
them on me and I was offered the job the next morning at 8:00am. I was
excited and thrilled. Now I had to figure out what to do.

EIGHT

BACK TO THE BIG DAY, getting out of our dressing room to the bus after the shoot-around was much harder than getting to the dressing room. Several hundreds of our fans, beside themselves with enthusiasm and love of their school, screamed and unwittingly pummeled their young heroes as we coaches and players worked our way from the dressing room to the bus. The crowd gathered around the players shaking hands, exchanging high-fives, even a few bear hugs in the lobby, introducing an element of danger to our exit that I did not appreciate. After too much pushing and pulling, we escaped to the bus. The last one on, I was thrilled to be onboard, and was about to sit down when Doc Adams called me to join him in the back. Doc had been through big games and big crowds more than once, and I had a funny feeling walking back, wondering why he wanted to talk to me at a moment like this. All kinds of scenarios shot through my mind, most of them dire. I knew it had something to do with injury or it wouldn't be Doc summoning me.

He didn't keep me waiting. "It's D'wayne, coach," Doc said. I turned and looked at D'wayne square in the eye and could tell he was upset about something. He had a condition some refer to as free bleeder's disease; though it's real scientific name is hemophilia. It is a condition where the stricken exhibit uncontrolled bleeding. It usually affects males and is transmitted from mother to son.

I said, "What happened and where is the cut?" D'wayne admitted he wasn't sure. He had been pushed to the ground and cut his knee on something, he didn't know what happened. But when he got on the bus, he realized he was bleeding. The injections used to control the condition were at the hotel but the team doctor would have to give the shot. That was a rule the university president had insisted on when we signed D'wayne. Everyone was afraid of liability issues with him, but Doctor Punching, our basketball team doctor, wasn't overly concerned. He was with the team for the shoot-around but he had not brought the injections with him. I had an early bad experience with Dr. Punching. He diagnosed me with leukemia when I fell sick in the fall. He tried to put me in the hospital and have a bone marrow test run on me, but I refused. Instead, I wanted a second opinion, and doctor number two found out that I just had a low white blood count, low but normal for me. I received some treatments and within one week was back to normal. Since that time my confidence in Dr. Punching had been shaken. It did not surprise me one bit that he had left the injections in the hotel.

D'wayne Hudson was one of a kind. He was a country boy, lived on a farm located on the outskirts of Denton, Texas. I had as much fun looking into him as with anyone I had recruited for the team. He was six feet seven inches tall, weighed around 230 pounds, but he wasn't just a good player but an excellent athlete too. He was the leading scorer in the metropolitan area that included Dallas County. I'm sure that stat was all that some recruiters knew about D'wayne. But the truth was he played on a terrible team, and they only won two games. He was the only one on the squad who could dribble and shoot. Anytime his team had the ball with an opportunity to score, it fell on D'wayne to shoot the ball. It was a nightmare to watch his team play because it invariably ended up with five players vs. D'wayne. He was a good offensive player, it's true, but the fact that it was a one-person show did have an effect on the stats.

I had become aware of him when one of my ex-players ended up serving as the preacher in his family's church. Lamar Odem was a young man who had played for me at Panhandle Baptist University and he was now the preacher at Mt. Zion Baptist Church on the outskirts of Denton. When Dwayne was in the ninth grade, Lamar wrote me a letter and asked me if I would help D'wayne get a basketball scholarship. One of the tenets of my recruiting philosophy was to always listen to all these great young athletes, both my ex-players and the current ones. I received better tips about players from them than any scouting service that I ever paid good money for. I remembered Lamar's letter when I heard that D'wayne was the leading scorer in the metro area; it was easy to see it was time for a recruiting trip to Denton. I took Jennifer with me because Lamar had been one of her favorites when he played for us. She hoped to visit with him during my stop to see D'wayne. Not only that, when she met Gracie, D'Wayne's mother, the two of them hit it off right away. Neither D'wayne nor I could get a word into the conversation. I felt the visit went well, but I am always on the lookout for negative feedback. D'wayne followed up by visiting North West State University that spring right after I took the head coaching position. He seemed happy the entire time he was on campus and we were all optimistic he was going to sign with us. Even Lamar felt we were his first choice. He had two more visits to make and told us that we were number one on his list. He was going to visit SMU and Baylor the next two weekends. I was happy but worried. Both big schools were so close to his home, and whatever you wanted to say about D'Wayne, he was a home boy.

As the April 14 signing date was fast approaching, we had not heard from D'wayne in two weeks. He had become close with Darryl, my top assistant coach, and they spoke regularly over the last two months. It was both unusual and worrying that D'wayne had just cut off communications. I told Darryl that something was up and sure enough, I was right. I had Jennifer call Gracie and we found out D'wayne had made a verbal commitment to SMU. It was his right to do so, but I was disappointed that he gave us no opportunity to respond to the SMU offer. I am sure he would have rather had it that way too. Disappointments are common in the recruiting business but you never get used to it. Dwayne was on top of our list and that just meant we had to scratch his name off and move onto the next guy. Of course, we had recruited other players with a similar skill set, but not with the same intensity as we had with D'wayne. He was a sincere kid. He was genuine; I was sure, not a phony in any way. Now we needed a tall slender swingman who could provide what D'wayne would have on the court.

D'wayne was strong in every area of the game, particularly rebounding. We already had a talk with Junior Boyd, out of Mobile, Alabama, our second choice. There really was not much difference in the two, I guess, except for the fact that I had put so much time into D'wayne, and that I knew him better. I knew his preacher, his high school coach, his principal, and his counselor. All of those sources gave me solid information about the young man I was recruiting, about his loved ones and his character. Junior's body and his skills compared well with D'wayne's on the basketball court. But I didn't know Junior as well so I felt a little insecure. <u>You can recruit the most outstanding player in America and it can turn into a flop if you haven't done your homework.</u> At any rate, we started in earnest scouting Junior and another player with similar skills to D'wayne's.

But all that changed when the Dallas Morning News hit the newsstands that Sunday. Texas sports were rocked: SMU was put on probation for recruiting violations. They had broken some NCAA rules in both football and basketball. The head coaches in both sports were fired on the spot. The story appeared to involve a booster club member who was providing extra funds for recruits on trips to Dallas. Names were withheld from the paper but it stated the college would understand if any prospect, for football or basketball, which had made early commitments wanted to change their mind. One week later, I was in the congregation at the Mt. Zion church waiting for D'wayne to sign an athletic agreement to attend and play for North West State University.

We didn't discover that Dwayne had hemophilia until after he signed. It was then that his mother revealed his condition. I guess she thought that it was too late for us to back out if we didn't know of the disease until afterward. I really didn't know what to make of any of this until I returned to campus to find a meeting had been scheduled with the school's athletic director and the president of the university about D'wayne. The team doctor took charge of the meeting and he informed us about the disease. He explained, "Hemophilia is when the blood fails to clot properly, which can therefore cause spontaneous internal bleeding. This can lead to subsequent organ damage, and even to death." Dr. Punching continued, "Protein injections of the missing clotting factor can stop the bleeding and create a normal blood clot, but fast action is critical. It's important that injection treatments of the clotting factor concentrate in adequate doses be administered immediately."

The President the spoke up, deciding, "Well, if that's the case, then you should be the only one to give the injections." It was a ruling I was unhappy with from the beginning. I would have felt safer with the responsibility falling to Doc Adams giving the shots, but it was out of my control.

As big a deal as we made out of hemophilia, it was largely a nonfactor for most of the season. I guess "D," as I called him, was used to it and had become naturally careful in how he did things, and it seemed it would never be an issue. And I was pleased it hadn't been a problem through all our games and all our practices. Some players could have been expected to baby such a condition, to expect easier treatment. But D'wayne was one of the most aggressive guys on the court. He was by far the team's best offensive rebounder, a punishing presence on the boards, and I just loved the guy. He always had a smile on his face and everyone just had a good feeling being around him. Things were going so well that when we played an exhibition game in Dallas early in the year, big "D" had every member of his family at the game along with the congregation of the Mt. Zion church. There had to be over 150 people in attendance just to watch big "D". The team warmed to all the excitement the crowd brought to the game. The show was all about big "D" during the pregame warm-up and he was having a fun night, shooting and dunking the ball for his fans. Coach Soapy got angry with him for showing off, but I really didn't hold it against him and was glad everyone was having such a good time. He was the only child and they all just loved him. On his last dunk before the officials came out on the court, however, big "D" cut his wrist on the goal. He rushed over to Doc in a panic and just placed his wrist in Doc's hands. Of course, Doc knew how to proceed under usual conditions, but Dr. Punching had not made this trip, so we rushed "D" straight to the local hospital for the necessary injection. I felt for everyone who had come to watch big "D" play that night, but they all knew and loved D'Wayne; they understood why we rushed him off during the game. We and our school were given high grades on our handling of their beloved native son.

Everything was smoothed over and there were no more issues with D'wayne's condition until one night around midnight in the early fall semester when I received a phone call from Ma Baker, the dorm supervisor. We housed all our freshman basketball players in her dorm. When I answered the phone, I recognized the voice right away.

She said, "Coach, you need to come to the dorm right now."

I replied, "OK," and hung up the phone. I have always made it a point of making sure that I responded quickly and without question when any of the dorm supervisors requested my attention. I found out over the years that they would work with you a lot better if they felt you supported them. Any kind of debate over the phone might create doubt in a supervisor's mind, and I did not want that.

When I arrived at the dorm, Ma Baker was at the door waiting for me. I got no niceties from Ma, no "How are you?" "Nice to see you," or anything like that. She said, "It's D'wayne," and directed me to look into the far corner of the room. With no information, I had no idea what to expect but my brain was in high gear and I was nervous. Curiously, however, I couldn't help but notice that several of the teammates were milling about the lobby, and watching every step I took. The strange thing was that although I knew I wouldn't be here unless there was a problem, they all seemed to have smirks or smiles on their faces.

Big "D" was in the corner just as Ma had said. He was huddled up like a little boy with both knees up near his jaw and his head down resting on his knees. He wore nothing but a T-shirt and his underwear. With a rough voice, I started, "What's going on, D'wayne?" He had learned quickly that when I called him Dwayne, I was angry.

He looked up at me and whined, "She bit me!"

"Are you bleeding, D'wayne?"

"Yes," the quick reply.

Catching my breath, I went on, "Where?" I needed to know.

The answer was quick and embarrassed: "On my pecker." Biting my lips, my tongue, and trying anything that might prevent the big smile from exploding across my face, I managed to keep myself from giving into the belly laugh I felt coming.

Finally, I said, "Go get your clothes on and I'll take you to the hospital." He hurried to his room and did as he was told and we quickly left the dorm. As we escaped the building, I could hear the guys in the lobby giving him a round of applause and all the encouragement they could manage.

Through an embarrassing and labored conversation on the way to the hospital, I was able to get the complete picture as to what had befallen my young star while maintaining most of my composure and poise. I did not know whether to laugh, be angry with him, or be embarrassed for him. One thing was certain: The people at the hospital thought it was very funny and the next day, it was all over the campus. I couldn't help but feel sorry for him, even if just a little.

NEXT UP ON THE BIG DAY was the pregame meal. The pregame meal can be a headache for coaches and I made up my mind to change it up so it worked to our advantage. The hotel in New Braunfels offered to set up some food but I turned them down. Thinking that this was to be our last pregame meal together was a genuine reality check. We had decided to have the same kind of meal before each game once we started the playoffs in the Big 12 Tournament. I am very nervous about changing anything when the team is winning, and I wasn't about to alter any part of our routine now. We used to host a high-end quality pregame meal, but I had recently instituted a new routine. We ordered Subway sandwiches, drinks, chips, fruit, and candy and decided the team members and coaches would watch game film of our opponents while we ate. One thing that wasn't new was that pregame meal attendance was mandatory: We had never had a problem with anyone skipping this team requirement until we were getting ready to play Baylor in our first game of the Big 12 Tournament. We felt good about our chances to win, even though Baylor had a higher rating than we did. We split with them during the season, with each team winning a game at home, so this would be the first neutral-site game. Tonight we'd play the first of a series of games that would define our season. We win and continue to play, or lose and go home. Everyone was at the gathering except Big Time. I knew he was pretty full of himself and beginning to think he was too big for our team, but I was shocked that he would blow off the pre-game meal.

I asked White Shoes, his roommate, "Where is Big Time?" and he responded that his friend was asleep in the room. It's a team rule that every guy on the team is responsible for each other, so I asked White Shoes why he left Big Time in the room without telling his teammates or any of the coaches.

He explained, "Coach, he said he was too sick to come down and told me that he needed his sleep." It got very still and quiet in the room and I could feel the tension rising in the players, particularly from White Shoes. I instructed Eddie, one of our assistant coaches, to go check on Big Time.

But no sooner had Eddie gathered the room key than White Shoes said, "Coach, can I talk to you in private?" I agreed of course, and we walked out of the room and closed the door.

White Shoes began, "Coach, you will not find Big Time in the room. He is not there, and we're not sure exactly where he is. He called me on my cell phone about an hour ago and said he was with his girlfriend and that he was going to miss the pregame meal. He asked me to cover for him. I tried to protect him but I knew you guys were going to catch him and I even told him that." Then he continued, "Coach, Big Time's head is getting way too big for his britches and you need to do something about it."

I assured him, "Thanks for being honest, and you can count on it. Something will be done." This was the opening of the Big 12 tournament, the key moment of our season, and I was angry with our number-one big-time player, and the one recruit, I was quite sure, who was being paid the most, "Big Time Hawkins." He had been named to the Big 12 All-Conference Team, and I guess he felt he could do anything. I suppose if I was getting paid as much to play as he was I might feel the same way, but I was not going to let him get away with this behavior. He had let his teammates down and he was going to pay for it, even if it meant my job.

We went back in and the team watched the film and ate our sandwiches. I let the team go and told them to be ready to go at 5:30, and to meet in the lobby wearing white. "When Big Time gets back," I said, "send him to my room." Around 4:00 p.m., Big Time knocked on the door and I told him to come in. We sat down and talked for a moment and I let him explain his side of the story. He knew he was in trouble but he also figured that we needed him if we hoped to win the big game this night. Honestly, I didn't think we could win without him either, but I was not about to let him know that. He started telling me his story, which was that he gotten stranded across town with his girlfriend and he did not have enough money to get a cab and so forth. I couldn't listen anymore and just cut him off. Perhaps I was wrong not to hear him out and listen to his whole story, but sometimes as a coach, you just lose it. I certainly did, attacking the details of what he was saying, and everything about him that I did not like. Then I told him in no uncertain words that he would not play tonight against Baylor, and he might have played his last game for the Black and Gold Lions. I told him if he wanted any chance to play anymore, that he had better put on his best coat and tie, join us at the game, sit on the bench, and be the best cheerleader on the court tonight.

Once I dismissed him, the word got out quickly to the players, the boosters, the press, and everyone else associated with the team. It was such a critical game. Some people simply assumed that I had lost my mind. Almost everyone was critical of the step I had taken. *Run him extra when you get home, make him do extra work, or come up with anything but do not punish the other players because of Big Time's lack of discipline.* Of course, I had to admit that my critics made some sense, and I gave it a lot of thought. I had learned there were two sure ways to discipline a big time player so it hurt, and one of them is not running. Take away playing time or the money in their pockets, and you get to them.

Just before the team took the floor, JJ McFather came by to see me. The team was in the dressing room and he asked if we could talk in private. He looked like he just stepped off a magazine cover, wearing the best money can buy. His cuff links were diamond-cut stones beautifully marked and he wore alligator shoes. His tie was black and gold and not a hair was out of place. JJ's clothes probably cost more money than I made in a year's time. He was a handsome man, and he carried himself with class; he simply looked great.

As usual, he got right to the point. He asked me what had happened with Big Time and I told him everything. He said that many of the boosters and particularly his father were upset with my decision. He went on to say that the boosters had invested quite a bit in Big Time and that I needed to find another way to discipline him for the good of North West State basketball. He suggested some other less dire punishments, and I heard him out as though none of this had occurred to me. It was too late for that, I told him, and that I was sticking with my plan. This was the first time JJ and I had ever had disagreed so strongly whatsoever; we were good friends but feeling defensive with one another. We went back and forth, and finally he lowered the boom: "Well, it's clear that you have made up your mind, so let me be clear and direct in return. You will be looking for another job if this backfires on you tonight." He wheeled around and walked away without saying another word.

A big boy from a town called Rule, Mississippi, Big Time's given name was Oscar Williams. He was six foot seven inches tall and he weighed close to 220 pounds. He was a true big-time athlete who could play the game of basketball. He was listed by Basketball Times as one of the top ten recruits in the country. Without a doubt, he was going to be a pro if he could mature and develop consistency in his game. I nicked named him Big Time right away, and he warmed to the name. He was full of himself already and had no problem letting anyone know how good he was. Once others heard that I had taken to calling him Big Time, everyone started referring to him in the same way. Truthfully, his attitude was hard to take and I meant the nickname sarcastically; I was trying to make fun of him, but it backfired because when people called him Big Time, he ate it up. I had first tried recruiting him in junior college as coach at Great Plains College. I saw him play in the Mississippi State Tournament. What I witnessed was outstanding basketball play on his part, and I was impressed with his quickness and his ability to score in a crowd. He was by far the best basketball player that I saw play that year. He was only a junior then and by the time his senior year came around, he was no secret to most of the basketball scouts. He did not have the grades to graduate from high school, which really concerned me, but he was worth the gamble. At least, that is how I justified how I decided to proceed.

My brother Mike and Tom and Linda Bingo were very good friends and both owed BQ Places, Mike's in San Antonio and Tom and Linda's in Gulfport, Mississippi. The first place that Mike went to visit when he was trying to learn about the BQ business was to Gulfport at Tom and Linda's Bingo BQ Joint. When my dad was stationed in Gulfport, Mississippi, our family ate at Tom and Bingo's joint every Sunday. Before long, we got to know Tom and Linda. Tom and Linda had two girls and they went to school at Rule High School, Rule, Mississippi which was fifteen miles from Gulfport. Rule was a nice safe school that had a strong tradition in basketball. It was no surprise that Tom and Linda were huge basketball fans and followed the Rule team wherever they played. Tom and Linda were fans of Oscar Williams and the entire Rule team. The Williams family would often eat at Tom and Linda's BQ Joint. In fact, Tom and Linda would host the entire team for free barbeque after the state tournament. They would invite all their friends, the entire team, coaches, and some boosters. This is how I first got access to Big Time. It was the only way I could get the opportunity to even talk to him. There was a long line looking to recruit Oscar. I had my connection with Tom and Linda thanks to my brother and that allowed me the chance to get to know his family, giving me a little edge in the recruiting process.

Off the court, by himself, Oscar was deep down a very nice young man but when he was around a crowd he changed into a monster attention-seeking person. I finally got a home visit and it went very well. We arranged a visit for him to Great Plains College and I was excited because he was only going to visit five schools. In the National Junior College Athletic Association (NJCAA), there is no limit on visits like the NCAA enforces, and I have seen some kids make up to 15 visits. Most generally flunk out of school, or just drop out. Oscar visited our school and to my surprise, he liked what he saw, and he really liked the players. In fact, he and White Shoes became instant friends. When he left, he told us that he wanted to come to our school, but he needed to visit two more competitors. When the time came, he did not sign on the day scheduled for that, but rather told me that he was going to sign on his birthday, which was exactly one week away.

On the day that he had designated as the one on which he would sign, I few to Gulfport, rented a car and drove to his house, only to find two other junior college coaches waiting outside. I had expected to be the only one coming and I had everything ready, so I was disappointed. I knew the other two coaches involved, which did not make it any easier, believe me. It would be a challenge to top both opponents because Oscar was hearing the usual offers: so much money to sign, then more when he arrived on campus, and then again if he stuck around for a year and with other monetary benefits and freebies too. I had tried the same selling job on Oscar and his family that had worked with Skunk's mother, but I had a deep knot in my stomach on this one. When I knocked on the door, Oscar was all smiles and invited me to come on in and meet the family. I entered into a house full of people, some I knew or had seen before, and some not. Oscar had me sit down and offered me a drink of water, and then his mother Lucy took over. She explained the situation to me.

Lucy said, "Coach, we appreciate your interest in Oscar and I hate to tell you this but we are having trouble deciding whom he should sign with." She went on, "Because you have been so nice to Oscar and all of us, we decided to wait to make a decision until one hour after you arrived. We are going to sign with one of you three so we would like for you to leave and come back in one hour and we will tell you our choice. There is a Whataburger down the street. If you guys would just go hang out for an hour and come back, we will have a decision."

I didn't know what to say. I finally gathered my wits about me and thought, *Hey, I'm just lucky to be in the final three,* and said, "Thanks for giving me a chance and for waiting for me. I'll be back in an hour." All three coaches, two black men and one white guy went to Whataburger, ordered something to eat and just stared at each other as we ate. The hour finally dragged by, and we all three returned to the house, walked into the living room, sat down, and waited for the announcement. With no hesitation at all, Oscar told us that he had chosen Mississippi State Junior College (MSJC). The assistant coach from the winning school was elated and he jumped in the air and started hugging the family members. I was disappointed, but I felt I had done what I could and I held my head up. I congratulated Oscar, his mother, and his family; got in my rental car; and left.

Now, two years later, Oscar was the leading scorer in the NJCAA and was in line to graduate from MSJC. White Shoes later told me that Oscar made over $15,000 signing: $5,000 each to sign, then when he arrived, and again when he stayed a year. Once I became the head basketball coach at North West State, I wanted to try to recruit Oscar yet again. Because experience told me that Oscar would be a hard sell, I knew I had to get Mr. Steven McFather interested. The way to get the older McFather involved, I knew, was to talk up JJ. I contacted Oscar and his family and told them about the North West State University position and that I wanted to recruit Oscar to North West State. Of course, I had a huge advantage as I knew everyone in his family and they felt very comfortable with me. I did not even have to make a home visit, as Lucy told me that if I was involved she trusted me totally. By this time we had already signed White Shoes and Oscar really liked the thought of playing his last two years with his friend. The two had stayed in touch the last two years and I was surprised how they both seemed to accept each other's talent and personality.

In the NCAA, when an athlete visits a university, the coach is not allowed to set up any drills, schedule pickup games, or stage any activity on which to base an evaluation of their potential. It is strictly off-limits and everyone knows it. But I knew if JJ could see Oscar play, he would feel exactly like I did, so I had to take a chance. I knew from what had gone down two years before that money was going to play a huge part in Oscar's decision. I sat down with White Shoes and explained my problem. He understood where I was coming from and he was as eager to have Oscar join us as I was. He wanted him on the team.

We all met at 11:30 p.m. on the Great Plains Campus in Pampa, Texas, in the basketball dome. It was six guys from State, Oscar and six guys from Great Plains. I got the keys from the AD and set up a pickup game for 11:45; they played until 1:00 in the morning. I had JJ along with some of his father's friends with me watching them play. Needless to say, Oscar put on a clinic and thirty minutes in JJ said, "We must get this kid and I want to be involved." He was smiling and I knew, of course, that he was as excited about Oscar coming to State as I was. I shared my former experience trying to sign Oscar with JJ, how big part money had played and how he turned me down the last time. JJ said not to worry, he was calling his father.

For this second time, Oscar wanted to repeat the same ritual that he had used when he signed to play in junior college. He waited until his birthday and invited three coaches to his house. It had come down to being a choice among UNLV, North West State, and North Carolina State. I did not travel to Rule by myself this time, but instead I had a representative from Steven McFather come with me. The elder Mr. McFather was supposed to be on the plane in New Orleans and I was supposed to pick him up. But instead, he sent a Mr. O'Malley, vice president of McFather Enterprises. We arrived two hours early this time; I had learned my lesson. I had already told Lucy and Oscar that I was bringing Mr. McFather with me and we wanted to have some time with them alone. As soon as we arrived at his house, Oscar opened the door and we both walked in and sat down when invited to do so. Lucy offered us something to drink. As I explained who Mr. O'Malley was, right away he asked if they had a beer in the fridge. They answered that no, they did not, but they could offer him a vodka and orange juice, which he accepted.

After Mr. O'Malley finished his drink, he looked at me and said, "Coach, I would like to visit with Lucy and Oscar alone. Would you mind leaving and please come back after about an hour?" I left but I was worried that he was drinking alcohol in front of a recruit and his parents. As a professional recruiter, that bothered me a lot but I was in no position to say anything about it. I went to the same Whataburger and ordered a diet coke and a burger. I didn't enjoy the wait, but it wasn't as bad as the one I had experienced two years before. After an hour, I went back to Oscar's house not at all sure what to expect.

As I entered the house, I noticed that O'Malley had another drink in his hand and he seemed relaxed and at ease. The phone rang as soon as I sat down and Oscar answered it. It turned out it was White Shoes, and he and Oscar talked for a little while. Then Oscar said to me, "Coach, White Shoes wants to talk to you."

The phone was over by the breakfast counter, and I picked it up and greeted my young player. White Shoes said, "Coach, are you surprised?"

I said. "I am very surprised and happy to hear your voice."

White shoes then said, "Look down on the counter and tell me what you see."

I looked down and answered him, "I see the scholarship papers that we sent Oscar from North West State" I paused briefly, and then yelled, "They are signed! You rascal you." I hung up the phone and started hugging everyone in the room. I felt sorry for the coaches that had not arrived yet, but not very sorry.

On the way back to the New Orleans, I asked Mr. O'Malley how he got the job done. He said, "It was simple, I just made them an offer they could not refuse." Mr. McFather had invested a great deal in Oscar. I did not know the details, but figured it had to be substantial to have put a stop to the other two visits and gotten Oscar to sign.

It turned out that Oscar was given a job selling football programs at all Tech games. Rumor had it that he would make anywhere between $500 and $1,000 per game for his "efforts." He would sell a program and someone would hand him a $100 dollar bill and tell him to keep the change. Also, on Saturdays in the early part of the season, JJ would pick him up early in the morning and bring him back later in the afternoon. He had put him to work at his office, or somewhere on one of his many ventures. I understand he would get paid $100 per hour.

Knowing all this, I was not surprised how upset he was with my suspension of Big Time, but I did not expect them to threaten to fire me.

The game with Baylor was our biggest one yet. I don't know if it was because of the suspension of Big Time or if it was just the opportunity that the other players received, or what, but I do know it was the turning point of our season. Just as my college coach had done, I play an eight-man rotation. I usually take the best eight players and try to fit them into a team that understands and knows their roles. I play more than eight but it is usually when I am forced to because of injuries or fouls. Big Time was our leading scorer with an average of 18.5 points per game. He would be missed and I knew that. I had to move David Garcia, a six foot six inch swingman, into the rotation. He was a carryover from last year. Dave was a very good player and I liked him a lot, but he was having a really hard time adjusting to the defensive intensity required by me.. He rebelled over the running grade sheet I kept on defensive performance and felt it did not give him the opportunity to use his basketball ability. He was a foreign player and he was a little soft, but a great shooter and playmaker.

Dave would have to take Big Time's place. My starters were Smooth Sammy at the point, White Shoes playing shooting guard, "D" at the swing position, Skunk at the power forward with Bubba in the post. That gave us a line- up of players 6'3", 6'2", 6'7", 6'8", and 6'11". I would back up Smooth with Jet One, sub Garcia for "D" and move D'Wayne to either Skunk's position or Bubbas spot. I could play White Shoes or Skunk at four positions if I had to, which gave me some flexibility. It was not like we could not adapt to certain situations. Still, I was nervous as one can be. I did not tell anyone what JJ had told me nor did I even want to think about it.

The tip went up and to my surprise; Bubba got the tip to White Shoes. He dribbled to the NBA three-point line on the far right side of the perimeter and, with no hesitation, pulled up and shot it. I was going crazy until it hit nothing but the bottom of the net. I was reeling inside. *What's going on? He never does that,* I thought. Baylor took possession and drove to the opposite basket, but Skunk came out of nowhere and blocked the shot all the way out to the regular three-point line, where Smooth grabbed it and sped to the other end for an easy layup. Baylor hurried the ball inbounds only to have Smooth Sammy snatch the errant pass, drive to the hoop, then wheel and pass it out to the perimeter where White Shoes nailed another three-pointer. Not even close to a minute in, here we were up 8-0. Now Baylor inbounded the ball and this time worked for a good shot, but when the ball was passed to the corner, Bubba and Skunk teamed to trap the Baylor player, who panicked and tried to pass. White Shoes got a hand on it, gathered it in, and then dunked the ball on an uncontested layup. With the crowd going crazy, Baylor called a time-out. The score was 10-0, White Shoes had eight points, and still the clock had barely moved.

My heart was racing so fast, my mind was in shock. I didn't expect this type of aggressive play, but I sure accepted it. At the half, the score was North West State University 49, Baylor 24. The game was over and I knew it. By the end, we had stretched it to a 30-point lead, and I was able to get everyone, with one notable exception, into the game; the team had fun. The 94-68 victory drove our growing number of fans in the crowd crazy. White Shoes scored 33 points, Smooth Sammy 15, and Skunk had 15 points with 12 rebounds. It was really good news for the team too that Garcia had netted 9 points, all coming from the three-point line. He was happy and I was glad. He had been the leading scorer on the team the year before, but North West State University finished last in the Big 12. Needless to say, the dressing room was buzzing; we all knew something special had taken place. As we were enjoying the fruits of our win, Big Time asked me if he could speak to the team. I called everyone to order and the big guy began, "Guys, I made a huge mistake and I am sorry. I love each one of you; let's win this thing!" The place went crazy.

When I exited the dressing room, the first person I ran into was JJ. The grin on his face was enough to make me feel welcome and appreciated. To this day, I truly believe that he was delighted that things worked out for the best doing it my way. But there was no time for thoughts about that. The celebration was on. When we got the players on the bus, I told them that I had a surprise for them. I was taking them to the best dining place in town. The games were played in the newest arena called "The Maverick Center," which seated about 18,000 spectators. The home of the Dallas Mavericks, the city's representative in the NBA, it was owned by May Arrington, and he had arranged for us to have a special dinner at May's Restaurant. The guys were really excited, and so were the coaches. Not only was the food the best, it was all you can eat. Every player ate until he could barely walk. Mr. Arrington organized the meal so that we got to dine and party alone, as a team. No media, boosters, family, or friends intruded on this team moment. He totally understood getting away from it all. We lacked for nothing in a true one-of-a-kind sit-down celebration, and I was so impressed.

It was Doc's job to pay the bills but this time I and all of the coaches went with him. We wanted to express our appreciation for such a fine meal, so we all followed Doc to the cashier. I went back and thanked the cooks, and the other coaches followed me and we all gave them high-fives, just basking in the moment. As we got into a conversation with May, a large crash from the dining area got our alarmed attention. We all ran back to find Joshua crouched behind "D" in a defensive posture while Donnie Sullivan, a guard from last year's team, held a chair in his hands ready to hit somebody over the head. As we entered I could hear "D" yelling, "I can't get cut, some-one help me." Just then, Skunk jumped in among the three of them and grabbed a hold of the chair that Donnie was brandishing.

I yelled, "Stop!" as soon as I entered the room. My only immediate idea was, *This has to stop.*

Donnie turned to me and pleaded, "They are picking on me, and they put hot pepper in my tea."

"Put the damned chair down, Donnie," I yelled back. Once he did, I continued, "Everybody, get the hell back on the bus and we will talk about this just as soon as I'm done paying the bill." They filed out of the room in a hurry and I looked at Doc and I just shook my head. I was pissed. What an embarrassment for the school and the team. The coaches and I made our way back over to Mr. Arrington and apologized for the actions of the group; we were mortified. He was really nice about it, however, and insisted we forget about it. He said he understood and it was nothing he hadn't seen before, and all I could think was, *Wow, do the pros have these kinds of problems too?*

We paid our bill, leaving a huge tip and left the restaurant in hopes we'd find the team on the bus, somewhat subdued, with each player in one piece. As we got on the bus to go back to the hotel, they were quieter, but the way they were milling around as a big group in the middle was unusual, I noticed. They were already in trouble for the next day, as I was sure they could tell. I would give them a lot to think about both before they retired to their rooms and the next morning, but something more had transpired on the bus, I suspected. It was easy to see that they all knew I was mad, and that they were in the wrong, but I could sense something else. It is a second sense that you develop as a college coach, one you need sometimes just to survive.

Donnie was another young man who had played for and was a starter the year before at North West State, and he just wasn't good enough to hang with the new talent I brought into the program. He was extremely vocal about his unhappiness, and how he felt that I was the cause. He complained that I was treating him unfairly, and I was forced to meet with his mother several times. The fact that all the players had taken to calling him a crybaby didn't help the situation. I did not trust him, and I had my reasons. When I took over the job at State, he knew I was recruiting new players and he also realized his position on the floor was in jeopardy. He would be a senior and I told him he could transfer or he could stay and we would honor his scholarship, as long as he was loyal to our program and to North West State. Scholarships were a one-year deal to be renewed annually and Donnie knew that. Since this was to be his final year, I told him we would keep him on the team but aside from that nothing was guaranteed except his scholarship. I told him to expect less playing time, even less if he failed to change his attitude about the transition and about me, unless he could find a way to come out better in my defensive ratings. When he left for the summer, I felt we both understood one another.

That summer, I received phone calls from three different coaches concerning Donnie. They were all coaching for Division Two schools, each knew me well, and each said the same thing. Donnie was trying to find another school where he could play basketball. That part was understandable, and it didn't bother me. What did anger me, though, was that he was painting me and the North West State University basketball program in a very unflattering light. We left him out in the cold and tried to freeze him off the team. He even made strong statements that I had mistreated him in workouts. He went on to claim that players were mistreated, how some players received more benefits than others, and just blasted Northwestern State. I called him as soon as I talked to the coaches and challenged him on all accounts. He said he was sorry but he did feel mistreated and he was really angry with me.

I probably should have cooled down first but as soon as I hung up the phone, I wrote him a firm letter spelling out exactly what I had said to him in earlier meetings. I thought it best to put it all in writing. Little did I know, but rushing ahead to send it out without having my secretary check the letter for mistakes would come back to haunt me. The letter I wrote was clear, I thought, and it spoke right to the heart of the matter, and directed all I had to say at him. I did act a little impetuously, but it was clear from my viewpoint that he had displayed a total lack of loyalty to the school and to the team.

A week later, North West State AD James Jones called me into his office. Jones had held this position for twenty-five years, and he and I had already discussed Donnie several times. He was a good guy, and I liked him, but he was a politician. He worked to please all sides, and he was not going to take the heat for anyone if he could help it. Jones began, "Coach, we have a problem," handing me a letter he received in the mail.

"Go ahead. Check it out," he said. I recognized the letter as soon as I saw it: I was stunned. It was a copy of the same letter that I had sent to Donnie. The disgruntled player had taken the time to point out every embarrassing grammatical error and misspelling in what I had written with a dark felt-tip pen, and then mailed a copy to every professor on the North West State University campus. Also, he had included a note on the letter to the effect, "Is this the man you want as your Head Men's basketball coach?" I was speechless and just stared back at Jones in disgust. There was nothing I could do. To my surprise, however, the ploy had backfired, and the AD said that he had already heard from several professors. "As of now, the faculty agrees that you did nothing wrong, that the letter was not that bad, and that you are the wronged party. The consensus on campus is that Donnie is very disliked, as was his attitude in the classroom. He questions the syllabus in most of his classes at one time or another and he has created problems for several professors." After a rough few minutes, I was able to walk out of Jones's office a lot more relaxed than I thought I would be when I first saw the copy of my letter.

As the team filed out of the bus at the hotel that night following the meal and the fight, we had a team meeting and I tore into them. I was furious, and I'm sure some of my comments crossed the line, but I let them have it with both barrels. At the end I established lights-out at 11:30 that night, and I warned them that I would be in the hall waiting for anyone who felt like daring me to send them back to Amarillo that moment. As I spoke, I noticed that Donnie had a cut over his right eye, and he was covering it with ice. When I asked him what happened, the whole group of players got quiet, and he just said that he had an accident. Later, when we were alone, a few of my assistant coaches filled me in. While we finished paying for the food and apologizing, Smooth Sammy took Donnie to the back of the bus and punched him out. The team was really upset about what had happened, and they all blamed Donnie for the incident. It seems it was true that Joshua did dose his tea with hot chili pepper when he was not looking, but it should not have provoked such a violent outburst. To the team's way of thinking, Sammy had settled things.

The next night, we played Texas in the semifinals. On the other side of the bracket, Texas A&M was playing Kansas. If we could survive, we would play the winner of that game for the Big 12 Championship and an automatic bid to the NCAA tournament. Coming off our fourth-place finish in the conference, we had hope that we could prevail in the tournament, but it wasn't a very realistic one. But now it was close to becoming a reality. I was excited as were the players. The first game was Kansas vs. Texas A&M and, to everyone's surprise, A&M beat the top seed, 79-76. Kansas played with no energy at all and A&M was just on fire. There was no doubt in anyone's mind Kansas had the better team but this time of year, strange things happen. Kansas had been in the top ten in the country the entire year. They were ranked number six in the nation before entering our tournament, and won the conference, with just one loss, falling to Texas in Austin. I think winning is fun, but pressure does build; it gets to the players sooner or later and it's like they hit a wall. I was hoping the same thing would happen to Texas in our game. My gut feeling told me we would play as well as we could, regardless of what Texas did. Texas, too, had had a very good year, and they were ranked in the top twenty the entire season, finishing ranked twelfth in the nation. They had defeated us both times in conference play, 76-71 on our court, and then at Texas by a 93-84 score. Of course, a contrite Big Time got the start in this game, and he responded with a career game with 42 points and 18 rebounds. We never trailed and defeated Texas going away 81-75.

It was like a dream come true. I had to pinch myself to make sure it was real. We would play Texas A&M for the Big 12 Tournament

Championship, with the winner guaranteed an automatic bid to March Madness, the NCAA tournament. We had split two games with A&M on the year, beating them at home and later falling to them at A&M. We were pretty evenly matched in talent, and it was quite a surprise that these two schools were playing in the conference tournament championship game. It was unlikely either team would have received a bid to the NCAA tournament without the automatic entry that the tournament victory would bring. A&M had a record of 18-10, while we finished 19-10. Both teams were lucky to be where we were, and the two fan bases were enjoying every moment. Big 12 powers Kansas, Texas, Kansas State, and Oklahoma were expected to receive bids into the coming field of 64, and we were delighted to have the chance to join the group.

One good thing about playing the A&M Aggies is that they always brought the Corps of Cadets with them. It could be intimidating for the opponent, but it made for bigger and louder crowds, a great atmosphere for playing basketball. Like the cadets, a huge and storied student military organization on the A&M campus, or not, they always brought excitement to an athletic event. My guess was they had between 3,000 and 5,000 cadets assembled, looking like a fighting force in their uniforms. ESPN was in full coverage mode, as was every radio station in Texas.

The game started off very ugly as neither team was as sharp as the night before. I anticipated this but regardless, as a coach I never learned how to handle it. Still fired up about the restaurant incident two nights before, it didn't take much for my anger to begin burning hot. I can usually tell in the first five minutes of the game where we are in terms of fire and concentration. For whatever reason we were flat; the team's intensity level was low and we were not playing very sharply at all. Fortunately, A&M was in the same boat, with both teams struggling after big victories the night before. I benched the entire group of starters after calling a time-out, trying anything I could to motivate them to snap out of the doldrums and kick it into gear. It was at the 12:34 mark and we were down 18-14. I let them sit on the bench for a few minutes after spraying a few choice words over the whole group, hoping to ignite a spark somewhere, anywhere. I usually don't substitute for so many starters at once, but the way they were playing, it wasn't going to make things much worse. With no one playing up to par, I figured it was time to let someone else play.

For the next few minutes A&M did outplay us, but they couldn't get their shots to fall, so by the time I put the starters back in the game the score was 25-20, A&M. The next seven minutes my guys picked it up and played a lot better but by this time, the poor play had taken a toll on their confidence. They were getting good looks at the basket, but our shots were not falling either. A&M took a 33-30 lead into the half.

Although unhappy about the first-half play I also knew we had performed better going into the break, only not with a lot of confidence. When we hit the dressing room, I concentrated on what we had done right in those last few minutes. I made the point that if they kept it up and were patient, those shots were sure to start finding the net. I felt that success in the game was all about putting your best talent on the court and getting them to play with the proper intensity and concentration. All the talent in the world will not bring about success unless your players go about their business with the right attitude and desire, and do it on the court in a game situation. The mind wins most of these contests; <u>how an athlete thinks will determine how well or poorly he or she performs. Get their heads straight and the bodies will follow.</u> Physical drills are critical, yes, but we spend a great deal of time trying to get each of my player's minds in good shape too. Honestly, it is the toughest part of my job. Get a player physically strong and ready to play for hours and they'll be able to reproduce it the next day. But outside factors that a player or a coach faces can take a player who is psychologically prepared one day, and damage or destroy the mind-set it took you months to prepare and create the next. Print media and the broadcast press are also two dangerous factors. They can take a well-tuned mind and plunge it into destructive thoughts. They can convince a good player he is not very good, and a player who needs work that he's ready to go. And it's not just the press. It works both ways with officials, friends, family, boosters, girlfriends, teammates, and coaches too. They can affect a player's performance in both positive and negative ways simply by affecting how he thinks.

The second half started off better for us than the first. Following his

42-point outburst against Texas, Big Time had yet to score a basket. They were defending him closely, but it is still beyond me how you can net 42 points one night and not get a sniff of the basket the next. Skunk and Bubba were carrying us, but it was all inside on good feeds or put backs. We got our first lead with 15:20 to go, when we inched ahead, 40-39. Finally Big Time hit a three, and was fouled in the process. The made free throw and four-point play had us up, 44-39. By the 9:45 mark we were winning 52-47. White Shoes and Smooth Sammy were starting to get into the flow, particularly on defense. White Shoes was a big factor, guarding their best player and doing a super job of keeping him off balance. At the 5:10 mark, we led 58-54 as the game was now heading into the stretch. We turned it on the next three minutes and had a 65-58 lead and the ball with 2:37 to go in the game.

I felt we had A&M on the ropes because now we were at the point in the game where our biggest strength should come into play, and that was shooting free throws. The starting five guys had compiled a composite 85 percent free throw shooting percentage, a ratio any coach would love to have. With that in our bag of tricks, I always felt if we had the lead, we could win at the end.

The officials made a questionable charging call on Smooth, and the bad news was compounded when A&M quickly pushed the ball back down court and hit a huge three. That woke up the cadets and the place was bedlam; all of sudden, it seemed the "Aggies" had the momentum. With a 65-61 score and 1:58 to go, A&M fouled D'wayne, putting him on the line for a one and one. But even though he made these at an 88 percent clip, I didn't have to watch; I could hear the first attempt clang off the front of the rim, with A&M collecting the rebound. They didn't waste any clock, taking the ball to the hoop where we fouled them. The two made free throws cut into our lead. We had the ball and all you could hear were the cadets. Everyone, all 16,200 of those in attendance, were on their feet. With 1:12 on the clock, I called time-out. The score was 65-63. We wanted to draw a foul if we failed to score a basket. We planned to execute our red-four-to-score game. Anticipating that we would be in late tight situations like this, we had developed what we called a red game and a green game. In our red plan, no shots would be taken but layups or put backs. If the call had been to play our green game, which meant you could take your shot anytime you were open from anywhere on the court. With the game this close this late, I felt we had had to penetrate, and work the ball to the basket. The plan worked and we got the clock down to 34 seconds left when they fouled White Shoes. With our 91 percent free-throw shooter on the line, I relaxed. I would trust my life with him at the line. As it turned out it was a good thing that it wasn't life or death, because somehow he missed the front end of the one and one; and A&M rebound yet again and they hurriedly called a time-out.

I lost a regional championship one time by trying to be cute and fancy in this situation, but I wasn't going to make that mistake again. At least that is what I told myself, but of course, I changed my mind because I felt I knew what A&M was going to do. They would run a set play for their best, Alex Rodriguez, to shoot the ball. You did not need to be a rocket scientist to figure that out. I wanted A&M to recognize that we were in a zone defense, which would, I was sure, cause them to change the play they had decided to run. At the same time, using the time it took them to react to this would eat up some clock. I wanted to put A&M on the defensive even though they were the team with the ball in their hands. *Make them stop and think,* I figured. I am a big fan of the term, "Paralysis by Analysis." But what it really came down to was no easy baskets and no stupid fouls. Now this is easier to call than to implement on the court, which I realized, but what else can you do but direct them to take a defensive approach at this point in the game?

A&M inbounded the ball and quickly went to work on the play the coach had set up, but when they saw we were in a zone, they called their last time-out. Now that they couldn't stop play again, I switched back to our basic defense, a man-on-man approach, though our plan was to disguise it as a zone, but then play the man. Following the time-out, the clock read 26 seconds when they inbounded the ball. They looked confused and disorganized for a moment, unsure of what they wanted to do, and Smooth deflected a pass. Players converged on the loose ball, a collision ensued and, when play was interrupted by a foul call with 15 seconds to play, it could have gone either way. The foul was on us, with the officials claiming Bubba had pushed from behind.

Now we had one time-out left, and I had a decision to make: Either use the last stoppage to try and ice the A&M shooter, or conserve the time-out. I knew we going to get the ball with 15 seconds to go, and I felt we could make better use of a play stoppage in those last few seconds, so I decided not to call one. A&M made both free throws, tying the score at 65-65.

This gave me time to think and I called a set play from the bench, one that my players knew well. We called it "pro"; it was a basic play where we set a screen for Big Time or White Shoes with either Skunk or Bubba. The clock started with our long throw-in and we quickly went into pro. Smooth went to White Shoes' side of the court with Bubba setting the screen. But somehow the ball came loose and went out of bounds. Still, A&M touched it last so it was our ball. I called that last time-out and we set up our play. With just 10 seconds left now, the players were confident we could score off an out-of-bounds play called No. 3. It was nothing new to the game; nearly every coach in the USA executes one like it in one form or another. It was a screen on a screener. White Shoes, set to inbound the ball, would slap the ball, sending Skunk to set a screen for D'wayne, who would then use the screen go to the basket looking for the ball; at the same time Skunk would receive a screen from Bubba and Smooth would back out in case things went awry. Nine out of ten times, Skunk would be wide open. With those lonely ten digits left on the clock, White Shoes slapped the ball, movement and screens occurred, bodies attacked each other. But no one came open. White Shoes passed the ball out to Smooth but A&M made a nice play, deflecting the pass, then picked it up and headed toward the other goal with a convoy of three players arrayed against poor Sammy all by himself. Somehow, someway, Smooth deflected the dribble and the ball bounced off one of the A&M player's hand and right into Smooth's hands. He quickly whirled and made a baseball pass to the other end to our basket where Bubba was waiting all by himself. Our big guy had not even run to the other end as he thought the game was over. Bubba made the layup as the buzzer sounded. Everyone in the building went crazy, including me. It was wild. We had just won our way into the NCAA tournament with a 67-65 victory over Texas A&M.

NINE

BACK AT THE BIG DAY, when the team arrived at the hotel in New Braunfels after the shoot around it was close to noon. We scheduled the pregame meal for two o'clock and announced we would leave for San Antonio at four-thirty later that afternoon. As we exited the bus, I advised the players to use this time wisely. I said, "You have between now and the pregame meal to visit with family and friends. After the meal there will be no contact with anyone except your teammates and your coaches. All cell phones will be taken for safekeeping." The game was scheduled for a 7:15 p.m. tip-off, something entirely dictated by CBS, which had the TV rights. The 7:00 o'clock window was obviously the one that worked best for them. With the few hours I had, my thoughts went to my family whom I had not seen in two days.

They must have been as eager as I was as my wife and girls were the first ones to meet the bus when we returned from the shoot around. They drove in late Sunday night and spent the night in another room. I had advised them to sleep in this morning while we took care of business. I was so proud of them and so excited that they could be in attendance for this game. Jennifer was a junior high drama teacher so she had to get an excuse from her principal. Each of the girls was in high school: Ann a senior, Nicole, in her junior year, and Renee, a freshman, so Jennifer needed to get permission from their principal for them to miss school as well. Why the NCAA plays this game on Monday is a mystery to me, but I am sure TV is one of the reasons.

If you tried to build the perfect coach's wife, Jennifer would have come close. She has been a primary factor in any success I have achieved, and she has been a great mother to the girls too. I couldn't be happier with how well she has helped me survive in the competitive world of college coaching. It's a job fraught with conflicts finding enough time for both coaching and family; it's a demanding position. Behind every successful male college coach, you'll likely find a strong wife supporting him. Jennifer was the best, something I never tire of telling my colleagues about. When they would ask what made her so special, I would reply, "She is a tremendous mom, she is a wonderful wife, a great cook, and she is a better recruiter than I am, to start with. But the big thing is she is a God-oriented woman who keeps me on track."

Jennifer and I went to high school together in Amarillo at Polk High School. I was a senior and she was a sophomore. We met through her best friend, whose brother was one of my buddies. That made it a natural fit for us to get together off and on during our high school days. A beautiful young lady, she was highly intelligent, and came from a wonderful family. We dated some in high school, and then became closer when I went off to college.

Even though this involved long-distance dating, it seemed the separation of my being in college and she in high school moved us closer to one another. There were intermittent times during this period when we would become serious about our relationship. Then when she went off to college, we not only continued to date off and on, we actually saw each other more frequently. We talked about marriage, raising kids, our spiritual life, our parents, and life in general; it was so easy for me to talk with her. I actually mentioned marriage before she did, but she was not quite ready; then when she brought it up, I was the one unsure. Things were very comfortable between us, but that was when I made the biggest mistake I ever have. One night after we both had graduated from college, I told her I thought I was in love with someone else. It hurt her badly, and I'm sure now that if she had owned a gun, she would have shot me. I had never seen this side of her, but I sure found out about it that night. My offhand comment really shook her, and I cursed myself and my big mouth. After eight good years of dating, I had disrupted both Jennifer's and my own life.

Dallas hosted the Texas Coaching Convention that summer and I attended with a group of fellow coaches from Albany. As the high school's Head Boys Basketball coach, my school paid my way at the clinic. Early in my career, I was thrilled, but even more excited because Jennifer was living in Dallas. She was an English teacher at Samuel High School. She had an apartment close to the school and I knew exactly where it was located because I had been there many times. I called her before I left to attend the clinic and when I told her I would be in Dallas, she answered, "Don't come over when you get here, because I do not want to see you anymore. You do nothing but complicate my life." I told her how terrible I felt about what I had said, and apologized over and over, but nothing I said had any effect. She kept warning me not to come by, and I insisted repeatedly that I wanted to talk to her and I was coming over regardless of what she said.

When I arrived in Dallas, the first place I went to was her apartment. I knocked on the door of her apartment, but nothing happened. Calling out her name a soft tone, and then progressively more loudly, elicited no response either. Retreating to the pay phone at the Seven-Eleven across the street, I dialed her number. She answered the phone, but told me to go away. I said I would camp out on her porch if need be, but I felt I had to talk to her. She warned me away again, threatening to call the police if I came back to her house. Undeterred, I went back anyway, and started knocking on her door more loudly this time. Resigned, I slumped to her front step, but before long, a policeman drove up and stopped. I was stunned that she had followed through with her threat; it hurt that she refused to see me. The police told me to leave or they would have to arrest me.

That Christmas, I had a break from school and basketball and went to my parent's home in Amarillo. I was hooking up with a buddy named Nick Ashmore, and we were trying to find dates for New Year's Eve. I told him that Jennifer and I had broken up and I highly recommended he give her a call. Nick had always had a crush on her, as many of my friends did, and I thought I was resigned to the fact that Jennifer and I were through. Nick called Jennifer and she accepted the holiday date. Meanwhile, the two young ladies I tried calling were both already committed that night; I couldn't find a date with New Year's Eve fast approaching. Being the great people they both were, Nick and Jennifer assured me that I could tag along with them; the three of us would end the year together and have a good time. I took my car and met them at the party because I was going to have to leave early in the morning. It was basketball time again, and my first practice was scheduled for three o'clock the next afternoon. Yes, I know it was New Year's Day but it had to be done because we played in a tournament the next morning at 10:00am. That is way they do things in Texas.

As long as I live, I will never forget that night. Immediately it was like I was hit between the eyes with a baseball: I was deeply in love with Jennifer and just hadn't realized it. I could not take my eyes off her, nor could I conceal my jealous feelings inside too much longer. I couldn't stand watching Nick hug her, and the very thought of the two of them holding hands and kissing made my blood boil. I had to leave because I was afraid of what I might do before the night was over. I thought the world of Nick but I was madly in love with Jennifer, a lethal combo as the third wheel on a date. How stupid not to realize my feelings until after suggesting Nick take her out. I kissed her on the cheek and left, wishing them both a good night and a good year. I had made it only as late as 10:30 p.m.

The next morning at 6:00 o'clock, I was on the road to Albany but all I could think about was Jennifer. I kept pinching myself to see if I was dreaming or awake. I had never felt this way about anyone. I met with the team in Albany, we worked out, and soon my schedule was back to normal, coaching teams playing high school games every Tuesday and Friday and junior high games on Mondays and Thursdays. Two weeks passed and Ron Tubb, one of my old high school buddies, dropped by to say hello. He and Jennifer were close, and he had just come from Dallas where the two of them had had a long visit. In truth, Ron had always had a crush on her, he wasn't much of a friend to me, and he seemed to enjoy the fact that Jennifer and I had split up. He came by mostly to brag a little about how much better Jennifer was doing since I was out of the picture. I really had no choice though; I had to visit with him to find out what was going on with her. And what he told me changed my life forever. Ron calmly informed me that Jennifer had become engaged to a guy in Dallas the week before. He went on and on, but I didn't hear a word once the first words out of his mouth put me in an immediate state of shock.

As soon as he left, I went straight to the school phone and called Jennifer. This was totally out of character for me, because we were never allowed to use the school phone to make personal calls. I didn't care. I let the phone ring and ring, but there was no answer. Rushing home after practice, there was still no answer when I called again. It was a pre-cell phone world back then, and my inability to reach her was driving me crazy. Finally, when I called at 10:30 p.m., she picked up.

I kept my cool at first and we talked a little about New Year's Eve, which was the last time I saw her, but before too long I got into it. I told her about my visit from Ron and what he had revealed. She told me that, yes, she was engaged to a wonderful guy. His name was Bill Paxton, he was a lawyer, and she was so excited. The happiness and excitement in her voice was like putting a dagger in my heart. I asked if she would allow me to come to Dallas and talk things over with her. She made it clear again that she was over the breakup, and asked me not to complicate things, to just be happy for her. She was set on her life path; she knew what she wanted now. She said she did not want me to come, that she was happy and afraid I would try to ruin it. I broke down and told her that I loved her and at least wanted a chance to talk to her before she got married. She owed me at least one last opportunity to visit with her, I pleaded. I truly hadn't planned this, but before I knew it I was telling her that I was on my way right now; that I would be there before she knew it. I hung up the phone, hurried into the car, and took off. When I arrived at her house I had shaved the forty-five minutes off the three hour, forty-five minutes it usually took to get there from Albany. I knocked on the door and this time, she let me in. I hugged her and behaved like a total gentleman; at least until I broke down and told her how deeply I loved her and wanted to marry her. I confessed how bad I felt, and that I knew how big a mistake I had made back on New Year's Eve. I told her how sorry I was for being so stupid. With tears streaming down I continued that my life would be empty without her by my side. I must have finally gotten through, because on Sunday, she called Bill Paxton and told him that the wedding was off.

Jennifer and I did not wait to have a formal wedding but rather we eloped, not asking or waiting for parental consent or letting anyone know. We ran off to New Mexico and got married. We were very much in love but we were both nervous about things. It was my fault more than hers because I was the one who pushed for running off and getting it done. It was an immature thing to do, I know, but I just didn't want a formal wedding and she went along with me. After all, look at how close we had already come to missing out on sharing our love. Looking back, it was one of the most selfish things either one of us had every done to our parents. But we were on an emotional roller coaster, and we just wanted to make our union official before the ride came to a halt. I guess I was also nervous, knowing that lots of my own friends secretly had a thing for Jennifer. How would they react when they heard she had broken off the engagement?

I'll never forget that morning in late March, we both said we were going to attend a teacher convention for our parents' benefit. I was dressed in a dark black suit, while Jennifer looked beautiful in a dark blue outfit. We asked Jennifer's best friend and her brother to be our witnesses. They took pictures and we were excited. We drove to Clovis, New Mexico, about 90 miles from Amarillo. After the wedding, we returned to town, setting out to take care of our first joint act, the task of telling her parents what we had done. I was scared right from the start, and did not know what to expect, and Jennifer demanded that I remain in the car while she could break the news herself, the way she thought would be best. It didn't go well, as all hell broke out when she announced our nuptials to her mother and father. She came back to the car in tears, saying, "Let's leave, my parents are very upset." It hurt me to see the tears in her eyes but she felt it was better to leave so we did without my having visited with them. As I was pulling out of the driveway, the enormity of what we had done hit me for the first time.

Our parents' homes were not very far apart, and we had to collect ourselves pretty quickly before we delivered the big news to my folks. I knew I wanted her by my side for this, so I asked Jennifer to come in with me. Once we had said hello and sat down, I told mom and dad that we had just gotten back from Clovis, and that Jennifer was my new bride. We were relieved, as they both celebrated our happy news with us right away. My mother and father accepted Jennifer as if she was one of us and we all had a good time together. I was very happy, and I can't tell you how proud I was of my parents and how they accepted the news. Sometime during the celebration, my Dad even pulled me aside and said, "I didn't think you had enough sense to finally marry that girl!" Sad but true, he was so right on both counts.

We were a good fit right off the bat. Jennifer was such an asset, but she did have one early problem being a coach's wife, and that had to do with how she would develop a comfort level attending my games. She hadn't had time to work on her game face before there she was watching games from the stands all the time. To start with, she was too nervous to sit still and rarely sat in any one seat for more than five minutes. If I wanted to visit with her during a ball game (which I was officially prohibited from doing anyway), I would be standing there talking to myself, because I could never find her. However worked up I became at a ball game; I couldn't touch Jennifer's intensity. She nearly got into a fight with one particular fan that harassed me during a game. Starting in the third quarter, this guy really let me have it the rest of the game. Jennifer would not put up with it, and eventually two administrators at that arena had to separate them. One of them even came into our dressing room as soon as the game was over and told me to get out there quickly because your wife is fixing to get into a fight. Another time she almost got the entire family attacked when she refused to back down in an argument at a road game against some hostile hometown fans. We needed a police escort just to get off campus that night.

Eventually, she settled on one particular spot from which she liked to watch our home games. And if someone happened to be sitting in her spot, she wouldn't hesitate to go to the AD and raise a fuss about it. I remember coming home after one game, and she was so excited that we had won, that when I acted nonchalant about the game's outcome, she started throwing anything she could get her hands on at me. During games, if she overheard fans questioning my decisions or yelling something about the coach, she would get up, stare at them and walk across the way and sit. No, she was not your typical coach's wife once the ref blew the whistle and the game was underway. She felt the highs and the lows just as strongly as I did, and we all know what a toll that can take.

So she initially had to feel her way at games, but off the court, she couldn't have been more supportive of the team right from the beginning. She would cook Thanksgiving dinner for all the players and coaches, would fix brownies for certain players when it was their birthday, and would even volunteer to go pick a player up at the airport or bus station in the middle of the night. With her teaching background, she would help a player pass exams in English and in other subjects; she would be there for them whenever they were sick, or even just homesick. And she helped with cookouts in the springtime when we would have some potential recruits pay the school a visit. But most important, she was always there for me when the going got tough. That was what really separated her from many coaching wives. Yes, Jennifer was one of a kind, we made a good team, and I was one lucky man.

It didn't help, I'm sure, that I was involved in one athletic event or another when each of our three girls was born. I was on a football field when I learned that Jennifer was about to deliver Ann, who was born in Tyler, Texas. I was at a baseball game when it came time for Nicole to arrive and I was on the road getting ready for the state basketball tournament when Renee was born. Our girls never experienced the seasons as fall, winter, spring, and summer. Rather to them it was football, basketball, track, and baseball season. But I never felt cheated or regretted that we did not have a boy, as some men in my position might have felt. Come to think of it, our family situation had me always feeling quite blessed. Here I was, the only male in a growing family that included our dogs. How could I not enjoy the unique status I found myself in?

Even though all three children were born to the same two parents, and in a similar type of environment, they were as different from each other as night and day. Ann was a classic overachiever. She never received any grade but an "A," and she always felt that there was not a mountain out there that she could not climb. She was smart, pretty and a person easily able to motivate herself when there was something she wanted. She played on two state championship teams in basketball. She wasn't ever the best player though, only the best leader. She was the type who was always patting the coach on the back, assuring him that things would be OK. She played under Hall of Fame high school coach Dan Wesson. A legend in the Texas panhandle, I liked and looked up to him because he was tough and did not give in to parents' demands. Coach Wesson established some hard and fast rules, one of which was that he would not allow a girl to play basketball and be a cheerleader at the same time. He had never allowed anyone to do it. But when Ann decided her senior year that she wanted to be a cheerleader as well, she asked Jennifer to approach the coach about it. Jennifer refused, feeling it was a matter between the two of them, and Ann went and talked to the coach, who surprisingly relented and said yes, she could do both. That told me that deep down Mr. Wesson was one very smart coach. Even though Ann was not even one of his top seven players, he could see she was a winner and a leader, a positive influence. He knew he needed her leadership and I really gained a lot of respect for him when he showed that flexibility. So Ann was a cheerleader-basketball player, a National Honor Society honoree, homecoming queen, favorite, and a beautiful girl just like her mother.

Nicole was "Miss Personality" of our little group, and used the characteristics she had at dealing with people to get whatever she wanted. She had a way of giving you no choice but to love her. With more friends than the rest of us had altogether, she was our social butterfly. Her grades were only average and she didn't play basketball, but she did participate in theater. She was a very good drama student and actress, and I loved to watch her perform in plays. She could play almost any kind of part that interested her. I particularly loved to see her do comedy. She was a natural born actress with great timing. She was beautiful, but in a different way than Ann. But Nicole had no trouble holding her own. She was competitive in everything she did, particularly when Ann was involved, but she did not want anyone to know it. Nicole had so much going for her that she sometimes forgot just exactly who she was. She was conflicted about athletics and played until eighth grade. Then she came to me and asked if it was OK if she decided to quit. I had no problem with her choosing not to participate, but what I did not want to see was her start something and then quit. I told her it was OK if she did not play, but deep down I don't think Nicole believed me.

When she was an infant, Nicole had the worst case of colic I've ever seen. She would get quite sick at night and fight it all night, then sleep most of the day. Jennifer and I took her to one specialist after another and each one recommended a special medicine or treatment that would cure it, but none of their remedies worked. Nicole would work herself up into a coughing fit until, exhausted, she would just cry and cry, racked with more and more coughing. Sooner or later, she would just fall asleep from exhaustion. That would last about an hour and then she would start all over. Finally one early morning around 2:00 a.m., I couldn't stand it anymore; I just decided I had to try something. I called a friend and asked if he kept any bourbon or whiskey in the house, and he replied that yes, he had. He invited me to stop by without hesitation. When I got there, he said, "What's the matter?"

I replied, "I have a problem at home, and let me borrow the bottle of whiskey for a day or two." He gave me the bottle and I hurried home. I took Nicole's pacifier and dipped it in the whiskey, then handed it to her. She sucked on it for a little while and soon fell asleep, and then she slept through the entire night. It would be an understatement to say that our little Nicole was wound a bit tight.

Renee was the passive one of the family, clearly the easiest one to get along with. She was controlled by her older sisters; she never really had a chance but to react to them. It did not bother her one bit, however, and she just did her thing. She was a beautiful girl, skinny and tall with a pretty face. She tried her hand at every sport, but although she didn't have much success, she would not quit. She just wasn't much of an athlete. She was book smart on the one hand, but a little short in common sense on the other. For instance, one day when she was in the sixth grade, she and a friend just decided that they would skip school that day. They walked about three miles to my office, strode in, and just sat down like nothing was amiss. I asked her, "Is there something wrong? Why are you two not in school?" as I was puzzled myself to see them in my office. Renee came back with, "We just decided that we did not want to go to school today, Daddy, and we had no place to go so we came to see you." She showed no fear on her face, no remorse, and I couldn't keep from smiling. When I called Jennifer, however, she went crazy. Of course, now I needed to adjust my attitude as well, to act really angry and disappointed. I took them back to school and let the principal handle it. Renee was always the one who stayed with her father when things got tough. She realized she was the "Daddy's Girl" of our group. Renee was proud of me for being a coach and her father. One thing was certain: Anytime I needed something, she was the first to volunteer.

The three girls were my biggest fans, but I was their biggest fan too. We enjoyed a very nice relationship; I loved them so much but I did feel guilty much of the time because I had to depend on Jennifer to do most of the parenting. So much of my job was recruiting, which led to me being out of town much of the time. This caused me to come to think that whenever I had opportunities to spend time with them, as I had now briefly, I would try to make the most of it. I saw it as a case of quality vs. quantity. My opportunities to be a good father came too few and far between as it were. When I had the circumstance to be able to spend time with my daughters, I worked hard at getting it right.

Thinking along these lines as everyone was exiting the bus, I was thrilled to see Renee running across the street to hug her father, followed by Ann, then Nicole, and finally Jennifer. Of course, they weren't just happy to see Dad because they missed him and were proud of him. They were all very hungry too, and they knew when it came to food, I was a softy. They all wanted to go to Furr's and have a bite to eat. Furr's Cafeteria was a tradition in our family, particularly for Renee, as she always ordered the same thing. She loved the chicken fried steak, gravy, mashed potatoes, green beans, and macaroni and cheese. Up or down, she never changed, and neither did her order. We all knew her preference by heart. Mealtime was catching-up time for our family. It was the only time we all got together where we could listen and talk at the same time. I would find out about boyfriends, teachers, coaches, homework, favorite and worst subjects, and, most important, their most pressing needs at that given moment. I always enjoyed these moments together; it really relaxed me to get away from the intensity of the basketball that so dominated my days and nights.

Ann was just two months away from graduation, so that was the most pressing issue we had to deal with at this point. She was nervous about her college choice and her future, as any normal high school senior would be. She had received an offer of an academic scholarship at Angelo State, but I could tell she was not sure she wanted to go there. When she had visited the school, someone had been rude to her and that put a bad taste in her mouth about the whole situation. I had learned in my own position that little factors can determine how high school seniors think when they are trying to decide on a college to attend. I got the feeling that Ann did not want to go to Angelo State but that she didn't know if she would get a better choice. A free education is a free education, and I was only hoping that something else might break for her while there was still time.

When we entered the restaurant, there was a long line, which neither bothered me nor surprised me; the place was very popular. But what did throw me for a loop, however, was that we ran into three ex-basketball officials from my hometown of Amarillo. Their names were Ricky Jones, Harlan Kile and James Voyles. They actually recognized Jennifer, which did not surprise me. When they saw me coming out of the bathroom after drying my hands, you would have thought we were long-lost cousins. All three had called many a game that I coached, and I had a deep respect for each of these guys. They were on the way to the Final- Four themselves and had stopped in New Braunfels to get something to eat. All three were ex-division one officials who had done their jobs well over many years; they were men of excellent character. I often times had thought how good it would be for everyone involved if we could bring them back into the game, because good officials are not easy to come by. All three officials called many basketball games that my basketball teams played. Each one at some time or another had to tell me to go sit down and shut up, more than once I assure you. But what separated them from others in the profession was that they were fair and consistent in their calls. I felt that with officials of that quality and integrity calling games, it cleared the way for me to be an even better coach. With them deciding things, I might have the opportunity to be in a class by myself.

I had always been fortunate that I learned early on how best to handle and work with basketball officials. Back when I was playing college basketball, my coach always preached to us about the guys with the whistles and the striped shirts. He would say, "You can count on one hand how many mistakes they make while you are making mistakes on the court all the time. Until you are perfect, something I've yet to see in a player, I don't want to hear or see any negative reactions to the officials, or their calls" It was a good lesson, happily learned early, and it still holds true today. Over a lot of games I am sure officials make very few mistakes when all is said and done. I use video in my coaching and I watch and study game action all the time. I find it to be about a 97 percent chance that when I disagree with an official call, and then go check over the video following the game, I was the one who was wrong. That covers about 30 years of coaching. We cannot control the emotion of the game, which is huge, and it usually blocks out good judgment. During decades of coaching college round ball, I have had my share of run-ins. I think officials have the toughest job in basketball, and that it is the most difficult aspect in any sport. The crowd is all over you, the coaches are within easy reach both verbally and physically, and the players can be in your face at any minute. Regardless of the call you make, it is 50 percent wrong. Calling a game can be an emotional nightmare, which has to be tough, because I know that some of these men love the game as much, or even more than, any of us. Even when I'm just trying to officiate a basketball scrimmage among my own players, I invariably get mad at someone. I'm just not good official material. Before every game we play, I don't only say a short prayer that we play well and that I do a good job, I also pray that I keep my head about calls I do not agree with, that I don't question every on-court decision they make. Then I go into the game and get angry, and lose it over some isolated judgment call. It happens every time unless I trust the officials running the game. I do not need to agree with the calls, nor do I have to be happy with them; I let myself experience whatever emotions the game brings on.

But I need to keep my emotions under control. Officiating a game is a job that needs to be done by a special kind of person if it is to be done well. I have the deepest respect for the truly good ones. Of course, some coaches are terrible, players too. And there are some terrible basketball officials as well. All my miles and hours of recruiting travel across the country give me a unique perspective. I watch thousands of games in which I have no interest in the outcome. I'm just there to see the players. When I'm viewing it from that perspective, I can be a pretty good judge.

Interestingly, I have noticed that different states seem to breed different kinds of officials. A basketball player can't really develop into the best he can be unless he gets the chance to play against the best. And the same holds true for coaches. Any coach worth his salt becomes a better coach every time he faces a team that plays better, and is coached better, than any he has ever seen before. And officials hone their games in the same way. When they have to decide who made the better play between the best players out there, on the best teams, they become better officials. So in states where basketball is all the rage, the players get better, they get coached better, and they play their games in front of the best officials in the country. And it ends up making for a better and more enjoyable experience for spectators as well. It is one reason why America is so caught up in March Madness and the Final Four. You see the best of all worlds.

But one more thing about officials is that they need to understand that while they are a huge part of the game, they are not the game. They need to take on the responsibility of this difficult job for the good of the game and the good of the kids playing the game. An official who is unable or unwilling to check his own ego before calling the game will hurt more than help. Of course, he needs to be a strong advocate for what he is doing, he needs to have an ego that allows him to see what he sees, to believe he saw it correctly, and to call it that way regardless of the opposition the calls receive. Without strong officials, you do not have a basketball game. In many ways, they can be more important than coaches. But officials are not there to determine the outcome of a game. If they do, then you have poor officials, and it unfortunately happens more often than people realize. Mistakes are made. Some missed or incorrect calls cannot be avoided. The wrong call on a big play at the wrong time will turn the game. But that is part of the game too. What cannot be part of the game, however, is an official letting their own ego determine the outcome of the game.

I give clinics across the country about the game, and I talk to young coaches about officials. I tell them that they must learn how to handle parents, administration, boosters, and officials, and not in that order. Coaching is easy compared to the other jobs out there really. I use key words in my presentations. When I talk about parents to coaches, I always tell them to remember what it would be like if it was your child you were coaching. I try to impress upon them that if you coach every player like he or she is your child, you will always be successful. When I talk about administration, I always start with the saying that an ounce of loyalty is worth a pound of cleverness. Loyalty is crucial when dealing with the administration and being a team player. When the discussion moves to boosters, I discuss firmness and honesty. I talk about standing up for your program and players within the program. And when I talk about officials, the key word is invariably respect. "You give respect, you will get it back," I advise every single time. "If you don't give officials respect, you're going to catch all kinds of hell."

TEN

ACK AT THE BIG DAY, the video we watched during our pre-game meal was the semi-final game where Memphis defeated North Carolina to reach the finals. I hated to admit it but Memphis was really good. They just didn't defeat North Carolina; they beat them in every aspect of the game. They out-shot them, out rebounded them, had fewer turnovers, and made more positive plays than North Carolina. North Carolina was the defending national champs and that was all NC had going for them. Memphis only lost two games with a total of three points, one to Tulsa by one point and two to Kentucky by two points in overtime. As I watched the video for the tenth time, I began to wish I had not started this video tradition. I only hoped I was not intimidating my own players.

One of the biggest question marks about me according to the North West State University Athletic Director, James Jones, during the interview process for the Head Coaching position at North West State was whether I could win big time games in the NCAA. I had already proven that I could win big in the NJCAA but for some reason that did not mean anything to the athletic director at North West State. He felt I would be over my head with the amount of talent I had to compete against on the NCAA level. Of course my counter to this was that I had won at all levels of basketball. This seemed odd to me because he was an ex-basketball coach and had never won too much on the big screen. I thought his insecure feelings were projected toward me and that bothered me. In my opinion, I had about as good of an education in winning as a coach could get. I did it the hard way but in the process, learned because I had a burning desire to know what it takes to win. Very few coaches start at the junior high school level, go to a small high school, win big, and continue to win at each and every level they coach. Of course, most coaches don't go up the stairs from level to level like I did.

The biggest turn-around for me in learning how to win was when I went to Panhandle Baptist University. Panhandle Baptist was a member of the National Athletic Intercollegiate Association which governs small four year colleges and universities that can't qualify for NCAA. It was on this level of competition that I got my bubble busted and had to sink or swim. I would not advise anyone to go through what I did in order to learn but it worked for me. The best players in the country usually sign to play at the big time NCAA level, high division one schools. The second best players usually sign just below that level but with a smaller type of division one NCAA school. The next best athletes usually sign with a division one junior college or at a division II NCAA school. After that, most often the next group signs with large division one NAIA schools. Finally the next level of players sign with small division one NAIA schools and Panhandle Baptist University was an example of that level of play. Of course, it does not always happen in that order but statistics prove this to be true. It kind of like a pecking order where a school like Panhandle Baptist waits their turn and then recruits what is left.

Panhandle Baptist University was a small division I NAIA school in Plainview. The town had about 25,000 people in the southern part of the Texas Panhandle. Plainview was a farming community with a strong conservative mind set on athletics. Although it was hard for my family to pack our bags and move from our new home and church in Odessa, the move was relatively easy. The people of Plainview, Panhandle Baptist and the First Presbyterian Church helped us make it easier. Jennifer really liked Plainview and that helped the move a lot. We bought our eighth house in Plainview. A nice three bed room home with two baths and a basement. The geographic location of Plainview was in the heart of what weather people call 'Tornado Alley' so the basement was essential. Ralph Sorrels was our next door neighbor and he just happened to be a Psychology

Professor at Panhandle Baptist University. He and his wife Jerry were the best neighbors one could have. They had two little girls so we all became very close and enjoyed each other's company.

The only bad part was that Ralph loved to work cement and to build stuff with cement. He worked projects of home improvement in his house until he ran out of ways to use cement, so he started inventing projects of home improvement on our house. We built a walk around the entire fence area from the front to the back and then to the entrance of both the front and back. After all, the girls needed places to skate and it was less grass to mow. I had never worked cement but I soon learned how, because I had no choice. Soon, Ralph and I got to know each other very well. For some reason or another, our family fit into Plainview very well.

For the first time in my life, I was on the ground floor with the administration which was the main reason for my taking the job. I was the athletic director at Panhandle Baptist and proud of it. Panhandle Baptist was where the 'Flying Queens' originated. Some of the best female basketball players at the college level played basketball at Panhandle and the tradition was dying. Many years before women's basketball really started growing, Panhandle Baptist was a power house of women's basketball, competing with Texas, Southern California, UCLA, and other large universities. Panhandle Baptist was one of the first to give full scholarships to women in basketball and one of the first to fly their athletes to and from the games. They were called the 'Hutchinson Flying Queens'. The Hutchinson's were from Plainview, and provided the airline service for the Queens, hence the name "Flying Queens". Now this was a huge political and financial issue and one that the current administration made clear from day one that I was to handle. Whatever decision I made about the women's basketball program, was going to be half right and half wrong. The flying queens could no longer compete in the Southwest Conference, much less some power houses in Division II, NCAA. The "Flying Queens" were going down fast and someone had to step up and make a decision. The problem was complex and was over due to be fixed. If we did not fix it, the women's basketball program would end. I do not know why I said 'we' because I was already told by the President I was going to be on my own.

I flew to the NCAA headquarters and met with officials one entire day. We were trying to figure out if we could possible go division II, NCAA. I had to come back and make a report to the board and the administration. What I found out really bothered me. We could qualify on any level of the NCAA, but each level had certain requirements, and we could not meet any of the requirements at Panhandle Baptist. You had to have a certain number of sports and we didn't come close to meeting those standards. We had men and women's basketball, men's indoor and outdoor track and cross country track. To me, that left only one option for the "Flying Queens" and that was for the women to join the same organization that the men belonged to; the NAIA. Of course, all the fans of the Flying Queens did not want to drop their standards to that level. The real problem was that if the Queens did not join the NAIA, they would soon not be able to play anyone because NCAA rules were changing and soon all NCAA schools would be prohibited them from playing NAIA schools. We really had no choice. I made the recommendation that the women join the NAIA, and it was adopted. Needless to say, I became a negative target for Panhandle Baptist supporters, both good and bad from that day on.

Panhandle men's program was in bad shape which was indicated by a losing record for the last five years. They had not been to the playoffs in ten years and the last time they really had a good year was twenty years before. They were considered by the opposition as an easy win. It was a joke around Plainview that crowds would fill the gym up for the women's game and when the women's game was over, they would all leave, making the men's team play in front of few spectators. Panhandle men's basketball was losing respect and was hurting Panhandle in terms of money lost through attendance at school. The bottom line reason that Panhandle wanted me to be their basketball coach came from fact of the turnarounds at Albany, Hereford, Permian and Permian Basin Junior college. They wanted the same thing. They were tired of the men's program being the laughing stock of Plainview. Of course, I knew all this so I used it to my advantage when I was hired. I have never been one for demanding something but I did request a few changes in the program. One of those was a full time assistant coach. They did not have one at the time, nor did the women, nor did track. So when they met my needs for an assistant coach, they also had to give everyone else one. The other was a recruiting budget to be upgraded to meet the standards of the competition. The facilities were nice at Panhandle but there was no place for the athletes to hang out so we created and developed a room in the gym just for athletes. When we finished the room it had a large TV and lounge chairs, a place for computers, and a soda machine. They did not have a trainer, and I talked them into giving scholarships for student athletes who wanted to become trainers. Each sport would get a student trainer and the school would send them off to be trained once a year. Of course, the final thing I pushed for was a complete drug testing program. They did not go for that, but insisted that drugs would not be a problem at Panhandle Baptist. I thought, well maybe not in a Christian school, I thought, "Who are you kidding?"

Again, the first thing I always do when starting a new situation is to figure out what was wrong with the old situation. There is a famous saying that I like to quote; "A problem cannot be solved by the same level of thinking that created it." I evaluated the problem and this is what I came up with: One) The talent level was not on the same level that I had at Permian Basin College, Two) The players in the program were soft and spoiled, Three) There was a great degree of selfishness in the program, and Four) It was hard to win because you had to play eighty-five per-cent of your games on the road. Now playing on the road on this level of college basketball was brutal. Not only do you play in front of a hostile crowd, you play with the home officials. You have no choice what-so-ever and you have to accept the officials regardless of the situation.

I started off with a really strong off season with weights, weighted vests and everything. I came across tough and short. It did get some of the guys attention as several talked about transferring. At the same time, I tried to recruit better talent. I did have a small advantage because I knew where to go to look for guys who might be interested in playing basketball at Panhandle Baptist. It was clear to me I needed to recruit better players. I hit it big with my own players that I coached at Permian Basin College as several signed with me to come to Panhandle Baptist. I knew the junior college scene well so I used that a lot. I recruited five transfers, three from

Permian Basin and two more from other junior colleges and then signed three players just out of high school. I felt good about the players that I signed and felt they would make an impact on the team.

That fall, I put the basketball players through the hardest workouts I knew. We ran miles, lifted weights, worked out with weighted vests, and ran sprints, worked on defense each day as I demanded intensity. I was trying to harden them up. To my surprise, most all of the players responded very well, but we did have to start taking trash buckets out on a daily basis in order that some of them could throw-up in the trash cans, instead of on the floor. Of course, I knew the Permian Basin guys could take it because I had put them through it before but there were some other guys that stepped up also. To my simple way of thinking, if you have to play twenty-five of thirty games on the road, you better be mentally tough. The only way I know to find out who can handle it and who can't was to put the players through situations that did not seem fair, being even brutal at times. There is such a fine line, but it had to be done and I had become pretty good at it. I was most impressed with Dirk Beasley and Randy Cooper. Dirk was a good guard and only needed confidence and time. Randy was really a unique offensive basketball player. He was only six-foot-five but had great focus and concentration. He had the ability to get his shot off even when the person guarding him was much taller, and his shots usually went in. The only problem I had with Randy was that he was strongly loyal to his last coach. He would not accept me being the coach without a fight. The fight was worth it as he turned out to be one of our better players and one of the better players in the region. He led the nation in field goal percentage with fifty-eight percent. Not bad for a six-foot-five skinny white kid. Two freshmen, Leland Lucas and Darryl Wrenn were both outstanding perimeter shooters and good players. They both knew how to win as both came from very good high school programs. I felt we had the makings of a very good team and I just needed to figure how to put it all together. It was tough because I had brought in transfer guys to take the place of guys that played before. This is one experience that helped me in the North West State University job, because I had done it before. Jealousy played a big part in the transition for all the players but I felt it was normal and not something that I could control. To put a stop to all of this, I just concentrated on the best team players and told them that. The team had to come first and foremost. I still used my grade-out system and that alone provided all the players a chance to get playing time.

I have told many a coach in basketball clinics that where I learned how to win was at Panhandle Baptist University. Plainview is in no man's land in the panhandle of Texas. To get teams to come play Panhandle Baptist at home was almost impossible. The closest competition that would play us on a home and home deal was Lubbock Christian University in Lubbock and McMurry College in Abilene. That was it. We couldn't get anyone else to come to Panhandle Baptist on a regular basis. However, we could travel just about anywhere to find people to play. Our conference schools were Texas Wesleyan College, in Fort Worth, Dallas Baptist College, in Dallas, Midwestern State University in Wichita Falls, and Lubbock Christian University. That would give us five home games out of thirty, not including the play-offs. You better be able to coach if you are going to play that many games on the road. The other thing that was tough about playing on the road was you had little choice in the selection of officials. In those days we did not have commissioners assigning games for officials but instead, the home school was responsible for assigning officials. It is not that the officials cheated but it is better to say that the officials were very prejudiced in their calls simply because they usually were home town guys and had a steady job. I learned from experience that the first ten minutes of a game and the last two minutes of the game, were the times that road officials were consistent. They were always fair at first and then somehow they would be influenced one way or another until the last few minutes of the game. For some reason, officials usually called a fairer game in the last two minutes of the game. Another factor at this level was that most of the teams were about even in talent. Every once in a while you could find some teams with high quality players but not very often. So the challenge was simple; you would be playing on the road in opponent's gyms, with their officials and against equal talent. Coaching always made the difference and that created a lot of pressure coaching at this level. I did some of the best and some of the worst coaching I ever did in my life at Panhandle Baptist.

Since players are basically even, the attitude of the team is very critical and the ability to play as a team is paramount. What all this taught me in my efforts to win was how to play with the ball more than the opponent. We called it 'Milking the Clock' and I developed it from Dean Smith's four corner offense, Bobby Knight's passing game and Hank Iba's delay game. We called it '4 to score'. Each possession is critical and the ability to keep your focus and poise is the utmost importance. That was the only way we could keep the officials and the crowd out of the game at the same time. What started off as just a survival game turned into a huge winner for us. It was simple but yet hard to defend against. At this time, there was no shot clock for men. The NBA had a shot clock and women had a shot clock but the men did not have one. We would pretend to try to score until the clock made a complete revolution from one minute to the next. An example would be like when we got the ball and the clock read 13:44; we would not shoot until the clock read 12:59, and only then would we attempt a shot, the rest was just fake basketball. It shortened the game from a forty minute game to a thirty minute game or less which was to our advantage on the road. It gave us the knowledge of when we were going to really do something on the court. Of course, if we could get a lay-up or a put-back, then milking the clock was off. Several things happened in this process: A] we became good at faking shots, faking passes and faking drives to the basket. B] We got very good at offensive rebounding. C] Our turnovers were lower because we seemed to know exactly when we were going to attack and D] our shooting percentage was much higher when we knew we were supposed to shoot. The next thing we learned to do was what you call "Gimmick Defenses" such as a "Box and One", "Triangle and Two" and other types of defenses that were not the norm. We learned how to hide defenses and that was the only way we could keep the opponent off balance. I learned that knowing how to control a game on offense and defense is the thing that you must learn or you will be beaten every game. When we played at home, we didn't worry about all that stuff and sometimes I wished we would have although we did not lose many home games. Of course, we did not play many home games.

Since NAIA teams were so spread out over Texas, we played under what they called 'The Gallup System'. The Gallup System is complicated and not easy to understand but it goes hand in hand with learning how to manipulate a game. Here is how it works: At the start of the basketball year, all teams were given a ranking. After the ranking was established, each game played after that would determine your ranking until the end of the season. If your team was ranked twenty-seventh and you beat another team that was ranked fifteenth, you would get points for that win and when the next ranking appears, you would probably move up. Points were determined by where your opponent was ranked, how many points you won or lost by, and by home court or visiting court. There were other factors involved but the bottom line was winning by the point spread which was given for each game played. If you lost but stayed within the point spread, you did not really lose according to the Gallup System. Next, another important aspect was where you played. At the end of the year, your rankings would determine if you made the playoffs and would determine if you played at home or on the road. If you played a really high level NCAA school and played them well, your rating would go up.

We had a good start for the new program as we won our first three games. I finally won Randy Cooper over as I left him at Wayland in the Abilene Christian win. He was late for the team bus so I left him. What made it better was that Abilene Christian was supposed to beat us by fifteen points according to the Gallup Poll. They were a strong division II NCAA University and we beat them by five points. It was not an easy win as we were behind fifteen points after the first ten minutes of play and it looked like a run-a-away for them. We came back, got the lead and beat them down the stretch. It was a really nice win. We then went to Eastern New Mexico and won so we were riding high. We were scheduled to play West Texas State University in the Amarillo Civic Center. West Texas State was a low division I school and they gave us ten thousand to play them in Amarillo. We were beaten but did not lose by the Gallup poll and I hated every moment of the game but we made money. I hated that kind of deal but it was necessary in order to make ends financially meet. We played well at McMurry and won and then we went to Oklahoma. Oklahoma clearly plays the best NAIA basketball in the nation. We lost three games in

Oklahoma and came home to regroup. Cameron University had won the NAIA National Championship the year before so I wanted to play them. They beat us by twenty-five but I learned a lot by playing them. The next year, I scheduled Cameron for a home and home deal. They would come to Panhandle Baptist and everyone thought I was crazy. At any rate, we finished the regular season third in the Gallup poll so we got to host the first round playoff game. It was with McMurry and the legendary coach High Kimball. He was a fantastic basketball coach and great human being. Panhandle Baptist had not won a playoff game in twenty years so we were trying to make history. McMurry could not handle us as we beat them by twelve points and advanced to the second round. It had been thirty years since Panhandle Baptist had been this far in the playoffs so we were proud of ourselves. We had to play in Ft. Worth against TWC. Joe Bob Overton was the head coach and we were very good friends as he was an ex TCU basketball player. Joe Bob had one of his best teams and they were the favorites to win according to the Gallup poll. We beat them on a last second shot by Leland Lucas from a pass from Dirk Beasley. History was being made!

Now, we had to travel to Wichita Falls to plays Midwestern State ranked #1 in the Gallup poll for the championship. The winner advanced to the national tournament. Of course, Panhandle Baptist had never been this far before. We played a great game and soundly outplayed Midwestern state but they won by three points. We could not keep them off the free throw line as they made thirty of thirty-seven attempts and we made ten of twelve attempts. I thought we got a bad deal and I was upset. It was one of those deals where they let them play but would not let us play. It's all a matter of view point and that was my viewpoint. It was something that neither I nor the players will ever forget. I was so upset; I stayed in the dressing room for one hour trying to avoid the press. I knew I would say what I felt and I knew that was the wrong thing to do. Three days later, I watched the video and the officiating was not as bad as I thought. That was why I did not want to talk to the press. They were better than we were but it was close. It was a great turnaround and the best season that Wayland had in men's basketball in over 30 years. I was named 'Coach of the Year in the district and was nominated for Texas 'Senior College Coach of the Year'. There were only three of us nominated so I felt good about that. When we got home late the next day, a crowd of Panhandle Baptist people met us and gave us a royal welcome. It was nice and music to my ears. We had broken the ice. One of my hero's in basketball was Dean Smith. He was a different kind of coach and because of his four corner offense, the rules changed. Another coach that I admired and respected a great deal was Hank Iba. I studied him and wanted to be like him particularly from the defensive standpoint. I developed a philosophy from both of these guys on how to win games.

As a reward for the outstanding year we had in basketball, Panhandle Baptist University Administration told me that they wanted me to go to the National Basketball Tournament in Kansas City, Kansas. What made it great for me was they allowed me to take my wife at their expense. We were excited because we had never been to Kansas City and excited to just get away by ourselves for a few days. I made reservations through the National office, the school provided a school car, and we were off to Kansas City. The games started on Wednesday and ended on Saturday night, but more than anything, it was a chance for Jennifer and me to get a little rest and relaxation. The drive was not that bad except for all the toll-gates. I was not used to paying to drive on a highway. We arrived in Kansas City around 4:00pm. The hotel was located in the middle of downtown Kansas City. I parked the car and we went in and checked in. Jennifer followed with some clothes and we went up to the room. When we opened the door, I thought we were in Old cowboy-western days of Roy Rogers. The room looked like a picture from an old western movie with a bed and a bathroom. The bed was small, hard, and smelled like mildew. The bathroom was not much better with an old tub and no hot water. We tried the air conditioner and it didn't work. I thought, this cannot be the place that the National Tournament suggested you stay. "Surely, there is a mistake." I went down stairs to talk to the office and found out that the headquarters for the National Tournament was in the hotel next door, and when that hotel filled up, they would move people to this hotel. We decided to stay for at least one night, make the best of it and then relocate.

It was about time to eat so we decided to go somewhere nice to eat. We had to park down the street because of parking space so I volunteered to go get the car and come pick her up at the front door. I went to get the car but couldn'tfind it. I looked everywhere and visualized my parking before going into the hotel. After searching for a long time, I realized that the car was gone. I panicked and thought someone must have stolen the school car!

Finally, I went back and told Jennifer I could not find the car. This time, she went with me and couldn't find the car either. We went to the hotel front office and reported a stolen car to them and asked them to call the police. The front desk clerk looked at me in a funny way and asked, "Where did you park the car?" I said, "On this side of the street down about seventy-five yards." He came back and said, "Sir, your car is not stolen but it has been towed by the police for parking in a tow away zone." By this time, I was getting upset, and said to him, "'There are no signs to that effect!" and he replied, "Yes there is a sign, but the sign is at the end of the block." I sprinted back to where I parked and sure enough, there was a sign about twenty-yards from where I parked saying that this area was a tow away zone from 4:00pm -6:00pm. By now, I was pissed off and trying to control my emotions and attitude. Jennifer and I went back up to the room and I called the police. I ask them if they had towed away my car. Of course, I did not know the plate number as it was not my car; it was the school's car. He was not going to give me the information because I did not know the license number. It was then that I lost it and told him what I thought of his city, the hotel and the toll roads. He hung up with anger but I still did not know if my car had been towed.

I know when I am beaten so I called back, and asked him again in a civil way and he answered my question. He said, Sir, your car was towed and we have it stored here at the police station". Then he paused for a long time, and said, "Sir, there is a problem." I said "What?" and he said, "When the tow truck was towing the car, the car fell off the hook of the tow truck and rolled down a hill into another car." I was not ready for this and I went blank for a long time. Finally, I lost it and said "What the hell am I supposed to do now?" He said, "Sir, I would come down to the police station and sign the papers for your car so that you can get it fixed". As soon as he said that, I asked where the police station was located, and he told me just around the block from where you are staying. I took off like a jet airplane. I was so angry that I did not notice the neighborhood that I was going into as I was walking fast and furious. Finally, I found the police station but not before I started getting tired and realized, I was in a rough area where the houses were not so nice. It was a neighborhood where I did not want to stick around very long. I am sure they were wondering what I was doing in their neighborhood. Of course, the police station wasn't just around the block but more like ten blocks.

At the police station, I calmed down only because I was too tired to fight and we settled any disputes that we had. First, my car could not be driven until it was fixed and they would fix the car but it would be until Friday before we could get the car. Second, I had to pay a ticket for parking in a no parking zone and a huge fine because the car had to be towed. Last but not least, a police car took me home because they said it was very dangerous to be walking in the neighborhood that I just walked from. It was now late at night; we had not eaten and were tired.

After that, the trip was not eventful but as far and Jennifer and I were concerned, it was over. We got the car on Friday and left for home as soon as we got it. I was tired and really upset. Jennifer was a trooper but she was fed up with this trip as much as me. Nothing had gone the way we wanted it to. We came to the last toll gate in Kansas and I stopped to pay. They always ask for your ticket and then you pay. You get a ticket at the toll gate ahead, then you give them your ticket and they know how much you owe. The guy at the toll gate asked for my ticket. I always keep the ticket in the visor on the driver's side, but it was not there. I said, "Just a second as I have misplaced it." I said to Jennifer, "Have you seen the ticket?" She was tired and said, 'What ticket?" I said, "The "toll gate ticket!" She said, "Here is the only ticket I know about." I said, "I don't need that stupid police ticket!" We started laughing at each other. We were so tired and so frustrated that we didn't care what happened next. I guess it was the frustration of the trip but we just started laughing and crying at the same time. By this time, a line of cars and trucks were lined up behind us as far as you could see.

They started honking and the toll attendant got nervous and said, "Please sir, let me see the ticket." I said once more, with a shout, "I have lost the damn ticket and cannot find it! Further- more, I am going to stay here until hell freezes over until I find the damn ticket!" Five minutes later, it was a stand- off and the poor guy did not know what to do. Finally, with trucks and cars honking he said, "Just go, and get out of here!" He opened the gate and we left laughing and crying about the ticket.

One positive thing about the trip was the Tournament itself. If anyone ever doubts the quality of NAIA basketball, they have never been to Kansas City and watched the National Tournament. I saw some of the best teams ever, regardless of the level. It was fun to watch.

As always, my second year was much easier than my first year. We played well from start to finish. We were consistent and good. We did four things that year that had never been accomplished. First, we went to the Marry Mount Tournament in Kansas. Marry Mount was a powerful NAIA school always in the top twenty. They had never lost a tournament game in the history of the school. We beat them in the finals of their tournament by ten points. We ran four to score the entire game and they could not handle it. Second, we beat Cameron on our home court, who was #1 in the nation at that time without four to score. We should have beaten them in Oklahoma but blew a ten point lead in the last two minutes. Third, we beat Midwestern State University in our gym for the first time in several years. Dr. Bass, one of the top administrators came on the court and had tears in his eyes when the game was over. He was so excited for us.

Last, we ended the year with the number one ranking in the Gallup system for the first time in the history of Panhandle Baptist. We finished the season with over twenty wins and the best won-lost record in the history of Panhandle men's basketball. We played McMurry in the first game of the play-offs again. We won on a last second shot by Cubby Kitchens. We were lucky to win because McMurry outplayed us. Since we played so poorly against McMurry and did not make the twelve point spread in the Gallup poll. That meant we really lost the game so we now had to travel. We had to go to Paul Quinn, an all black college close to Waco. We played poorly again and lost to Paul Quinn on their home court.

Again, I was nominated as senior coach of the year but did not get it. The one thing that I could count on was the fact I was becoming a good game coach and I learned how to coach the point spread. I was learning how to win games. I would never be the same and knew it. I wanted a division one job and felt ready.

Southwest Texas State University, a small division one school had a head men's basketball position open. I thought I should take advantage of my last two years and make a move now. I was named one of the hot young coaches on the move by the Dallas Morning News and I felt the timing was right. I signed a three year contract with Wayland when I came on board but I knew that they would understand my desire to advance my career. Little did I understand how difficult this venture would be? There were one-hundred-twenty applicants for the job. It was a very good basketball position. The football team under Jim Wacker had just won a National Championship in division IA football. They were building a huge basketball complex and the location in San Marcos was as good as it gets. They had about 25,000 students and bragged about having three girls to every boy. On top of that, South Texas and North Texas are as opposite in weather as an orange is to an apple. South Texas is beautiful, green, and warm. I informed both my superiors and bosses, Dr. Bill Thompson, and Dr. Don Allen of my intent to apply. They both appeared to understand my situation and we all talked about it for a long time. Jennifer was not happy as she loved Plainview. She was head of 'Meal's on Wheels' and was really enjoying the attention from being the director. For the first time, she was getting as much attention as me. She deserved every bit of it. Everyone loved Jennifer and she was good at what she was doing. On top of that, she was a wonderful mother and wife.

One afternoon, I received a phone call from the Athletic Director of Southwest Texas State University Vernon Windsor asking me to come for an interview. They had narrowed the short list down to six people. The plan was for the interview to take place one day, and then they would keep two applicants over the next day to visit with the President of the university. They would offer the job to one of those two. I was thrilled to death to be in the group of people that they interviewed. I was the only one being interviewed from an NAIA school. Four were head coaches from lower level division one schools and one was a coach from high school in Houston. That spring, before all this happened, I went to Kansas City as the Head Key-Note-Speaker of the NAIA National Tournament. I gave a two day clinic associated with the National Tournament. That prepared me for this interview and gave me some confidence in the process. During the interview, Jim Wacker, the head football coach and I hit it off right away. He liked me and my approach to the game, building and maintaining a program. All I did was use the same material that I used at the National Tournament clinic and it paid off. I made it to the final two but I had to go against Tom Newberry who was the head coach at Sam Houston State University, a small division one school in Huntsville, Texas. We both went to the president and he visited with both of us for over an hour. I knew Tom very well because he had recruited some of my players at Permian Basin. He was successful everywhere including Sam Houston State. I had a great visit with the president and he was honest with me. He liked me a lot and really liked the fact that everywhere I had been, I improved the program. He and Vernon said that they could not find anyone to say anything bad about me. He told me that he was going to have to go with Tom because of his experience and the fact that he had already proven he could win on a division one level.

Case closed and I went home sad but happy. I was proud that I competed that well with so many people but sad I did not get the position. I figured out that I had better start recruiting for next year as we lost lots of good players. At that time, I learned another hard lesson about recruiting. The rumor was out that I was leaving Panhandle Baptist and my opponent used that to convince players not to be interested in coming to Panhandle Baptist. Just as I was about to get into recruiting and visiting players, I received a call from the athletic director from Sam Houston State University. He had talked with Vernon Windsor, and the President of Southwest Texas State University about me and they were interested. He asked me if I would come down for an interview. I was stunned and agreed I would come down. I talked to Dr. Allen, my supervisor again about going to interview at Sam Houston State. He tried to talk me out of it and I could tell, he was not happy with my decision to pursue this opportunity. He told me that God wanted me at Panhandle. I told him that I was not getting the same message from God he was getting. Everything was different this time as Sam Houston paid for my entire family to come down and visit. We had the opportunity to look at housing, and really get a feel of the city. I hate to admit it but this time around, Jennifer and the girls weren't happy campers. I was alone on this deal and I knew it. The interview went well and they offered me the position. It was a $12,000 raise and an opportunity to get my foot into Division one basketball. I was excited but could not tell anyone because they had to get it approved through the proper channels. They told me that they would call me Monday and let me know all the details.

I received the phone call Monday afternoon. It was from the office of the President and he told me that he was sorry but they could not hire me. He said that when Sam Houston called Dr.Inser, the President at Wayland, Dr. Inser went off on them and threatened a law suit for stealing their basketball coach. Dr. Inser said, "He had not been informed and that I still had one more year on my contract." Sam Houston made it clear to me that they would not even think about hiring me under those conditions. I was more disappointed than I have ever been in my life. I was mad, and upset with Panhandle Baptist. I felt cheated about my situation. I felt I had gone through the proper channels and had professionally done what was necessary. I was angry and I went straight to the president's office. He was a really nice person, but not a good president. He was a foreign clergyman from Africa and knew nothing about the education business. He was a great Christian man and had a PHD in Education. He told me that God wanted me at Panhandle Baptist and that Panhandle needed me. I was upset and did not argue but threw my keys down on his desk and told him that I would finish out my third year and would be gone after that. Then I walked out but not before I told him what I thought of Dr.Allen and his proper chain of command. After that, I was never the same at Panhandle. I went home and told Jennifer about everything and as always, she was upset with Panhandle even though she did not want to move to Huntsville.

I really liked my team coming back and learned a huge lesson about coaching that year. We weren't going to be as good as we had been but I still liked them. We had great chemistry. Lucas had really developed into a good basketball player and Beasley was an outstanding leader along with the rock, Wrenn. Lyndon Mansour was strong and played hard. Ken Peters was a very effective off guard and could shoot the ball as good as anyone we played. We had some other guys that could be good backups and I felt good about all of them. We worked hard and they all had good attitudes about team play and work, but the key was Lucas and Beasley. They were the best leaders I have ever had. Two players from the past, Cooper and Kitchens stayed on as graduate assistants. Both were working on their Masters Degree and both would soon get it. This was a first for me at Panhandle and I was pleased with the administration allowing me to keep those two guys on board.

I thought if we had a big man, we could win it all this coming year. We got a huge break when Fred Montrose a 6'10" 290 pound post became eligible after dropping out at the University of Kansas. He was an Amarillo high school graduate and an ex-teammate of Ken Peters. One thing led to another and soon we signed Fred. As I stated in an early chapter, when you sign a player of Fred's talent level, there is a price to pay. Jennifer went out on a limb and got Fred's wife a job in Plainview. We had to twist some arms to allow married housing to open up a spot for Fred and his wife, and I had to beg, wine, and dine the registrar to allow Fred's transcript to be acceptable. I really believed that Fred would work out. The guys on the team were excited and I was excited.

Not only was I not the same toward Panhandle Baptist, but I was not the same period. My mother was very sick and I did not think she was going to make it. My dad was getting worse in a nursing home in Big Spring so often I had my mind in other places besides basketball. It was so sad concerning my mom that Baylor Medical Center in Dallas told us that we would have to move her out because they no longer could do anything for her. The bottom line was that they could no longer give her the morphine she needed. Neither my brother nor I had a clue as to what we could do. Finally in the late summer, some people in our church at Plainview helped me get her accepted in a nursing home in Plainview. I had her transported by ambulance to Plainview. I remember that ride back to Plainview as I followed the ambulance the entire trip. I was sad about many things, I really got depressed and one thing for sure, I was not myself.

As soon as the fall workouts started, I did not like what I was seeing in Fred Montrose. He had really good skills and he was huge but his work ethic was very poor and he was too big and could not move because he was overweight. The worst part of it was that Fred had a poor attitude. His attitude was the same as all athletes that think they are big time. "What's in for me"? I knew in a week why he did not make it at Kansas University. Of course, what I was seeing was exactly what everyone told me before I signed him. I didn't have anyone to blame but myself. Not only that, but what made everything so complicated, Fred was a smooth talker and knew how to manipulate situations so that he came out looking good. He had the complete support of the team and that bothered me. His powerful influence was affecting the team without them knowing it. I could see it, but my hands were tied except when he screwed up and then I would let him have it. Not only that, I let too much stuff go on, without stopping it. I had too many other things on my mind. It was a horrible mistake to recruit him and I could see it happening. I was so upset with myself for allowing this to happen. Beasley and Lucas were the captains and they loved him so I thought, "Maybe, it is just me." Kitchens and Cooper were student assistants and they would not say anything at all but they knew what was going on. I could tell that they did not trust Fred at all and when I would ask them if I was wrong in my evaluation, both would agree with me.

Finally, Fred made a mistake that gave me the opportunity to do what I needed to do. We had a luncheon dinner downtown where the city was giving us a special lunch provided by the Plainview Chamber of Commerce. It was a big deal and Fred did not show up. The only problem was that Peters did not show up either. Peters would have never done that before but I knew what was going on with Fred. He knew that I would not kick Peters off the team because he knew I liked Peters so he convinced Peters not to go simply because he did not want to go. The next day, I called both in my office and removed them from the team for not showing up for a team function. Of course, Fred had all kinds of excuses just as he had before on other issues. Neither thought it was fair and in some ways, it was not fair. One thing for sure, it was long overdue on Fred's part. I couldn't care less. That next day, after practice, Beasley and Lucas came into my office and talked to me for an hour about letting both Fred and Peters come back on the team. I told both of them the truth about what was happening. Neither could see it the way I saw it. They both felt that kicking Peters off was unfair and I agreed with that, but it was not unfair with Fred. They promised me that if I would let them come back, I would not have any more trouble from Fred. Finally, I told them that I would let them come back on the team, and the only reason I was doing it was for Beasley and Lucas. I also told them that I would hold those two accountable for Fred's attitude the rest of the year. They both agreed and we were back as nothing had happened.

We had the most up and down year that I had ever had since I started coaching. We could not beat teams we were supposed beat and beat teams we were not supposed to beat. After the suspension, Peters was not the same and of course, Fred was still the same, just smarter about what he did and did not do. We had some really great highlights as we beat Oklahoma City at Oklahoma City in overtime. They were ranked #2 in the nation at the time. We beat Cameron at Cameron and Chaminade at Chaminade when they were #1 in the nation. Then we would turn around and get beaten by LCU, McMurry, and Eastern New Mexico. Really, the season was a blur to me as I was hurting inside for my mom and dad. Both were slowly dying. My mom had turned so bad she could not even recognize me when I would visit her. My Dad was a little better but it was just a matter of time for him.

To help our recruiting and make our program better, we created a trip to Hawaii for both the women's team and the men's team. It was a wonderful trip as we stayed eight days, played three games and had time to enjoy Hawaii. Panhandle Baptist had a university in Hawaii so we had Panhandle people make all the plans and arrangements. It was an easy deal for me. We had been playing so badly and I decided not to fight it anymore. We did not even workout before we left on the trip. Our first game was with Hawaii Hilo on the Big Island. To my surprise, we played well. We were beaten but played well which was something that we had not been doing lately. The next night we played Pacific and easily beat them. Again, we played well. That same night, the University of Tennessee with Ralph Sampson played Hawaii Chaminade. Tennessee was ranked #1 in the nation by all polls in the NCAA and Chaminade was ranked #1 in the nation by the NAIA. ESPN covered the game and made a big deal out of it. To everyone's surprise, Chaminade beat Tennessee by two points.

It was Sunday and we all went to church in an outdoor church by the ocean. You could hear the waves and the birds. I asked God to take my mom for she had suffered enough. The next night we played a box and one on Chaminade's leading scorer, and executed the four –to- score offense. We beat Chaminade by two points. It was a huge victory for Panhandle Baptist University and the basketball program. The next day, ESPN stated that since, Panhandle Baptist University beat Chaminade and Chaminade beat Tennessee, in their opinion, Panhandle Baptist University should be #1 in the nation. It was a great occasion for the people back in Plainview and Panhandle. I did not have much time to enjoy as my mom died two days after I returned from Hawaii. Too make things worse, when my brother and I told my dad, that mom had passed away, he died three weeks later.

We finished the season just under a twenty win season. I performed one of my worst coaching jobs ever in my career. We lost in the first round of the play-offs. When the season was over, Beasley and Lucas came into my office one day, they closed the door and both said that they wanted to apologize to me. Of course, I thought I knew what they were talking about but made them spell it out. They both broke down and told me that I was right about Fred and we would have been better off without him. He had completely destroyed the team and they both knew it. The truth of the matter, I was the one that destroyed our team because I allowed him to stay on the team. Those two guys would never know how terrible I felt about this particular year. To this day, I have stayed in contact with Beasley and Lucas. They are two of my most beloved friends in the world.

That spring, I started looking for a job. As I stated to the President, I was going to finish my contract out and resign. Of course, they wanted me to stay, but it would be a cold day in hell before that would happen. I had a recruit named James Ashmore from Hale Center that I recruited out of Henderson College, in Kilgore. While I was recruiting him, he told me how much he liked Henderson College. So, when the head men's basketball position opened up at Henderson College I applied. The high school principal at Plainview offered me an assistant principal's position in the high school and the athletic director of Lubbock Independent School District offered me the head basketball position at Monterey High School. After going for an interview at Henderson College and being offered that position, I had to make a decision. I had mixed emotions about all three positions but had to make a decision. As always, I talked with Jennifer and she encouraged me to take the Henderson College position. Reason being, she said there was a "Glow of excitement and energy in my body and face when I returned from Henderson College". East Texas, here we come again!

ELEVEN

T HE SUN DAWNED ON THE BIG DAY, and the time had come for us to leave for the game. I was nervous but anxious not to show it, so I made sure to try to establish some eye contact with each team member as they were getting on the bus. The mood was somber among the players and the entire staff. One by one, they filed in, each looking elsewhere, glancing in the opposite direction, anything to avoid the eye contact I was trying to make. They each wore game faces, sure, but not ones I had seen before. I started wondering if we had just gone too far with this group and they were about to crack. Each group of players has a breaking point; they can only overachieve so long before their performance suffers. It's a simple fact. You can just play your best so long before you break down, particularly fighting against superior competition game after game. I began to worry that this team had indeed hit that wall. That we had overachieved couldn't be denied. Had we played to our level we would not even have won the Conference tournament championship, much less be competing in the field of 64.

We did receive a few lucky breaks on our path to the finals, something almost anyone who knew anything about basketball was aware of. When sportswriters would hint that we had caught a break in our draws and fortunate in the way the contests that determined our coming opponents played- out, I repeated over and over, "I'd rather be lucky than good." Of course, I wanted to coach the best team, but if you don't have some luck, it is very difficult to survive March Madness. The NCAA selection committee set us up in the West Regional side of the bracket for the Division I Men's Basketball Championship. Our ninth seeding was a blessing for us in that we would begin play in Philadelphia against Washington State, the eighth seed. Opening games are tough on favorites. Not only were we not the favorite, the first game against a mid-bracket team, a superior team perhaps, but not overly so, was the biggest break yet. Bubba and Skunk had fantastic games against Washington State, and we won easily 76-64, with White Shoes and Smooth making clutch free throws down the stretch. Bubba had 18 points and 11 rebounds and Skunk scored 12 and pulled down 14 boards. D'wayne had a great game on the defensive side, stealing the ball five times by himself, with two resulting in resounding slam dunks. They were real crowd-stirring plays. I felt good about the win, yes, and even better that the boost in confidence from winning the Big 12 tournament was much in evidence. The celebration would not last long, however, as we watched our opponent for the next game, Michigan State, destroy Cleveland State 103-62. The MSU Spartans were the second seed, and they were ranked No. 8 in the country. We were scheduled to play in two days, so at least we did have some time to prepare for them.

Michigan State was poised, confident, and ready for us. They attacked our four-to-score setup with tremendous pressure and lots of help-side defense. You could tell they had used their time wisely: They must have practiced against the way we preferred to play, and it showed quickly in the game as they zoomed to the lead. At halftime, Michigan State was up 35-23. We had not played that bad; they were just that good. State was led by an All-American center named Victor Banks who was a returnee from the year before, and he already had 15 points and 8 rebounds at the half. We could not stop him, regardless of what we tried. In addition, as a team they were double-teaming our three guards out front and forcing the ball to the corners. From there we were not getting any points, except for a few times that the corner guys dribbled and penetrated with individual moves. In other words, they were forcing our big guys to each make a play every time down the floor, with no real passing option. Their game plan was working as we were really finding it impossible to score with any consistency.

We responded by putting Big Time into the back corner from where he was a real threat at the three-point line, and then substituted Skunk for Bubba. We couldn't keep State's big guy, Victor, from scoring anyway, so I decided to go with four guards instead of three. We came out of the break with lots of intensity, as did Michigan State. The teams traded baskets for the first three minutes with White Shoes knocking down a three-pointer and then getting fouled while driving to the basket. On our next possession, Smooth drove the lane and passed the ball to the corner where Big Time hit nothing but the bottom of the net. Then back at the other end, we created a turnover, and this time White Shoes repeated that play, passing the ball to Big Time, who buried another three-pointer. Michigan State's time-out halted play with them up 45-39.

I knew they would try something different, but going into a zone defense would have been my last guess. Studying lots of film, I hadn't seen a zone from Michigan State the entire year. They were an aggressive man-to-man team, it was the coach's style, and they had pride in their defense. They came out in a matchup 2-3 zone and, to my surprise, it worked; our players froze in their tracks and acted like they hadn't seen this alignment ever before. Spartan steals blunted our next two possessions, but they missed on both opportunities to score. You could see they were a different team though, as the zone gave them a lift.

With 12:30 to go and Michigan State up 49-41, I called a time-out. I took Skunk out of the game and put Dwayne in because he was a better zone player than Skunk. Dwayne just had a knack of getting to the right spot and finding the open man with the ball. Sure enough on the next possession, Big "D" passed the ball inside the zone to Big Time under the basket for a quick score and foul. It was the fourth foul on Banks, sending State's best player to the bench. It was huge for us, a turning point in the game. We had been losing ground but the momentum swung dramatically back toward us. Dwayne followed by claiming an offensive rebound and passing out to White Shoes, who nailed a three-point basket. With 8:10 left, and the score 58-53, Michigan State called another time-out.

My gut instincts told me it was now or never. I felt the Spartans were too good a team for us to be given a chance if we trailed going into the last few minutes. We had to do something to catch them off guard, and then hope for a good finish. I told the team that we had two minutes to do something or the game would be decided for us. I set up a full-court trapping press that we'd use until the 6:00-minute mark. The next two minutes we were going all-out now to see if we could swing the game our way. The ploy worked as the unexpected switch had an immediate effect, and we stole a Michigan State inbounds pass, and cashed in a layup. State urgently attacked our press, but they hurried an off-target shot, and Big Time rebounded the miss and fired an outlet baseball pass to Smooth for a breakaway and yet another layup. I was tempted to back off the press now but I had said we were going to press two full minutes, and I decided to let it happen. It did not take Victor long to get back into the game. Michigan State could feel the momentum swinging back to us and they called a time out. After the time out, you could see determination on the faces of the players from State. They knew it was now or never. On the first possession, Michigan State broke through clearly on the next possession and got the ball inside to Victor, who was ready to take charge. The Spartans' star player went to the basket with so much intensity, however, that he slipped executing a dunk and fell on his back, screaming loudly in pain. The entire arena came to a standstill and became eerily quiet. As the valiant Victor was carried off to a standing ovation from the crowd, we all tried to gather our wits and stay in the game. The loss of State's best player yet again was a break, but it did stop our team when they were playing their best. But the delay did give us time to consider the situation. Down just 58-57 to State, the two teams had 5:48 left to play. I called off the press; it just seemed the time to do it. If you are a gambler or a player, there are times to push and times to ease up a bit. You have to know when to back off, and I felt it was time.

We had possession of the ball and I was sure that they would go back to their man defense, so I switched, reinserting Skunk in favor of Dwayne. With Victor out, we did not have to double-down on the post and that gave us more flexibility to pressure their guards. We worked the clock down to 4:46 before we shot the ball. White Shoes missed a running layup, but Bubba got the offensive rebound and passed out to Smooth, who quickly raised his hand with only four fingers showing. We now worked the ball until 3:52 showed on the clock before taking a shot. Smooth drew a foul this time. When he made both ends of the one and one, it gave us our first lead, 59-58, almost 37 minutes in. State came down the floor determined to score, which they did, but not before using close to a minute off the clock. Passing inbounds at 2:46, we milked it down again and shot the ball with 1:56 remaining, but missed and State rebounded.

Michigan State called a time-out. Although it could be argued that it didn't look good for us, as they had the lead and the ball, this is really the situation that we had played for from the start: We wanted a close game with a chance to win at the end. Michigan State certainly would have preferred to be ahead by a big score. We were in our element, and not frustrated at all. With their one-point lead, they went into their stall game and we responded with what we call Lightning, which was an all-out double-team with a safety under the basket to draw the charge. I inserted Jet One into the game because of his speed and quickness and we went with five guards. But our dogged defense was using too much time on the clock, and when it got down to 35 seconds to play, I started yelling *"Foul now!"*

The guys didn't hear me though, and with less than 10 seconds to go, a Spartan drove toward the basket, attempting the easy layup and the three-point outright win. The clock read seven seconds when Skunk came out of nowhere to block the layup. Not only did he block the shot, he pinned the ball up against the backboard and came down with the rebound. State's player was so angry and frustrated that his shot was blocked that in his frantic reach for the rebound, he knocked Skunk to the floor; the official whistled a foul. That put Skunk on the free-throw line for a one and one at the free throw line with two seconds left and Michigan State clinging to a 60-59 lead. They of course tried the obligatory time-out to see if they could freeze Skunk.

It's hard to know what to say to a player who already knows the game is riding on him with two tiny ticks left on the clock, so you might as well just be yourself. We end every practice by having the players run lines, and each of them has to make free throws or the entire team has to run. It may not be championship game pressure, but this kind of peer pressure may even be more intense. Skunk was always good when he had to be, so I just looked at him and said, "One and one, the team runs if you miss." He and the guys all laughed and I felt good about him going to the line.

The first free throw hit the front of the rim, and caromed to the backboard and bounced back into the basket. The crowd went crazy. The score was 60-60, with those same two ticks left on the clock. Skunk's second free throw hit the back of the rim and came off the goal long. But Big Time somehow got inside position and jumped his highest; he couldn't control the ball for a rebound but instead made a mid-air slap at it back toward the goal. The ball hit the front rim, bounced to the backboard, back to the rim and circled around the goal as the buzzer rang, the lights came on: The ball dropped through the net. NWS 62, Michigan State 60.

The crowd went bananas. People I'd never seen before in my life rushed the court, screaming and yelling for all they were worth, "Go NWS Go!" I was just shell-shocked. I came out of a haze in the locker room with Athletic Director Jones beaming into my face, his head shaking, wondering how we were doing what we were doing. I didn't know any better than he did, but I certainly was enjoying the ride.

We were in the Sweet Sixteen and needless to say, we were excited. Our confidence in each other was at an extreme high and the players had bonded like no other team I have ever coached. Even the players who had a problem with me because I had changed so much and made so many player adjustments were enjoying this ride. The biggest reason it took us so long to jell was the fact that I was playing seven new faces and the old faces were not getting to play many minutes. As far as playing time goes, earlier we had gone back and forth with some of the guys from the team the year before and some of the new guys but the chemistry was just not good. Everyone was uneasy and even the freshmen were wondering if it was worth it. Certainly, I did not anticipate the chemistry problem and I really didn't have much of an answer either.

Finally, I got fed up with the griping and bitching one day and told them that we were going to have a game to decide who plays and who does not. "It is time to put up or shut up," I said. I was so confident in the group that I recruited that I let the players returning pick who they wanted on their team. The only rule I had was that they could not pick any player who had any Division One basketball experience. Of course, that limited them from picking any of the new recruits because none had played any competition against NCAA Division one teams. All the new recruits had either played on the high school or junior college level but no division one competition. On one team, you had the newcomers and on the other team, you had last year's group and some holdovers that played the year before. The old guys were not bad and I was a tiny bit concerned. The media made a big deal of this showdown and the guys that played last year were excited about the opportunity to show me up. It was our preseason scrimmage and open to the public. Although this was a gamble for me, the newcomers won easily, beating last year's players in front of about 5,000 spectators 103-55. The complaints from the vets became a rare phenomenon since then.

The West Regional Sweet Sixteen bracket was to be played in Glendale, California, where we were to face Purdue. They had beaten Marquette 66-61 to get to this point. Purdue had a team very similar to ours in that they were not one of the favorites. Actually, Marquette was favored to beat them, but as we had already proved, it just didn't always happen the way the experts predicted. Totally unlike Michigan State, Purdue played an up-tempo game and depended on their guards to do the scoring. They had two big-time guards who could play for anyone. The two were twins, in fact, from South Carolina, called Moe and Doug Adams. Both stood six foot three inches tall, and both were all-American candidates. The team also fielded a front line of two, six foot eight inch guys, each quick and athletic. They backed that up with a young freshman point guard who was a McDonald's all-American at six foot one inch. I decided to have my team run with them as I felt we were as good as they were and I would wait until the final twenty minutes of play to see where we stood, and make any adjustments at that point.

At the start of the Purdue game our confidence from the Michigan State win was something to behold as we came out shooting from the NBA line. And to my surprise, the guys were making everything they shot. The halftime score was 47-40 in favor of North West State University. We were playing so well at that point in the game, I really didn't know what to say except, "Good job," and "Keep on doing what you are doing." It's the kind of speech I hate making because you know that things will change sooner or later but you really can't dwell too much on what might happen, when things are going so well. You have to play the game in the present but a good coach always needs to be prepared for the future better than his opponents are. I was expecting a letdown and, sure enough, we started the second half very flat. Things began spiraling out of control: Our shots were not going in the basket, our defensive intensity was lacking, and all hell was about to break loose. With 17:30 to go in the ball game, and the score now 47-46, I called a time-out. I chewed the starters out with a few choice short words, and threw a fit, meaning that I did nothing to fix the problem other than to release my frustrations. We went back and forth with Purdue, until the 11:05 mark, when I called a time-out again, with the score 60-59 in our favor. Taking into account that we were playing with no shot clock, I put it to the team as simply as I could: We would execute our four-to-score play with the greatest intensity we have ever had. "No one has worked harder for this opportunity than you have and now is the time to do just what we have worked on in practice for at least 1,000 hours. It is your game to win, so just go do it."

Purdue had not been as effective against our four-to-score as Michigan State had, and we just ate the clock, made a few shots, buried our free throws, controlled the clock, and won the game 75-66. The locker room was wild and fun. We were now one game away from the Final Four. I had to pinch myself to make sure it was real. AD Jones made his now customary visit with the huge smile, shaking his head again and wondering how we were doing it. It was really fun to see him have to repeatedly eat his words about me and I was enjoying myself immensely. He had expressed his concern that I could not win big-time games or recruit top-flight players during my interview, and I wasn't about to let him forget it.

Our win over Michigan State had been huge; a victory over a top-ten, nationally ranked team, but it suddenly looked pretty small when Arizona defeated No. 1 seed Connecticut. We all watched the game because it was right after our win over Purdue. Arizona played perfect basketball on the one hand, and if I had to guess, I'd say Connecticut was a little too overconfident. The Wildcats trailed the Huskies the entire game but at the end came up with some huge three-point shots, and then finished the game making eight of eight from the free throw line to seal the victory. It takes just three long hoops to cut a nine-point deficit, and that is exactly what they did. U-Conn wasn't just the No. 1 seed in our bracket, but the third-ranked team in the nation. Their upset loss set the scene for us to play Arizona for the right to advance to the Final Four. Of course, everyone was picking Arizona. That was OK with me; I loved the underdog role. I think the point spread was nine points.

The game was a sellout with over 18,000 fans watching the battle. Our guys were excited and I was as nervous as can be. If anything, we were a little cocky I thought, but some of that just comes with winning. I had a gut feeling about Arizona when I was watching the celebration after they beat Connecticut. I just couldn't see them mounting the same inspired play against us. The situation was so different. I know, and I feel almost every coach who has been in the game for a long time would agree with me, that it is almost impossible to duplicate the fire, the emotion, and the effort two nights running against two different opponents. And things really get dicey when the second game is against a team you are supposed to beat. Players rarely think they've being overconfident; they're just sure of the outcome, they'll tell you. That is when you can almost smell defeat. Anytime the focus is more on the outcome rather than the process, the team simply does not play up to par.

My hunch was right, and Arizona had neither the energy nor the swagger in our game that they had shown against Connecticut. It was a blessing, because my team went into the game tight. I can't explain why, except I guess the pressure does add up over a period of time. So we couldn't get loose, and Arizona's play lacked fire and enthusiasm. Neither team played championship caliber basketball as we both struggled at the line and from the field. Sadly, the offensive struggles were not the result of great defense. At the half, we were trailing by the score of 29-26. White Shoes was blanked, and Big Time had scored just 3 points. Dwayne led the way with 7 points. I had sat the starter's midway into the first half and we got lucky because the bench players came through with 8 points. We were just not playing on all cylinders, but neither was Arizona.

The second half picked up where the first left off. Smooth let fly with an air ball and I thought the fans were going to kill him, and Bubba missed two free throws that did not even come close. I thought to myself, *the end is near.* Arizona was not responding to their coach, who was yelling about how lazily they were playing; he was constantly on them about lack of energy. Of course, they had the lead so why should they worry? It wasn't a very good game and with ten minutes to go, they still held the lead at 44-40. I finally became resigned to the fact that it was going to be a sloppy game to the end. I just quit fighting it, and tried to figure out a way to energize our team. When the Wildcats extended their lead to 49-42 at the eight-minute mark, I called a time-out. I had gotten into the guys' faces already about lack of focus, but now I could see it was really not that; rather it was that they were trying hard not to lose, and that was creating tightness. On the next play, Smooth drew a charge, but the ref called it a block, hitting my guy with the foul. I went crazy toward the official, who was briefly taken by surprise by my reaction; it caught him off-guard. In actuality, the only good team on the floor was the officiating team. They were doing a better job than both sets of players on this particular night. Of course, he had no choice, and I was assessed a technical foul. Our players were shocked; I hadn't been whistled with a "T" all year long. As the Arizona guard shot the technical's, I just looked at our starters and said; "Well, at least I am trying to do something to make it happen right now. What are you doing?"

The Cats made both free throws for a 51-42 lead. When their coach called a time-out, it gave me the opportunity to explain myself to the players. While Arizona was setting up a special play, I told them, "It's not about focus or effort, but instead about you being more concerned with the score at the end of the game rather than playing the game possession by possession." I continued, "You have a few minutes to make something happen. Let's go Black 32 on defense and Pro on offense for two minutes. I want to see you in the paint and not on the damned perimeter hoisting up some fancy three-pointer."

Black defense was a run-and-jump full-court defense and 32 was a triangle-and-two set, a gimmick defense used often just to create confusion for the other team in hopes they'll do more thinking and less playing. Once thinking takes over, paralysis invariably follows in its footsteps. Pro was a simple pick-and-roll offense. I wanted penetration, and movement and action in the paint. We needed to get to the foul line.

As expected, Arizona had drawn up a special play, but it was directed through their best guard, who was being checked one-on-one by Smooth; the Cat guard forced the ball and turned it over. We went down the court; White Shoes penetrated and made a basket as they fouled him. On the next possession, Arizona came down and tried to force the ball inside, but we had it covered with one player in front and one behind. Their pass was deflected and Big Time came up with the steal, following with a perfect pass to Smooth for an uncontested layup. Not letting up at all following the flurry of points, Big Time stole the ensuing inbounds pass, and was fouled hard by Arizona for his trouble. The officials huddled and made what I considered to be the correct call and ruled it an intentional foul. Arizona Head Coach John Roberson went crazy, as did the flagged player. A technical foul was added against the player, and the official told John to sit down. Big Time made the one-and-one nice and easy. White Shoes usually shoots our technical free throws but since Big Time was there at the line, and had his rhythm, I pointed toward him. He smiled, turned, and made both without hesitation. Due to the intentional foul, we retained possession, and we inbounded the ball too, but not before I called out a special play designed just for Big Time to score. We called the play (BT). We threw the ball in play, set a staggered double screen for him on the baseline so he could get open sprinting to the other side of the court. The inbounds pass went to Smooth; who dribbled to the other side, and then, nearly out of bounds, he fed Big Time cutting off the screens we had set. No sooner had the big guy received the pass from Smooth than he hit nothing but the bottom of the net. We now had our first lead of the game at 53-51 with 5:48 to go. We had come out of our shell and you could see the life on the faces of our players.

In a state of shock, Arizona called time-out, trying to regroup. At this stoppage in play, I told our players we would play the remainder of the game in two-minute sessions. The idea was to adjust our play according to what happened in each session. Each two-minute interval was like a game within itself. This helped us stay more focused on the game instead of the end result. We changed back to 10 TT on defense and also to our four-to-score on offense. The "10" referred to an all-out man-to-man defense, while "TT" stood for tough team. It was just a figure of speech, really, but the concept was that each player would get tough on defense for the good of the team. It was not a special strategy at all, but each player was handed a certain responsibility, and they knew it. They had to be tough, to be responsible for the team, and not to break down, so the team defense held. It couldn't be any more basic: <u>When each team member plays defense for the good of the team, the team becomes that much tougher to beat.</u> Arizona couldn't buy a basket. Responding to our renewed focus their attention to detail quickly sharpened, but they just couldn't score. They were now in a panic and rushing their shots. Our defense was solid now and all we had to do was get the ball and hold it.

At our next possession, the clock stood at 5:30 and by the time we shot the ball, it was down to 4:47. Bubba was fouled collecting an offensive rebound off a missed shot by Skunk. He made both foul shots, increasing our lead to 55-51. Arizona responded with a special play, one that worked very well; their best player got a wide-open look from the top of the key, but he put up an air ball anyway. It had become one of those nights for Arizona. We got the ball with 4:10 to go and I yelled, "Skip a possession," which meant that we were going to hold the ball for an extra possession before we shot. Next year, the NCAA would be instituting a thirty-five-second shot clock. I was just glad that that was still in the future.

Finally, at 2:55 we let go with a terrible shot, and then we were called for a foul under the basket for pushing from behind, trying to get the offensive rebound. Arizona went to the line but missed the front end of a one-and-one, and we rebounded with 1:43 on the clock. We attempted another shot, but missed it. We moved the score to 57-51 anyway though, because Skunk got another offensive rebound and converted. We felt very good about our chances. Arizona called their final time-out, and came out onto the court with a strong sense of defeat in their eyes. We went back and forth from the free throw line, but we ended up winning the game by the

score of 61-57. We enjoyed yet another celebration in the dressing room.
James Jones came in with nothing but a huge grin on his face. After all,
we were making money for the school and the conference with every win
and every day we stayed alive in the tournament. I think we had already
added somewhere around $1,900,000 to the coffers for the school athletic
department. He was a happy camper, I was a happy camper, and the team
was filled with happy campers. We were going to the Final Four in New
Orleans. Bourbon Street, here we come.

It always seems that when things are going so good, something bad
has to happen to dampen the mood. Two of our players, both guys from
last year's team, spent the night we beat Arizona in jail. Rick Champion
and Ned Fowler had both been starters off and on during the previous
NWS season. They got drunk in a bar downtown somewhere in Glendale
and picked a fight. When they were asked to leave, they made a scene
arguing with the bouncer, and the bartender called the cops, who locked
them up. This establishment, I was told, was a bar located near UCLA and
some UCLA players were also involved. The respective athletic directors
at the two schools got together and talked it over. My first involvement
was through a 2:30 a.m. phone call from AD Jones, and he and I went
down to get the boys out of jail. When we got there, we discovered that
the two sets of parents had already bailed the boys out and taken them to
their hotel in town.

Rick was a skinny six foot two inch white kid from Shaw, Oklahoma,
a nice enough kid and a very good basketball player. As a matter of fact,
he was Mr. Basketball for his classification in Oklahoma, which was 2AA.
But he had developed a bad habit of drinking with his frat brothers and
he had been in trouble with the dean several times. On one occasion in
particular I stood up for him when the dean wanted to kick him out of
school. Once the authorities caught both Rick and Ned with alcohol in
the dorm, the dean was tired of giving him more chances to get his act
together. Rick promised me he would not touch the stuff again and he
convinced me to give him a second chance. I punished him with extra
drills and some running, and then I forgave him and welcomed him back
on the team.

Ned, however, was a totally different case. A black kid who stood about six foot three inches tall, he was very athletic and was good enough to play and start on our team. His attitude was poor, though, and it cost him a lot of playing time. He was not a team player in any sense. He hailed from Dallas and, unfortunately, he was a spoiled brat. A classic prima donna, Ned quite simply thought he was better than he was. He thought he was better than everyone else, and he set himself apart; he was not liked by his teammates except for Rick. He swore I had cheated him out of a pro career and his family had threatened a lawsuit against me because they felt the same way. Ned was a major irritant in my life. I was just trying to make it until the end of basketball season when I would be able to dismiss him from the team. He would not attend class, and he was the most difficult player to deal with on our team. Ned was in trouble with the dean because he had cut so many classes, and he had been put on disciplinary suspension because of his drinking and because of his attitude on campus. Both boys had already received their last warning from me a month before when they were caught in the dorm with girls and alcohol, both of which are prohibited.

I met with the AD and school president for breakfast later that morning. Both officials felt strongly that a statement from me needed to be issued to the press addressing what had taken place. Broadcasters and media people already knew about it, and everyone was watching to see what I was going to do. I made it very clear to my bosses that I was very upset with Rick and Ned and that I had written records and backup documenting their repeated bad behavior. Both the AD and the president encouraged me and told me to work whatever I decided through the dean. I talked the situation over with all of our coaches, and asked each of them what they felt we should do. To a man, they all believed we owed neither player anything; we had all bent over backwards to just maintain their status as students and team members. We went back and forth between a complete suspension and a partial one. There was a track record and some precedent for such an action, as we had already had to suspend Skunk early that year for drinking and for causing property damage. We suspended him for three weeks and put him to work in the cafeteria both as a punishment and so he could earn the money to fix what he had broken. We all reluctantly agreed that we would do the same with Rick and Ned even though they had been in trouble before. On the flight back to Amarillo, I discussed the suspensions with both students at length, explaining the punishment and the reason for it. Neither had much to say, but I knew this would not be the end of the story.

I arrived in Amarillo, Texas to find two phone calls awaiting me, one from each set of parents; they weren't pleasant calls. I was painted as the villain in all of this, and how dare I pick on their son[s]. Ned was really the first black kid that I had a hard time dealing with. I found in my years of coaching on the college level, if anything, black parents were more supportive of the coach in difficult times than their white counterparts, particularly if you gave them a heads-up in advance that trouble was brewing. But if you had to confront them after the fact, out of the blue, then no, they were very difficult to handle. I cannot tell you how many preliminary calls I have made to a black parent as a precaution, only to see the young man turn it around and get his act together. One time when I was coaching at a junior college, I called the mom of one of my black players and told her that her son was partying too much and spending too much time with his white girlfriend. Mother and son were in my office the next day, with her dragging him in by the ear and making him apologize to me.

Rick, on the other hand, was just a spoiled middle class white student, a good kid inside who was just feeling his frustrations with a lost season and the reality that he was really not as good a player as he thought he was. His parents were not as angry or upset with me as Ned's parents were, but they were unhappy about what had happened to the boys. On Tuesday morning, the AD was back in my office and, taking a seat, confronted me with a glum look on his face that I did not like.

"Coach, I have some bad news for you that you aren't going to like. The Champions have filed an injunction for Rick and Ned to be reinstated back on the team."

I just looked at him for a long time and finally replied, "So what does that mean to us?"

"It looks like they will get their wish because I talked to the judge in his chambers this morning. There is nothing we can do about it because it is the law. Their argument is that going to New Orleans for the Championship is an once-in-a-lifetime event and keeping them from going would just create undue damage to the young boys in terms of their self-esteem and egos."

Of course, I was furious, and starting yelling, "What about my ego, what about my self-esteem, what about the team's ego, what about the school's reputation, much less my reputation?"

He said, "Calm down and do not think for one minute that I do not understand the way you feel. We will support you 100 percent in this, I guarantee it."

"Do I have to play them or just let them rejoin the team?"

"No, you do not have to play them. Who plays will be totally up to you."

I gave him a hard look, and replied, "The press is going to have a field day with this, and you know it."

"Let me handle the press."

I said, "You'd better, because if I have to deal with them I will tell them the whole truth."

"Now coach, we have to be careful how we handle this because we could be facing another suit from the Fowlers."

I agreed to let him handle the press and I agreed that I would allow them back on the team but I did not promise anything other than that.

We took more of a beating from the New Orleans press about Rick and Ned than we did from the local media. In small headlines, and below in small dark print, there was an article, all slanted from the players' side. It read something like this:

It seems as though North West State University Head Basketball Coach Ron Young has put winning ahead of character. Judge for yourself, but it seems to me that when players get in a brawl in a bar and are thrown in jail, a strong statement should be made by the coach. As far as we can tell the only thing these two young men missed was one day of practice last week. Even the pros have better discipline than that.

I read the article and my blood pressure went sky-high again, so I stepped outside and felt the nice cool New Orleans breeze. That will take your breath away and make you forget lots of things. What I couldn't forget, however, was the upcoming competition. Louisville had beaten Pittsburgh 78-76 to reach the Final Four. Louisville was by far the better team, but Pittsburgh battled them to a standstill and hung around until finally Louisville put the game on ice with excellent ball handling and perfect free throw shooting in the last two minutes. Anytime I became impressed with a lot of talent, all I had to do was to look at Louisville. That was one talented team. Every player was an outstanding athlete who could run, jump, and shoot. They were as well-coached as any team I have ever seen and I couldn't find a weakness in anything they did. They were huge, fielding players who stood 6'10", 6'8", 6'7", and 6'6", with a point guard who measured in at 6'3". They scored an average of 92.5 points per game, and I felt sure the only way we would have a chance at beating them would be to take the air out of the ball. We were not going to throw in the towel by any means, but it was only smart to realize that our chances to win the next game were just two: slim and none. We spent the whole week working on special plays from out of our four-to-score set meant to succeed against zone traps and man-to-man pressure. If Louisville had any weakness at all, it was the fact that they did not shoot as well from three-point range as some other teams we had played. The best outside shooter was the point guard but he had a habit of looking to pass first and shoot second. That would give us time to adjust to his shot. The other two guards, both huge for guys playing that position, were hoisting up these bombs at a twenty-nine percent clip. With that in mind, we worked all week long at trying to make players shoot over us, at not playing so aggressively on defense, but rather just trying to keep our man between their guys and the basket.

One thing that I noticed all week long was a different attitude among our players. They were not uptight about anything. Not the uproar over the barroom fight, not the media distractions, not the excitement of the Final Four: It seemed like none of it was getting to them. I had never seen them so relaxed, yet determined and enthused about playing basketball. In workouts this week, the intensity level was so high that I had to calm them down several times. Usually I am on them about being too lackadaisical in practice. Even in the pregame warm-up before the tip-off, I noticed a level of confidence that I admired and appreciated. It was real: My guys really thought they were every bit as good as Louisville. I certainly wasn't going to tell them anything different.

The opening tip was controlled by Bubba, which is usually a good sign. It did not take long to know I was right, as White Shoes drove the lane, pulled up for a short jumper and hit nothing but the net. It was like Louisville was not on the court. Now the real test came as Louisville had the ball for the first time. They quickly moved the ball from side to side and passed the ball inside to one of their posts. He passed it back outside for a wide-open three-pointer. Big Time came out from the paint to contest the shot just enough to force the miss, Skunk rebounded, and hit Smooth for a three-point shot from the corner in transition. His shot hit the rim, but he got a good bounce and it fell in. We had an early 5-0 lead. This was our 36th game together and I had never seen this group so relaxed, yet so intense. At the half, we were up by 45-40 and not a bit timid about things. Going into the break, I just knew that I wanted to keep on trucking. I wasn't about to try to fix anything, as it showed any sign of being broke. "Basketball is the most over-coached sport in America," I heard Bobby Knight say that once at a clinic, and the older I become the more I understood what he meant. All I did at this halftime was to be a cheerleader and compliment each player on what they had done so well. The positive feelings were contagious as each player started telling each other how well they'd done, slapping each other on the back and so on.

We came out from the half fired up and ready to continue. So did Louisville because they came right at us to start the second half. Their outside jump shots strategy was shelved as they started attacking the basket. Bubba got into foul trouble early and sitting him for a bit hurt us somewhat, but "D" and Skunk were holding their own, playing with flair, quickness, and determination. At the 10-minute mark the score was tied 65-65. Both teams were playing great basketball and neither team was holding anything back. Anytime there was a loose ball, you would see five or six guys going after it. On any missed free throw, the blocking out was like two tanks trying to go through one another. The defense was so aggressive that the officials could not decide who was gaining advantage and who was not, and pretty much let them play. It was like two championship fighters battling it out to the very end hoping to gain an edge somewhere.

With two minutes to go, Louisville finally got an 83-80 lead and the ball. We went to our trapping defense but they scored, giving them an 85-80 lead with 1:40 left on the clock. I called a time-out as the Louisville fans started in with, "It's over--on to the final four!" and continued it throughout the break: "It's over--on to the final four!" It was so loud I had a hard time communicating to our players what I wanted done, and that was from a couple of feet away. We inbounded and quickly went to work. By now Bubba was back in the game and he set a high screen for Smooth out around the three-point arc. Usually Bubba would roll to the basket but this time I had explained to him that I wanted him to pop out and knock that shot down. He grinned and he did just like I wrote it up, which doesn't happen very often. He drained the shot, and with 1:12 to go we had closed the Louisville lead to 85-83. They went into their delay game and we fouled early, which is what I wanted if we couldn't manage a quick steal. Taking the free throw line, the Louisville guard made one of two, moving them ahead by 86-83. We now had the ball but that incessant "It's over--on to the final four!" was deafening. I'm sure our fans must have been cheering too, but we couldn't hear them, or at least I couldn't. With 48 seconds left Smooth passed the ball inside to Bubba, but he missed his shot and they rebounded. We fouled right away, and I called time again. The idea was to try to ice the shooter, but also make sure everyone knew the plan for the next two possessions. Putting our best offensive players on the floor, I hoped we could score the next time we had the ball, starting with another special play for Bubba again. Louisville canned both free throws, which gave them an 88-83 lead with 40 seconds to play.

We quickly ran the floor to set up the same pick and roll, the same step back for Bubba, designed to get the same shot, but this time, it was a fake. Bubba received a back screen from Skunk, and then went in for an alley-oop dunk, thundering the ball through the hole and getting fouled in the process. *Now*, I could hear *our* fans go crazy. And our bench was whooping it up too. Bubba missed the free throw and the score was 88-85, Louisville leading with 22 seconds left in the game.

We employed our full-court black press, but Louisville handled it well, except they got in a hurry and mishandled the ball. Still, they recovered the ball under the basket, and their best guard fired at the basket. But he missed both the shot and, in his effort to rebound the ball, committed a fouled going over Dwayne's back. Before "D" got to the line, Louisville called for time. Down by three, I realized the two free throws wouldn't get us even and time was running out. This was the time for prayer, but that would not help right now, so I just settled on a smile and a vote of confidence toward "D". One thing for sure, we acted like we knew what to do. After all, we'd been making big plays throughout this run. Maybe we were bulletproof after all. And "D" missed the second shot, all right, but not until after he missed the first too, and things were looking bleak when they rebounded and followed with a successful outlet pass. But Smooth came through again; he deflected the outlet pass and stole the ball putting up an unbalanced shot with no time left from the three point line. He hit the board, and the ball banked into the basket. If I live to be 100, I don't believe I'll ever hear that loud a roar from a crowd again. You just have to take a breath to get your bearings as you wonder just what really happened. With the score apparently tied at 88-88 we were thinking overtime. The officials did not have reliable replay in those days, so they conferred with the timekeeper, and the call on the floor stood: tie game, heading for OT.

Of course, Louisville shot out of the gate in the overtime too, running off the first five points of the extra session. We were trailing 94-89 with 3:21 left when we finally scored our first basket, a tip-in by Big Time that closed it to 94-91. But Louisville answered with an open three-pointer, 97-91. Here it came again: "It's over--on to the final four! It's over--on to the final four!" I was beginning to think they had a point, but as long as there was time on that clock, we had a chance. Pushing aside any doubts, I began to become convinced that we were destined to play in the championship game.

With 2:35 left on the clock Smooth drove the lane and was hacked on the forearm. He made the front end of the one-and-one, but missed the second one, with Louisville grabbing the rebound. With a 97-92 lead, they were content to stall for the last 2:20. After they worked some time off the clock, we fouled going after a loose ball. The two foul shots ballooned the lead to 99-92 with 1:50 to go, and the crowd for Louisville went even crazier now, if that was possible, screaming the same chant at the tops of their lungs. We had heard about as much of that refrain as we could stand, but somewhere, somehow, someone was going to have to make some great plays or it was over. The time-out I called was to settle everyone down, but also to make them realize that this game was far from over. Time was the key, and we had enough of it. "Forget that the clock reads minutes at all," I told them. "Focus on the seconds. Go out there and outplay them for the next 50 seconds. I demanded urgent play, driven play, from this point on," I continued, "nothing but sprints and quick moves."

My guys went straight to work, as Smooth missed a three-point attempt, but Bubba claimed the offensive board and put it back in. With 40 seconds left and Louisville holding a 98-94 lead, we threw our "All hell broke loose" defense at them. The sudden change in tempo startled Louisville, and they walked with twenty-five seconds remaining. But they pressed us on the inbounds pass, which caught us off-guard; we quickly turned it over, and Louisville had the ball and the lead just 18 ticks from the end. I was relieved when the officials whistled a Louisville time-out. I thought we had a chance to cause a turnover before the clock resumed even. Barring that, I told the players to go after the ball aggressively because a foul was needed quickly if we failed to get the ball on a steal.

I have spent many years trying to come up with the right thing to do under all kinds of circumstances, but I've learned you just cannot predict what is actually going to happen when play resumes. As if validating what I was thinking, a foul was called as they set up to throw the ball in. There was uncertainty among all the players, but the side official demonstrated that Smooth had drawn an offensive foul while jockeying for position, and he would be going to the line. Smooth had lots of great basketball qualities but shooting free throws was the weakest part of his game. Still, he knocked both shots down to narrow the Louisville lead to 98-96. They had the ball, the lead with 18 seconds to go, which pretty much dictated our strategy: We had to foul them as soon as the ball was thrown in, which we did. With 12 seconds left, their player made both, allowing Louisville to regain a four-point bulge at 100-96. Sometimes in a game like this, a litany of things happen that are so unpredictable that it is hard to remember one from the other but what followed was so outstanding that I do not think I will ever forget it. With time running out and players knocking each other down scrambling after a loose ball created by a Louisville deflection, White Shoes snatched up the ball and heaved a three pointer, draining it with two seconds to go. All I can remember on the play is that he was falling to the floor as he let it fly from a bump he had received while gathering it in. The foul was clear-cut and once the ref made it official with his whistle, we were down 100-99 with a free throw to come. White Shoes calmly arced in the shot, sending the two teams to a second overtime session with a 100-100 score.

The second set of extra play was just a true gut check, the kind we had survived so many times, and I guess we just outlasted them, as we jumped on Louisville and scored six quick points for a 106-100 lead. That we were back in our four-to-score set from that point spelled Louisville's fate. We milked the clock down on each possession, and since it was just a five-minute period, we retained complete control. We won the extended affair 110-105 to advance to the Championship game of the Final Four. Wow!

Making it to the final game of the Final Four was the most exciting moment I have ever experienced. *Nothing will be the same in my life from this point on*, I thought. The high was something that you dream about as a kid, winning the game on a last-second basket, catching a touchdown pass with no time left on the clock to win it all. The best part is that you get to share this excitement with so many friends and family. Quite simply, everyone was in seventh heaven, with huge grins on all their faces; our collective eyes shone like it was the Fourth of July.

It was Saturday night and before I released the players to family and friends, I did give them a short reminder about being a good example for North West State University and what our expectations were for Sunday.

I gave each player a schedule of events with times and so forth. Since they were with family I tried not to worry about them but the many things that can go wrong off the court were always in the back of my mind. I then went to the lobby and met with over fifty friends and family to greet and thank them for coming. That celebration took about two hours and it was now quite late. Jennifer and the girls were already in bed and I was headed to the room when someone grabbed my arm and jerked me away from the crowd, which was now down to about twenty people.

To my delight, it was Conrad Hogan and Everett Smith, two young guys who had played for me at Henderson Junior College. They did not have to drive very far because they lived in New Orleans. It was an unexpected surprise and I was happy to see them. Conrad was a six foot five inch, strong and thick guard-forward type young man that I recruited from this city, while Everett, though also six foot five was just the opposite, skinny, unsubstantial, lacking in brute strength, and also from New Orleans. Conrad said, "Coach, you can coach Talent now?" We both smiled and he continued, "I saw several big-time athletes on the floor tonight and North West State University had their share."

All this time Everett was smiling and shaking his head, sharing my joy. I just hugged them and said, "You guys are right and only you two know how I learned to coach talent. I owe everything to you two, and other guys like you, two rag knots from the flats of New Orleans who taught me not to be scared to work with talent, and taught me how to win big. I owe you guys." We laughed and started talking about the Henderson days.

The higher the level of play, the greater the talent must be. That is not just something that I made up but a fact that all coaches who have won big have come to understand. You cannot win the big game if you do not have the talent to get the job done when the game is on the line. Talent is the ability to run, jump, catch, move quickly, and overpower an opponent. Size is just another form of talent. Skill is the ability to shoot, to handle the ball, dribble it, and pass it to a teammate. You can have a great team that plays well but it depends on the level of your competition whether you can win big or not. The higher the level of competition, the higher the level of talent and skill that is required.

My early years in coaching were spent on the high school level. I was so naïve that nothing mattered to me at that age. I just loved coaching and being around the players, trying to develop each one to his maximum. When I started coaching in college, I still did it for the game and the players, but I was starting to understand what having great players meant to a college team. At first, I did not really switch my focus to recruiting talent over other aspects of the game. I got lucky and more of less by accident managed to recruit some very promising players without going very far out of my way. I learned that it takes a different skill to handle and coach a big-time athlete rather than average players with some skills and a desire to be the best they can be. Also, I learned and studied those coaches who succeeded handling and relating to front-line talent, and those who failed to. The toughest job as a college coach is handling and coaching the exceptional players, the ones who can turn the game around.

When I first got my start in the business, it was the weakest aspect of my college coaching. I didn't want to talk about it but I knew deep down, I had a problem. One of your first clues is to watch a college coach and notice who he or she recruits. The typical excuse for avoiding the truly special athletes is, "It will cost us too much," or "I will be wasting my time," or "They will never adapt to my coaching style." There are other excuses but the bottom line is that the coach does not want to deal with the rejection he/she fears. I had lots of experience by the time I got to Henderson, but I had only recruited six relatively big-time players, and had just a modicum of success with just three of them.

When I arrived at Permian High School I learned what a real program was and that experience helped me everywhere I have been ever since. I knew what I expected and wanted from the way I had things set up, and then I learned how to adapt my program to whatever situation I came into contact with. When I went to Panhandle Baptist, I learned how to win games. It was something that just happened but it was an experience that helped me going forward. You can say you are learning by watching or being an assistant coach but the real training happens when you are the one making the calls and you are the one who has the responsibility. That is what I finally learned, and it was to my advantage. But what I still had was a deep-down fear of big-time talent and how it blended with my need to control every situation. I knew if I was ever going to be successful, I had to change. But I also realized that that is easier said than done.

TWELVE

When I went to Henderson College in Kilgore, Texas it was nothing but rebellion toward Panhandle Baptist University in Plainview. Little did I know that this move was going to be the final chapter of my learning curve to prepare me for "The Big Dance." All the girls loved living in Plainview and none of us were really excited about living in East Texas again. Jennifer hated humidity, heat, and insects. I felt guilty because this move was created because I could not deal with the Panhandle Baptist Administration. It was the first time in my life that I was leaving a place with hard feelings. After I resigned from Panhandle Baptist my assistant coach resigned, then two other coaches resigned. Panhandle fired the primary administrator overseeing the athletic program. I might have stayed if they had done that earlier, but it was too late. We were headed to Kilgore, home of Henderson Junior College and I was determined to make the best of it. Feeling guilty as I did, the first thing I tried to do was make-up with my family.

I knew only time would repair those feelings but we needed something to get excited about so I just decided that we would buy the neatest house money could buy. We purchased our 9th house in Kilgore. It was a four bedroom, 2½ baths, a huge fireplace, sunken living room, across from a small pond with more than fifty pine trees surrounding the house. It was a dream home and all of us were proud and it was isolated in a rural area away from city life.

Jennifer and Renee left early to get the house ready for us to move our furniture in a rented moving van. Ann and Nicole stayed with me to help with moving the furniture and the clean-up detail. I became angry with both of them because they were not being much help. They are so spoiled; "I was thinking" as I would command an order to "go do that and go do this". Needless to say, they were not happy when it came time to leave in the moving van. The last thing I had to do was make a place for Candy, our dog. Candy was a full grown large gentle German shepherd. I fixed a spot in the back of the moving van just for her, but worried about the heat since it was a warm June day. At any rate, we were headed for Kilgore, which was a nine hour drive. We were moving along when I noticed a storm headed our direction. Storms in the Texas Panhandle area can be very dangerous and this storm was a scary, dark, black one coming right toward us. I made the decision to stop and get a motel in the next city, which was Seymour. From experience I knew there was a small cabin-like motel outside the city limits of Seymour, kind of like the Bates Motel in the movie "Psycho". Suddenly like a bomb, the storm hit and it started raining and hailing hard. I pulled up to the office and ran into the building and got us a room. I sprinted back to the van and we drove on a dirt road to our cabin. Candy had been in the back for almost four hours and I knew she needed to get out and go to the bathroom.

As soon as the rain eased up, I went inside the motel and opened up the door for the girls to go into the motel. It started raining hard again, and since I was already wet, I when to the back of the moving van and opened the back door. Candy jumped out and I put a leash on her. I took her to the front of the motel room out of the rain. I told the girls to watch Candy while I got our overnight gear into the motel. All this time it was raining and all of a sudden, lightning came out of the sky; thunder as loud as a train-wreck and Candy broke away from the girls. Running and jumping in the mud and rain, the girls chased Candy while I was yelling at Candy first and the girls second. Candy was now full of mud and then she sprinted back to the motel room, jumping on the beds and all over the room. Mud was everywhere including on me, Ann and Nicole. We were all tired and I let everyone in arms distance know exactly how angry I was. I made the girls take Candy into the shower and clean her and themselves.

Then I made them go get some extra towels. Nicole was scared to walk to the main office and so I had Ann go get the towels. By that time if Nicole or Ann had a gun, I would have been dead. They were very angry with me. The only one who was happy was Candy. After using all our towels on Candy, we did not have enough towels to dry ourselves, and the anger started over again. It was clear to me that the teams were me and Candy vs. Ann and Nicole. Fortunately for me, I had the keys to the van, and the money so Candy and I won.

That night, it stormed all night long but it did not bother anyone, except Candy who was locked in the bathroom. The next morning, I got the girls up early before sunrise and off we went to Kilgore. It wasn't until six weeks later when the girls stated making friends, we joined the First Presbyterian Church, our life in our house was back to normal, before they forgave me.

Henderson College had an old school tradition. They had won the national championship in men's basketball in the mid-fifties. They were always in the hunt for the championship up until the last ten years. Since then, Henderson had not had a winning season and had lost their competitive edge in the conference. Of course, that edge was their tradition. Kilgore was an old oil town and once had a lot of money. The facilities were average, but not in comparison with the facilities in the in the Western Junior College Athletic Conference. Junior college basketball was something that the community in Kilgore understood. People could talk about the players coming back, the teams in the conference and the coaches in the conference. It was important to the town and the community that Henderson Junior College has a good basketball team. Henderson College had football, track and women's and men's basketball. They had the famous Rangerettes and an athletic booster club.

It was totally different than Permian Basin College. Henderson College would have a pep rally and appreciation days. The budget was better than Permian Basin College, and I had a large office, with an unlimited long distance phone service. I really was glad that we had football because I liked it but I discovered another advantage in having football. When trouble on campus occurred, the administration couldn't just turn to the basketball team, they also had to look at the football team. Another thing I liked about having football is that it gave our guys something to do on Saturday night.

When it came to championships Henderson had been there before and wanted to be there again. As I always do, I had to figure out why Henderson had fallen on bad times in men's basketball. One, the talent level was down. Compared to Panhandle Baptist or Permian Basin College, the level of talent did not measure up. That was a puzzle to me because East and South Texas was full of talent right on your front door. Dallas was about a 1½ hours, Houston 3 hours, Shreveport 1 hour and New Orleans 4½ hours. That was a piece of cake compared to traveling in the West Texas area. Second, there seemed to be a strong political fight going on between the president of the college and the president of the booster club. Three, the faculty overall and most all of the community were prejudiced about black athletes and their role in the academic arena. Four, the other teams in the conference faced the same problems but just had more talent.

From my viewpoint East Texas was the opposite from West Texas concerning black athletes. I felt I was in old Mississippi. An example of what I am talking about was when I got into a recruiting war over a black player that was 'All-East Texas' out of high school. He called and wanted to transfer to Henderson Junior College from a Division one school in Mississippi. He was unhappy with certain situations, all related to being married. I did my homework and found out that he was the real deal as a basketball player. The reason that he wanted to transfer was because his wife was about to have a baby and they wanted to be close to their home at Longview. Longview was about ten miles from Kilgore. He was a super guy and I liked him a lot. I told him after checking on grades, attitude and all the things that I felt were important, I would take him. I will never forget what he said. "Coach, you will not be able to find a place for us to live in East Texas, but I will come if you can." I laughed inside because I thought, this kid doesn't know me! I started working on this project as soon as I hung the phone up and started inquiring about places to live that were nice and decent. After three weeks of trying to find him a place to live, I found out, he was right. People would always be very nice and thoughtful concerning my wanting to find a place for an athlete to live but when I would tell them that he was black, they would change their mind. Their common answer was "I am sorry but we just can't allow that in this neighborhood." I was shocked and mad. Finally, I had to tell him to go elsewhere and I recommended Dallas Baptist or West Texas State. Two weeks later, he called and thanked me for helping him get a scholarship and a place for his wife at Dallas Baptist. They had married housing and they took care of him and his wife.

I loved East Texas when it comes to recruiting. The coaches in the Eastern Conference would get angry with me but the truth of the matter; they are spoiled by their location. They aren't lazy, but just spoiled with recruiting being so much easier. I was in hog heaven as athletes were everywhere and all you had to do was work at recruiting and you would get someone, even if you were a terrible recruiter. I was late in the recruiting process and pulled in some athletes that I was recruiting in North Texas, but hit pay-dirt when I recruited Conrad Hogan's, a six-foot-five player that was not happy with the division one offers he had and wanted to try and go bigger. To this very day, Conrad remains as one of my favorites. He was one of a kind from the standpoint of character, poise, intelligence, and loyalty and I forgot, he could play basketball. Conrad was from New Orleans and with his help; I recruited two other guys from New Orleans and one from Shreveport.

We had a first good year. I usually struggle with my first year but the New Orleans guys kept me on target and we won more than we lost by a large margin. We made the play-offs but were defeated by East Texas College out of Paris, Texas in the first round by 15 points. I was upset, hurt and was wondering what was wrong with me. I could not figure why when my teams go to the play-offs, we can't finish it off. One day in the spring, I was in my office when Conrad Hogan and Everett Smith came by to visit with me about recruiting. We talked about the year we had and about the teams coming back, the most talented players and so forth. We had a really good honest talk and then Conrad got the courage to ask me if we were going to play the slow down game again next year. We had to spread the court out to win most of our games. We ran what I called 4 high [which was the same as four-to-score] and the games that we could win were usually low scoring games. I simply broke down and told them, "I did not want to do that again but I ask both of you, how do we win if we don't slow the other team down?" Conrad said in a low tone of voice, "Coach, it's simple, recruit better players." They both went on talking at the same time. "Coach, the players that you recruit are good players and they are good enough to compete in league play and maybe the play-offs but they are not good enough to get us past the playoffs and to another level of play." I knew they were right; finally I broke down and told them my story and my attitude about Big Time players. I told them about the Big Time players I had coached and how much I hated coaching most of them. I was impressed with their attitude as they listened to me and my complaints about the Big Time players. I was afraid I could not coach that kind of player and I knew the challenges that went with that kind of athlete or at least I thought I knew. Conrad said to me, "Coach, we understand what you are talking about and both of us want you to recruit better players. We will make a commitment to help you recruit and help you handle the players that you recruit. Not all Big Time players are the same." From that point on, I made a deal with those two guys, that with their help and the others on the team. I would recruit better players. The deal was that we were going to get better players and I would let them play, and not slow the game down. We made a pact and set up a game plan. Every Wednesday and Sunday night from 6:00pm till 11:00pm, we would meet in the coaches' office and start making calls to players that we felt could lead us to a national championship.

We had drug problems at Henderson College just like the other place I had been but it was covered up by everyone and no one would admit it. I knew if I could keep my guys straight, we could be conference contenders. I made up my mind that I was going to do something about our problem. I read enough to learn that Jimmy Button, the Head Basketball Coach at Arkansas had a drug program that the university installed concerning substance abuse and how to control it on a college campus. So, I went to the University of Arkansas and found out what they were doing. I liked what I found out and came right back to Henderson College and met with our athletic director. I told him what I wanted to do. He met with the president of the college and we all had a meeting. I was excited with how far this had gone, but after the meeting, I was disappointed. The administration at Henderson concluded that they did not have a drug problem, could not afford drug testing nor would they support it. The administration was clueless to what I was trying to do even though I explained it. Drug testing is not just about catching people that abuse drugs but more about providing athletes an excuse to say no. I was not happy with the attitude of the administration so I came back with my own game plan. I would pay for and administrate the tests and do whatever it took to keep my players clean. They came back and told me that I could do that but if it backfired, they would take no responsibility for my actions. My attitude was that I was looking for a job when I got this job so I continued with my plan.

To make the money for the tests, I conducted a women's and men's basketball camp. I made good money because most coaches did not give camps in those days. My brother came up to Henderson and helped me and we had a very successful camp.

That was just the start, and with the help of the players returning, we recruited two six-foot-nine players, Gene Adams and Nathan Nash, both from Louisiana, two six-foot-seven players from Louisiana who were big time athletes, two six-foot guards from Mississippi that were better than any guard coming back. Then I stole six-foot-six post from East Texas who was a blue chip player with poor grades. Please do not forget that I had three starters back from a playoff team to go with this. To be honest in my opinion, I had the best recruiting class of any junior college in Texas. I had too much talent but knew once I started drug testing, some were going to have to leave. The funny thing about this recruiting class was that I told them about everything up front and the guys on the team were up front about everything, so it was not like they did not know what was going to happen.

It would be a normal day for us to have ten to fifteen college recruiters in during our off season workouts. After all, we had four future NBA players. It was amazing, and I really got to know so many college coaches.

Of course, they all wanted to wine and dine me as I was the key to getting the information they needed to recruit our players.

The first day of official practice we put our practice gear on and everyone started shooting. I came on the court and told them to put the basketballs on the rack because today was the first day of drug testing and I was going to handle it myself. I would call three at a time and give them a test tube to pee in. I would go to the bathroom with them and watch them pee. They would give me the sample tube and I would place it in a container provider by the hospital which I had already contacted concerning this procedure. It went fine except I had three that said that they could not pee. I told them fine, that I would be there all day and all night if needed. After a long time of bluffing, they gave in and pissed. I told all of them that we would have another test the next month but I would not tell them when.

I missed the entire day of workout but from then on, I did have their attention. I paid for the results and everything from the basketball camp money without the support of the administration. The same three that had a hard time pissing, all turned up positive. I wasn't easy on any of the three and two quit. The third was Gene Adams, one of the outstanding athletes we recruited. He was very sure of himself, almost to the point of being disrespectful. He was cocky and acted as though he did not care until I said that I was going to tell his grandmother about the results. He went crazy, cried, dropped to his knees and begged me not to tell her. He said that it would kill his soul and her soul if she found out. I told him that I would not tell her unless he tested positive again. I believe to this day that Gene became one of the best players in the nation at that point in time.

Now, the next big issue was getting two guys past the GED. Neither graduated from high school because of bad grades, but they were not dumb. They were just not motivated and very immature. Both were very sensitive and the instructors at the education center were very prejudiced in their approach to learning. They had black people figured as dumb and did not really care to work with them. I asked Jennifer to work with them. After all, she got me by the English usage test in graduate school. Jennifer worked with both of them for two weeks and they both passed all parts of the GED.

One night during the fall semester, I received a phone call from Robby Andrew's mom. Robby was one of my New Orleans guys and he was special to me. After I finally woke up, I realized who I was talking to and she asked me to do her a favor. It was 3:00am in the morning and I could not imagine what she wanted. She said that she could not get in touch with Robby so that is why she called me. Robby's brother who lived in New Orleans had been executed by a drug gang. It was horrible and I had to go tell Robby. I went straight to his room, woke him up and told him what had happened. He went crazy and it took both me and Conrad Hogan, his roommate to keep him from harm. He tried to beat his head on the wall, and then just went crazy with emotions and finally cried and cried. After the dust cleared, Conrad and Robby told me the entire story. The story is long, but the bottom line was that Robby's brother was a drug dealer. He had very little choice in the matter because that was the only way he knew how to survive and make ends meet. Robby's brother took care of the family and particularly his younger brother. He told Conrad and Robby if he ever caught any one of them with drugs, he would beat them to death. One drug dealer in the family was enough. Robby's brother was totally against his own family being a part of the drug scene, but since he was making good money for the family, he was going to stay with the drug market. Somewhere he made a mistake and it cost him his life.

We finished the year at 29-3, second best record in Kilgore history, won the Conference Championship and made it to the Semi-Finals of the playoffs. I was named 'Coach of the Year' and Gene Adams was named player of the year. We would have won the entire business but Conrad injured his knee and didn't play in the play-offs. He was such a leader and his teammates depended on him for so many things, we just could not continue long without him. I learned that coaching talent in games is easier than coaching over-achievers, if you know what you are doing. It was a thrill to coach those guys and I loved every minute of it. We were defeated in the semi-finals but it was not due to lack of performance or talent. We got beat because of a situation where it was almost impossible for us to win. We beat Rose County the last game of the year at Tyler. It was close and the third time we had beaten them that year. That was on a Saturday night, and then we had to turn around and play them on Wednesday night again in the play-offs on their home court. If they were a bad team, we could have done it but they were very strong and it was hard to overcome that situation.

The season did not come without scars, as I had to handle several situations that occurred off the court. We had our normal suspensions, our ups and downs but our practices were as good as I have ever had and we had the talent to win every game we played. I found out that the key was how I handled everything and the tone in which it was handled. I learned to be more patient and to be a better listener. I also learned to be tougher and not to baby anybody at any point in time.

In January, I received a call from Dick Little, my long lost buddy. He now was the Athletic Director at Great Plains College. He was in the process of firing the current head basketball coach. It seems that the President demanded that Dick fire the current head basketball coach. He also demanded that Dick hire someone who could turn the program around. To put it honestly, Great Plains College was lower than Permian Basin College when I first took over the program at Permian Basin. It seems that Great Plains lost 23 and won 6 that year. The other years were not much better and the President hired Dick to turn the men's basketball program around. Dr. Larry Barker was the president and he had tried in his way to hire people to get the men's basketball program turned around and had failed for over twenty years.

Of course, I knew a lot about Great Plains. I had coached in the same conference and while coaching at Panhandle Baptist, Great Plains and I crossed paths many times. In all my years in the conference which started in the early seventies, I was not impressed with Great Plains. Dick and I talked about it a lot and he knew how I felt. He asked if I would be interested in taking the job at Great Plains and at that time, I was not interested and said so. We kept talking back and forth during the basketball season and soon I became interested. I thought, I had the best players in the country coming back, and we were just now getting adjusted to East Texas, why leave? Now, make no mistake about it, I did not like the administration or the attitude of some of the boosters at Henderson

College. Finally, late February, Dick called me one day and told me he was flying to Dallas and then driving to Kilgore to offer me the job. He knew Jennifer and the girls as well as anyone as he had been at our house many times before. They all loved Dick as he was a very loveable guy. Easy to talk to and smart about anything you want to talk about. By this time, I was getting a name in college coaching. I did not tell Jennifer that Dick was coming because I really did not know what I was going to say. I will never forget when Dick came because it was the day that we had to play Athens County Junior College coached by Lynn Williams. Both had a tradition in winning. Dick flew into Dallas just as he said, but he had a guy with him. His name was Mike Young, my brother, and they were in Kilgore, to recruit us to Pampa, home of Great Plains College. We beat Athens County and we all ate B.Q. ribs after the game. Deal was done. We were headed to Great Plains College for an interview with the president. When Jennifer and I went to Pampa for the interview, the winds were blowing around sixty-seventy miles per hour and the dust was so bad that you could not see ten yards in front of you. It was one of those days in West Texas that you wish you could forget. We all hit it off from the start and Jennifer was in on the interview. What surprised me was when Dr. Barker turned to Dick and asked him, "Well, if you are willing to hire Ron, are you willing to fire him also?" Dr. Barker was a great guy but he wanted a winner and he was very negative about whether it could happen. He simply did not believe it could happen. He had been hurt so much that he blocked it out.

After the last game of the play-offs, we were going to Pampa as a family so the kids could see where we were headed. Kelly Dawson, the Athletic Director at the University of Texas at San Antonio sent word that he would like to talk to me after the game. I told Jennifer to go to the car and I would join them later. Kelly's best friend, Tim James lived in Kilgore, Texas. They would come to our practices or games and we would visit about basketball on a regular basis. I got where I enjoyed their company. Right after the game with Rose College, Kelly offered me the Head Men's Basketball position at the University of Texas at San Antonio on the spot. I was stunned, as I did not expect it and was speechless. Of course, I was proud and thrilled at the same time, but I came back and said "I have already made a commitment to go to Great Plains College. " Then one thing led to another in the conversation and finally he said "You mean to tell me that you would go to a junior college over a division one school?" I said, "At this point in time, yes." He then said, "Well, I am glad that we missed on you, because you are not what we thought you were." I walked out of the building and got in the car and headed toward Pampa, Texas, home of Great Plains College.

THIRTEEN

B
ACK AT THE BIG DAY, it all took on the appearance of being in
a dream: the trip to the dome, which took only thirty-five minutes
because we had police escorts; the parking lot filled with over thirty-
thousand vehicles one hour before game time; people standing in line for
tickets, as if any were left; others hurrying to try and get the best seat; ticket
scalpers in force trying to make a buck. There were crowds of spectators
pushing and shoving trying to get pictures of the team. Flashbulbs popped
from all directions as spectators tried for an angle from which to take the
perfect team picture. Entering the dome, we were treated like we were the
most important people in the world. People stepped back, clearing plenty
of space for us so we could make our way. You could hear the crowd in
the stands and the fans in the halls, the stairs, and the concessions, as
we filed into the locker room. Excitement abounded, and the team was
having a ball. Cable TV setups were everywhere with built-in tables and
chairs for an impressive group of commentators and analysts. Security
lined the court and the halls, which gave me a nice safe feeling. Bands
and cheerleaders were finding their proper places and getting organized,
readying themselves to provide their part of the coming entertainment. The
San Antonio Marine Color Guard was there for the opening ceremonies.
Everyone was waiting for the entrance of the teams.

In our locker room, all was normal with Doc doing the taping and
the assistant trainers performing muscle rubdowns and other training
and game preparation. Guys were taking care of bathroom needs, shoes

were being tied up just tight enough, and the players quietly exchanged small talk. I was at the front of the blackboard writing reminders about our game plan and objectives for the big game. Everyone on the team was very attentive and focused on the task to come. We had already gone over every detail many times in the hotel but this was just yet another last-minute reminder. The game was scheduled for a 7:15 p.m. tip-off, and the facility had a routine worked out for both teams due to the requirements of both the TV coverage and the in-house crowd; after all, this was the Final Four Championship. We were to make an appearance out on the court first at 6:30 and start our warm-up. Memphis would follow us at 6:35. Then we would retreat to the locker room at 6:50 with Memphis doing the same five minutes later. Memphis would appear next, taking to the court again at 7:00, with us to follow soon thereafter. Starting players were to be introduced at 7:15 p.m. Between 7:05 and 7:15, time was set aside for pregame festivities like the singing of the National Anthem, TV interviews with important people and commercial spots filled the big in-house screen.

To me it was nice to be the favorite in spirit, and not in point spread. We were an eleven-point underdog according to the San Antonio Times. The paper explained that that was the largest pregame point spread in the history of the Final Four. On the other hand, the paper also reported that two out of every three people interviewed were pulling for North West State University. Since we had not been picked to win any game, including in the Big 12 tournament that was a precursor to this one, being the underdog was a role we warmed to. We had gained much respect and many supporters along the way and I was beginning to feel increased pressure to win this one for our fans as much as for our team. We even had some sportswriters who had believed we didn't belong in the NCAA Championships relent and join our bandwagon. The press coverage we were getting was outstanding and it was 100 percent positive even if they were writing about how we had surprised everyone getting this far.

It started with the Baylor game in the Big 12 tournament where we first raised eyebrows by winning 94-68. That was a shocker, not so much that we won but how convincingly we did it, and without our all-American

Oscar Williams, the player I generally refer to as Big Time. The upset victory over Texas 82-71 followed, and the come-from-behind win against Texas A&M 67-65 to win a berth in the NCAA Championship Division One Tournament really got people looking our way. Right about then, the word was that we were one of the hottest teams coming into the NCAAs, but still almost everyone felt we wouldn't last long. It wasn't the 76-64 victory over Washington State in the first game but rather the Michigan State victory, where their all-American, best player, and team leader hurt himself. This was the turning point in the tournament for us. The 61-59 upset victory over Michigan State helped our team gain confidence and we rattled off wins over Purdue, 75-66, and Arizona, 61-57. Topping it all off, the double overtime victory over Louisville 110-105 now found us set up to play the powerful Memphis basketball team for the national championship of NCAA Division One Basketball. It was like a train speeding along: There were times I wasn't thinking win or lose at all, but whether or not that train was ever going to stop.

When we ran on the court, it seemed like all 45,000 people were standing, clapping, and cheering for our benefit. What a pleasing rush for the players, though it was deafening to our ears. As far as you could see, there were so many rows upon rows of people that they seemed to be stacked on top of each other, and they were all giving us a rousing ovation. Chills went down my spine and my heart sank to my feet. I wondered if the people in the additional stands that were added just for this event could even hear the ball bounce or see the numbers on our jerseys. It didn't seem to bother anyone as they were into the game just like the lucky ones sitting right behind our bench. Five minutes later, Memphis came on the court and the crowd gave their team the same wonderful treatment. I thought, *people are here to see a wonderful event, two great basketball teams squaring off for the right to say they are the National Champs.* The electricity generated among the spectators, the TV people, the sportswriters, the teams involved, and the workers in the dome was exhilarating and overwhelming. I literally pinched myself to make sure it was not a dream.

I couldn't even think as both teams lined up for the tip-off. Frozen into stillness by the magnitude of the moment, I started wondering just how I had gotten here. That thought hardly lasted though, as the tip went to a Memphis guard on the right side of the court and he drove straight to the basket. Smooth was back and he was in great shape to draw a charge but he never had a chance. The Memphis player acted like he was going to continue with the layup, but instead flipped the ball back behind him, high up toward the goal, an alley-oop pass to their all-American big man, Thomas Cane. Standing six foot nine and tipping the scale at two-hundred ninety pounds, he thundered in a dunk right over Smooth. It was a ferocious dunk that instantly got 45,000 fans on their feet. Thomas came down like a gorilla with a wide white-toothed grin and, assuming a fierce, aggressive posture with both fists clinched, yelled to my players, "Welcome to Big-Time Basketball!" Taking the ball inbounds, White Shoes was double-teamed and threw a panic pass to Smooth Sammy underneath the basket but a Memphis player intercepted the ball and converted a layup on the other end. I called time-out. With 20 seconds gone, we were down 4-0 and the game looked totally out of control. When I looked into our guys' eyes, I could see something that I had not seen the entire year: fear. I tried to calm them down and put my foot down about playing the next two possessions aggressively, letting nothing stand in our way. They weren't cringing in fear really, but rather reacting more like a deer in the headlights; to a man they were startled.

We panicked and began playing like we were stuck in quicksand. We went out on the court looking like our old selves, but the look was deceiving. Memphis looked like men and my players looked like little boys beside them. We took a bad shot; Memphis rebounded and went straight at the bucket for another thunderous dunk. This time Smooth stepped in front to draw the charge. The resulting collision was both scary and ugly; Smooth was knocked down, and he stayed down. Doc ran on the court and checked him out. He finally stirred after a little time and some smelling salts, but it was clear he had been knocked out cold by the hit. Also, though it may have been the least of our problems, to make matters worse, Smooth was called for the foul for moving underneath.

This was trouble for us. You can survive the loss of some players, even some very good ones, and the team will adjust, but losing Smooth was a real blow. White Shoes was no point guard, but I felt I had no choice; I had to try him there because our only other point guard option was young Jet One. He was only a freshman and much smaller than most of the players on the court. But what really worried me he hadn't seen a lot of court time, playing backup most of the time. I thought it would be too much for him to handle. Of course, that was a decision that was rethought for me, because in the next five minutes White Shoes tried to do too much with the ball. After three straight turnovers, I took him off the point and inserted Jet One to run the offense. Much to my surprise, he handled the pressure so much better than I thought he would and didn't appear to be overmatched on the court at all. I thought to myself, *I am worse than my players, I think too much.*

With ten minutes gone in the first half the score was 22-4; a Memphis rout was on. I called time-out, and it was no more Mr. Nice Guy this time; I chewed them out thoroughly, and did not worry about hurting anyone's feelings. One thing was certain: Nothing I said could have made things any worse. Following the time out, the team did come back and start mounting some semblance of an offense, but we couldn't stop them from scoring.

At halftime, the score was 46-24. Smooth had a concussion but was on his feet in street clothes. The mood was somber and quiet. I paced around a little, trying to figure out what to say. We simply did not show up for the game the same way Memphis had. There was nothing complicated about it. We were in a game playing like we did not belong, while Memphis was demonstrating why they were ranked No. 1 for most of the year. I saw no clear way for us to turn the corner, but what would have been the point of not at least trying? I confronted each one of the guys personally, attacking their manhood, telling them they were scared of the big bad boys from Memphis. "If I am wrong," I said, "you can prove it, because we are going after them with all we've got. We're going to press them full-court, pressure them man-on-man, and rotate with the intention of making a play, and then sprint to the proper defensive position; not trot; not jog; *sprint.*" We talked about rebounding, and what we had to do, and about getting open shots and how we could work free for good looks at the basket. When the locker room huddle broke up and we emerged onto the court, I was exhausted and felt terrible about having gotten down to such a personal level. I had to challenge them though; it was our only hope.

NWS came out for the second half as an assemblage of pissed-off players. They were pissed at their coach, not the score. Memphis got the ball on the sideline, drove the lane and Bubba slipped going for the block, accidentally tackling the Memphis player with the ball. Luckily for us, the ref agreed with my take, and no intentional foul was called, but rather just a two-shot shooting foul. Their bench went crazy, their fans too, but I felt it was a good call because the contact would not have taken place had Bubba not slipped; there was no purposeful aggression. They missed both foul shots, and when rebounding, Bubba was fouled, struck by a hard right to the face with an open hand from the hulking Thomas Cane. An intentional foul was called this time, and now they were all really riled up, including the Memphis fans. Bubba made both free throws and we got to inbound the ball. We ran our special inbounds play to Big Time and he missed his three-pointer but he was fouled, another hard foul. Big Time went to the line and made all three free throws. Memphis was emotional now, and clearly showing their displeasure with the officials. They inbounded the ball and Jet One stole it from one of the Memphis guards, passed in the corner to Big Time, who drained the three-point shot this time. Just like that the score had narrowed to 46-32. Memphis called time-out and, trying to make nice, I had to admit to all the guys that they had done exactly what I had asked them to do; they had gone out on the floor and made a difference. I praised their effort and told them not to panic because there was lots of basketball left.

We needed to cut the lead a little at a time and then try to make a huge run at the end. We all agreed that playing the game in two-minute segments would be good for our concentration, right until the last few minutes of the game. We executed that plan for the next two minutes and, to my surprise, we played Memphis even to a 51-37 score. The next two minutes it got better: We outplayed them and closed it to 54-43 with 13:40 to go in the game.

Everyone could feel the team coming back. We had been playing with our backs to the wall, then forging ahead for weeks now; this game was no exception. I felt it, the players felt it, and so did the fans, though Memphis would surely have something to say about it. At the 8:00 minute mark the score was 63-52 and it looked like Memphis was still in the driver's seat. They called for time, and I made adjustments to our press, opting for a half-court trap. I knew that the next four minutes were critical if we were to have any chance of winning the game. I gambled with our odds and told the guys to be ready to match up and switch to playing man-on-man defense after the next trap. Memphis was blessed with very good guards so the half court trap might not bother them; perhaps a match-up man defense would get them off their game. Unfortunately, we couldn't use the four-to-score set, because it's designed with the premise that you have the lead. You need to have the other team in a situation where they are behind and they have to defend, so unfortunately our best, and most practiced, set was not an option. The half court press had worked to some degree as we outscored Memphis 5-2 in the latest two-minute period. With the score 65-57 and 5:56 left on the clock, I called time-out. We changed defenses again just to try and keep Memphis off balance. We needed to be able to continue outscoring them in each short period. It worked as we outscored them 6-3 and at 3:43 the scoreboard read 68-63. We were now in striking distance and I could feel it. Memphis had the ball and they worked the clock and the ball down to 2:55 before taking a shot. We fouled them in the act of shooting and they made one and missed one. We took that rebound and finally got it inside to Skunk, who made a great turnaround shot. It was a shot from heaven, one I had never seen him shoot before. Now the clock read 1:47 and the score was 69-65. Memphis spread the floor and started stalling the ball. The clock read 1:01 when we fouled.

They made both free throws for a six-point lead. We quickly drove the lane, and "D" was fouled while shooting. He made the basket and the free throw to close it to 71-68 with 45 seconds left. Memphis stepped on the inbounds line on the throw in and now it was my turn to signal time. We went over a special play where Bubba gets the ball off a pick he himself sets. We also went over the last few seconds and what we wanted to do on the defensive end. As expected, when Bubba set the screen for

White Shoes, Memphis went all out and left Bubba wide open. He took the shot but the ball hit the front of the rim and fell away from the basket. Memphis rebounded and we fouled quickly, which was part of our game plan. They made both free throws with 20 seconds left for a 73-68 lead. We had the ball and I was out of time-outs. We called a play, the same play but this time White Shoes did not pass to Bubba but instead shot the three, falling down with a Memphis player draped all over him; the sound as it "swished" through the net was a thing of beauty. Memphis called time with the score at 73-71 and 12 seconds to go. We got a piece of the ball on the inbounds pass but they came up with the loose ball and in the process, we fouled a Memphis player. They canned both free throws, which pushed the lead to 75-71. We quickly threw the ball in and gave the ball to Big Time who penetrated the lane and was fouled. Down 4 points with 7 seconds left, we talked it over while Memphis called their last time-out. The four points we needed would require two possessions. I told Big Time to make the first and miss the second; maybe we could get the board and pass it outside for a three. It worked to perfection…almost. Big Time hit his first shot, missed his second short where Skunk was there to rebound the ball. He hit "D" with a pass, and he let the ball fly from beyond the arc with two seconds remaining. It looked good and I was excited that our plan had worked, but the ball caught a bit of the back of the rim and bounded high above, with Memphis collecting the winning rebound. It was a final: Memphis 75, NWS 72. We had lost the National Championship.

When you put your heart and soul into something and things do not go the way you want them to, you pout, you yell and shout, you point fingers, you cry, you drift off into a daze, you frown. Or you take it just like it was supposed to be that way. We were all just devastated. No one knew what to say or do. They say you should win just like you lose. Well, "they" did not play for the NCAA National Championship, and lose, so what do "they" know? I tried to keep my poise and I shook everyone's hands although I didn't remember doing so the next day. The celebration was on for Memphis and I was wishing it was us instead of them. They were a very good team, a worthy opponent, one that I respected. After all, they had just beaten us, and no team seemed to be up to that of late. In our dressing room, the scene was like a funeral. Some of the guys were just in a corner by themselves with tears in their eyes; others were more demonstrative and did their crying out loud. Some hugged one another with a gentle feeling of satisfaction, knowing they had done so much right, though it was now over. Still, all of us were hurt deeply by the loss.

But it did give me some faith as to why I believe in athletics. Although we could hardly have been hurting more from the letdown, we gained a lot from the experience, and in the long run it would make us stronger for the rest of our lives. The sacrifice, the commitment, and all that goes with this price we all paid can influence young and old hearts alike in such a positive way. It will carry over into the players' adult lives sooner or later. From what I've seen, it usually exerts a strong positive influence. I told the guys to go out and enjoy their families and enjoy the memories and never--and I repeated never--get down about tonight and the loss to Memphis. "You came in as champions and you leave as champions. Itinerary will be left on the bulletin board outside the hotel for tomorrow. Enjoy the night."

I did not keep the players very long but let them go early instead. I wanted time with my family because I knew that would be a healing process in itself. After talking to the media, the hometown press, and many of my extended family and friends, it was time to be with my wife and daughters. I knew the morning sun would rise as always and frankly I couldn't wait. Jennifer and the girls were great as always but they couldn't help being sad and down about it too. We went out for a bite at a late-night eatery where we bumped into several North West State University fans. The girls were excited that the fans found out we were there but Jennifer and I would have preferred to eat alone as a family. After several minutes' worth of cheers for the team and the school, and some nice words and congratulations to me, most of the fans respected our privacy and left us alone. Of course, we did get a freebie, as someone was kind enough to pay for our meal. My only thought was, *Another violation for me to deal with.* When we got back to the room, it was close to 1:00 a.m., but most of the patrons at the hotel were wide awake. Hundreds of supporters were in the lobby, most had been drinking, and it was pretty wild. The North West State fans had time to get over the loss and all they could think about was the fact that their team played in the Final Four, and that they were damned happy to have witnessed it. I was the hero for the time being and they loved and honored the team, but very few team members got to enjoy this celebration. I sent Jennifer up to the room with the girls and they went to bed. I stayed up with the fans until around 4:00 in the morning, enjoying the moment.

Our team had an 11:00 a.m. flight out of San Antonio, which was to arrive in Amarillo at 3:00 p.m. We were all exhausted but we were glad it was finally over. We had to change planes in Dallas, deplaning only to discover there was a large group of North West State University fans awaiting us. It was fun and they had put snacks out for us and made us feel welcome in Dallas. It was unexpected but this was a welcome surprise. After being the center of attention at Love Field in Dallas, the trip to Amarillo International Airport was filled with anticipation. As we exited the ramp into the airport, all we could see were black and gold banners and thousands upon thousands of State supporters. They were so excited about it all that they were inadvertently blocking the passengers and crew from getting off the plane and the aircraft prep and cleanup crew from approaching it. Finally, airport security cleared some space by forcing the supporters back so people could get where they needed to go. It was a wild scene, one that we all watched and enjoyed.

JJ McFather had gathered the Black and Gold Booster Club, and they organized this with JJ in control from the beginning of the rally to the end. A microphone and speakers were set up, and as each player picked up his bag and headed outside, a man serving as master of ceremonies would call out his name and the crowd cheered them and stamped their feet. The airport security people were having a tough time with all of this, but the North West State people were totally oblivious of that. After each player and each coach was introduced and cheered in the parking lot, I was asked to say a few words on behalf of the team. I took the microphone from JJ and blurted out. "It's not so bad coming in second after all!" This got the crowd going, which got security nervous, so JJ looked over at me and said, "Finish it off quickly before we all get thrown in jail."

I went back up to the mic and continued, "Thanks to the greatest fans on the planet and to the greatest city in the world. God bless you all!" People were just thrilled to be there, so whatever I said was going over well. I hurried to collect everyone and get them on the bus, and then we set off for the university. Our next stop came as another surprise, a huge one for all of us. Once on campus, instead of delivering us to the dorms and apartments, the bus took the team straight to the Golden Spread Dome, home of the North West State University basketball team. The entire student body was apparently in the dome, which seats about 10,000 students. The scene was unreal; everyone and everything moved in slow motion, like in a dream. Banners were stretched everywhere and the cheerleaders, the band, several school dance groups, and every administrator were all there. The tumultuous scene and the cheers of the huge gathering of students eased some of the pain of having lost the final game. The players were excited too. You could see they were feeling better about themselves. The fans started chanting for individual players to speak and each player got a few minutes to address the happy throng. We all got to experience their appreciation, and it felt wonderful. The Mayor of Amarillo was there, and city councilmen who took the podium in turn and made speeches, all praising the team and all that we had accomplished. When the President of North West State University took his turn with the microphone, he added that on behalf of the school, he wanted to express his appreciation and share the joy over the improbable string of victories this group of players and coaches had posted. He finished up, "Today, we celebrate our men's basketball team and their huge run at the National Championship, during which they gained the respect and admiration of the entire world. In recognition of that, tomorrow North West State University will celebrate by cancelling all classes. Thank you all for being here to share this big moment." The students were happy, of course, they were cheering, hugging, and high-fiving one another. Then they started an oft-repeated refrain of "Black and Gold, we love you!" over a pulsing beat that spread the joy and happiness. One thing was certain: We wouldn't have to work the next day, and I was happy about that.

After we got everyone back where they were supposed to be, I was finally able to calm down. We were all very tired and I told each coach to go home and stay there, and we would meet Monday morning to get organized and back on track for the next year. We all shared hugs, which was understandable. It was the end of quite a long journey we'd taken together, and both spoken and silent thanks and congratulations were shared all around. The next few days, I slept until at least 7:30 a.m., which qualifies as big-time sleeping in for me. Jennifer went back to work, and the girls resumed their daily classes, so I had the house to myself except for our dog Bingo. He was a black and white screw-tail bulldog, which is really nothing but a Boston terrier. He was great company, though not as much after three or four days had passed. Bingo and I became very good friends as my main activities that week were sleeping, eating, and playing with him for four days, all things Bingo agreed were great ways to fill a day. Of course, I did spend some time scanning the Internet for the sports commentary, editorials and reports concerning the big game with Memphis, and the run that preceded it. Again, we came out smelling like a rose. I do not think I saw one negative comment about our team or anything concerning our program at North West State University. As I read, I was already thinking about recruiting for the next year, and press coverage has a lot to do with how potential recruits see a school and their basketball program. I couldn't help myself; I was already forming a plan about the coming year and what we needed to do in the off-season on both the recruiting front, and in doing workouts.

When the last Big 12 team is eliminated from the NCAA playoffs the All-Conference teams are announced. Although we had made such a long run in the big dance at the end, our guys didn't figure to receive a lot of recognition from the Big 12, as we finished fourth in the conference. Big Time did make the First Team all-conference team, White Shoes was named to the second team and Bubba merited a third team selection. Both Skunk and Smooth received Honorable Mention congratulations. Kansas Head Coach Vincent Smith was acknowledged as the Big 12 Coach of the Year. Kansas also had the Player of the Year, the Newcomer of the Year, and the Defensive Player of the Year. None of this came as a surprise to me, although many of our fans felt NWS was ripped off. I considered it far more telling that several pro teams had already contacted me regarding several of our players. We may not have scored the most honors in the Big 12, but someone out there had noticed how our players performed. Given a choice between a conference trophy and a chance at the pros, I feel confident that each of my guys would have picked the latter.

When the Associated Press came out with the All-American lists, Big Time was second team and I received NCAA Coach of the Year honors. It was also very cool that White Shoes was selected to the Honorable Mention all-American list. These honors were big news in our area, something on virtually everyone's lips. Before we knew it, we had all become the subject of repeated TV mentions and radio reports, and we were being honored by local service groups. I lined up a long list of speaking engagements, and additional invites from all over the country. Of course, I was overcome by all of this, and suddenly found myself needing a full-time secretary to help me keep my appointments and make all my travel arrangements. I rebelled somewhat: I would rather be off on recruiting missions and not doing public relations work. But a few of my assistant coaches reminded me that PR really was recruiting, so I ended up agreeing to most of the requests for interviews and other appearances that I was asked to make.

One thing I learned about advancing to the Final Four Championship: It puts your school on the map, and on the radar screens of millions of people, both young and old. Recruiting was now easier. Players wanted to talk to us. Heads would turn when we arrived and walked the red carpet at many an appearance. On the other hand, rivals knew all about us; they would deride our method of play, and warn recruits against signing with us. We had a good number of players returning probably, including every starter and the first two subs coming off the bench, both of them underclassmen. New recruits might not get to play often. We anticipated all of this and ignored it, and went to work like it was just another year. There was no reason to let anything get in our way as far as recruiting was concerned. The rumor was that Big Time was going to apply for the NBA draft and I was just proud that we finally had a player who could actually do that, and perhaps succeed at it. NCAA signing day, April 14, was fast approaching, and we hadn't finished playing until April 5.

That was just part of the problem, because three of our coaches were also talking about taking on different jobs too. Soapy had been in touch with North Carolina A&M, a school that had all but offered him the head basketball coaching position. I was certain he was going to take it. They were a division one school, they played in a good conference, and it was closer to home for him. They started talking to him last year at the Final Four convention and the process was ongoing. Soapy had worked hard, and he deserved a shot at being a head coach; I was proud of him. He had kept me apprised of all the talks. Decision time was approaching for old Soap. They had given him 24 hours. Darryl, too, had received several calls about coaching, but he was more interested in serving as the Director of High School Sports in Alabama, a position that had opened up. His wife was from Alabama and he was interested in job security and in spending more time with his young family. The job was with the Alabama State High School Coaching Association. As director he would be in a position of responsibility, controlling all aspects of high school athletics in the state. And finally, Eddie had already committed to a head football coaching and Athletic Director job at a small school just outside Ft. Worth: It was in the town of Throckmorton, Texas. He was excited about it though he would wait until recruiting season was over. I wasn't sure how I felt about all of this. I was happy for them, but I dreaded losing all these guys from my staff. I decided to just keep focusing on recruiting so I didn't spend too much time thinking about it.

April 14 came so fast that it was hard to be prepared. We signed two guards that day. One was from North City, Oklahoma, a six foot three inch scoring type of player who averaged 28.8 points per game. He was an outstanding shooter and one thing we all agreed the team needed was more outside shooters. The other player was a local kid named Reggie Johnson, just six foot tall, but he was a great athlete with good high school numbers. He averaged 18.9 points and 8.1 assists over the last two years, and led his team to back to back state championships. We were talking to two big-time players from South America as well. Vladimir Martinez stood seven feet tall and weighed 295 pounds, while Jay Hernandez was only a bit smaller, six feet nine inches and 278 pounds. We felt we had a good chance to sign both in the next few weeks. NCAA rules allowed us to recruit no more than two foreign athletes and we felt good about these players. We were also hot on the trail of New Mexico's "Player of the Year," a guy named Darryl Hunter. He was waiting to see whom else we signed, while we felt he might be able to take Big Time's place should he opt to go to the NBA.

My family life was just about back to normal and I was enjoying my stay away from the big-time lights. I have never been one to hog the spotlight and attending and speaking at so many events following the team's success had me feeling pretty uncomfortable, out of my element, and even a bit depressed. The girls were really enjoying being in the spotlight and having fun playing the part of minor celebrities. We still couldn't go anywhere without people approaching us, usually just to say congratulations, but sometimes wanting to discuss specific plays in some of the games. They were generally very appreciative, and wanted to thank me for my efforts on behalf of the school and the area. Of course, every once in a while someone would just have to start playing coach, second-guessing some of the decisions I had made, but that wasn't very often. It was funny, though; more often than not I found myself agreeing with these fans. So, with life back to normal, and everyone adjusting to a new year, I started planning for the coming season. Little did I know that my life was about to take a completely different turn.

FOURTEEN

It was the first Monday in May when James Jones, the AD, came over to my office, which was across the campus from his, opened the door without knocking, closed it, sat down, and just looked at me. He informed me that he had told our secretary to hold all phone calls to my office because he wanted time alone with me. James pulled a letter from his jacket pocket and handed it to me. I looked at the letter and it was from the NCAA investigation chairperson. Reading slowly because I did not want to miss a word, I looked up and James was staring at me intently. He said, "Well, what do you have to say?"

I asked, "About what?"

He responded loudly, "Hell, the allegations in the letter are pointing toward the fact that some of our guys received extra financial benefits to attend North West State U. Do you know if that is correct?"

I said, "Not to my knowledge, but I would not put it past any of them."

James replied, "Well, the NCAA is coming to Northwestern in force Wednesday morning at 8:00 a.m., and they want to meet with you, me, JJ, and four players. The players are Willie Warnell, Bubba Peek, Sammy Burelson, and Oscar Williams.

"Who filed the complaint?" I asked.

James said, "They wouldn't tell me, just as I expected. But since I have served on that committee for five years I think I can find out. It seems that someone within our group came forward with impressive evidence concerning improper behavior on the school's part. The NCAA investigation group has already done quite a bit of research and they are very positive that we have several violations. The word is that they are coming at us with everything they've got. You need to tell me everything that you know right now so we can get organized and be on the same page when we meet with the NCAA."

It was close to lunch and I begged off, telling James that I had a luncheon date with my wife that I could not break, but I would get back with him later that afternoon. I told him that I would come by his office and we would talk. He said, "That's fine, but make sure that you get the players together for Wednesday morning at 8:00 a.m. in the board room."

I had no plans with Jennifer but I had to get away and try to get my act together. This was my worst nightmare and it was coming true. I had to decide to face up or just lie about what I knew. I thought about everything: my family, my church, my players, my coaches, my life as I knew it, and I started crying. My first thought was, *how do those other schools get by with cheating?* Then I just told myself that I had to toughen up and deny everything just like all the other guys I've known had done. *That's it,* I decided, *I have to deny everything from the start to the end.* I called the players and told them about the investigation and to my surprise, they were calm about the entire issue. Then it occurred to me that of course they would be calm; they would only get a slap on the wrist, and most of their peers would be impressed with them to boot. I was the one who would take it head-on, the one who had the most to lose.

Wednesday morning was a day of infamy for Ron Young. There were four investigators from the NCAA and they started interviews at 8:00 a.m. on the button. First, the boys were interviewed and that took until 9:15. The investigators then assembled together and compared notes for an hour. At 10:30 a.m., they interviewed me, JJ, and James. The first question they asked me was if I knew the boys were getting extra financial support to attend North West State University. Their aggressive approach told me they knew everything. I was wondering the entire time what they could know, and how. First, they attacked the jobs that Sammy and Bubba held in order to pay for their room and board, tuition, and fees at the school during the year I was not at North West State. It seems that the two players had managed to pay almost $35,000 that they owed in one way or another. Of course, both those guys had received government grants that were worth a lot of money, but that alone couldn't account for the expenses they had covered. Funny thing, they owed nothing. Everything was paid off.

Then they hit me hard about Sammy's father being represented on his indictment trial for murder by a lawyer who graduated from North West State University. The trial went on for months and the big question was who paid for the lawyer? I honestly did not know the answer, but some things were coming clearly into focus. Another area of concern revolved around how Bubba's mother was allowed entrance into an expensive first-class Alzheimer's/Dementia clinic in Canyon, Texas. Canyon was only about 20 miles from Amarillo. The investigators asked me pointedly, "Did you know that it cost $1,500 a day to stay in that clinic? That is very expensive and we cannot trace who is paying for it. But we know that the family does not have that kind of money."

Of course, I didn't know Mrs. Peek was in Canyon. It was the first I had heard of it, so that was an easy one to answer, but I was now slipping into a state of shock. They followed up with questions about Willie Warnell and how his mother was driving a new 2009 Toyota pickup while being on welfare. They also demanded to know how Willie was able to have an expense account at the Hub Clothing store located downtown. "To this point in time, he has spent over $3,500 in clothes and we cannot trace any money transactions. Everything was paid for in cash."

Next they came at me hard about Oscar Williams and his ability to buy clothes at the Hub, and drive a brand-new LX 2009 Lexus. They also questioned his alleged work with Toyota, saying he was getting paid for work he didn't do. They blindsided me with questions about his school job selling programs at football games; it was estimated he had made between $5,000 and $10,000 a game. I had so many emotions going, none of them good, and I did not know where to begin. Of course, I denied everything but they certainly had access to many facts that I did not know anything about. When I was leaving, I spied White Shoes exiting one of the rooms. As it was clear he was leaving the interview process, I ask him how it had gone. He pleaded, "Coach, I'm sorry but I had to take care of my family first. Family first, coach, I am so sorry, I love you man." I was floored, but somehow I walked out the door.

I went home that night with my head down, just wanting to have a drink. I told Jennifer and as always she came to my defense. I could not figure where the NCAA received all the information they had. I was totally in the dark about some things, and had some clue to others, but now I was really wondering what the truth was. Of course, bad news spread quickly and my phone was ringing from the time I got home until I went to bed. I was most concerned about my assistant coaches and I tried my best to calm them down. I wouldn't have acted so brave and disinterested in my own fate if I had known what was coming next.

The following day, the interviews were conducted in reverse order. James, JJ, and I went first with the players to follow. All investigators were in on each meeting with each scheduled one hour apart. I went first, and that it started with me wasn't the only thing that was a little different. It was more casual, and right to the point. I wondered if everyone was being handled the same way. It was becoming clear that they already knew how they expected the process to conclude. I did not and I was wondering. What I discovered in this session was that I had been made the scapegoat of the entire deal. They came after me from all different directions and no doubt, I was frustrated. Players had identified me in all the wrongdoing and said nothing about Steven McFather. It was very clear to me that he had bought everyone off without me knowing about it. JJ McFather was only mentioned as a guy from whom they could borrow money when they were in a bind, but they had to pay it back. According to them, I was the guy tasked with finding boosters to pay for the players' needs. Their responses to questioning indicated I was the guy who set up most of the payments when a player need arose. What bothered me most is that the NCAA was not a bit interested in who the boosters were, but instead just wanted to know who contacted them and who gave them the information on how to get the job done. I could see what was going down so I agreed to tell them the entire truth if they would tell me who was behind all of this.

Rather than its scheduled hour, my interview dragged on for two. I started with my first meeting with Mr. McFather in Dallas. I told them the entire story as I knew it. I had no clue as to how North West State University got Bubba and Sammy to sign, and that was the truth. I did some background work for North West State and contacted the players for the school but that was it. I did try to influence them into coming to the school but I did not pay or bribe anyone to ensure their attendance at North West State University. Yes, I did tell Mr. McFather how to get it all done. He asked me how different programs got the big-time players and I answered him how other schools had recruited some of my players that I had coached before, and how I had been beaten by opponents in the recruiting wars. I knew nothing for sure, but did suspect that NCAA rules had been violated. It was not my place to question Mr. McFather. I knew that no money had been transferred directly from my hand to those of any players, which was the truth. Of course, the NCAA investigators did not believe me. They told me that all four players pointed the finger at me saying I was behind each violation and that I knew about each one. I realized then that McFather had gotten to them the way he gets to everyone. I said, "There is no telling how much money he is spending to keep those guys pointing the blame at me." I was hurt and shocked that the players would turn on me after all we had been through, and then I remembered Willie and what he had said the day before. I should have realized when he said he was sorry but that he had to do what was necessary, which was to take care of family. I told the investigators that I would take a lie detector test, I would take any kind of oath they needed but I was not as totally guilty as they were saying. But I could tell that they were not buying anything I was selling. I then said, "Ok, I have told you the truth, you don't believe me but at least tell me how you found out about all of this."

They replied, "We received three letters from parents of your players giving us the total rundown on these violations. It appears their sons came home for spring break and revealed the entire story. Oscar Williams got it started. They were all at a party, and Oscar had a few drinks, and then started bragging about how much money he made this year. He implicated some other guys, as his story went on. Some of the parents felt cheated and together decided to go after you and North West State University. One thing led to another. We got to Oscar at home later in the same spring break and broke him down. He told us everything. He did mention Mr. McFather but we thought he was speaking about the son. We sent a letter to JJ McFather explaining that we were coming to North West State University to investigate these violations. That was about three weeks ago."

It hit me hard but now I was sure as I thought to myself, *so that is how Steven McFather found out before I did. That is how he got to each family and that is how they all knew what was coming.* I was shocked and downtrodden as it all sunk in. I'm pretty sure I've never been hurt so deeply. I decided right there that I would never coach again the rest of my life, regardless of how this all played out.

The next day, I received a phone call from James and he asked me to come over to his office. I had expected this summons, and I was scared but I had to face the music. He fired me on the spot with the approval of the president and the booster club. I knew it was coming. There is a clause in the contract that if I knowingly violate any NCAA rule, my position would be terminated immediately. Little was said. I could tell James believed every word of the report being prepared by the NCAA. I was crushed and I certainly did not want to go over every detail again. It was only a matter of time until everyone knew about my getting fired and the shocking revelation that I had cheated to win.

The first person I had to tell was my wife, Jennifer. It was the hardest thing I have ever done in my life. My one true love, someone who has looked up to me, was going to find out how big a cheat I had become. Racked by guilt and embarrassment, I approached Jennifer. But the tears in my eyes and my negative body language got through to her first. "What has happened to you?" she asked. I broke down, had a good cry and slowly laid it all out, just as it had happened. I felt so guilty and ashamed. As usual, she came through big time and listened to my story attentively.

When I finished, she said, "When the girls get home tonight, you have to tell them the same story you just told me, the same way." I agreed it had to be done, and later that night, the Young family had a team meeting with me as the center of attention. I felt an inch tall but they had to be told right now before they learned of it from the morning paper, which surely was going to execute me. The girls took it even better than Jennifer, but they really did not understand how much of a life-changing event this was: They were just too young. I knew that when they arrived at school the next day they would begin to understand that from this point on, things were going to be different. The next morning at 6:00 a.m., I read the front page of the Amarillo Globe Newspaper. In big bold black letters, it reported:

Coach Young Fired at North West State University for Violations of NCAA Rules

The NCAA has found several violations of the NCAA code in the North West State University basketball program while under the supervision of Coach Ron Young. It is said that several players received benefits for signing with North West State University and those benefits continued as long as they played for Northwestern. Coach Young denied several allegations but admitted that he knew some of the violations were happening. North West State University fired coach Young yesterday hoping that the NCAA will take notice of that action on North West State University part in the consideration of the penalties headed toward North West State because of the violations.

That night, the girls shared the mean way they were treated by several students with smart comments about how they had a cheat and a fraud for a father. Ann said that most of her friends could care less, and it seemed that the teachers were more upset than the students. Some were very sympathetic with her feelings and those of the family in this dark time. I felt we probably needed to move away before the NCAA entered the penalty phase of the violations process. It all seemed to hurt Renee the most, as she cried both nights. Nicole was the most embarrassed of the three while Ann was the most indifferent to it all.

One thing was certain: We had had a pretty good ride here, but we would not be the toast of the city any longer, something clearly illustrated when we attended church the following Sunday. Up to that point, it was usual that the preacher would make some kind of comment about the Gold and Black Lions. And we had even brought the entire team to church several times. Fellow church members would volunteer to take different players home with them for a good home-cooked meal. The preacher loved it and the church loved it. It was a good fit for all of us. It got us out of our comfort zone, but feeling good. But this Sunday, we were receiving the cold shoulder from almost everyone. I am sure most just didn't know what to make of the news, or what to say about it. But the entire morning we experienced none of the friendly faces who had smiled at us in the past. I felt so guilty because I knew I was the reason that we were being treated differently. Something needed to be done, so I got up and walked to the front of the church when the preacher asked if anyone wanted to come forward at the end of the service. Jennifer had no clue that I was going to do this, nor did the kids. The truth is I'm not sure I did either. I was weary of the coldness and felt it was up to me to do something to break the ice.

The preacher and I were good friends by now and I think he already had figured out what I was up to. Something just told me I had to walk up front. I told him that I wanted to confess my sins before God and the congregation. He understood and when the concluding song came to an end, he told those assembled that I had something I wanted to say. I was never one for getting up in front of crowds and talking. I would always get tongue-tied or just forget the words I had planned to use. Jennifer always made fun of me because I could get up in front of thousands at a coaches conference and speak but when you put me in front of a few hundred church people, I would simply choke. The preacher turned on the microphone and I began, "Dear God, please forgive me for my sins, particularly the ones that have made front page news. I am truly sorry and I ask for everyone's forgiveness. I became power-hungry with greed and had no regard for my family, for you, for anyone here. I am guilty of losing sight as to what is important and of going into the world of men with the intention of gaining false recognition and glory. Please forgive me and please give everyone in my family the strength to deal with what my sins have wrought. Last but not least, please give me the strength to forgive myself. I need to look myself in the eye, to be able to accept your forgiveness because I know it will always be there. Amen."

When I finished, the congregation fell silent, but then they started clapping, and the preacher and I hugged. I started crying, Jennifer and the girls ran up to the front with tears in their eyes and we engaged in a group hug. Members lined up to shake my hand as though I was joining the church, or celebrating something. It was a moving experience, and a healing one. After church, we all went out to eat at Furr's Cafeteria and to our surprise, we did not feel one bit of rejection from anyone in the crowd there. I thought to myself, *Thank you God!*

The very next Monday, I was back at North West State University clearing out my office and saying my good-byes. As I was preparing to leave for home for the last time, I received yet another visit from two men wearing suits and ties, and brand-new shoes. There was something lawyerly looking about these two, I felt. They inquired about Ron Young and I confessed that that was me. I continued by telling them that if they were from the NCAA, I wasn't going to talk with them this time. I had had enough of the NCAA. When they pulled out badges, I knew this was a different kind of visit.

The nearer gentlemen said, "I am Mark Atkinson, FBI," and offered me his hand to shake.

"Tom Melrose, FBI," said the other, and he gestured as if to greet me as well. I was taken back a little by the FBI paying me a visit at this moment with all my troubles. My first thought? *What the Hell have I done now?* Agent Atkinson continued, "Mr. Young, we need a few minutes of your time. Can we please sit down?" We moved some chairs inside the room and agent Melrose inquired if I felt we could have a sufficiently private conservation.

"Last week I would have said yes," I replied, "but I'm not so sure anymore. Lately, I wonder."

"In that case, let's go for a ride and we can talk." I climbed into the front seat of a black Lincoln with dark windows and nice leather seats. Atkinson drove to the parking lot of the football stadium and parked the car in the middle of a host of empty spots. He got things started by saying, "Mr. Young, you need to know that everything we say here is being recorded for FBI purposes. We have reason to believe that organized gambling has been going on during your basketball games. We know for a fact that more money was won and lost in nine of your recent games than we've seen change hands in the history of gambling in college athletics. Don't ask us how we know, but please trust us that we do know. We know how much money was exchanged in every game up till the Final Four championship game. Some people became wealthy predicting accurately whether or not you would cover the point spread in your games. It seems that your team never lost by the point spread. We have reason to believe that a Mr. Steven McFather is working with the Mafia in organizing much of this gambling. Do you know Mr. McFather?"

"Yes," I admitted.

Agent Melrose spoke up: "Can you recall for us how you came to meet him and when that transpired?"

I said, "I believe it was about this time last year when he flew me to Dallas when I met him for the first time."

Melrose continued, "What was the nature of your business?"

"I was trying to convince him to support me in my desire to succeed to the head basketball coaching position at North West State University. We talked about nothing but basketball the entire time."

"Did he contact you or did you contact him?" Atkinson asked.

"He contacted me after a basketball game I coached at my last job a year ago. He sent two of his employees to make the invitation."

Melrose pressed on, "Mr. Young, we need to know what was said in your first meeting. Remember, this conversation is being taped so please be as specific as possible."

I said, "I thought it was going to be a short meeting where I would introduce myself and explain why I would be a good candidate for the position. Instead, it became a four-hour lesson in basketball and I was impressed with how much he really understood the game. First, we discussed how to recruit big-time players into an organization and different ways to attract them to North West State. I left nothing out and told them everything I knew. He wanted to know how the other schools got the talent they have and I told him everything I knew. I was surprised that he had some really solid ideas to complement what I had to say. Second, we went over the philosophy of offensive basketball. He wanted a ball-control type of coach who managed his players and the game closely. I told him what I believed in and how I would coach at North West State University if I got the chance. I believed that you had to play offense in a manner that would be extremely difficult to guard, to play the game in such a way that gave a hard-working underdog an excellent chance to win every game. I went into detail about my offense and what it took to win. I continued with how important it was that the players on the court buy into this offensive approach. Once they did, it is almost impossible to keep the team from having a chance to win because the score is going to be low. If we can get talented players, we can win: I was convinced of it. Next we went over the defensive side of the game. I was thoroughly impressed with his attention to little details concerning the way the game of basketball is played. He asked literally hundreds of questions and I answered most of them. We continued by going over the top players in the country, and started discussing plans on how to recruit those types of players to North West State. He blew me away when he turned the conversation to me. He knew my history in coaching from the day I started right up until the present. He seemed to know more about me than I did about myself."

"Have you had any other contact with him since then?" Atkinson wanted to know.

I said, "No, but if I want something, I generally go through his son, JJ McFather."

"Tell me about your relationship with JJ."

"He is president of the booster club and he was the chairperson on the search committee to find a new head men's basketball coach. He is a friend of mine and I trust him even after all that has been said and done to me. We were on the same page as far as North West State University basketball is concerned. As far as I know, he keeps his father informed of everything that is happening concerning our basketball program but I can't even think for one second that JJ would be involved in organized gambling."

Atkinson intervened, "Mr. Young, if it helps, as far as we can tell, JJ is innocent of all wrongdoing in this. He is just a fanatic North West State University fan, who has a dad who happens to be a crook."

Then Melrose handed me three prints and asked if I knew any of the people in the pictures. "This picture was taken by an undercover agent when you guys were playing an exhibition game in Dallas. The picture was snapped at a place called Thousand Island, a strip club there. It is one of four that Mr. Steven McFather owns. His son has no clue that his dad owns these clubs, not to mention two casinos in Mississippi and two in New Mexico. Can you identify anyone in the photo?

I looked it over and replied, "Yes, I can identify everyone. The person on the left with a bottle of beer in his hand is Patrick O'Malley, Mr. McFather's right-hand man. He accompanied me when I recruited Oscar Williams. Next to him is Willie Warnell and there is Oscar. Next picture please." As he handed me yet another, Melrose told me that this second picture had been taken in Los Angeles, at a nightclub called Sugars' known for gambling and sex shows. He went on to say that it too was a McFather property. I identified everyone again, and then came the third photo. This last picture, I was told, was taken in New Orleans when we were at the Final Four.

"Please look at it and identify whoever is in this picture. We took it at Pete's, which is well-known for gambling and drugs."

I looked this picture over and immediately felt sick to my stomach. Sitting next to two beautiful girls were Willie and Oscar again. "You know who those three are," I said, pointing to Willie, Oscar, and Patrick. "The other two with them are Bubba Peek and Sammy Burleson." I guess I still wanted to believe that these two were my guys, that they had remained faithful to my program. I felt sick again, and wanted to leave but I just toughed it out until Atkinson started the car and drove me back to my old office. We pulled up, and we were all three very quiet. No one said a word. I was exhausted and I wanted out but I had to know a little more. Exasperated, I looked at the two of them and asked, "What have I got to do with all this and what is going to happen with this information?"

Atkinson replied, "You are a witness and may be called upon for just that if we can get enough evidence to convict Steven McFather. But other than that, you'll have no problem from us. The boys in the pictures are free because no one can prove that they threw a game, just because the point spread was covered in every game. We are sure that they received benefits from McFather but we cannot prove that they did anything for him for financial gain. Your team made Mr. McFather over two billion dollars. We know his tactics and we will catch him because sooner or later as he will make a mistake." Mark continued, "He finds innocent coaches and uses them to his advantage to make money. Whether it has negative or positive effects for them is of no importance to him. You were easy for him. He did not have to bribe your players to miss some shots and so forth. Your offensive philosophy determined the games would be close. This is not the first time for him to find a coach, get him fired and then continue to make money off high-percentage gambling. You must admit his plan is a difficult one for us to beat but we are going to get him."

I shook their hands, got out of the car and left. I was crushed even further, my ego shredded even more. In my life, I had never been so down. Not only had my coaching integrity come up short, I felt so used in the process. McFather was a very smart man and he knew that we would win the game by beating the point spread if we played the game the way I drew it up. He knew my past, knew I was not the kind of person that said one thing and did another. My God, the man was so smart that he had the FBI on the run. Further, he knew that if I had the talent to compete, collected enough big-time players together with some really good ones already on the team, his gamble presented no real risk at all. Rather, it was almost a sure thing. He kept everyone happy and he convinced the players that everyone wins if we can beat the point spread. The biggest sale for him was to convince the players that my style of playing basketball was the best way to do what was needed. I had foolishly convinced myself our players bought into my strategy both because I was a convincing teacher and that it was the best way to win. In retrospect, the ease with which they were all convinced to play just as instructed had given me pause now and then. Now, it was clear to me how little influence I had exerted, that it was more the work of Willie, Oscar, Sammy, and Bubba, but the bottom line was

Steven McFather's money. It all makes sense now and I am sure that those four all made more money than I did this past year. I just cannot prove it. All this time I thought the players were playing my way because I had convinced them it was the way to win, they were actually just doing what Steven McFather's money said they should. I kept smacking myself in the forehead and telling myself how stupid I was. I was more convinced than ever of just two things: I wanted to get out of Amarillo as fast as I could, and I wanted no part of anything to do with big-time basketball.

FIFTEEN

My brother, who had coached with me during some of the early years, lived in San Antonio and owned Mayb's BBQ Shop, a nice little barbecue restaurant located on the river close to downtown. He actually married into the business, tying the knot with a San Antonio girl named Betty whose last name was Mayberry. Betty's father had gotten off to a slow start in the BBQ business quite a few years earlier running a small van selling barbecue along the Guadalupe River and especially at the New Braunfels Schlitterbahn Water Park Resort. He would drive his van close by where people would be returning from tubing the river, and he would make a killing. After all, they were not only tired, but both thirsty and hungry. Emerging onto the riverbank on a hot day, the pickin's were easy. The strategy was the same at the Water Park. Make sure you caught 'em just coming out of the park, looking for something to eat and drink. As a matter of fact, that is how Mike came to discover and fall in love with the BBQ business, as well as Betty, by just cooking out with her father on weekends. One thing led to another, and before long, Betty and Mike were engaged and then married. When Betty's father died, Mike not only took over the business; he took it to another level. Mike found an old shack along the river, bought and rebuilt it, then started a BBQ business right there.

Devoted to perfecting his fare, Mike would travel across the country to learn as much as he could about the business, and how to run it successfully. Any place famous for their BBQ, palace or dive, had something to teach him, he figured. Not every place was eager to give away any trade secrets, but Mike had a way of finding out. He would sneak behind the counters, talk to the cooks, share a few words with the manager, and visit with paying diners inside each place. He had as strong a thirst for barbecue knowledge as I did for basketball. We would share tales about our favorite BBQ spot in East Texas between Kilgore and Tyler. The County Line's barbecue, for instance, was outstanding, but it was their attitude that most caught Mike's attention. They served the best, but it was nothing but BBQ--no sides except onions and pickles and two thin slices of bread. Come try our Baby Back Ribs with a little sauce on the side, and if you don't like them, well, there were other places. Even Mike, who had been all over the world sampling barbecue, loved eating at a place like that. And now, after years of hard work, Mayb's BBQ was famous in the San Antonio area. It was a hangout for coaches, and not only them. The key was Mike and his personality. He was salesman, politician, and cook all rolled into one. Needless to say, Mayb's (Mike's, really) was a huge success.

Mike called me when he heard the news about my getting fired. I had already told him about much of it so he was up to date on what had happened. He asked me what I was going to do and I told him I did not know but it was not going to be coaching. Mike continued, "Well, I have a job for you at Mayb's. Do you want it?"

This was a no-brainer, and I rushed to reply, "Yes!" That June, I went to work at Mayb's BBQ in San Antonio as a manager. Though happy for me, Jennifer insisted that we not sell our house. She would continue to live in Amarillo. Nicole was entering her senior year, and that would have been too much to move her at such a turning point in her young life. I agreed with Jennifer, so I moved in with Mike and Betty and started to work at Mayb's. Following the death of Betty's father, her mother had become seriously ill, and Mike and Betty had had to put her in a nursing home. That left them with a huge two-story house with an additional cottage on the side where Mike and Betty had been living. With them in the bigger house now, I just moved into the cottage, which was quite nice and contained five rooms: a master bedroom, living room, dining room, kitchen, and bathroom. I paid Mike and Betty $400 a month in rent so I could live in the cottage.

If you think owning and managing a popular BBQ place is fun, then you have another think coming. I wanted to get away from coaching and I sure found the answer. Working at Mayb's was an around-the-clock job. I had to make sure the cooks did what they were supposed to do the way Mike wanted it done. I usually went to work around 7:00 a.m. and returned home on a typical day a little after 8:00 p.m. We would start our cooking early in the morning and continue all day long. The aroma from the wood and BBQ attracted more customers than the food itself, which was just the way we wanted it. Let the customers smell the cooking before they tasted it. Mike had a special way he wanted his meat cooked and I was the enforcer who saw to it that it was done just that way. Hiring people to do the cooking and serving was easy, but getting them to buy into our exact process wasn't. Mike would usually arrive at Mayb's around noon and he would stay until closing. He was the show. They came for the food, but people enjoyed seeing Mike make it work too. The day would start in earnest around 10:30 a.m. for the first big wave of customers, and from then it was nonstop cooking and serving until there was a short lag about 3:00 p.m. The next group, the early dinner types, would start showing up around 4:30 and that rush would carry through without slowing down until almost 9:00 p.m., which was around when Mike would generally start closing up. He didn't want Mayb's to become a club, a bar, or anyone's hangout so he would close Mayb's a little after 9:00 p.m. He was open to keeping the place open longer if he received a special request, for a big family party or for an organization or company group dinner. We both worked on Fridays, Saturdays, and Sundays. Those were the restaurant's biggest days so we made sure that one of us was around throughout the day. We would alternate taking off two days in a row: Monday, Tuesday for one, then Wednesday, Thursday for the other. Thanks to my job at Mayb's, the time just flew by quickly for me.

Getting so involved in Mayb's left me virtually no time to think about North West State University basketball, although the occasional e-mail or call from old friends would remind me from time to time. I had very little contact with the situation: Each of my assistant coaches had been replaced as well. Each one took the jobs we had talked over together, and

I did hear from them often. They were happy and really involved in their work, which was all to the good. North West State University had hired a really good coach from Louisiana Tech named Jerry Long. He was a good coach and I had no regrets at all. I found it easy to e-mail him, give him my congratulations, and wish him luck. Oscar declared for the NBA and from what I had heard through some of the guys who eat at Mayb's, he was doing well with the Suns in their early workouts. I did hear from Willie, as he ran into my wife at the local Furr's Cafeteria. Willie said that he was leaving Northwestern and going back home to UCLA where he would sit out a year. I traveled to Amarillo quite often to see my family, and they would make the opposite trip to see me every so often. The big news was that the NCAA was not taking any drastic action against Northwestern State. Once North West State University had quickly fired me, the organization penalized them by reducing the number of athletic scholarships they could award by two a year, for two years. What did surprise me was that Northwestern was to be allowed to continue competing for the playoffs. Although I agreed that was fair, I wished that Stephen McFather would get caught, but I doubted that would ever happen. The school had a really hard time in the Big 12, finishing in ninth place in the conference. From what I hear they lost the first game in the Big 12 tournament to Iowa State, which brought their season to an end.

It was Easter Sunday and we closed Mayb's for the special holiday. I flew home just to be with Jennifer and the kids. I was going to take Monday and Tuesday off so it would be a three-day break for me and I was excited. We went to church that Sunday and the place was packed. Of course, there was nothing unusual about that at Easter, the biggest Christian holy day. The preacher delivered a powerful sermon about the need to fulfill God's mission for you. His talk really affected me, and a light bulb turned on in my head. He talked about how God had a purpose for everyone and it was up to us to follow that plan. I totally believed what the reverend was saying, that God gives each of his people specific talents, and it is up to each of us to use those talents to the best of our ability, both for God's purposes, and for those of man. Following the service we went to Furr's as we often had in the past, and after our meal had gone on for a while, I announced to the Young family that I had made a decision: I was going to get back into the coaching business. They all just stopped eating for a moment and just looked at me. I said, "Look, I am too young to retire and I feel I am wasting my talents at Mayb's. I have decided to go back into the coaching business. But this time, I have decided that I want to coach girl's basketball. I can't go back into the NCAA because of my past, but I can contribute to coaching on a high school level." To my surprise, the whole family was happy with what I was saying, even Jennifer.

She asked, "Why girls basketball?"

I said, "It would take a long time for me to heal again working with boys and I do not feel I am ready to do that just yet. I have always enjoyed working with our girls, so I figured, why not?" I confessed I had no idea where and when an opportunity might present itself, but that I believed God would open a door or two for me somewhere along the line. "I'll continue working at Mayb's until I get a chance that feels right." I flew back to San Antonio and, for the first time in a long time, I felt good about myself again.

The instrument of my return to the ranks of coaching eventually came along. His name was David McNey and he was the superintendent of schools in West Mora, New Mexico. It is a small city not far from the Mescalero Apache Indian Reservation next to Ruidoso in the same state. I had coached David at Hereford High School. He was a very good basketball player after I toughened him up a little. David's father was a highly paid physician and his family didn't lack for anything they needed when David was a boy. He was a little spoiled, and he knew about the finer things in life. He was a great kid but very soft, something anyone paying attention could have figured out.

I was the lucky coach tasked with the job of teaching David toughness. I will never forget when he was a junior and we were working on a defensive drill. The drill was set up with a dribbling ball handler at the top of the center jump area while his counterpart on defense would start at the baseline. There weren't a lot of Xs and Os involved in this one. The object for the dribbler was to get to the basket and score; the defensive player's job was to stop him before he got there. It was a simple enough drill, but it was all about contact so I would string chairs across the free throw line to cut down on the space that the dribbler and the defender would have available to them. We would set it up so there was five feet of space between the chairs. What I wanted to get from the drill was a solid stop of the dribbler by the defender, something that wasn't going to happen without some body contact. The drill was for the ball handler as well; I wanted him to get past the defender with the ball and score. All my players wanted to do well, but I had to put a little more on the line: To make it more competitive, the loser in this drill would have to run a down-and-back after giving me 10 quick push-ups. I, and no one else, decided who the loser was in this drill.

David had already run a down-and-back three times and had 30 push-ups behind him when he finally got his bellyful, and complained, "Coach, what is the purpose of this drill?"

Not liking his put-upon- tone, though I could see he was frustrated, I replied, "It's just for you, David, I am tired of watching guys dribble around you like you were a ghost."

"If I step in and stop him, I will foul so what's the point?"

Angrily I had replied, "The purpose is to get you to make contact on the dribbler, which you need to learn to do. I know you are going to foul him but you are never going to learn how to handle this spot until you do foul. You have to learn how to make contact without fouling. Now get in there and stop the dribbler."

At six foot five and about 210 pounds, David had little to fear. He literally destroyed the dribbler with a full body tackle to the chest. I said, "It's a tie. Good job, David!" We became close after that. He went on to become our very best defensive player and he eventually attended school and played college basketball in Eastern New Mexico. And now, he was the Superintendent of Schools at West Mora.

I sat in his office and we talked about old times. I had looked on the New Mexico Web site and saw that there was a girl's basketball coaching position open, with the instruction that those interested should contact David McNey. One thing led to another and we were now talking about my becoming the new head girl's basketball coach. We talked about everything from my getting fired and why I decided I wanted to coach girl's basketball to his family of four and his wonderful wife, Mary.

He still referred to me as he had years ago. "Coach," he said, "the job is yours if you want it; we can certainly fill your plate. You will be assistant cross-country coach, assistant football coach, and assistant boy's basketball coach, assistant junior high track coach, head girls basketball coach and head golf coach. You will have to teach five biology classes. Your wife is welcome to accept a job teaching kindergarten if she wants it." I had already talked it all over with Jennifer, of course, and she wanted me to take the job if they offered and if they could find a spot for her. Jennifer had taught David McNey freshman English at Hereford and he was crazy about her, so I had reason to hope for such an outcome. As a matter of fact, he said that she was the best English teacher he had ever had. I was scared to death about the work load, scared about coaching girls for the first time and about the entire deal. But I tried my best not to not show it and agreed to David's offer.

We sold our house in Amarillo and moved to the mountains. West Dora had a population of 1,095, and the school system provided housing for teachers at a small monthly fee. We paid $250 per month for our three-bedroom cabin, located right on the edge of the White Mountain wilderness. Jennifer fell in love with it; it was so isolated and beautiful. It was cold at night, cool in the morning and hot in the afternoon. Ann and Nicole were attending college so leaving Amarillo did not bother either of them one bit, but Renee was going to be a junior and she had her doubts. Little did she know I had my doubts too?

We started cross-country drills on August 1. I was shocked to see every girl on the basketball team sign up for cross-country as well. Head Coach Lynda Moore was totally focused on the sport. We would meet in the mornings around 5:30, get on a bus, drive out about 10 miles, then have the girls run back into town and to the school. In the afternoons, we would work on sprints and form running and conduct different types of training for long-distance running. The girls would lift weights before going outside in the afternoon. On August 15, football started with two-a-day workouts, one at 7:00 a.m. and one in the late afternoon starting at 6:00 p.m. I loved the football staff as they were a really good fun-loving bunch of guys, all quite serious about the game. Expectations were high because last year's football team had posted a 7-3 mark, and everyone was back for another go of it. Football fever was rampant in the school, and we in the Young family were no exception.

Needless to say, I was a busy beaver in August. School classes started up in late August and I began preparing each day for my biology classes at 7:00 a.m. First period was open for me, which gave me plenty of time to prepare my biology lessons. Jennifer was wild about her kindergarten classes and Renee was enjoying meeting new people. She was happy and excited, which sure made me feel better. Everyday, I would get my basketball girls in a class period designed just for them. They continued to surprise and impress me. Not only did every one of them play basketball and run cross-country, every starter on the team was a cheerleader too. They all had a great attitude about the school and were excited about the schools coming up on the team's schedule later in the year.

I was totally enjoying myself and never even thought about how busy I was or anything remotely like that. Coaching and teaching had become fun again and I looked forward to every day. We had been in school about two weeks and our first football game was coming up on Friday. I had been working the girls out on basic fundamentals and basic shooting and passing drills. I alerted them that we would have a play day that coming Friday, since there was a big pep rally that day and football that night. Rather than put them through full drills, we would have a free day to have some fun with the game.

Friday came, and all the cheerleaders went all out and trying to look as good as they could in their spiffy new uniforms. Our workouts require that they change into physical education (PE) clothes, not my rule, but a school one. If they don't dress for the sport, they don't get credit for the day unless I excuse them. I told the cheerleaders not to dress out and just take the day; we would catch up on the drills. But to my surprise, every one of them suited up, and then came out onto the court. It was impossible not to be impressed; I was very pleased even though I had told them not to bother with the PE outfits. They all spoke as with one voice: "Coach, we wanted to do it."

About that time, a runner from the front office came to me and handed me a note. It said that I was needed on the phone. I had mixed emotions. I take coaching seriously and did not want to leave my team without supervision. I was afraid of what might happen if I was not around. I had never left a team for any length of time without supervision in the past, and the few times they had even a few moments to their own devices, I was sorry to see how they behaved. This message said the phone call was an emergency so I left the gym, went to the phone in the main office, picked it up and said, "Coach Young speaking," identifying myself in a manner that sounded totally unfamiliar to me.

Mike replied, "How you doing, big brother?" He quickly assured me that there was no emergency, but he was dying to know how things were going. He really just called to talk. I assured him everything was fine; as did he, for a few minutes, but the whole time we spoke I was worried about the team I had left in the gym all by them-selves. Finally after convincing my brother that I was as happy as I had ever been, he let me go. Almost twenty minutes had passed, so I headed straight back to the gym, recalling as I did some of the scenes I had come back to in years past when I left my boys to themselves, even if just for a few minutes.

I walked into the gym to find two groups of girls neatly organized on either end of the court. The younger girls were on one end while the veterans had gathered across the way. They were working on a drill we had been practicing the last two weeks. Relieved but confused, I sat back and just watched. It sent a strong message. I thought I had died and gone to heaven.

AUTHOR'S NOTE CONCERNING THIS BOOK

I am compelled to defend the NCAA, and do so with all the energy I can gather. The NCAA does everything they can do to clean up violators of Division one basketball. They are limited with limited resources and they cannot be everywhere all the time. Hall of Fame basketball coach Bob Knight recently was quoted saying "Integrity of college basketball needs to be cleaned up". I could not agreed more but how you clean it up is a huge question.

All characters herein are purely fictional. Any similarity to a real person is coincidental, although real stories have been used to get the reader's attention, but the names of the people are not real. The Junior Colleges are not real but the Universities are real except North West State University. Any negative perception that comes from the book toward any College or University is only in the perception of the reader because that is not the intent of the book. This book is about college basketball and basketball fans and because of that, the real names of the major Universities were used. Basketball fans across the United States identify with several powerful basketball programs and most are mentioned in this book.

Any cheating involved concerning a particular University was a fragment of my imagination. I just made them up. Also, any suggestions concerning unprofessional behavior toward anyone person or school are totally fiction, nor are there any underlying plots of criticism intended.

In another life, I was a college coach for twenty two years and I did not have to do research to write this book. This book is about my life as a high school and college coach. I must say that there is a lot of truth in this book particularly about cheating. The issue of cheating to get ahead is common. As long as winning brings big bucks into schools and winning adds to attendance, the tactics will remain. Because of that, the results in this book are not far off the mark.